THE
Forest
OF
Vanishing
Stars

ALSO BY KRISTIN HARMEL

KRISTIN HARMEL

THE
Forest
OF
Vanishing
Stars

WELBECK

Published in 2022 by Welbeck Fiction Limited, part of Welbeck Publishing Group
Based in London and Sydney
www.welbeckpublishing.com

Copyright © Kristin Harmel Lietz, 2021
Cover design by www.headdesign.co.uk
Cover photographs © Marie Carr / Arcangel Images (Woman);
Yolande De Kort / Trevillion (forest); Shutterstock.com (grass)

The moral right of the author has been asserted.

*All characters and events in this publication, other than those clearly in the public
domain, are fictitious and any resemblance to real persons, living or dead,
is purely coincidental.*

First published in the United States by Gallery Books, an imprint of
Simon & Schuster, in 2021

A CIP catalogue record for this book is available from the British Library

Paperback ISBN: 978-1-80279-362-8
E-book ISBN: 978-1-80279-363-5

Printed and bound by CPI Group (UK) Ltd., Croydon, CR0 4YY

10 9 8 7 6 5 4 3 2 1

To Kathy Trocheck (Mary Kay Andrews),
Kristy Woodson Harvey, Patti Callahan Henry,
Mary Alice Monroe, Meg Walker, Shaun Hettinger,
and all the members of our Friends & Fiction community.
You filled a dark year with light, love, and friendship,
and I will be forever grateful for all the ways you saved me.

CHAPTER ONE

1922

The old woman watched from the shadows outside Behaim-strasse 72, waiting for the lights inside to blink out. The apartment's balcony dripped with crimson roses, and ivy climbed the iron rails, but the young couple who lived there—the power-hungry Siegfried Jüttner and his aloof wife, Alwine—weren't the ones who tended the plants. That was left to their maid, for the nurturing of life was something only those with some goodness could do.

The old woman had been watching the Jüttners for nearly two years now, and she knew things about them, things that were important to the task she was about to undertake.

She knew, for example, that Herr Jüttner had been one of the first men in Berlin to join the National Socialist German Workers' Party, a new political movement that was slowly gaining a foothold in the war-shattered country. She knew he'd been inspired to do so while on holiday in Munich nearly three years earlier, after seeing an angry young man named Adolf Hitler give a rousing speech in the Hofbräukeller. She knew that after hearing that speech, Herr Jüttner had walked twenty minutes back to the elegant Hotel Vier Jahreszeiten, had awoken his sleeping young wife, and had lain with her, though at first she had objected, for she had been dreaming of a young man she had once loved, a man who had died in the Great War.

The old woman knew, too, that the baby conceived on that autumn-scented Bavarian night, a girl the Jüttners had named Inge, had a birthmark in the shape of a dove on the inside of her left wrist.

She also knew that the girl's second birthday was the following day, the sixth of July, 1922. And she knew, as surely as she knew that the bell-shaped buds of lily of the valley and the twilight petals of aconite could kill a man, that the girl must not be allowed to remain with the Jüttners.

That was why she had come.

The old woman, who was called Jerusza, had always known things other people didn't. For example, she had known it the moment Frédéric Chopin had died in 1849, for she had awoken from a deep slumber, the notes of his "Revolutionary Étude" marching through her head in an aggrieved parade. She had felt the earth tremble upon the births of Marie Curie in 1867 and Albert Einstein in 1879. And on a sweltering late June day in 1914, two months after she had turned seventy-four, she had felt it deep in her jugular vein, weeks before the news reached her, that the heir to the Austro-Hungarian throne had been felled by an assassin's bullet, cracking the fragile balance of the world. She had known then that war was brewing, just as she knew it now. She could see it in the dark clouds that hulked on the horizon.

Jerusza's mother, who had killed herself with a brew of poisons in 1860, used to tell her that the knowing of impossible things was a gift from God, passed down through maternal blood of only the most fortunate Jewish women. Jerusza, the last of a bloodline that had stretched for centuries, was certain at times that it was a curse instead, but whatever it was, it had been her burden all her life to follow the voices that echoed through the forests. The leaves whispered in the trees; the flowers told tales as old as time; the rivers rushed with news of places far away. If one listened closely enough, nature always spilled her secrets, which were, of course, the secrets of God. And now, it was God who had brought Jerusza here, to a fog-cloaked Berlin street corner, where she would be responsible for changing the fate of a child, and perhaps a piece of the world, too.

Jerusza had been alive for eighty-two years, nearly twice as long as the typical German lived. When people looked at her—if they bothered to look at all—they were visibly startled by her wizened features, her hands gnarled by decades of hard living. Most of the time, though, strangers simply ignored her, just as Siegfried and Alwine Jüttner had done each of the hundreds of times they had passed her on the street. Her age made her particularly invisible to those who cared most about appearance and power; they assumed she was useless to them, a waste of time, a waste of space. After all, surely a woman as old as she would be dead soon. But Jerusza, who had spent her whole life sustained by the plants and herbs in the darkest spots of the deepest forests, knew that she would live nearly twenty years more, to the age of 102, and that she would die on a spring Tuesday just after the last thaw of 1942.

The Jüttners' maid, the timid daughter of a dead sailor, had gone home two hours before, and it was a few minutes past ten o'clock when the Jüttners finally turned off their lights. Jerusza exhaled. Darkness was her shield; it always had been. She squinted at the closed windows and could just make out the shape of the little girl's infant bed in the room to the right, beyond pale custard curtains. She knew exactly where it was, had been into the room many times when the family wasn't there. She had run her fingers along the pine rails, had felt the power splintering from the curves. Wood had memory, of course, and the first time Jerusza had touched the bed where the baby slept, she had been nearly overcome by a warm, white wash of light.

It was the same light that had brought her here from the forest two years earlier. She had first seen it in June 1920, shining above the treetops like a personal aurora borealis, beckoning her north. She hated the city, abhorred being in a place built by man rather than God, but she knew she had no choice. Her feet had carried her straight to Behaimstrasse 72, to bear witness as the raven-haired Frau Jüttner nursed the baby for the first time. Jerusza had seen the baby glowing, even then, a light in the darkness no one knew was coming.

She didn't want a child; she never had. Perhaps that was why it had taken her so long to act. But nature makes no mistakes, and now, as the sky filled with a cloud of silent blackbirds over the twinkling city, she knew the time had come.

It was easy to climb up the ladder of the modern building's fire escape, easier still to push open the Jüttners' unlatched window and slip quietly inside. The child was awake, silently watching, her extraordinary eyes—one twilight blue and one forest green—glimmering in the darkness. Her hair was black as night, her lips the startling red of corn poppies.

"*Ikh bin gekimen dir tzu nemen*," Jerusza whispered in Yiddish, a language the girl would not yet know. *I have come for you.* She was startled to realize that her heart was racing.

She didn't expect a reply, but the child's lips parted, and she reached out her left hand, palm upturned, the dove-shaped birthmark shimmering in the darkness. She said something soft, something that a lesser person would have dismissed as the meaningless babble of a little girl, but to Jerusza, it was unmistakable. "*Dus zent ir*," said the girl in Yiddish. *It is you.*

"*Yo, dus bin ikh*," Jerusza agreed. And with that, she picked up the baby, who didn't cry out, and, tucking her close against the brittle curves of her body, climbed out the window and shimmied down the iron rail, her feet hitting the sidewalk without a sound.

From the folds of Jerusza's cloak, the baby watched soundlessly, her mismatched ocean eyes round, as Berlin vanished behind them and the forest to the north swallowed them whole.

CHAPTER TWO

1928

The girl from Berlin was eight years old when Jerusza first taught her how to kill a man.

Of course Jerusza had discarded the child's given name as soon as they'd reached the crisp edge of the woods six years earlier. Inge meant "the daughter of a heroic father," and that was a lie. The child had no parent now but the forest itself.

Furthermore, Jerusza had known, from the moment she first saw the light over Berlin, that the child was to be called Yona, which meant "dove" in Hebrew. She had known it even before she saw the girl's birthmark, which hadn't faded with time but had grown stronger, darker, a sign that this child was special, that she was fated for something great.

The right name was vital, and the old woman couldn't call Yona anything other than what she was. She expected the same in return, of course, a respect for one's true identity. Jerusza meant "owned inheritance"—a reference to the magic she had received from her own bloodline, and a tribute to being owned by the forest itself—and it was the only thing she allowed Yona to call her. "Mother" meant something different, something that Jerusza never would be, never wanted to be.

"There are hundreds of ways to take a life," Jerusza told the girl on a fading July afternoon soon after the child's eighth birthday. "And you must know them all."

Yona looked up from whittling a tiny wren from a piece of wood. She had taken to carving creatures for company, which Jerusza did not understand, for she herself valued solitude above all else, but it seemed a harmless enough pursuit. Yona's hair, the color of the deepest starless night, tumbled down her back, rolling over birdlike shoulders. Her eyes—endless and unsettling— were misty with confusion. The sun was low in the sky, and her shadow stretched behind her all the way to the edge of the clearing, as if trying to escape into the trees. "But you've always told me that life is precious, that it is God's gift to man, that it must be protected," the girl said.

"Yes. But the most important life to protect is your own." Jerusza flattened her palm and placed the edge of her hand across her own windpipe. "If someone comes for you, a hard blow here, if delivered correctly, can be fatal."

Yona blinked a few times, her long lashes dusting her cheeks, which were preternaturally pale, always pale, though the sun beat down on them relentlessly. As she set the wooden wren on the ground beside her, her hands shook. "But who would come for me?"

Jerusza stared at the child with disgust. Her head was in the clouds, despite Jerusza's teachings. "You foolish child!" she snapped. The girl shrank away from her. It was good that the girl was afraid; terrible things were coming. "Your question is the wrong one, as usual. There will come a day when you'll be glad I have taught you what I know."

It wasn't an answer, but the girl wouldn't cross her. Jerusza was strong as a mountain chamois, clever as a hooded crow, vindictive as a magpie. She had been on the earth for nearly nine decades now, and she knew the girl was frightened by her age and her wisdom. Jerusza liked it that way; the child should be clear that Jerusza was not a mother. She was a teacher, nothing more.

"But, Jerusza, I don't know if I could take a life," Yona said at last, her voice small. "How would I live with myself?"

Jerusza snorted. It was hard to believe the girl could still be so naive. "I've killed four men and a woman, child. And I live with myself just fine."

Yona's eyes widened, but she didn't speak again until the light had faded from the sky and the day's lessons had ended. "Who did you kill, Jerusza?" she whispered in the darkness as they lay on their backs on the forest floor beneath a roof of spruce bark they'd built themselves just the week before. They moved every month or two, building a new hut from the gifts the forest gave them, always leaving a crack in their hastily hewn bark ceilings to see the stars when there was no threat of rain. Tonight, the heavens were clear, and Jerusza could see the Little Dipper, the Big Dipper, and Draco, the dragon, crawling across the sky. Life changed all the time, but the stars were ever constant.

"A farmer, two soldiers, a blacksmith, and the woman who murdered my father," Jerusza replied without looking at Yona. "All would have killed me themselves if I'd given them a chance. You must never give someone that opportunity, Yona. Forget that lesson, and you will die. Now get some rest."

By the next full moon, Yona knew that a kick just to the right of the base of the spine could puncture a kidney. A horizontal blow with the edge of the hand to the bridge of the nose could crush the facial bones deep into the skull, causing a brain hemorrhage. A hard toe kick to the temple, once a man was down, could swiftly end a life. A quick headlock behind a seated man, combined with a sharp backward jerk, could snap a neck. A knife sliced upward, from wrist to inner elbow along the radial artery, could drain a man of his blood in minutes.

But the universe was about balance, and so for each method of death, Jerusza taught the girl a way to dispense healing, too. Bilberries could restore circulation to a failing heart or resuscitate a dying kidney. Catswort, when ground into a paste, could stop bleeding. Burdock root could remove poison from the bloodstream. Crushed elderberries could bring down a deadly fever.

Life and death. Death and life. Two things that mattered little, for in the end, souls outlived the body and became one with an infinite God. But Yona didn't understand that, not yet. She didn't yet know that she had been born for the sake of repairing the world, for the sake of *tikkun olam*, and that each *mitzvah* she was called to perform would lift up divine sparks of light.

If only the forest alone could sustain them, but as the girl grew, she needed clothing, milk to strengthen her bones, shoes so her feet weren't shredded by the forest floor in the summer or frozen to ice in the winter. When Yona was young, Jerusza sometimes left her alone in the woods for a day and a night, scaring her into staying put with tales of werewolves that ate little girls, while she ventured alone into nearby towns to take the things they needed. But as the girl began to ask more questions, there was no choice but to begin taking her along, to show her the perils of the outside world, to remind her that no one could be trusted.

It was a cold winter's night in 1931, snow drifting down from a black sky, when Jerusza pulled the wide-eyed child into a town called Grajewo in northeastern Poland. And though Jerusza had explicitly told her to remain silent, Yona couldn't seem to keep her words in. As they crept through the darkness toward a farmhouse, the girl peppered her with questions: *What is that roof made of? Why do the horses sleep in a barn and not in a field? How did they make these roads? What is that on the flag?*

Finally, Jerusza whirled on her. "Enough, child! There is nothing here for you, nothing but despair and danger! Yearning for a life you don't understand is like staring at the sun; your foolishness will destroy you."

Yona was startled into silence for a time, but after Jerusza had slipped through the back door of the house and reemerged carrying a pair of boots, trousers, and a wool coat that would see Yona through at least a few winters, Yona refused to follow when Jerusza beckoned.

"What is it now?" Jerusza demanded, irritated.

"What are they doing?" Yona pointed through the window of the farmhouse, to where the family was gathered around a table. It was the first night of Hanukkah, and this family was Jewish; it was why Jerusza had chosen this house, for she knew they would be occupied while she took their things. Now the father of the family stood, his face illuminated by the candle burning on the family's menorah, and though his voice was inaudible, it was clear he was singing, his eyes closed. Jerusza didn't like Yona's expression as she watched; it was one of longing and enchantment, and those types of feelings led only to ill-conceived ideas of flight.

"The practice of dullards," she said finally. "Nothing there for you. Come now."

Yona still wouldn't budge. "But they look happy. They are celebrating Hanukkah?"

Of course the girl already knew they were. Jerusza carved a menorah each year from wood, simply because her mother had commanded it years before. Hanukkah wasn't among the most important Jewish holidays, but it celebrated survival, and that was something anyone who lived in the woods could respect. Still, the girl was being foolish. Jerusza narrowed her eyes. "They are repeating words that have likely lost all meaning for them, Yona. Repetition is for people who don't want to think for themselves, people who have no imagination. How can you find God in moments that have become rote?"

Neither of them said anything for a moment as they continued to watch the family. "But what if in the repetition they find comfort?" Yona eventually asked, her voice small. "What if they find magic?"

"How on earth would repetition be magic?" They still needed to procure a few jugs of milk from the barn, and Jerusza was losing patience.

"Well, God makes the same trees come alive each year, doesn't he?" Yona said slowly. "He makes the same seasons come and go, the same flowers bloom, the same birds call. And there's magic in that, isn't there?"

Jerusza was stunned into silence. The girl had not bested her at her own game before. "*Never* question me," she snapped at last. "Now shut up and come along."

It was inevitable that Yona would begin wondering about the world outside the woods. Jerusza had always known the time would come, and now it was heavy upon her to ensure that when the girl thought of civilization, she regarded it with the proper fear.

Jerusza had been teaching Yona all the languages she knew since she had taken her, and the child could speak fluent Yiddish, Polish, Belorussian, Russian, and German, as well as snippets of French and English. *One must know the words of one's enemies*, Jerusza always told her, and she was gratified by the fear she could see in Yona's eyes.

But she had more to teach, so on their forays into towns, she began to steal books, too. She taught the child to read, to understand science, to work with numbers. She insisted that Yona know the Torah and the Talmud, but she also brought her the Christian Bible and even the Muslim Quran, for God was everywhere, and the search for him was endless. It had consumed Jerusza's whole life, and it had brought her to that dark street corner in Berlin in the summer of 1922, where she'd been compelled to steal this child, who had become such a thorn in her side.

And though Yona irritated her more often than not, even Jerusza had to admit that the girl was bright, sensitive, intuitive. She drank the books down like cool water and listened with rapt attention whenever Jerusza deigned to impart her secrets. By the time Yona was fourteen, she knew more about the world than most men who'd been educated in universities. More important, she knew the mysteries of the forest, all the ways to survive.

As the girl's eyes opened to the world, Jerusza insisted upon only two things: One, Yona must always obey her. And two, she must always stay hidden in the forest, away from those who might hurt her.

Sometimes Yona asked why. Who would want to hurt her? What would they try to do?

But Jerusza never answered, for the truth was, she wasn't sure. She knew only that in the early-morning hours of July 6, 1922, as she hurried with a two-year-old child into the forest, she heard a voice from the sky, sharp and clear. *One day*, the voice said, *her past will return—and it will alter the course of many lives, perhaps even taking hers. The only safe place is the forest.*

It was the same voice that had told her to take the girl in the first place, the voice that had always whispered to Jerusza in the trees. Jerusza had spent most of her life thinking the voice belonged to God. But now, in the twilight of her life, she was no longer sure. What if the voice in her head belonged to her alone? What if it was the legacy of her mother's madness, a spark of insanity rather than a higher calling?

But each time those questions bubbled to the surface, Jerusza pushed them away. The voice from above had spoken, and who knew what fate awaited her if she failed to listen?

CHAPTER THREE

It was two years later, and 150 kilometers south, when Yona finally dared disobey Jerusza's orders.

By then she and Jerusza were deep in the Białowieża Forest, the Forest of the White Tower, and though autumn was teetering on the edge of winter, the ground was still thick with mushrooms, the days punctuated by hammering woodpeckers and plodding elk, the stillness of the nights broken by the howls of roaming wolf packs. It was a magical place, and Yona, who had grown to love birds, had trouble focusing with all the white storks and streaked bitterns soaring overhead. She imagined lifting off into the sky herself, seeing for miles, having the ability to simply fly away from here, to go wherever she wanted. But that was just a dream.

It was a late October day, the air sharp and cold, and Yona was out gathering acorns in a large basket. She and Jerusza would store them for the long winter ahead; they would leach, dry, and grind most of them for flour, but they'd also roast some in honey from the hives Jerusza had a knack for finding within the walls of crumbling trees. She was so distracted by the sudden *ja-ja-ja* of a rare aquatic warbler overhead that she had her guard down. The man was only a hundred meters from her when she spotted him, and with a gasp, she shrank back into the willows.

He hadn't seen her, hadn't heard her move. Yona had grown accustomed to rustling with the trees, so calmly in sync with them that her movements flowed with the wind. She reached instinctively for the knife she always kept strapped to her ankle, the one Jerusza insisted she sharpen each week, just in case, and her heart raced as she stared.

The man wasn't as old as she'd thought at first glance. In fact, he was barely more than a boy, perhaps a year or two older than she. His hair was as white blond as hers was ebony, his skin as tanned as a cowhide. His shoulders were broad, and he walked with an assuredness that told her he knew the forest.

But where had he come from? She and Jerusza had been camped here for three weeks, and they hadn't seen any sign of other people. Did he live in the trees, too? Her heart thudded against her rib cage as she allowed herself to taste the possibility of a kindred spirit, just for a second. The ache it created in her chest was a symphony of longing and loneliness and fear, and it made her reckless. Slowly, before she'd had a chance to think it all the way through, she took her hand off the hilt of her knife, straightened, and stepped from her hiding place in the trees.

"Hello," she said, but he didn't turn, and she realized that she hadn't actually said it aloud, though her lips had traced the word in the air. The second time, she summoned her breath, and when she repeated the greeting, it came out too sharply, and the young man spun around to stare at her.

"Hello," he said after a few seconds. His voice was deep, his eyes wide with curiosity. She wondered what he was seeing. She knew from occasionally glimpsing her reflection in gurgling streams that her eyes—each a different color—were large for her face, her nose long, her cheekbones high, her lips a rosebud bow. Her skin was impossibly white, though she spent her life outside, and her hair was a curtain of black smoke, tumbling to her waist. She had sprouted like a weed since her sixteenth birthday in July, and her legs were now as long and gangly as a fawn's. It was the first time in her life she'd been conscious of her body, which, until now, had been merely utilitarian.

He seemed to be waiting for her to say something, and so she coughed to clear her constricted throat and forced out the first words she could think of. "Why are you here?" she asked.

He raised his eyebrows—which were so blond they were almost invisible—and laughed. "I suppose for the same reason you are. To gather food for the winter."

She had a million questions. Where had he come from? Where was he going? What was the world like outside the forest? But all the queries battled for space within her head, and all that came out was, "I've not seen you before."

He laughed again, and she realized she liked the sound. It was different from Jerusza's laugh, which was jagged, raspy, and steeped in all-knowingness. There was nothing Yona could do to shock Jerusza, and she understood now that there was power, maybe even joy, in surprising someone.

"I've never seen you before, either," the young man said. He took a step closer, and reflexively, she stumbled backward. He stopped instantly and held up his hands. "I'm sorry. I didn't mean to startle you."

She forced a smile. "Oh, you didn't." The lie tasted salty in her mouth.

There was a moment of silence as he regarded her. "You live around here?"

"Yes." Then instantly, she amended the answer. "Ah . . . no." She could feel her cheeks grow warm.

The young man hesitated, studying her. "All right. Well, I live in Hajnówka."

"I see." Yona had no idea what that meant.

"On the edge of the forest," he clarified. "About a day's walk from here."

"Of course." The feigning of knowledge she didn't possess tasted like another lie. Jerusza had made her learn all the countries of the world; she could pick out Brazil, Nepal, Tripura, on a map, and sometimes she dreamed of taking flight like a bird and soaring far, far away to another land. But she knew little of the villages just outside the forest, which she suspected was Jerusza's intention. Knowledge was temptation, and Jerusza's refusal to show her maps of the local region was a way of ensuring that there was nowhere tangible for Yona to go.

"And you?" the boy asked. "Where do you live?"

"We—" She stopped abruptly. She had been about to say that she lived in the forest, but hadn't Jerusza told her not to tell people that? That men might come to harm them? She didn't think this young man would do something like that, but she had to be cautious. "I am from Berlin."

She didn't know why she'd said it. Jerusza had never said a word about Yona coming from anywhere but the woods. But at night, when Yona slept, she sometimes dreamed of a city, a wooden bed, plush blankets, parents who loved her, and milk that tasted different from that which Jerusza sometimes procured from wandering goats. The word—*Berlin*—didn't taste like salt, though, and Yona wondered if somehow it could be true.

"Berlin?" The young man's eyebrows shot up. "But that's six, seven hundred kilometers east of here."

Embarrassed, Yona shrugged. Of course she knew that from the maps she had studied, but why had she named Berlin? It was a world away, a place she could see only in her imagination, a place Jerusza would never take her. What a foolish thing it had been to say. "I know," she mumbled.

The man frowned, his forehead creasing with doubt. "Well, maybe I will see you again."

Yona knew she was losing him, that he was about to leave, and she felt suddenly desperate to make him stay. "Who are you? Your name, I mean."

He smiled again, but only slightly this time. His brow was still heavy with his lack of trust in her. "Marcin. And you are?"

"Yona."

"Yona." He seemed to roll her name carefully on his tongue. She liked the way it sounded. "Well, Yona, I'll be back here tomorrow if you are around. My father and I are camped nearby."

"All right." And because she didn't know what else to say, Yona backed away slowly, melting into the forest, until she couldn't see the boy at all anymore. Then she turned and ran. It took her an hour to double back and head in the direction of the hut she shared with Jerusza, for though she was intrigued by Marcin, she wanted to be sure he wasn't following her.

That evening, over a dinner of sweet honey mushrooms with wild garlic, Yona had to bite her tongue. She knew that if she mentioned the young man, they would move immediately.

"You're very quiet tonight," Jerusza said as they walked down to the stream nearby to clean their dishes, stolen long ago from a farm at the edge of the forest. They had accumulated most of their things that way: their clothes, their boots, their pots, their axe, their knives.

"No, I'm not," Yona said right away, which of course made Jerusza's eyes narrow in suspicion. Yona could have kicked herself for being so carelessly transparent.

"Usually you tell me about your day—the creatures you saw, the things you gathered. Usually you talk incessantly, in fact, for you aren't wise enough yet to know the best tales are told in silence."

Yona forced a smile, though the words stung. "An aquatic warbler!" she said too quickly, too brightly. "I saw an aquatic warbler."

"Ah." Jerusza's eyes were dark slits of skepticism. "Like you, a bird that cannot be caged. A sign, perhaps, that you came too close to civilization, and that if you're not careful, your freedom will be taken from you."

Yona looked up, startled. "I—I didn't get close to civilization." The salty taste was back.

Jerusza's expression was knowing as the shape of her eyes finally returned to normal. "Of course you didn't. We're in the middle of the trees. You couldn't have made it to a village and back without—"

"Berlin!" Yona blurted out, desperate to change the subject.

"Pardon?" All at once, Jerusza was very still.

"Berlin," Yona repeated less confidently. "Did we live there when I was young, Jerusza? In a house with beds and blankets and fresh milk?"

Jerusza's lips puckered, the way they did when she tasted a sour berry. "You foolish girl. Can you imagine me in Berlin?"

Yona's heart sank. Sometimes dreams were just dreams. "No."

"Then don't ask me such questions."

That night, Yona didn't dream of Berlin. She dreamed of a boy named Marcin who approached and touched her on the cheek. But then, before she could say a thing, he turned into a warbler and lifted off, soaring above the treetops while she stayed rooted to the ground.

It was three days before Yona saw Marcin again. When he looked up and saw her coming toward him from among a cluster of oaks, relief swept across his features.

"Well, I thought you were gone forever," he said as she approached.

"I was not gone forever." It was a foolish response, and she knew it the moment she'd said it. She was glad when he laughed.

"Yes, I see that. So where have you been? Did you go back to Berlin, then, German girl?"

She could see amusement in his eyes, so she allowed herself a small smile as she took him in. His clothing was worn, his shirt too small for him and torn at the elbows. Yona was startled by the impulse that ran through her then, the urge to mend his sleeves. There was something else, too, something that unsettled her even more—a desire to touch his skin, to see if it burned as hot as hers did. "No, I did not," she answered abruptly.

His smile slipped a bit. "I was only joking."

"Of course. It is just . . . I have not . . ." She trailed off helplessly. How could she explain to him that she had never in her life spoken to anyone but Jerusza? That she didn't entirely understand jokes, because Jerusza never made them? That her only glimpses of the world outside the forest had been on the few occasions each year that Jerusza had allowed Yona to follow her into a village in the dead of night?

"It's all right." Marcin's tone was gentler now. "It was a bit of a silly joke anyhow. Berlin wouldn't be a good place to be now."

"Why not?"

He blinked at her a few times. "Surely you've heard about the things that are happening there."

"What things?" She had a bad feeling suddenly, a glimpse of storm clouds moving in, a sense that whatever he was about to say was something she already knew in her bones.

His smile was gone, but his eyes were still kind. "I should not have assumed. It has been in the newspaper. Can you read, Yona?" The question was not cruel. He thought she was simple, uneducated, a girl from the woods who had lied about the only distant city she had heard of.

But he was wrong. The problem was that the books Jerusza stole from the libraries in the towns and villages outside the forest, or from churches and synagogues, were chosen according to some plan that Yona didn't understand. Her education had been limited to histories of the world and scientific texts on plants, herbs, and biology, as well as multiple readings of texts from various religions. Life, Jerusza said, was an endless search for the true meaning of God. "Yes, I can read."

"I'm sorry. Of course you can . . . I just thought that . . ." Marcin trailed off, but he looked chagrined.

"It's all right. I—I do love books most of the time. They are . . ." She hesitated, the right words dancing on the tip of her tongue. "Books are magic, aren't they?"

"Well, in Germany right now, the people in charge would disagree. They would say that books are dangerous."

"But how could a book be dangerous?"

"Don't know." He shrugged. "They are burning them there, in your Berlin, you know. That's what I was trying to tell you."

"Burning books?" Yona blinked at him a few times. "But why would anyone do such a thing?"

"I suppose they don't believe people should be able to read books they don't agree with, written by people they don't agree with."

It sounded a bit like the way Jerusza thought of things—a righteous sense of deserving control over others' thoughts—but Yona doubted the old woman would go so far as to incinerate knowledge. "How terrible."

A faint call came from somewhere in the distance, the call of a man's deep voice, and Yona stiffened, her hand going instantly to the knife at her ankle. Marcin heard it, too, for he cocked his head in the direction of the sound and sighed. "My father," he said. "Do you want to—"

"I should go," Yona said quickly. And though she wanted to stay, though she wanted to ask Marcin what else was happening in the world, and what his life was like, and what he had read in books and newspapers, she was suddenly terrified. Marcin seemed like a friend. But what if his father was one of the people Jerusza had warned her about? She had already stayed too long. "I—I'll return tomorrow."

"Yona, please don't run away again," Marcin said, taking a step forward.

But she was already gone, vanishing into the trees like a gust of wind, until it was as if she had never really been there at all.

When Yona returned to camp that afternoon, her heart was throbbing with regret. Why hadn't she stayed longer? Had the courage to ask more?

She was so lost in her own thoughts that it took a few seconds for it to register that Jerusza was in the midst of tearing apart the hut they had called home for the last three weeks, stripping the bark from the roof, uprooting the wooden stakes with furious jerks of her hands. Yona stopped and stared. "Why—" she began.

Jerusza spun on her. "You think I wouldn't find out about the boy? How dare you disobey me? You don't know the world, and you haven't the wisdom to make your own choices, you careless fool. What if he had followed you?"

"I didn't—"

"Enough!" Jerusza cut her off, her voice a sharp knife of disappointment. "What have you done?"

Shamed into silence, Yona gathered her things and tried not to cry, but it was useless. As they trudged through the forest, away from where Marcin would be waiting for her the next day, Yona's tears slipped and fell, silently watering the earth. "He was kind, Jerusza," Yona said after they'd passed an hour in silence. "He didn't mean me any harm."

"You know nothing," Jerusza shot back. "Men can be cruel and heartless and cold. And the mistakes we make follow us all our lives."

"He was my friend," Yona whispered.

"Was he? Or did he want things from you?"

Yona was confused. He had seemed to want nothing but conversation. "What things?"

Jerusza spat. "In this world, you keep your power as long as you keep your legs closed."

Yona just blinked at her, completely lost. "I—I don't understand."

Jerusza stared at her in disbelief. "Come on, child. Boys want things from girls. It's the oldest story in the book."

And then, in a flash, Yona understood, and heat raced to her cheeks. "But it wasn't anything like that!" She knew about the mechanics of sex—*an unfortunate necessity to perpetuate the human race*, Jerusza called it—but in her mind, it had nothing to do with feeling like one had common ground with another person. They had only talked, which had nothing to do with their bodies.

Then again, she had longed to draw closer to him, hadn't she? Was that nature at work? Or was it simply desperation to have someone see that she was alive, whole?

Later, as the years passed, and she and Jerusza made their way north and then east, she thought of Marcin sometimes and wished she'd been brave enough to touch the skin of his arm, just so she'd known, if only for a second, what it felt like to connect with another human being.

But there were no more humans to be found where they were, and life lapsed into predictable monotony for a time. Each day, they foraged for food and herbs. Each night, over a small fire, they cooked what they had found. They moved at least once a month so they left hardly a trace if anyone came looking. In the late summer and autumn, they gathered and smoked food for the winter; by the time the leaves turned, they began building a shelter, dug deep into the sandy earth and supported by poles hewn from tree trunks. In the winter, they huddled together around a small fire inside their cramped dugout, emerging only to refill their meager larder with mud loaches, beetle larvae, and frozen berries as their supplies dwindled, and to shovel freshly fallen snow into pots for fresh water. Each spring, Jerusza ventured into villages to steal clothing, shoes, blankets, knives, and axes— leaving Yona behind now, with firm instructions not to move or there would be dire consequences—and on each expedition, she brought back books, which Yona inhaled ravenously, longing to imagine what life was like outside the forest. In the summers, they found their way to deserted Russian encampments left behind during the Great War and dug in the earth until they found treasures like magnesium sticks and ferro rods, which made it easy to build fires. In time, they accumulated a small sack of them, which they took with them wherever they went, for it would provide easy light and heat for years.

But something was happening, and by the time Yona had turned twenty, the world around the forest had grown angry. The earth growled, and airplanes rumbled overhead with increasing frequency, breaking the stillness of the sky. There were sometimes explosions far away, and sounds Jerusza explained were shots from soldiers' guns, and though Yona begged Jerusza to tell her what was happening, the old woman's answers were obfuscating. "God is angry," she would say, fear glimmering in her eyes. Or, "We are being tested." Whenever Yona asked more, Jerusza grabbed her by the shoulders and hissed warnings such as, "As long as you are here, Yona, you are safe. Do not forget that," or, "The forest will protect you." But how could Yona find protection from something she didn't know, didn't understand?

There were more people in the forest now, too, and that seemed to frighten the normally unflappable Jerusza. "These men, they will hurt us if they find us," she whispered one night as they cowered in the darkness of a three-hundred-year-old hollowed oak, each of them clutching a knife, listening to heavy footsteps nearby.

"Who are they?" Yona asked.

"Bad men. The horror has just begun." But Jerusza would explain no more. Later that night, long after the footsteps had faded, they began moving again, this time to the east.

"Where are we going?" Yona asked, her voice low, as she struggled to keep up with Jerusza, who was traipsing through the darkness with purpose.

"East, of course," the old woman said without breaking her stride, without turning to look at Yona. "When there is trouble, you must always move toward the beginning of the day, not the end. You know this, child. Have I taught you nothing?"

In the summer of 1941, bloated black logs fell from the sky one bright afternoon, shaking the solid earth, frightening the birds from the trees, scaring the rabbits underground as the ground quaked and rolled.

"Bombs," Jerusza said, her voice as hollow as a dead oak. "They are bombing Poland."

Yona knew about bombs, of course, for they'd fallen two years before, too. But she had never seen them like this, clouding a bright blue sky. "Who?" Yona felt cold, despite the heat of the sun. In the distance, there were more explosions. "Who is bombing Poland?"

"The Germans." Jerusza did not look at Yona as she replied. "Come. There's no time to lose, or we'll be directly in the path of Russian deserters."

"What?" Yona asked, completely confused, but Jerusza didn't answer. Instead, she gathered their things, thrust a few knapsacks into Yona's arms, and started off into the woods as quickly as Yona had ever seen her move.

It took them two days and nights of walking, stopping only to sleep for a few hours when their feet couldn't carry them anymore, before they reached the edge of a seemingly endless swamp, just to the west of the forest's heart.

"Where are we?" Yona asked.

"Somewhere safe. Now take off your packs and be prepared to carry them above your head. Your knife, too."

Stunned into silence, Yona scanned the horizon. The swamp stretched farther than the eye could see and seemed to Yona to be an optical illusion; it was dotted with islands, but it was impossible to tell from the edge which parts of the swamp were solid ground and which were swirling with deep, murky water. Was it Yona's imagination, or could she hear the water hissing the word Jerusza had just spoken? *Safe*, it seemed to be saying. *Saaaaaaafe*.

"But won't you get sick?" Yona asked as Jerusza began to lead the way into the deepening swamp, the water already up to their hips. After all, the old woman was a century old, and just the week before, she had begun to cough and shake at night.

Jerusza choked out a mirthless laugh. "Have I not taught you by now that the forest takes care of its own?"

"But why are we doing this, Jerusza?" Yona had asked an hour later as the water reached their necks. Around them, the swamp continued to hiss. They carried their packs on their heads so the turbid muck wouldn't soak their things.

"Because you must know this forest inside and out, her heart, her soul. Now you are in her belly, and her belly will keep you safe."

It took them two days to reach an island in the center of the swamp, where they found mushrooms, bilberries, and startled hedgehogs that were easy to catch. They remained there for a month, until they had picked the island clean of its sustenance, until they could no longer hear explosions or the *rat-tat-tat* of gunfire in the distance.

As they finally made their way back to a more familiar part of the forest in early August, Yona summoned the courage to ask a question that had been weighing on her for a long while. "What do you believe, Jerusza?" she asked as they walked, the old woman several strides ahead of her, leading the way. "You call yourself Jewish, and we mark the Jewish holidays, but you scoff at them, too."

Jerusza didn't turn to look at her, nor did she slow her pace. "I believe everything and nothing. I am a seeker of truth, a seeker of God." It wasn't an answer. Finally, Jerusza sighed. "As you know, my mother was Jewish, and so according to Jewish law, that means I am, too. You know these things, child. Why are you forcing me to waste my breath?"

"I—I suppose I'm wondering about myself."

"What *about* yourself?"

"Well . . . what am I? You are not my mother, but you raised me. Does that make me Jewish, too?"

The silence hung between them as they walked. "You are what you were born to be," Jerusza said at last.

Yona clenched her fists in frustration. It should have been a simple question, but somehow, even after all these years, it wasn't. "But what *was* that?" she persisted. "Why do you never give me a clear answer? *What* was I born to be?"

"I wish I knew," Jerusza shot back. "I wish I understood why the forest called me to you. I wish I could understand why I've had to spend the final years of my life with an ungrateful child. I suppose you're fated for something great, but at the rate you're going, I'll be long dead before you fulfill whatever destiny that may be."

Yona's head throbbed with confusion and hurt. "But if you could tell me something about where I came from . . ."

"For goodness' sake, stop!" Jerusza finally turned to glare at Yona. She chewed her sagging lip for a long moment before adding, "You're asking the wrong questions, child. Never forget that the truth always lies within you. And if you can't find it, maybe the forest was wrong about you. Perhaps you're nothing more than an ordinary girl, after all."

CHAPTER FOUR

By the time 1942 dawned, frigid and empty, Yona had grown used to her own company, for Jerusza, now 102 years old, hardly spoke at all anymore. Yona was nearly twenty-two, and she knew everything there was to know about the earth beneath her feet, and the things that sprang from it, but nearly nothing about the ways of mankind. She hadn't seen another human in nearly three years other than occasional glimpses of the bad men from deep within the trees. She held conversations with red squirrels and mountain hares. She cooked, she cleaned, she spoke to a God she couldn't understand. But venturing outside the forest had grown too dangerous, even for Jerusza. The deeper into the Nalibocka they went, the more the world outside disappeared.

Before she knew it, it was March, and the cold was seeping back into the ground, the snow melting, the frost releasing its hold. On a day when the sun rose above the treetops in a cold, cloudless sky, Jerusza, who hadn't moved from her reed bed, summoned Yona.

"Today," Jerusza said, her voice raspy, breathless, "is the day I will die."

Yona's eyes filled with tears. She had known the time was coming, for Jerusza's body was slowing, growing colder. The birds, reemerging to look for signs of spring, had kept their distance like never before, and Yona had felt a shadow looming over their home dug into the earth. They'd been living there since November, the longest they'd stayed in a single place.

"What can I do?" Yona asked, coming to kneel beside her.

"Prepare me some linden tea." The old woman drew a trembling breath.

Blinking back her tears, Yona scrambled to do as Jerusza had asked, brewing a strong concoction made from the dried flowers of linden trees, which she and Jerusza had gathered last summer. It would bring Jerusza's fever down and help with the pain, but it wouldn't slow her transition to the other side. As she waited for the flowers to steep, Yona tried to focus on how to keep Jerusza comfortable, but dark thoughts kept creeping in at the edges; what would become of her when Jerusza was gone?

When she knelt again beside Jerusza a few minutes later, a steaming cup in her hands, the old woman's breathing had grown noticeably shallower, but still she recited the *vidui*, the prayer of confession, before taking the cup in her trembling hands.

"Jerusza, what will I—" Yona began to ask, but Jerusza cut her off.

"There are things I must tell you." Jerusza took a long sip of the tea. She blinked a few times, and when she turned her cloudy eyes again to Yona, she looked stronger and more alert than Yona had seen her in months.

"I am here." Yona leaned in and put her hands over Jerusza's, an expression of solidarity, but Jerusza shook her off.

"First, you must never venture outside the forest. Not while the world is at war. You must promise me, Yona."

It was the deal they'd had since the bombs had begun to fall two and a half years before, and Yona had stuck to her side of it. But once Jerusza died, she would be all alone in the darkness. What if she craved human contact once in a while? "But if I need food . . ."

"The forest will provide, child!" Jerusza let out a great, hacking cough that shook her whole body. "The forest will always provide. You must give me your word."

It would have been so simple to just agree, but Jerusza had taught Yona long ago never to lie unless her life was in danger and an untruth was the only way out. "I can't do that," she whispered.

Jerusza struggled to sit up. Her eyes were blazing, even as the life seeped slowly out of her. "Then you are a fool, and you will put yourself at great risk."

"But maybe great risk is the only way to a better life," Yona said. "Isn't that what you've told me about our existence? Life in a village would be easier, but we take the risk of living in the woods because it gives us a bigger life, here under the stars."

Jerusza's upper lip curled. "It appears the student has become the teacher at last." Her voice was raspy and growing weaker. "Well then, I suppose there is something else you should know, too. Of course you are already aware that I am not your real mother."

"Of course." A sudden ache of loneliness shot through Yona. She had tried asking about where she'd come from several times over the years, but Jerusza had always stormed off, calling Yona an ungrateful wretch. Yona had come to believe, over the years, that she must have been abandoned by heartless parents in the woods, and that the old woman had saved her life.

"I stole you," Jerusza continued, her tone even. "I had no choice, you see."

Yona sat back on her heels, sure she had misunderstood. "You *stole* me?"

"Yes. From an apartment in Berlin. From a woman and a man you were not meant to belong to." She delivered the blow as calmly as if she were remarking on the weather.

"*What?*" Yona stood abruptly, shaky on her feet, disbelief mixing with an inkling of a sense that there was a small part of her that already knew the story. *Berlin.*

"Sit down, child. There's no time for your dramatics now."

Yona took a few gulps of air, her body tensed to flee into the forest, where she wouldn't have to swallow the pain of whatever Jerusza was about to say. But she couldn't. She knew she couldn't, because the old woman would be dead before she returned, and she would never hear the things she needed to know. "What did you do, Jerusza?" she whispered, sinking back down.

"What did I *do*? I saved you, child." Sweat was beading on Jerusza's forehead now, and her breathing was becoming more labored, a series of staccato swallows and hisses. "Your parents were bad people, you see."

"How could you possibly know that?"

"The way I know everything." Jerusza's words bit like a whip. "The forest told me. The forest, and the sky."

"But—"

"Their names were Siegfried and Alwine Jüttner," Jerusza continued, rolling right over Yona's grief-stricken protest. "They lived in an apartment at Behaimstrasse 72 in Berlin."

The apartment with the wooden bed and the warm blankets that haunted her dreams. Yona swallowed hard a few times, a thousand questions bubbling within her. The one that forced itself to the surface, though, was, "Am I meant to go back to them now? Is that why you're telling me this?"

"No!" The old woman's eyes flashed, and she sat up. Her torso wobbled unsteadily, like a blade of wheat in the wind, and Yona resisted the urge to reach out and steady her. She didn't deserve that. "No!" Jerusza repeated, her voice so loud and sharp that Yona could hear a startled congress of crows lifting off outside, squawking in outrage. "You must not."

"Then why tell me at all? And why now?"

"Because it is . . ." Jerusza trailed off, her words dissolving into a wet cough that wracked her body. ". . . knowledge that may spare your life—or another's—someday."

"What do you mean?" Yona leaned forward.

"We are all interconnected, Yona. You know that by now. Once fates intertwine, they are forever linked. Lives are circles spinning across the world, and when they're meant to intersect again, they do. There's nothing we can do to stop it."

"Are you saying I will see my parents again?"

Jerusza looked away. "The universe delivers opportunities for life and death all the time. I am giving you now a chance for life, just as I did when I took you."

"I—I don't understand." Yona could feel desperation closing her throat. She wanted to shake the old woman, who, even on her deathbed, was talking in smug, impenetrable riddles. "A chance for life? What are you saying, Jerusza?"

"You will know." Jerusza drew another difficult breath, then sighed and sank back into her reeds. "You will live until the first new moon of your one hundredth year, Yona, if you do not forget the things I have taught you. *You will know.*"

Yona sat back and stared at her. The old woman's prediction—so certain, so sure—would have sounded outlandish if Yona didn't know that Jerusza's talent was infallible. The earth spoke to Jerusza in a way that Yona had never understood, but it never lied, and neither did Jerusza. That was why Yona knew she had to ask the question that had been burning within her for years.

"Do you love me, Jerusza?" she asked in a small voice, ashamed that it mattered so much. "Please, I must know."

Jerusza stared at her, and her expression was not one of tenderness or even regret. It was of disgust, revulsion. "Love is a wasted emotion," she said at last, her voice fading. "It makes you weak. Have I taught you nothing? Love is for fools."

Yona looked away before Jerusza could read the pain in her eyes. "But what if the parents you took me from loved me?"

"And so what if they did?" Jerusza's voice had waned to a whisper. "Would you have traded the life you've had with me for one with evil parents, just because it came with love?"

"I don't know," Yona said. "You never gave me the chance to choose." At that moment, Jerusza closed her eyes and breathed her last, and a single tear rolled down Yona's cheek for all that was lost and could never be found.

Yona was reeling from the revelation of her origin, but still, she dutifully did the things Jerusza had asked her to do, the rituals the old woman had taught her, a combination of Jewish tradition and Slavic witchcraft as mysterious as Jerusza herself. "*Baruch Atah Ahdonai, Ehlohaynu, Mehlekh Haolam, Dayan HaEhmet,*" she murmured over the body of the woman who had raised her, a woman she had never really known at all. *Blessed are you, Lord our God, king of the universe, judge of truth.* She lit candles made from beeswax and nettle and placed them above Jerusza's head. She recited the Twenty-third Psalm and then sat beside Jerusza, the only mother she'd ever known, for a day and a night.

When the sun rose high the next day, Yona washed the old woman's body with frigid water from a narrow nearby river, gently, carefully, wringing out the rags into pitchers, and then poured the water into a shallow grave, the best she could do when the ground was still cold. Then she wrapped Jerusza in a white burial shroud and carefully lowered her into the earth. After she had shoveled the dirt back into Jerusza's resting place, she stamped it down carefully, for she knew that ghosts could escape from loose earth. She hoped that Jerusza's soul would find its way to its next home, whatever that might be, but that it would fly far from here, for though she dreaded being alone, she feared the prospect of being haunted by Jerusza even more.

For seven days, she stayed to sit shiva, not bathing, not changing her clothing, hardly moving from her spot on the cold earth, and reciting the mourning prayers three times a day as Jerusza had taught her. When the prescribed period of mourning was done, she destroyed the earthen roof of the dugout, gathered the few things she could take with her—two bags of acorn flour, three shirts, three pairs of trousers, and a tattered wool coat Jerusza had stolen for her from a village long ago, a mug, a plate, a pot, an axe, and the knife she always carried on her ankle—and walked away without looking back, leaving Jerusza, and everything that belonged to their life together, behind her forever.

For two months, Yona wandered the forest alone, setting up camp in a different spot every few months, just as Jerusza had taught her, but gradually coming closer to the forest's edge, too, flirting with danger in a way that made her heart race. What if she ventured into a village, a town? Could she choose a different life than the one Jerusza had given her? After all, who was Jerusza to choose Yona's fate, her future? But fear held her back—fear and a memory of the explosions that had shaken the forest the summer before. Jerusza's words still rang in her ears. *The horror has just begun.*

By late April, the spring sun burned the afternoons, and Yona, accustomed now to the predictable silence of her own company, had moved into the northern depths of the forest, leaving both the mysterious swamp and her dreams of civilization behind. In the summer and autumn, one was never really alone among the trees, for that was when the creatures of the forest were most active. Each day she walked deeper into the woods, and at the coming of each twilight, she made a simple camp beneath the stars. When the nights were mild, there was no need to build a shelter; the sky was her roof, the world her walls. In the mornings, she talked in a gentle whisper to the long-billed snipes that came to drink from the clear brooks, and sometimes, if she stayed still enough, she could lock eyes with a sleek spotted lynx for a long moment before each of them went their separate ways in silent understanding.

At night, when she closed her eyes, she reached for long-lost images of her parents in her mind until she could just make them out through the fog of time, their familiar faces hovering above a cradle. *Siegfried and Alwine Jüttner.* Who were they? What did they believe had become of their lost daughter? Did they still think of her, wonder about her fate?

On a crisp morning after a heavy rain late in the month, Yona was just about to emerge from the hollowed-out oak trunk where she'd sought shelter from the storm the night before, when she heard a rustling in the trees. She had seen a flock of cranes the previous afternoon and thought they might be returning, so she held her breath and listened for their distinctive bugle calls. But the flash of color behind the trees wasn't the muddy white of a crane, and immediately, Yona's chest seized with fear. It was too small to be an elk or a bear. It was too small even for a fox. It took Yona a few startled seconds to recognize that the creature moving into the clearing was a slight, dark-haired child, a little girl in a threadbare dress, her hair matted, her arms and legs mud-caked, her face white as a cumulus cloud.

Yona ducked quickly behind a tree and watched as the girl staggered closer. Yona hadn't seen a child in years; the glimpses she caught of other humans in the forest were always of older boys or men who had ventured beyond their villages to hunt, or of the bad men Jerusza had warned her about, the ones who wore tattered uniforms, fur caps, and scowls. Yona couldn't guess how old the child was—old enough to speak, perhaps, though certainly not old enough to be roaming the woods alone—but she could tell instantly that something was wrong. The girl's eyes were wide as full moons, unfocused, and her legs seemed ill-suited to carrying her tiny frame as she wobbled to and fro.

Yona took a step forward, then froze. Surely there would be a protective mother nearby. But Yona waited a minute, and then two, and no parent arrived. The girl wobbled a bit more, and then her eyes rolled back into her head, and she collapsed with a noise that sounded like both a sigh and a gasp, pitching headfirst into a jagged tree stump.

Yona was running toward the child before she could stop herself, driven by an instinct she couldn't name, which overrode her caution. Before she knew it, she was on her knees beside the child, lifting her up, feeling for a pulse in her tiny, limp wrist, sighing in relief at the strong *tap-tap-tap* from the child's radial artery. She put a hand on the girl's forehead and withdrew it quickly with a sharp intake of breath. The girl was burning up. Yona picked her up gently and then hesitated. What to do next? The child needed something to bring her fever down, but where were her people? Parents didn't let children this young wander into the wilderness, for they would disappear forever there. She waited only a second more before calling out, "Hello? Anybody?"

Two white-backed woodpeckers lifted off from a tree nearby, their startled *kuik-kuik*s piercing the quiet of the forest, but nothing else moved. Yona looked down once more at the little girl in her arms. Her hair was tied with a bow; her little blue sweater, though shredded to rags, had a yellow fabric star carefully stitched on. There was someone out there who cared about her. "Please!" Yona called out once more. "The child is hurt!" But her only reply was the shuffle of the branches and the faint echo of her own voice.

There was no one out there. Finally, with the child in her arms, Yona turned and hurried toward the tree where she'd found shelter the night before, a massive oak, hundreds of years old, with a hollow in its trunk large enough to lie down in and to stand without ducking. After reassuring herself that the girl's heart was still beating strong, Yona laid her down on a bed of leaves and dashed out to skin a long strip of bark from a willow tree. She raced to the stream a kilometer from her camp, soaked the bark in the cool water, and ran back to the shelter, where she knelt beside the girl and applied the compress to her head. "There," she murmured, "you'll feel better soon." She sat back on her heels, studying the girl's still, colorless face. "Please hold on," she added in a whisper.

After checking the child's pulse once more, this time just under the hollow of her neck, Yona stood again and made her way back outside. She started a fire as she always did, with one of the Russian magnesium sticks she treasured, then she stripped some more bark from the willow, dipped her pot in the stream, and set to work boiling water for willow tea. The smoke from the fire might attract people, signaling Yona's location, but it was a chance she had to take. Besides, if there were people in the forest, they might be the girl's people.

Then again, what if the girl had been running from someone? The thought made Yona's breath catch in her throat. The girl's clothes were shredded, her body bruised and scraped, her little frame nearly emaciated. What if it hadn't been the forest that had hurt her? What if the forest was protecting her from the demons on the outside that Jerusza had always warned Yona about, the ones Yona wasn't sure whether to believe in?

As soon as the water boiled, Yona hastily poured it into a cup, added the willow bark, and extinguished the flames. Maybe no one had seen them at all. She rushed back into the hollow tree and knelt beside the girl again, but now all her senses were on high alert. She believed in her ability to protect herself—after all, so much of her childhood had centered around learning the art of fatal self-defense—but she had never thought much about protecting someone else, not even when Jerusza was near death's door, for even then, Yona had believed in the old woman's protective magic.

"Wake up," she murmured, touching the girl's cheek, which felt a little cooler, a sign that the bark across the girl's forehead was working to fight the fever. "Please, sweet child, wake up."

And then, as if God had been listening, the little girl did just that, her eyelashes fluttering, her eyes opening—they were deep, the color of a bear cub's fur—and her mouth forming a tiny O of surprise as she registered the presence of a stranger looming over her. The girl sat upright and screamed, but the sound was barely audible and the effort of that alone seemed to exhaust her.

Yona put a gentle hand on her arm. "You are safe here," she said. "I won't hurt you."

But the girl just stared at her in confusion, and Yona realized she hadn't understood. She had spoken in Belorussian, because she knew many of the people in the towns that ringed the forest used the language, but perhaps the girl was Polish. She tried again in that language, but she was greeted by the same blank, frightened look. She tried German, then Russian, but still nothing.

Finally, the girl spoke. "*Ver bisti? Vu zenen maane eltern.*"

Surprised, Yona replied in Yiddish. "I am a friend. And I don't know where your parents are, but I promise, I will do all I can to find them. In the meantime, I will keep you safe."

The girl's mouth fell open. "You are Jewish, too?"

Yona hesitated, Jerusza's confused words from the summer before still fresh in her mind. *You are what you were born to be.*

But what *was* that? Jerusza had steeped her in Jewish tradition, had made sure she knew Jewish law inside and out, had read to her from the Torah even before Yona could read herself. Yona believed in God and saw him everywhere, and she believed the teachings of Jewish scholars and sages, but that wasn't enough, particularly for someone who had never set foot within a synagogue, though Jerusza insisted that God could be worshipped anywhere. "I don't know," she concluded helplessly.

"But . . . you speak the language of the Jews."

"I speak many languages."

The girl looked confused. "Your—your eyes are funny. They're different colors."

Yona blinked a few times. "Yes, I suppose they are." No one aside from Jerusza had gotten close enough to her to notice them, not even the boy she'd met in the woods years before. It felt strange to be face-to-face with another person, and Yona felt suddenly self-conscious, though the girl was just a child. "My name is Yona," she said after a pause. "What is yours?"

The girl hesitated, searching Yona's eyes. "Chana," she said at last.

"Well, Chana, I have made you some willow tea. If you drink it, it will make you feel better."

Chana regarded the cup in Yona's hands but didn't reach for it. "It will not hurt me?"

"I give you my word." Yona held out the cup, and after another second's hesitation, the girl took it and sniffed it uncertainly. "It will bring your fever down, and it will help with the pain," Yona added.

The girl took a small, hesitant sip, wrinkling her nose a bit, but then she drank again. "How do you know I am in pain?"

"You fell." Yona tapped the center of her own forehead. "You hit your head, just here. Can you feel the bump? And you have many cuts and bruises." She hesitated, watching the girl as she drank again. "What happened to you, Chana? What were you running from?"

The girl's face changed then, her eyes filling with tears. "I was running from the . . . the people who want to kill us."

"But who would want to kill you?"

The girl looked over Yona's shoulder, searching the woods for an invisible hunter. When her eyes returned to Yona's face, the sadness in them nearly knocked Yona over. "The Germans," she said. "The Germans who came to Volozhin."

Yona didn't understand. For all she knew about the forest, she knew nearly nothing about the way mankind worked. Still, she knew enough to realize that if there were people out there trying to kill an innocent child, something had gone very wrong in the world. "Why?" she asked finally. "Why would anyone be trying to kill you, Chana?"

"Because I am Jewish." The girl's voice was flat, sad. She touched the yellow star sewn onto her sweater. "They are trying to kill us all."

CHAPTER FIVE

For two days, Yona fed Chana a soothing stew made from fish bones, chanterelle mushrooms, and acorn flour, and each night, she waited until the girl was sleeping soundly before she let her own tears fall.

If an adult had said the things the girl had, she would have believed the person was lying. But Chana, just six years old, was guileless. Her voice had stayed low and flat as she told Yona, haltingly, of the terrible things that had happened to the Jews who lived in the villages around the forest's edge. Arrests and deportations of the strongest men. Ghettos where streets overflowed with human waste and garbage. Rampant disease, starvation, orphans with nowhere to go who froze to death in the winter, their hands still reaching for bread that would never come.

The realization of what was happening outside the forest swept over Yona like a virus. She dry-heaved in the mornings, out of sight of the girl. And when she smiled and reassured the girl that all would be well in the end, she could taste the salt on her tongue, just like when she'd lied to Marcin in the woods all those years before.

The Germans had done this to the child, and Yona couldn't stop thinking of the things Jerusza had said on her deathbed. She had stolen Yona from German parents. *Bad people*, she had called them. *Evil parents*. Is this what Jerusza had meant? Could people be so cruel to their fellow man? Had Jerusza been right to do what she had done?

"Please, will you take me to find my mother and father?" the girl asked just after dawn on the third day. She had gained some of her strength back, and she had told Yona that she'd been separated from them a week earlier, when they fled the ghetto together along with a dozen others through a tunnel they'd dug by hand. Germans had given chase, shouting words she couldn't understand, and when gunfire rang out, she'd been so frightened that she ran without looking back. When her legs faltered beneath her and she could go no farther, she stopped and found herself completely, terrifyingly alone.

Yona feared that the girl's parents were dead, but she nodded and forced a smile. "We will begin looking for them today. But the forest is large, Chana. It is possible we might not be able to find them. You must prepare yourself for that."

"They will be looking for me, too," Chana replied with certainty. "They are out there."

And so, although it went against Yona's instincts, they began moving that day toward civilization on the northern edge of the forest, the direction from which Chana had come.

It took them a day and a half, walking by the light of a full moon, sleeping in the day, before Yona picked up a trail. Two pairs of footprints led east, away from a riverbank, and one of the sets was too small to be a man's. Could they belong to Chana's mother? They were fresh, less than a day old.

Six hours later, just as the sun was beginning to rise, they found the footsteps' end. Set between two oaks was a poorly constructed lean-to with an inexpert roof of scattered branches that couldn't possibly have done much to keep out either rain or sun. The second Yona spotted it, she pulled Chana behind a tree and motioned for the girl to be quiet. She had to be sure that the people who had built it would not harm them. Chana looked at her with wide eyes and nodded her understanding, but after a few minutes had passed, a woman emerged, her long brown hair falling over her shoulders like a curtain, and Chana was off like a shot. "Mami!" she cried.

The woman turned, and Chana flew into her arms. Both of them were crying and talking at the same time, and as Yona stepped from behind the bushes, she was surprised to feel tears in her eyes. It was the sort of reunion she would never have; there was no one out there waiting for her.

After the woman let Chana go, Chana turned and pointed toward Yona, and the woman's expression changed from one of pure joy to one of guarded curiosity in an instant. "She saved me, Mami," Yona could hear the girl say, and after a second, the woman's face softened, and she beckoned Yona closer.

"Is this true?" she asked, her voice deep, strong. She spoke Polish, unlike her daughter. "You saved my Chana?"

"She was injured," Yona replied in Yiddish, the language the woman must have been more comfortable with, for it was the one she'd taught her child. "I promised to help her find you."

The woman stared at her for another moment. "You speak Yiddish. You were in the ghetto, too? I have not seen you before."

Yona shook her head. "I am only from the forest."

The woman studied her for a minute more. "You know how to help people who are hurt, then? Please. My husband, he needs help. Will you come?"

Yona nodded and, ducking her head, followed the woman toward the poorly built structure, Chana tailing behind them.

"Thank you," the woman added without looking at Yona. "Thank you for saving my child."

Chana's father was dying, his torso a bloodied mass, his face beaded with sweat. He lay on his back, breathing rapidly, his eyes half-open and glazed. When Chana came close, whimpering, he looked as if he did not know her, and her mother quickly pulled her back, wrapping her in a hug.

"Who . . . you?" he managed to ask Yona. He struggled to sit, but Yona put a firm hand on his shoulder and eased him back down.

"My name is Yona," she said. "I brought your daughter back to you. And I will try to help you."

He stared at her for a few seconds and then closed his eyes. "I am already dead."

"You are still alive. And I will do all I can to keep you that way." Yona spoke with a confidence she didn't feel, but she had to. It was the only way she could convince herself that she might be able to save him. She looked skyward and wished Jerusza were here to help her, for the old woman would know just what to do. Then again, the mere fact that Yona was here would have gone against everything Jerusza stood for. She would have told Yona that she was putting herself in danger. And Yona knew this, knew that the longer she stayed, the higher the risk was for her. But she couldn't simply abandon this family.

"This is a gunshot wound, yes?" she asked gently after examining the gaping hole in the man's abdomen. She had seen dead animals left behind this way by careless hunters.

He seemed not to hear her over his own labored breathing. But Chana's mother, who was hovering nearby, said in a raspy whisper, "Yes. They shot him."

"All right." Yona was struggling to sound as if she was in control rather than terrified. "Do you know the burdock plant?" Chana was crying, her face hidden in the threadbare folds of her mother's dress.

"Yes, I know it," Chana's mother said.

"You and Chana must bring me some as soon as you can."

Chana and her mother set off into the forest at a jog, and Yona realized too late that she had forgotten to warn them to be quiet. Then again, she and Chana had encountered no other signs of man on their trek here, and there was no indication that anyone was watching other than the creatures of the forest. She quickly scanned the area around her for something she could use to help Chana's father while she waited for Chana and her mother to return, and her gaze came to rest on some tiny white flowers growing thirty yards away. *Achillea millefolium*, yarrow. Her heart thudding, she dashed over to grab a handful of the buds. Racing to the stream, she chose a large stick and crushed the plant into a paste, adding a bit of water. Then, the rough mixture in her hands, she hurried back to Chana's father.

Inside the listing lean-to, his breathing had grown even more labored. As Yona knelt beside him, he didn't even look at her. "This will hurt," she murmured. "I'm sorry."

He grunted and writhed in pain as she turned him gently over to make sure the bullet had gone through him instead of lodging in his body. It had; there was a clean, circular hole in his lower back where the bullet had departed. She spread the paste around the outer perimeter of the exit wound, and then she turned him back over to spread it all around the jagged edges of his shredded abdomen, too, wincing at his screams. "It is going to get worse before it gets better," she murmured once he had again fallen back into a state of semiconsciousness. "But it will be your only chance to survive."

By the time Chana and her mother returned, pink burrs and leafy greens clutched in their hands, he was fast asleep, his chest rising and falling under Yona's palm as she watched the blood around his wound finally begin to clot, beginning the slow work of knitting his body back together.

"Isaac is still alive?" Chana's mother asked, staring at Yona with a blend of fear and respect. "What do we do now?"

"Now," Yona replied, "we pray."

Yona waited until the blood had stopped oozing from Isaac's gut before rubbing a mixture made from the leaves, stems, and flowers of the burdock plant on his wound to disinfect it. She gently turned him over, and he groaned in his sleep as she spread it on his lower back, too.

It was two days before he awoke, clear-eyed, and asked for Esta, his wife.

"Will my husband live?" Esta asked in a whisper as she slipped past Yona and into the hut. Yona had given it a roof and walls of spruce bark supported by pine poles, which would with-stand the wind and better blend into the trees. They would need to stay here for a week, at least, before Chana's wounded father would be able to walk on his own again.

"I think so," Yona said, but as she locked eyes with the other woman, an understanding passed between them. The words were not a promise, but Yona had done her best.

It was enough, though, and eight days later, Isaac, who had worked in a Jewish bank before the Germans forced it out of business, was walking around, albeit with difficulty, laughing with Chana, whose face had been transformed by relief.

The mirth in his smile didn't reach his eyes, though, and Yona could see pain there, pain and fear. The way they were all living now, focusing on his healing, was just a suspension of re-ality. They hadn't gone far enough into the forest to evade those who might be after them.

"Chana told me some things about the ghetto in your town," Yona said quietly as she examined Isaac's wounds on the eleventh day, while Esta and Chana waited outside. "Are they true?"

He winced as she rubbed a fresh paste around the large gash in his torso, which was still very much at risk of becoming infected. He didn't speak for a moment, and when he did, his words were heavy with sadness. "The Soviets came first, three years ago, and took away our right to practice our religion, any religion. That broke my heart, for the yeshiva was such a central part of our lives, of our town. It had stood for over a hundred years, since 1803—and the godless Soviets, they turned it into a bar. We thought it could not get any worse than that." He drew a trembling breath. "We were wrong.

"Last summer, the Germans came," he continued, his voice flattening into a monotone. "A month after they arrived, they moved all the Jews of our town into a tiny ghetto, in horrible conditions. We received no more than a piece of bread each day. And then they began to murder us, at random."

He went silent again, and Yona tried to hold back tears. "I—I don't understand."

Isaac's shrug was heavy, and he avoided Yona's gaze as he went on. "In October, they killed three hundred Jews for sport. It was no secret. They wanted us to know, to be afraid. They wanted us aware that, to them, our lives held no value, that we lived or died at their whim. But then the killing ceased for a while, and we thought perhaps they have had their fill of our blood. Perhaps we are safe now. Perhaps they wish only to demean us, to humiliate us, to keep us in squalor, which is all terrible, Yona, but at least we were alive.

"Then, just a few weeks ago, I received word, through a Belorussian policeman I have known my whole life, that there was a large *Aktion* planned. There were plans to kill more of us, thousands, maybe all of us. I told my wife, and she did not believe me. I wanted us to run, to try to escape with our daughter, because to stay seemed to be waiting only for death, now or later. Still, Esta said, 'It is not true. How could they kill thousands of us anyhow? Where would they put us? What good would it do?' Then, one day just two weeks ago, I was walking home from a job cleaning the toilets of the Germans when I passed a young mother carrying an infant; she was being teased by a German soldier. I did not know all the words he was saying, for he spoke his language, and it was clear she did not understand, either. He reached for her baby, a little girl, and the mother pulled away, but he reached in to tickle the child, who giggled. I will never forget the sound of that laugh, Yona, for it changed everything. It made the mother relax. It made her think the man was kind. So she reluctantly let him take the baby, who could not have been more than six months old, and, with a laugh of his own, he grasped the baby by her feet and swung her into the wall of the building beside them, smashing her tiny skull."

Yona let out a small moan of disbelief.

"The sound of the mother's scream will never leave me," Isaac concluded, finally looking at Yona. "The German's face never changed as he turned, shot the mother right between the eyes, and strolled away." He took a deep breath. "I took my wife and my child and slipped into the forest that night through a tunnel that had been dug beneath the wall. We joined an escape that had already been planned. Eleven of us made the attempt, and we were spotted; they fired upon us, and most of the others fell. Perhaps they thought they got all of us, for they didn't follow. And now, here we are."

Isaac seemed to know that there were no words to say after that, for he closed his eyes and settled back against the reed bed Yona had built to make him comfortable. After fifteen minutes had passed, his breathing lengthened, and Yona knew he had fallen asleep, the pain of recounting his terrible story exhausting him. But even after he had found peace in slumber, she could not move. She knew that Isaac's words had been true, but how was it possible? Even after years of being told by Jerusza that mankind was not to be trusted, the words shook her to the core. She had preferred always to believe in the things she had seen in the villages: the laughter, the hugs, the togetherness, the love. But had Jerusza been right about this, too?

For two nights, Yona could hardly sleep, for she could hear Isaac's voice in her head, and she could see the things he had told her unfolding in startling clarity each time she began to dream. On her fourteenth morning with the family, she awoke with a sense of foreboding deep in the pit of her belly. Something was lurking in the darkness, something just beyond their reach, and they were no longer safe here.

"We need to move today," Yona said as the family sat down around the remains of the previous night's fire to have a small breakfast of acorn coffee and berries. Isaac was improving by the day, and Yona was confident that he could keep up a slow pace through the forest if she and Esta helped support him. "I can feel it in my bones. It's time."

Isaac nodded in solemn agreement, but Esta's back stiffened and she glanced at her husband in disbelief before turning to Yona. "We are perfectly safe here. And my husband is not well enough to travel."

"I am, Esta," he protested. "I must be. Yona is right."

"Because she feels it in her bones? That is nonsense. No one is after us anymore. What do they care? Three Jews who escaped through their sieve, no matter. We are safe now."

"I don't think you are," Yona said after a long silence. She hadn't thought much about the future and how long she would stay with the family, but she knew she couldn't just desert them. *We are all interconnected*, Jerusza had said on her deathbed. *Once fates intertwine, they are forever linked.* "We are too close to where you came from. We must move deeper into the forest. We can go slowly, but we need to begin."

"*We?*" Esta repeated, her tone suddenly so bitter that Isaac flinched, his gaze flicking from his wife to Yona and back again in confusion. "You have helped us, Yona, but you are not one of us. How can we trust you?"

"Esta, my dear, Yona saved my life," Isaac protested. "She brought Chana back to us. She has given us two miracles. How can you doubt her?"

Esta's mouth was set in a firm line. She turned to her husband. "Didn't we trust that the Germans would let us live, too? And yet they have already killed my mother and yours, for no reason at all. We'd be dead, too, if we had stayed. No, Isaac, we trust no one but ourselves from now on. We made that promise. And she is not like us."

Yona blinked a few times. The words wounded her, though of course they were true. How foolish she had been to imagine a world in which she could protect them, a world in which loneliness would be a distant memory. But they needed her now, at least for a little while, for they didn't know the woods like she did. She opened her mouth to say that, but Isaac spoke first.

"Esta, please, don't disrespect her. Yona can show us where to go, where to hide. She can help us with what to eat until we know what to do on our own."

Chana's eyes were wide with fear as she watched her parents trade verbal barbs.

Esta's eyes raked Yona over once, and then, her jaw tightening, she turned again to her husband. "No. I will not make the mistake of trusting the wrong person again." She looked at Yona, her eyes alight with anger, before turning back to her husband. "Anyhow, you think I don't see it, Isaac? The way you whisper to each other while she's dressing your wounds?"

"I was telling her about the atrocities against our people," Isaac shot back. "Hardly words of seduction, Esta."

"She's a lonely woman in the woods. She has helped us, and we are grateful, but now we must go. It is our fate, not hers."

Yona's heart pounded as she looked back and forth between husband and wife, both furious. "Please, let me help you." She stood, and though she wasn't sure why she was begging them, she continued. "I—I have come to care for Chana. For all of you. Please, we must go south."

"I'm sorry, Yona," Esta said stiffly. "But I must protect my family."

"From a woman who has shown us nothing but kindness?" Isaac asked, his voice finally rising.

"Mami?" Chana ventured, but Esta ignored her.

"We will survive without her," Esta said. "We do not need her anymore."

"I—" Yona began.

"Thank you for all you've done to help us," Esta said as Isaac sighed and sat back down, muttering to himself. It was clear that Esta had won, but at what cost? "You can leave whenever you like, Yona. You must be eager to return to whatever it was you were doing before we interrupted you."

Yona stared at her for a long time. She could see a dozen futures unfolding for the family, none of them good. She couldn't leave them defenseless. "I will stay as long as you are here."

"Then we will go," Esta said abruptly. "Chana, help me pack our things."

"Please, you are making a mistake." Yona waited until Esta met her gaze. "The forest can be cruel if you don't know it, and—"

"Thank you for your concern, Yona." Esta looked away. "We will leave in an hour. We appreciate all you've done, but we can take care of ourselves."

Yona tried once more to talk Esta out of her decision, but it was clear the woman had made up her mind, driven by a deep distrust that Yona couldn't undo. She didn't understand Esta's decision, and she didn't know how to reverse it—nor did she have any idea if it was even her right to try. As Esta had said, whatever happened next was their fate, not hers. And so, as the family packed up—Isaac shooting her uneasy glances, Chana crying, and Esta avoiding her gaze altogether—Yona forced herself to walk away, beyond the clearing, so she couldn't beg them to stay any more than she already had, and so she wouldn't have to watch them go.

"Do we have to leave, Mami?" she heard Chana ask. "Can't Yona come with us?"

"Yona needs to remain here, my darling," Esta replied. "She is not one of us. Your father and I will keep you safe."

For a long time after their footsteps had faded, Yona wondered whether she should go after them, persuade them to stay with her for a little while more, perhaps even just give the girl one last hug goodbye.

But fate is part chance and part choice, and Yona understood that Esta had chosen a path for her family that didn't include her. Indecision paralyzed her for so long that by the time she stood, her heart aching, the family was long gone.

Yona spent the next four days telling herself that she'd made the right choice, although at night she dreamed of Chana's soul coming loose from her body, lifting up like an incandescent butterfly into a dark night, and she awoke each morning with a sense of foreboding. On the fifth day, reluctantly, she began moving east, in the same direction the family had gone, though she knew she wouldn't see them again. The forest was too vast.

It was midmorning when she heard three distant gunshots, each snapping the stillness of the forest, and when she doubled back in the direction of the terrible sounds, and found the family's bodies in a clearing, she knew she'd made a tremendous mistake. She watched from the shadows as two German soldiers walked away with Isaac's shoes, laughing and patting each other on the back. And then, when they were gone and the forest was still again, she slipped from the darkness and gently turned Chana over so that the girl's empty eyes looked up at the sky. She lay motionless between her mother and father, all three of them in a row. They'd been executed, at point-blank range, a single shot to the back of each one's head.

Yona let the tears fall as she stared down at the child's destroyed face. She hadn't been directly responsible for Chana's death, but she had failed her, hadn't she? She had let Chana and her family go out into the wilderness, knowing the dangers, and because she had done nothing, they had died. "I'm sorry," she whispered to the little girl. "I promise I won't make the same mistake again."

But it was too late for this family, who would sleep forever, becoming one with the unforgiving earth.

CHAPTER SIX

For the next month, as the summer sun ripened the forest, Yona lived in darkness, her dreams haunted by the image of Chana's still face in the field, the tinny smell of blood. She thought about the boy she'd once met, and his long-ago warnings of book burnings in Berlin. She thought of the terrible things Isaac had told her about the ghetto in Volozhin. She spoke to Jerusza in the stillness and sometimes heard an answer in the wind. And she gazed at her own face in the small rivers that ran through the forest and wondered about the parents she'd been taken from so long ago. Would she ever see them again? It seemed impossible, for they were miles away, in a country trying to take over the continent. But on her deathbed, Jerusza had whispered, "Lives are circles spinning across the world, and when they're meant to intersect again, they do. There's nothing we can do to stop it." Yona had played the words through her mind a million times, wondering if they meant her orbit would once again cross with theirs. She longed for it, though she knew nothing about them, nothing about the people they were. Still, they were her family, a place to belong.

As she moved from hollowed tree to hollowed tree, finding a different place to sleep each night, she could hear the buzz of aircraft overhead sometimes, and the movement of men through the trees in the distance. Germans ventured into the forest's edges on occasion, searching for Jews, but so far, the heart of the forest had remained safe. But would the Germans invade with their army at some point? Would they mow the trees down, take away the only shelter she had ever known? It sounded crazy, but so, too, did the systematic murder of innocent people Isaac had told her about. Perhaps the whole world had gone mad.

She had walked many kilometers in order to put as much distance as she could between herself and the way she had failed Chana's family, and by July, she was in the southern part of the forest. One cloudy morning, she had just begun to move again for the day when she spotted a man up ahead, standing by a stream, his back to her. Quickly, she ducked behind a tree and held herself motionless, watching him.

His clothes were threadbare, a stained and torn shirt stretched over his broad back and rolled at the sleeves, his pants pushed up to his calves. He was older than Yona, she thought, but not by much. His hair was the color of river silt, and it glimmered in the sifted sunlight filtering through the trees.

He was standing completely still as he stared at the water, and Yona held her breath, studying him. He looked strong, but his waist was too narrow for his body, someone who was accustomed to plentiful food but had recently learned to live without, she guessed. But what was he doing? Studying his own reflection in the placid stream?

Her question was answered a second later when, with a grunt, he dove headfirst into the water, splashed around for a second, and then groaned. "It got away!" he called out in Yiddish, shaking the droplets from his hair as he climbed out of the water. Yona shrank farther into the trees, motionless. Judging from his language, he was Jewish, too, like Chana's family.

"I told you," came another masculine voice, this one farther away. Yona held her breath. There were two of them? "You can't catch a fish with your bare hands."

There was the sound of footsteps breaking branches, and then the second man emerged in the clearing, across the stream from the first. He looked younger, slimmer, the lines of his face more sharply drawn, his hair as black as Yona's.

"I suppose you have a better idea?" asked the first man, again staring at the water.

"Berries?" the other man asked with a shrug. "Mushrooms?"

"We can't feed everyone berries for the rest of their lives, and you and I can't tell the poisonous mushrooms from the harmless ones," the first man said. "Give me a minute, Leib. I'll catch us something."

"Sure, or you'll make such a racket that you'll attract every disgruntled Soviet partisan in the forest."

"There's nobody out here," the first man grumbled. But Yona could hear the smile in his voice.

The one called Leib stood and watched, an eyebrow cocked, as the broader-shouldered man went still and silent once more. Again he pounced on something in the water, and just like the last time, he came up empty-handed, muttering to himself.

"We need a better solution, Aleksander," Leib said, and this time, the teasing tone was gone. "They're starving."

As the one called Aleksander stepped once more from the shallow stream, shaking the water off, Yona could see, even from a distance, that his expression had sobered. She didn't believe the smile he forced as he turned back to Leib. "I'll take care of it, Leib. All will be well."

Yona watched in silence as Leib walked away, shoulders slumped. As she turned her gaze back to Aleksander, she was surprised to hear him begin to pray softly, asking first if God was there and then telling the sky that he would give anything for a little luck, a little food. "They're counting on me," he concluded, his voice mournful as he looked to the water once more.

Yona wanted nothing more in that moment than to step from the trees and be the answer to his prayer, the proof that after whatever terrible things he had endured to bring him here, there was a God after all. But who was she to think she could save anyone from the darkness? She had failed with Chana's family. She'd likely been wrong to try to help them in the first place; hadn't Jerusza always taught her that she was better off alone? Then again, how could she ignore the pull of her heart, the part of her that couldn't turn away from a person in need? What if Jerusza's path hadn't been the right one? Who was the old woman to still be pulling the strings of Yona's life?

The man called Aleksander dove thrice more into the water, trying to catch fish with his bare hands, before finally sitting down hard on the streambank with a heavy sigh. His back was to Yona, and she could see the tension knotting it through his wet shirt. Water dripped from his hair onto his collar, and as he reached up to scratch his head, he let out an almost inhuman moan of despair. "My God, what will I do?"

"I—I can help." Yona heard her own voice before she had actually formed the intent to reveal herself. She spoke in Yiddish, because it was the language the man had been speaking moments before. The man scrambled to his feet at once and turned, searching the forest for the source of the sound before his gaze settled on her.

He blinked a few times, confusion washing over his features, as she forced herself to step from the trees. There was no turning back now. They regarded each other for a few long seconds. She could feel her heart thudding against her rib cage.

"*Amkha?*" he asked after a moment, his expression wary, uncertain.

It was a Hebrew word, one that roughly meant "the nation of people." He was asking if she was one of them, a fellow Jew, but the question was the one that had been tormenting her, the one she couldn't answer, so she merely shrugged.

"Where did you come from?" he asked at last.

She hesitated. This was a mistake. His friend would return at any moment, and then what? But in an instant, she saw Chana's face in her mind's eye and she felt the weight of her failure. She couldn't turn away, not again. "I come from the forest," she said simply.

A small smile pulled at the left corner of his lips. "I see that. I meant to ask where you came from before that."

"The forest," she repeated, and she watched as his brow creased.

"The forest." He scratched his head. "But you speak Yiddish." She could see him trying to puzzle her out.

"You do, too," she replied, but offered no explanation. "You need help."

"I—" He started and stopped. "I have people to feed. People who are relying on me. I—I was only a bookkeeper before this. If you need me to run some numbers for you, no problem, but surviving in the woods . . ." He forced a smile, seemingly trying to make the moment feel lighter, but his eyes gave him away, and finally, his gaze fell. "You see, they need me, and I don't know what to do."

She nodded. They stared at each other for a long time, and then Yona took a deep breath and started forward, her blood pulsing hot through her veins. "You are trying to grab the pike because they are larger, but that's difficult using only your hands. There are dace in the water, too, very small fish, plenty of them, much easier to catch. You just need to know how."

He studied her as she came closer, so close that she could feel the way his presence rippled the air between them. The current made her want to run away, but it also made her want to draw closer. Paralyzed, she stood frozen in place. "Who *are* you?" he asked softly, looking down at her.

It was a simple question, but it stilled her for a moment. How could she reply when she didn't know the answer herself? So she let her eyes slide away. "I am the person who will help you feed your people tonight. All right?"

He stared at her for a minute more before chuckling to himself, though not unkindly. He took a step back. "All right."

They locked eyes for a few long seconds; then she turned away and, with her back to him, quickly removed her boots, rolled her trouser legs a few times, and stripped off her shirt, leaving only a thin undershirt beneath. She could hear the intake of his breath as she turned back around and stepped into the stream. The water was cold, bracing, as it burbled around her ankles. She lowered her shirt into the water, making an opaque net of it. She waded deeper, not minding that she was getting her clothes wet. The sun was hot and would easily dry them, and they were in need of a wash anyhow. She stood still, hardly breathing, until the fish forgot she was there, wiggling all around her, their silver scales glimmering in the sun, catching the light. And then, so quickly that if the man had blinked, he would have missed it, she scooped her shirt up in one quick motion, curving it into a half-sphere so that nothing could escape over the sides as the water drained. Within the fabric, seven small fish gasped and flailed. She held them up to him and smiled. "See?"

His mouth hung slightly open as he looked from Yona to the bundle of fish and back. "How did you . . . ?"

"You have to become a part of the water."

He blinked a few times and then waded into the water beside her. He pulled off his shirt, revealing taut skin browned by the sun, stretched over sinewy muscles. She was suddenly very conscious of him as the ripples from his movement lapped against her legs. He stayed still for a few seconds, trailing his shirt in the water, but it wasn't long enough, and when he yanked the makeshift net out, the fish scattered, and he came up empty. "You made it look easy," he said, looking up at Yona with chagrin.

"I have been doing this nearly all my life." She realized only as the words left her mouth that she had just confided something to him, told him something about herself. She hadn't intended to. "You will learn." She felt exposed under his gaze, but she was surprised to realize that it didn't bother her, not like she'd thought it would. He was looking right at her, and there was something about being seen that reminded her that she wasn't just a ghost, a spirit in the woods. "How many do you need to feed?" she asked him.

He hesitated, and she could see him weighing his options, deciding whether he should be honest. That was good; he was cautious. He was right not to immediately trust a stranger, and she respected him for it. "Thirteen, including myself," he said after a long pause. "Fourteen if you count the baby."

Thirteen people and a baby, hidden somewhere nearby. It was almost incomprehensible. "You are many."

He nodded, watching her closely.

"You have come from the ghetto in Volozhin?"

"Volozhin?" He was still trying to puzzle her out, but after a second, he shook his head. "No. We are from the ghetto in Mir, to the south of the forest."

She closed her eyes for a few seconds. "And you escaped?"

"Yes, but to what?" he asked softly. "It is summer now, with enough plants to eat, but what happens when the winter comes? How will I feed them all? I convinced them to leave with me. I promised that I could take care of them. But what if I cannot? What if we were better off where we were?"

"You were not." The immediacy of her response startled both of them. "The forest will care for you better than the ghetto would. And you will learn."

Again he seemed to be trying to read her eyes. "You know the ghetto, then? In Volozhin? That's where you've come from?"

"No." She knew he was fishing for more, but she wasn't ready to be caught. "We will catch enough dace to feed your people tonight. Tomorrow, you will come back, and I will show you how to make a *kryha*."

"A kryha?"

"I don't know another word for it. It's—it's a net. You will catch a lot of fish that way. More than enough, and some pike, too, the larger ones."

"I don't know what to say."

Neither did Yona, so she slid the seven fish from her shirt and held them out to the man, who hesitated for a few seconds before holding his dripping shirt up like a basket. Yona slipped the fish into the fabric. She tried not to notice how his muscled chest and shoulders gleamed with perspiration. His body was different from that of Chana's father, and it elicited in her a reaction that she didn't quite understand.

In short measure, she collected another six fish and handed them over silently, her eyes sliding away as he watched with his mouth agape. Twice more, she gathered a half dozen, until she had handed him a total of twenty-five. They were small, but they would be enough until tomorrow. "You can pick some sulfur-shelf mushrooms, too," she said as he bundled the fish into his shirt, making a sack of it. She emerged from the water and strode to a nearby tree trunk, where dozens of flat, deep -yellow mushrooms grew right out of the bark, one on top of the other. "You will see these all over the forest this time of year. They are safe if you cook them and will taste good in a stew with the fish. Just take care if any in your group are feeling ill; mushrooms are hearty and will help you to survive, but they are sometimes difficult to digest." She promptly closed her mouth. Had she said too much? She busied herself with tearing two handfuls of mushrooms from the tree and crossing over to him, hands outstretched.

"I don't know how to thank you," he said, taking the mushrooms and examining them almost reverentially before ng back at her. When she finally met his gaze, she could his eyes, and it both unsettled and pleased her that of evoking such a thing. "I'm Aleksander," he

"I know." When he looked at her with confusion, she added, "I heard your friend say it."

"Ah, Leib."

"Don't tell him about me. Please." She spoke before she could think. She knew it must have seemed a strange request, but she already felt exposed. If Aleksander could keep his word, could keep her a secret a little longer, maybe she could summon the courage to introduce herself to his friend, too. But not now, not yet. This was already too much.

"I give you my word. Though he will be very confused to see me bring back so many fish, considering how unskilled I've already proven myself to be." Aleksander smiled.

She returned the smile shyly.

"You haven't told me your name," he said after a few seconds had passed.

She took a deep breath. "It's Yona."

He blinked a few times. "You have a Hebrew name."

"Yes."

"It's beautiful," Aleksander said, and she could feel herself blushing again. "Thank you, Yona. For everything. I will return tomorrow."

And then he was gone, and she found herself wondering if she should have said more, should have made sure he knew how to clean and prepare the fish. But it was too late—for both that and turning back time. Even if Aleksander and his people moved on after a few days, even if she never saw him again, she had crossed a line into a new life, one in which seeing Chana's lifeless body—and hearing of the horrors of the ghetto—had changed her forever.

"I'm sorry, Jerusza," she whispered into the wind, but th

was no reply, not even a rustling of the trees. Still, it mattered little. No longer was the forest a sanctuary where she could live out the rest of her days alone, preserving only her own life. She had to do something to help the people like Aleksander, who were just trying to survive.

CHAPTER SEVEN

Yona hardly slept that night, and she rose before the sun. After praying for guidance, and once again speaking to Jerusza without hearing an answer, she set out toward the stream in the graying darkness, intending to get to work making rope for the kryha.

But as she approached the streambed, her skin tingled, and her hair stood on end. Someone was already there, waiting in the darkness. She could feel an ash-scented presence, something that didn't belong. She tensed and ducked behind a tree, holding her breath as she listened, ready to run.

At first there was nothing, no movement. After a moment, though, a stick snapped, and she could hear footsteps. Silently, she pulled her knife from its ankle holster. And then, a voice cut through the darkness.

"Yona? Is that you?"

It was deep, uncertain, and she recognized it immediately. She took a deep breath and stepped out from behind the tree, still clutching her knife. "Aleksander."

In the east, above the thick canopy of trees, the sky was

beginning to pale as the earth spun slowly toward dawn. It was light enough now that she could see him standing by the water, looking for her. When his eyes met hers, he cracked a small smile, but she didn't put her knife away yet.

"Why are you here?" She took a step forward and then another. "I thought you were with your people."

"I was." He took a step toward her, but he stopped abruptly when she took an instinctive step back. He held up his hands. "I'm sorry. I didn't mean to startle you. I was just eager to get started this morning."

She studied him for a moment and then relaxed. What was wrong with her, feeling suspicious of a man who was merely eager to find food? Jerusza's words of warning rang in her ear—*Men can be cruel and heartless and cold*—but she pushed them away. The old woman was wrong. Humans had a responsibility to do more than just protect themselves. In the face of evil, they were compelled to save each other. It was the only way mankind could survive. "Were the fish enough to feed everyone last night?" she asked as she slipped her knife back into its spot at her ankle.

"You would have thought we were having the feast of our lives." He smiled. "They were very grateful, Yona. It felt wrong to accept their praise myself. I wanted to tell them about you."

She nodded. There would come a time when he would have to. If she was truly going to help, she would need to go to them, teach them how to survive. But not yet. "What do you have there?" she asked, forcing herself to take another step closer.

He held up a small bundle a bit sheepishly. "Rope. You mentioned making a net. I thought this might help."

Yona stared. "Rope?" She had planned to show him how to weave rope from nettles, which were plentiful in the forest. It would have taken the whole day, but it would be a lesson that would serve him well in the future. "Where did you get rope?"

"We took some clothing on the way to the forest." His eyes slid away. "Not much, but enough to prepare for the winter, from villagers who already had plenty. We decided as a group last night that it was worth it to sacrifice one sweater if it would help us to fish. Moshe is a tailor; he spent the evening unraveling it." He hesitated suddenly. "Were we wrong to do that?"

She could feel the tension in her chest dissipating. "No. We can use it. But in the future, keep your sweaters for the winter. You will need all the warmth you can get. I will teach you how to make rope from what the forest gives you."

They had both been taking tentative steps forward as they talked, and now they faced each other in the clearing beside the stream, just two meters apart. "How do you know all these things, Yona? Who *are* you?"

"I wish I knew." She let her gaze slide away. "Come. Let's build a net to catch fish."

By the time the sun hung high in the sky, Yona had taught Aleksander how to make a basic kryha, and then, because they had plenty of rope left over, she taught him how to make a gill net, too, showing him how to find two trees near the side of the stream, string a cord between them, and hang pieces of rope from the top down, knotting them methodically in a diamond pattern to create a one-inch mesh wall. They used the last of the rope to secure the net to the bottom of the stream with stones to weight it in place.

When they were done, they climbed out of the water, side by side, letting the sun warm their skin and dry their clothes. Aleksander stared in awe at the results of their handiwork. "Now what do we do?" he asked.

"Now we wait," Yona said. "The fish will come."

Aleksander shook his head in astonishment. "Yona, you're a gift from God."

"No." She looked away. "I am just trying to do what is right."

She could feel him studying her. "Well, I thank God, all the same, for sending you to us." He was silent for a few minutes more. She could feel herself breathing in the silence, so heavily that it was audible. What was wrong with her? "I make you uneasy," he said gently after a moment had passed. "I don't mean to."

"I—I'm not accustomed to people." She ducked her head.

"And I'm not accustomed to beautiful women who know the forest. But I think I could get used to it, if you could."

She looked up at him, confused, and saw him smiling at her. Her cheeks burned as she looked away and busied herself with collecting willow twigs.

"What are you doing?" Aleksander asked after a moment. "Can I help?"

"Yes." Her voice cracked. She felt strange, shaky. "See if you can find some birch bark. I'm making you a large basket to bring your fish back to your people."

He watched her as she began to weave together the most pliable twigs she could find, her fingers moving rapidly, expertly, for she'd done this a hundred times before. "Surely we won't need a basket that large."

"Are you certain?" She nodded toward the gill net. "Look."

Aleksander turned to look at the stream, and when his eyes met Yona's again, they were wide with surprise.

"There are already dozens of fish there."

"Yes." Yona allowed herself a small smile.

"But . . . with something so simple, I'll be able to feed everyone, all the time."

"Until the winter comes."

As the smile faded from Aleksander's eyes, Yona regretted the words. She should have let him revel in the realization that he could provide for his people after all. "It's all right," she said gently after a moment. "There are ways. I will teach you about foraging. About preserving your fish and meat. You can't stay in one place too long, either."

She could see the lump in his neck bob as he watched her. She had been weaving as they spoke, her fingers moving deftly around the sticks, fastening them together. As he handed her a long twig in silence and she wove it through the thatches, making a conic basket that would serve him well, she could see him searching for words. "Why are you helping me?" he asked as she handed the basket over. When she didn't answer, he added, "You're Jewish, too, aren't you?"

It was the same thing Chana and her parents had asked, a question Yona feared she would never know the answer to. "Does it matter?"

"It is usually something people want to know."

Yona thought about this. "But maybe it shouldn't be. Perhaps they need only know whether you are kind, decent, capable, well-intentioned. It is within your own heart that you find God. And we all walk our own path toward him. Don't we?"

He didn't say anything, and in the silence, she could feel her cheeks warming. It had been a silly thought, one that showed no understanding of society or the way it worked. Surely he was thinking that she sounded like a childish fool.

But when he spoke, there was only quiet admiration in his tone. "Yona, the world you describe would be a paradise."

"But it is not reality."

He shook his head, but again he didn't speak right away. Yona liked the silence, the easy feeling of space existing without words, and she appreciated him for not having to fill the void. "My parents died years ago. I am one of six brothers," he said at last, his voice so low it was barely audible. "All dead now, except me. All of us fought in the army. Three of us returned alive. After the German invasion last year, they came for the Jews in my town, forced us into the ghetto. In November, there was word that something was coming, a mass execution. I tried to talk others into leaving with me, but only a handful came. My brothers didn't believe me and so they stayed. We could hear the gunshots from where we hid in the woods. We were out there for days before venturing back; we lost one old woman to the cold, or perhaps to heartbreak, I don't know. We had to return, though, because we didn't know how to survive. When we left again a few weeks ago, because we'd heard rumors the ghetto was going to be relocated, perhaps even liquidated, I promised those who followed me that I would protect them. And maybe with your help, Yona, I can, at the least, make sure that they're fed. But how can I— how can anyone—protect them from a world that hates them because of what's in their blood, because of what's in their hearts?"

Yona was startled to feel tears stinging her eyes. "I—I don't understand how people could feel that way."

His smile was gentle, bitter, and sad, all at the same time. "Money. Belongings. Taking from one group to pad the pockets of another."

"But the hatred . . ."

"Is how they sleep at night, I suppose. If they convince themselves that we are not even worthy of the air we breathe, then it's easier to get rid of us, isn't it?"

The silence rolled back in, and this time it was both comfortable and full of words they didn't need to speak aloud. When Yona looked up, Aleksander met her gaze and held it for a long time. She didn't look away until they both heard a voice in the distance calling Aleksander's name.

Immediately, he jumped to his feet. "It's Leib," he said, scanning the forest.

Yona knew, from the space between the echoes, that they still had a few minutes before the younger man appeared. She could run, hide. There was still time to disappear into the forest.

But then Aleksander looked at her with a question in his eyes, and something in her shifted. "I will stay," she said. "I will meet him."

"Are you certain?"

"No." But somehow, she was. She could feel it in her heart, a deep certainty, all of a sudden, that fate had brought her here, that this was part of some greater plan she didn't understand yet. The wind whispered in the trees. "But it is the right thing."

Aleksander studied her for a few seconds before nodding. "I will go get him, then, tell him where we are."

Yona nodded, and though he held her gaze for a few beats more, as if waiting for her to disappear if he blinked, he eventually turned and moved into the woods.

In the silence left in his wake, Yona could hear herself breathing, could feel the stillness all around her. There was a slight lapping of the water against the banks, the fish struggling to free themselves from the net. The whisper came through the trees again, but it wasn't Jerusza's voice she could hear. *This is your path*, it said. She took a deep breath and got to her feet.

In the ten minutes before Aleksander returned with Leib, Yona had waded back into the stream and quickly, expertly collected most of the fish whose gills had become lodged in the net. She was holding the basket when they arrived in the clearing, and when Leib's eyes went first to it instead of her, she knew instantly that he was very hungry. Up close, he looked younger than he had from a distance, perhaps only sixteen or seventeen. He was slim, long-limbed, with a nose as sharp as a crow's beak, and a smattering of stubble on his narrow chin.

"Fish," she said in greeting, and when his gaze moved to her, he looked confused. "It's too dangerous to build a fire now, for the smoke could be seen from miles away on a clear day like this, but you will have plenty to eat tonight, I promise."

He blinked, looked uncertainly at Aleksander, and then turned his gaze back to her. He cleared his throat. "Aleksander tells me you have helped us. That the fish yesterday were from you?"

"Yes." Yona didn't elaborate. Instead, she gestured for him to sit down.

"Thank you," Leib said, his voice low as he settled across from her.

Yona nodded without looking up, embarrassed by his gratitude.

"Leib, this is Yona," Aleksander said. "Yona, Leib."

"Hello." Leib regarded her with curiosity.

"Hello." She didn't know what else to say, so she looked
hastily away, then she glanced at Aleksander, who was watching
her. He gave her a small, encouraging smile.

She turned back to Leib. "Um, you look hungry. I will pick
some berries. You can scale the fish?" As soon as she said it,
though, she wondered if he carried a knife. After all, why would
he, this village boy who didn't know the woods? But he surprised her by pulling a folding blade from his pocket and holding
it up.

"Sure."

"Where did you get that?" She hadn't meant to sound ac-
cusatory, but when he flinched, she knew she had. "I'm sorry,"
she mumbled. "I only meant to say that I'm surprised. I would
not have thought you would be allowed to have a weapon in the
ghetto."

"I wasn't." He glanced at Aleksander. "But once we were far
from Mir, Aleksander insisted we venture into a few villages and
take what we needed," he explained, avoiding her gaze.

"But *only* what we needed," Aleksander cut in. "The villagers, they are facing hard times, too. But there were things we
needed to survive."

Yona nodded her agreement, in awe that he had figured out
how to do such a thing—and apparently to do it with some level
of morality. "You have scaled a fish before, Leib?"

"I've seen my mother do it. I can try." He grabbed one of the
small fish by its tail and put the blunt edge of his knife against its

midsection. As he scraped, silver scales sparked into the air like a burst of light. "Like this, yes?"

"Yes, yes," she said, giving him an encouraging smile. "Just get the scales under the collar there, too. Good, good."

He smiled as he held up his fish to examine it. In just a few swipes, he had wiped it clean.

Yona smiled back. "You're a natural, Leib."

He looked down, the smile suddenly sliding from his face. "If my father could see me now. He teased me for having a book in my hand all the time. Said I'd never survive if anyone took away my stories."

A small silence hung over them, and then Aleksander patted Leib on the shoulder. "He would be very proud, Leib," he said, his voice deep and warm. Yona nodded, but still, Leib wouldn't look at them. When he finally turned, Yona could see tears in his eyes, which he quickly wiped away with a look of embarrassment.

"I'm sorry," he said, getting to his feet. He strode away into the trees without another word, and beside her, Aleksander sighed as they watched him go.

"The grief comes in waves," Aleksander said simply after a moment.

"I'm very sorry." Yona felt suddenly awkward as they lapsed back into silence. "The others who are with you," she asked after a moment. "Their grief is similar?"

Aleksander glanced at her. "Yes."

"And have any of them spent a winter in the wilderness before?"

Aleksander choked out a laugh like Yona had never heard, one devoid of mirth and filled only with disbelief and pain.

"No. We all came from comfortable lives in the villages out-side the forest. We were tailors and bookkeepers, shop owners and students. None of us could have imagined a day that our homes would be gone, and we'd be running for our lives into the depths of a forest we don't know at all."

It wasn't fair, any of it, and though the thought of being around more than a few people after a lifetime alone was enough to make her pulse race with fear, she wondered whether this was her path, the fate Jerusza had been talking about. "Your group," she said abruptly, and then she took a deep breath and dove off the cliff into the deep unknown. "I would like you to take me to them. Tomorrow. If it's all right with you. I—I would like to help."

Aleksander's brows rose. "I don't want you to do anything you're not comfortable with, Yona."

"I won't stay long. But the forest can be dangerous." She thought of Chana and her family, and she swallowed hard. "I will teach you to live—and to disappear."

Aleksander's gaze never left hers as he nodded slowly. "Thank you, Yona. But I—" He stopped abruptly and shook his head. "I don't want to disappear. I want to survive so we can tell the world what has happened."

"I don't want you to disappear, either." She was surprised by how vehemently she meant the words. "And that is why you must become one with the forest to survive." Just like a pack of wild animals, they would need to remain on the move as long as the weather was good, for the longer they stayed in place, the more vulnerable they became to predators—both man and beast. And Yona couldn't let that happen.

That night, after filling their basket until it overflowed with fish, Yona waved goodbye to Aleksander and Leib as they disappeared into the forest with their new fishing nets. She watched them as they went, somehow knowing, even before it happened, that Aleksander would turn around not once but twice to see if she was still there. Then she slipped back into the woods toward the hut she had called home for the last week.

She had little to travel with, so it took her no time at all to pack her things into the leather knapsack she'd used for years, the one that smelled like the damp of the forest even on the driest days. And then, when the moon rose overhead, bathing the forest in light, she stared up at it in the clear sky, listening to the sound of her own breath, the comfortable rhythm of solitude. Tomorrow, everything would change.

But for now, she was alone with her thoughts. Above her, the stars stretched across the heavens, a familiar canopy that would be with her wherever she went.

CHAPTER EIGHT

In the morning, Aleksander was waiting beside the stream, the woven basket next to him, when Yona arrived. He watched her as she approached, and when she was within earshot, he smiled and said her name. Two eagles lifted off from a nearby pine, and a crow squawked his protest over the interruption.

She continued her silent walk toward him, and when they finally stood just a few meters apart, she studied his face for a few seconds before speaking. "Hello, Aleksander," she said, her voice sounding strange and high-pitched to her own ears. She was nervous, and when he took a small step back, she wondered if he could sense it. Did he understand how profoundly her world was changing?

"Did you sleep well?" he asked, the question sounding strangely formal.

She nodded, though she had barely slept at all, her dreams punctuated by strange visions of Jerusza silently screaming in the darkness. "Did you?"

He smiled ruefully. "To be honest, I was worried about you."

"About me?"

"About whether I'm forcing you to do something you don't want to do."

She thought of Jerusza. Of a lifetime of being told what to do, how to feel. Of a stolen childhood, of a life of loneliness she hadn't asked for. "No. This is my choice." It felt good to say the words, to remind herself that she had the right to a road of her own choosing.

He hesitated, watching her closely. "Yona, have you ever lived outside the woods?"

She opened her mouth to say no, but then she thought of Berlin and the shadowy sketches she could sometimes see in her mind's eye of her life before Jerusza. A wooden children's bed. Billowy drapes the color of spring sunshine. A mother with brightly painted red lips, a father with a neatly trimmed mustache and grease in his hair. How could she still see them so clearly? In trying to make her forget, had Jerusza instead frozen the images in time? They were faces that felt like they belonged to a dream, but she knew they were real, vestiges of the life she should have had. "Yes," she said after a while. "A long time ago."

"And now?" he asked. "You are all alone?"

"I am. For almost half a year now." She took a deep breath.

"I see." Something in his expression shifted slightly, a recognition of pain. "You lost someone very recently. I'm sorry. What happened to him?"

His assumption that she had been sharing her life with a man was almost laughable because it was so far from the truth. He was the first man other than Chana's father whom she'd seen up close, if you didn't count Marcin, who had been just a boy, and who existed now only in her distant memory. "It was a woman

named Jerusza. She is the one who raised me. She died just before the spring."

"Oh. Yona, I'm sorry to hear that."

"It was her time. She lived to be one hundred two."

"One hundred *two*?" His brow creased in confusion. "Surely
not. People don't live that long. And certainly not in the wilderness."

Yona held his gaze. "She did." She turned before he could
ask more. How would she explain Jerusza? It was impossible.

"Well." He cleared his throat, at a temporary loss for words.
"Would you like to go see my people now, Yona?"

"No. Let's catch some more fish first. Then we can feed
them when we arrive."

He nodded and busied himself with helping her to unspool
and stake the gill net she had crafted the day before. As they
waded into the water together, they were silent at first, concen-
trating on the placement of the mesh. But as they moved to the
shore and Yona looked up, she found him studying the curves
of her body. It made her stumble and blush. He looked away
instantly and cleared his throat.

"You said you once lived outside the woods," he said.

"Yes."

"How long ago did you move into the forest?"

"I was only a little girl." She could feel him watching her again
as she looked west, where the sun set each night, where somewhere
there was a family that belonged to her. "I hardly remember it."

"But where did you—" he began.

"And you?" she interrupted before he could ask more questions she didn't know how to answer. "Where are you from?
You said you were a bookkeeper?"

He nodded slowly. "Yes. I was raised in Mir, and my parents were very firm that my brothers and I would have good Jewish educations. In school, we learned Latin, Polish, physics, chemistry, history, religion of course, even psychology. But nothing prepared us for what was to come. When the Russians arrived, it was terrible. They took everything; we were suddenly very poor. And though there were some refugees from the west who told us about ghettos in Germany, we hardly believed it. We actually thought things would be better if the Germans drove the Soviets out. At least then, we thought, we could make some money. Who could have known that instead of money, they would bring death? Within just a few weeks of arriving, they had allied with the local police, and together they brought several prominent Jews from our town seven miles outside the forest and stoned them to death after forcing them to dig their own graves. It was a warning to all of us."

The sunshine suddenly felt very cold. "Oh, Aleksander."

"Can you imagine such a thing?" He seemed to be talking only to himself. "It was not so long ago that I had a good business, a life in front of me, family I loved. And now . . . now, all of it is gone. I fear that those who chose to remain in the ghetto will die, but what guarantee is there that we will survive?"

"There is no guarantee for any of us," Yona said when she could finally find her voice. "But you *will* survive." She swallowed, the taste of the impossible promise bitter in her mouth. "You will hide here in the forest, and you will learn how to find food and shelter, and you will live."

"How can I believe such a thing?" he whispered.

She met his gaze. It was warm, and it seemed to penetrate her. No one had ever looked at her that way before, with a blend of gratitude, fear, and something else she couldn't put a finger on. "Believe in me," she said. "Believe that perhaps God has led me here to help you."

He looked at her for a long time. "I think maybe I do believe that, Yona."

And then, because her cheeks felt as if they were on fire, and because it felt as if his eyes were burning a hole right through her, she stood abruptly and turned away, heading for the stream. She had intended to check the net, but instead, the cool water greeted her, and she found herself wading upstream until the water was waist-deep. She took a deep breath and submerged herself. Only after she was beneath the surface did the heat flooding through her body finally disappear.

An hour later, her hair and clothes almost dry thanks to the relentless sun, Yona gathered another basketful of fish, and after packing up the net and handing it to Aleksander, she hoisted her rucksack on her back and made herself smile, though her heart was thudding in fear. This was it, the moment her life would change. What would his people think of her? How would they react? Would they want to cast her out, as Chana's mother had, because she wasn't one of them? She was lying when she took a deep breath and told Aleksander, "I'm ready."

He searched her eyes, nodded, and gave her a small smile in return. "Shall we go?"

They walked for the first thirty minutes in comfortable silence. Aleksander seemed to understand that Yona would need the solitude for a short time, at least, before her world opened up.

"Who is with you?" she asked abruptly as they paused to trudge through the shallow water of a stream. Dozens of tiny fish darted away from their footfalls, a silver starburst of fear beneath the surface. "In your camp, I mean."

"You're trying to prepare yourself."

"I suppose I am."

"Don't be afraid, Yona. They will all be as grateful as I am." He gave her a small smile. "Well, you've met Leib. His mother is with us, too. Miriam. She's a kind woman, but her eyes are empty now; the rest of her family—Leib's father, her two younger children—were killed. She—she seems in a trance sometimes, like she is somewhere else."

"I'm so sorry," Yona said, and Aleksander extended a hand to help her out of the stream. She didn't need it, but she took it anyhow, liking the way his fingers laced with hers, the strength of them, but also his gentleness. She didn't want to let go, but she did, for what use was holding hands on solid ground?

"Oscher and Bina are husband and wife," he went on as they began walking through the trees again. "It's a miracle they survived together, both with their relative health, though Oscher has a limp that slows him down. They are grandparents, but their children and grandchildren are all gone. Murdered." His tone was flat, empty. "Every one. Six children. Thirteen grandchildren."

He paused for a second, and in the space between his words, Yona tried to comprehend two whole generations snuffed out, an entire future halted before it had begun, a familial legacy that would never be.

"Moshe is the tailor I mentioned, an old man, older than my father was. Sulia is twenty-five or so. Her older brother was friends with mine a lifetime ago, so I've known her since she was small. Ruth is around the same age, and she has three young children with her: Pessia, Leah, and a little boy, Daniel, just a baby. Her husband died last year, shot while Ruth and the children were out of the home, visiting her mother. There's Luba, who is in her sixties, and Leon, who is seventy. They both recently lost their spouses to the Nazis, and they talk little, but they help with the cooking, the construction of our shelters. Leon, he was a shoemaker once, and so he helps to mend our boots. And then there is Rosalia. She has been helping Leib and me stand guard at night. I don't know much about her, but she is resilient, tough." He paused and glanced sideways at Yona. "You will like her, too, I think."

Yona felt uneasy. It was jarring to hear the names of the people she had vowed to take responsibility for. These were human beings who were being hunted, people who had already lost incomprehensible things. And the majority were older people and children, the two hardest groups to keep alive in the forest. "How old are the children?"

"Pessia is four, I think, and Leah is a year younger. Daniel is perhaps a year old, maybe less."

Yona nodded, taking this in. "And Oscher's limp? It is serious?"

Aleksander sighed. "When we were leaving the ghetto, I had Leib lead the rest into the forest. I stayed behind with Oscher and followed at a slower pace. He couldn't keep up. But he tries, Yona. And he's one of us."

Again she nodded. It was another problem. If the group had to move their camp in a hurry, he would hold them back. But Jerusza had been the same at the end, and Yona had simply become more cautious, more observant of her surroundings, more attuned to danger. She would teach Aleksander to do the same with Oscher.

"Is there anything else? Anyone who might be a problem if you need to move quickly?"

Aleksander thought about this for a moment. "Ruth's children are slow, but they're small. Leib and Rosalia carried the girls when we fled the ghetto and Ruth carried the baby. They made good time."

"All right."

They were both quiet for a while before Aleksander spoke again. "You don't have to come with me, Yona, if you don't want. I know this must be a lot for you."

"It is." Yona glanced skyward, where a flock of crows had just lifted off. "But perhaps God gives us the answers before we know what the questions will be. Perhaps I was meant to help you, if I can."

He accepted this in silence, and when he finally answered, his voice was choked. "Thank you, Yona," he said, and when his eyes met hers, they were damp with gratitude and pain.

It took them another twenty minutes before they reached the camp, and Yona could smell it before they arrived, which made the hairs on her arms stand on end in alarm. The scents of roasted fish, burning embers, and sweat hung in the air. They were all signs that humans were living here, had been living here for long enough that their guard was down. It would make them vulnerable if the Germans ever came to this part of the woods. "You'll need to move your camp, Aleksander," she murmured. "Tonight."

"What?" Aleksander looked startled. "But it is already mid-day. There isn't time to——"

"You are in danger here." She was walking more quickly now, worried about the people ahead, in danger because they didn't know how not to be careless. They were focused only on surviving, not erasing all traces of themselves. They didn't real-ize, though, that the two things were the same.

For the first time since they'd met, Aleksander's voice took on an edge. "Yona, I can't. They won't——"

"Aleksander." Again she cut him off. "Please, trust me. We need to move now."

He stopped and stared at her. After a second, she stopped, too, and met his gaze. "We?" he repeated.

She blinked a few times, startled by the question. "I will stay with you long enough to help you stay safe. And then I will go. But please, you must believe me now."

He was silent for a few seconds, but she could see the storm in his eyes. "All right."

They broke through a wall of trees, and suddenly the small encampment was in front of them, a haphazard scene of huts built inexpertly from leaning branches and leaves, a firepit in the middle ringed with mud, a large pot sitting beside it. Two old men lounged with their backs against trees, talking with their eyes half-closed, faces tilted to the sun, while a few women washed clothes in a small stream at the edge of the clearing. Yona's skin tingled. Though convenient, it was terrible planning to hide beside a stream; trackers would follow the waterways first. Two little girls were chasing each other around the out-skirts of the settlement, giggling, and a woman nursing a small boy watched them with sad eyes. Leib emerged from one of the poorly constructed lean-tos, followed by three women and an older man, and called out a greeting. All eyes went to Aleksander, and then immediately to Yona.

"Everyone, listen," Aleksander said, striding into the clearing, his authority over the little group immediately evident. Even the baby stopped nursing and turned his head to look. The young mother—Ruth, Yona recalled—hastily covered herself and stood up, lifting the baby to her shoulder. "This is Yona. She is here to help us."

"*Amkha?*" one of the young women with Leib asked, her expression unreadable. It was the same word Aleksander had said to Yona the first day she saw him trying to fish.

"Yes, she is one of us, Sulia," Aleksander answered firmly.

The woman's eyes flicked back to Yona. Her hair was the color of burned acorns, hanging to the middle of her back, and her waist was narrow beneath an ample bosom. After a long pause, she smiled. "Yona, is it?"

Yona nodded. She had been prepared for the strangeness of being around a group of people, but she hadn't expected the look of judgment in so many eyes. They were all assessing her, trying to read her, trying to see if she belonged, even the two little girls, who had stopped playing and were whispering to each other as they stared.

It was Sulia's gaze that seemed to penetrate the most deeply, though, so Yona was relieved when the other woman finally stepped away from Leib and walked across the clearing. She extended her hand. "Welcome," she said to Yona.

Yona had seen handshakes before from afar, but she had never engaged in one herself. As she reached out and let Sulia's hand encircle hers, she was surprised to feel how hard the other woman's fingers squeezed, folding Yona's fingers into an uneasy U. Yona tried to squeeze back with equal force, and Sulia blinked rapidly a few times before pulling away.

"So, Yona, you are from the area near Mir, too?" Sulia asked.

"No."

Sulia seemed to be waiting for Yona to say more, but she didn't.

"Yona, meet Ruth." Aleksander nodded to the young mother, who nodded back and gave Yona a smile that was small but full of light. "That's Daniel, and over there are Pessia and Leah, her other two children. Against the trees there, you see Leon and Oscher."

The old men both raised a hand in greeting as Aleksander continued. "You know Leib, and the women with him are Miriam, his mother; Bina, who is Oscher's wife; and Luba." A woman in her forties with dark hair framed by graying streaks—who must have been Miriam—nodded at Yona. The other two women—one with long, straight white hair, the other with twisted hair the color of silverfish—smiled and waved.

"And that's Moshe with them," Aleksander concluded. The man beside the older women nodded at Yona, his arms full of clothing. He appeared to be in his sixties and was nearly bald, with a pair of thick spectacles perched on the tip of his nose. He was the tailor, Yona recalled. She nodded back.

"Rosalia is still out on patrol?" Aleksander asked Leib, who nodded. "Can you go find her and bring her back?"

Leib's eyes flicked to Yona. "Why?"

Aleksander hesitated, his eyes roaming the small encampment. Everyone remained still, watching. It felt to Yona as if they were all holding one long, collective breath. "Because we need to move," Aleksander said at last, and there was a chorus of exhales, punctuated by a few soft gasps. "At once. We aren't safe here."

Leib tensed. "You've seen Germans? Where? How close?"

"No. Nothing like that. Still, we need to be on our way as soon as we can."

Frowning, Leib glanced at Yona, then nodded and slipped off into the woods without another word.

"What are you saying, Aleksander?" one of the old men asked, the one Aleksander had introduced as Oscher, using the tree he'd been leaning on for support as he stood. The white-haired woman, Oscher's wife, Bina, moved to his side, taking his hand and squeezing, as he added, "We need to move? From this spot that is comfortable and safe? Why?"

Aleksander hesitated and glanced at Yona. "Because we are too obvious here."

"But you said the Germans aren't coming," murmured Ruth, her eyes round with fear as she rocked Daniel. The little boy's eyelids were drooping, almost closed, his mouth slightly open, and Yona felt a pang of sudden fury at the thought that there were people out there hunting this defenseless child.

"Perhaps not today." Aleksander's voice was heavy with grief and exhaustion, and before Yona could stop herself, she reached out and touched his arm. The gesture of comfort seemed to surprise him; he blinked at her a few times before nodding and giving her a small smile. "But they will come." His tone was resolute now. "They will come, and we cannot be here waiting for them."

"You are being too cautious. We are fine here," Sulia said.

She glanced at Yona and added, "Aleksander is too worried sometimes, too careful."

The words felt proprietary somehow, but that hardly mattered, because they were so incorrect. "There is no such thing as being too careful in the forest," Yona said. "There is always danger."

"Ah." Sulia crossed her arms and glanced around at a few of the others in the group, her gaze resting on Aleksander for a few seconds before settling on Yona. "So this is your doing, yes? You have told Aleksander that we need to move our camp? And he believes you because you helped him catch a few fish?"

"Sulia," one of the other women murmured in warning, but no one else spoke.

Yona could feel her cheeks heating again. Her palms were sweaty. She wanted to run, but if she did that, she'd be abandoning these people to the same sort of future Chana's family had met. So she drew a deep breath. "Right now, you have been here too long. If your enemies come close enough by chance, they will find you."

"*Our* enemies?" Sulia repeated. "Do you hear that, Aleksander? We must consider what she's saying. She is telling us what to do, but she does not believe she is one of us."

"Of course she is, Sulia." It was Ruth who spoke. She had stopped rocking the baby and was rounding up the girls. "She is trying to help, which makes her a friend. We are all just trying to survive. Why not take the guidance of someone who can help us?"

"But who is she, anyhow?" one of the old men asked. "None of us know her from the ghetto, from our villages."

"Who cares?" another man shot back. "She knows the forest."

"Well, so do we!" the first man replied.

"Oh yes, Leon, you are going to lead us through the woods now, are you?" the second man retorted. "Feed us all? What's for dinner tonight, then?"

"Enough!" Aleksander cut off the bickering by raising his hand. "Yona, what should we do?"

"You must—" Yona hesitated, suddenly uncertain—not of the need to move, but of her right to dole out instructions to people she'd just met. But Aleksander nodded encouragingly, and she drew a deep breath before continuing. "*We* must destroy the shelters, pack up your belongings." She glanced at Ruth. "Do your girls know how to gather berries?"

Ruth nodded. "But I'm not certain which ones are poisonous, so I've been hesitant to let them."

"I will show them." It would keep the children busy, but it was also something they should know if they were going to live in the forest for any length of time. The right berries would help them to survive. The wrong ones could kill them, slowly and painfully.

Yona beckoned to the girls, who approached her slowly. Behind them, the older men and women had begun to gather things lying about—a frying pan, a pair of trousers drying on a large stone, a pair of boots, a tattered, leather-bound book— stuffing them into rucksacks. Yona watched Oscher limp across the clearing, and her concern deepened; his leg was in worse shape than she'd realized.

"Your name means 'dove,' you know," said the older girl as Yona knelt down to eye level. Her hair was straight and silky, even though it likely hadn't seen a comb in months. Her younger sister had tight, tangled curls, and both had rosy cheeks, thirst-blistered lips, and sun-bitten noses. But their dark eyes were bright and interested.

"I know." Yona smiled and turned her left wrist over, showing them her birthmark. Both girls leaned toward it in fascination, and the older one touched her wrist. "This is how I got my name."

"It looks just like a real dove," said the older girl.

"Do you want to know a secret?" Yona asked, and both girls leaned in, eyes wide. "I can feel this dove sometimes, when I'm hungry or sad or scared. It feels as if she's trying to fly."

"Whoa," breathed the younger girl.

"Yona," murmured the older one, still staring at the deep-maroon birthmark, which Yona could feel pulsing. "I love your name. I don't know how I got mine."

"And what is it?"

"Pessia." The little girl smiled tentatively. "And this is Leah. My sister. I'm older. Only by ten months, though."

Yona smiled as Leah kicked at the dirt. "It is wonderful to meet you, Leah and Pessia. Can I tell you another secret?"

Pessia's eyes widened and she nodded, leaning in. "What is it?" Leah still looked uncertain.

"The forest is full of good things to eat—and to drink," Yona whispered.

"But *Mami* says it's dangerous to eat from the forest," Leah said.

"Your mother was right about that when you were village girls. But now you are forest girls, and I will teach you how to find safe things. There is only one rule. You are never to eat anything you pick without checking with me or your mother first, until you learn. If you will promise me that, I will teach you. Is that a deal?"

Leah nodded, but Pessia looked skeptical. "Does that mean you are here to stay, then, Miss Yona?"

Yona glanced over their heads to where Aleksander stood in conversation with Oscher, Moshe, and the other older man, Leon. She watched for a second as Sulia helped Ruth pack up the baby's things, and as Miriam, Bina, and Luba began to pull down the leaves and bark from their makeshift shelters. Could she really do this? Give up her solitude, possibly her safety, to help this group to survive? It went against all Jerusza had taught her, but she had to, didn't she?

"Yes, Pessia," Yona replied, and just like that, the dove on her wrist beat against her skin, though whether in joy or trepidation, she didn't know. "I am here to stay for now."

Pessia studied Yona for a few seconds before a slow smile spread across her face. "Good. I'm glad."

"Yes." Yona stood and beckoned for the girls to follow her. "I think I am, too."

CHAPTER NINE

B y the time Leib returned with Rosalia, a tall, solidly built woman of about thirty with fire-streaked chestnut hair, dark eyes, a confident stride, and a rifle, the camp was mostly broken down, the group's belongings packed, the shelters destroyed. Yona had shown the little girls how to quickly and efficiently pick the plump, twilight bilberries that grew around the camp, and how to tell them apart from the poisonous herb Paris berries, which only grew alone, one to a plant. The girls were each filling a basket Yona had quickly woven from willow twigs and bark, and she kept an eye on them as she walked into the clearing to meet Rosalia.

Rosalia's grip was firm but not crushing, and her eyes were kind as she assessed Yona. "Leib tells me you are here to help us. And that you are the one responsible for last night's bounty of fish."

Yona ducked her head. "The fish were Aleksander's and Leib's doing, too."

"They were much appreciated, Yona. We've been very hungry."

Yona had the feeling she had passed some sort of test. "You have a gun," she said, gesturing to the weapon in Rosalia's hands.

Rosalia looked down, almost as if she was surprised to realize it was there. "Oh, yes. It belongs to Aleksander. He and I take turns guarding the camp. Leib, too."

"That's wise." Yona glanced around. "Of course Ruth has the children, but what about Sulia and Miriam? They're young, healthy. Do they not take a turn?"

"They are wary of guns." Rosalia's voice was a serene thrum. "It's just as well. Those who protect the group must be confident."

Yona nodded. Rosalia hadn't taken the opportunity to criticize the other two women, and she appreciated that.

"Have you used a gun before, Yona?" Rosalia asked.

"No."

"But how do you protect yourself out here? Leib said you'd been in the forest for a long time."

"I avoid people."

"Surely the forests are crawling with partisans now, though."

She thought of the footsteps she and Jerusza could hear in the forest, the way Jerusza had warned her to stay hidden, their journey to the swamp in the summer of 1941 to avoid Russian soldiers fleeing from the German onslaught. "I have learned to stay away. To keep to myself."

"That sounds very lonely."

Yona bowed her head. How could she explain that she had never really felt alone, because she didn't know what it felt like to be with people? She understood now, though, that her yearning to visit the villages on the forest's edge might have been exactly that, a longing deep within her, a loneliness she hadn't known a name for. "Perhaps."

"And yet you are here now. With us. No longer alone." The words weren't exactly a question, but Yona felt the curiosity in them. The other woman was trying to understand her. Yona wished she could explain, but she could hardly grasp the decisions she had made in the last twenty-four hours, which went against everything she knew.

"There was a family," she began, but then she didn't know how to explain Chana and the strange dynamic with the girl's parents, or the way she had let them down so terribly. "I failed them. I—I did not do enough. And they were killed."

Realization sparked in Rosalia's eyes. "They were like us. Jews."

"Yes."

"You are a Jew, too?"

"I was raised by one." She looked away, feeling a surge of guilt. How was she supposed to explain to anyone what it was to feel a part of a religion that would perhaps never be hers? "But we're all children of the same God, don't you think?"

"I think the Germans would disagree. I think they would want to know just what is in your blood." Rosalia looked as if she wanted to say more, but Aleksander interrupted by striding up to them.

"I think we are ready to move," he said.

Yona scanned the campsite. It had indeed been dismantled, packed away, and the girls were back with their mother, who was carefully picking through their basket of berries. But they couldn't go yet; the campsite was still full of signs that people had lived there, cooked there. It would be a poison arrow handed to the Germans, pointed in the direction the group had gone. "First," she said, "we must erase all signs that we've been here at all, as best we can."

Aleksander nodded and glanced skyward. "But it will be dark in a few hours. We should be on our way, so we can cover more ground."

Yona understood what he was saying. With a group largely composed of older people and children, it would be difficult to move without daylight. They would need to learn how to navigate by the stars, to walk by the light of the moon, but not tonight. "We will do our best here, quickly, and then we'll move. We will walk until twilight and find a place to settle."

It took a few seconds before he nodded. "Very well."

A few minutes later, with Rosalia standing guard and the two little girls perched on a fallen tree, eating berries with Leon, Oscher, and Bina, Aleksander called out to the group, "We must scrub the clearing of signs we've been here."

"It looks empty now," Leib said, looking around.

"Not to those who are accustomed to tracking," Yona replied.

"Tell us what to do, Yona," Aleksander said.

Yona took a deep breath and tried to ignore Sulia's pursed lips, the glances Oscher and Moshe exchanged, the way Miriam and Luba were regarding her dubiously. "Luba, Miriam, gather big branches and sweep away all the footprints you see in the dirt around the outskirts, working your way back to the clearing, making sure you erase your own prints as you go. Leon, Oscher, if you can manage, please scan the campsite for any burned logs, embers, and ash—any sign that there have been man-made fires here—and put them in a stack, over there. Leib, you take them to the stream and submerge them. Sulia, please sweep the places all of you slept for any trace that you've been here—imprints in the dirt, leaves in unnatural piles, even fallen strands of hair. Moshe, you and Aleksander should take the bark that you used for roofs and spread it around the forest floor so that it looks untouched."

"What can I do?" Ruth asked. She was rocking Daniel gently; his eyes were closed, and his mouth twitched in a dream.

"You have the baby," Yona said.

"Pessia can hold him." Ruth glanced at the older girl, who nodded, wiped her berry-stained fingers on her shirt, and reached for her little brother. The boy settled into Pessia's arms with a coo and a sigh, and Ruth turned to Yona. "I am ready."

Yona nodded. "Come with me, then."

From the pile of the group's belongings, Yona pulled two large pots. It was extraordinary that they'd managed to obtain such supplies, but she was thankful for it. The pots would allow them to boil water for herbal remedies, and soups when the weather grew cold. And now, it would allow her and Ruth to do a job that was necessary, though unpleasurable.

"We need to wash away the waste," she said, handing Ruth one of the pots.

"The waste?"

Yona's eyes drifted to the area just beyond the edge of the circle that the group had obviously used as a latrine. It was hidden behind a massive oak for privacy, and there were two large holes dug in the ground. A tracking dog—or a man who was experienced at searching the woods—would know it in an instant.

"Oh," Ruth said, following Yona's gaze.

But she followed Yona, and together, in companionable silence, they dumped pot after pot of water from the stream on
the area, then filled in the two holes with fresh dirt, using large
sticks as hoes. They finished with a few dozen more pots full
of water, going back and forth to the stream, and covered the
space with leaves and branches, until finally, the ground looked
untouched. Then they returned to the stream together to wash
the dirt from beneath their nails.

"You have been alone out here?" Ruth asked as they scrubbed
their hands with the cool water.

"Yes."

"Do you mind if I ask what happened to your family?" Her
tone was gentle. "Surely you had parents."

"I don't know what happened to them," Yona said after a
pause. She wondered where they were now, *Siegfried and Alwine
Jüttner.* They were strangers. "The woman who raised me died
earlier this year."

"I'm sorry." When Yona didn't say anything, Ruth added, "I
am glad you are here. With us."

Yona searched herself before replying. "I am, too."

Three hours before nightfall, they set off, moving slowly northeast through the trees. They were going deeper into the heart of
the Nalibocka, trudging at a pace that Oscher, who leaned on
Leib, was comfortable with. Ruth carried Daniel, while Miriam
held Leah, and Pessia trudged along holding Luba's hand, after
announcing to the group that she was a big girl and could walk
by herself. Ruth and Yona had exchanged looks of doubt, but

the child was keeping up just fine, a look of steely determination on her rosy-cheeked face, and Yona was impressed.

Yona and Aleksander walked ahead of the group, leading the way, and Rosalia brought up the rear, the gun still in her hands as she scanned the forest for danger.

"We're moving farther away from civilization," Aleksander said as they moved, ducking in unison under a low-slung oak branch. His boots crunched loudly through the underbrush, while Yona moved almost silently, her weight on the balls of her feet, as Jerusza had always taught her. *Move like a lynx*, Jerusza's voice sounded in her head. *Think like a fox. Track like a wolf.*

"Yes."

Aleksander cleared his throat. "Are you sure about this, Yona? I initially made the decision to stay within a day's walk of some of the towns at the forest's edge."

She glanced at him. His jaw, sharp beneath several days of dark growth, was set. "Why?"

"So that we could venture in if we needed anything."

"Like what?"

"Food—a few chickens, some potatoes, some jam. Glasses for Moshe." He paused. "It's where we got the pots we cook in, from a farmhouse not far from where we camped for the first few weeks."

She understood. "You stole those things."

He turned, his eyes meeting hers. "Some of it, yes. It was survival, Yona. We—it was hard to know how to eat at first. And Moshe's glasses were crushed by a German weeks before we left. He's nearly blind without them. And the gun. Yona, we needed a gun."

"You stole that, too?"

Their conversation paused as they reached a small stream. Yona tested it first, and then nodded, beckoning everyone forward. With cupped hands, they all drank the water, Leib in particular gulping it down in huge, desperate swallows.

"Slow," Yona said, reaching out to touch his shoulder. "We are all thirsty. But drinking too quickly will make you sick."

He nodded, but he continued to gulp the cool liquid, and Yona returned to her own spot on the bank beside Aleksander.

"It's getting dark," he said.

Yona looked up at the sky, which was fading to a shade of deep blue that sometimes reminded her of Kroman Lake in the southern part of the forest, where bream, perch, and pike swam. She and Jerusza had visited twice a summer when Yona was young, and the old woman had even permitted Yona to swim once while Jerusza fished. The water had been cool, bracing, and it had moved around her in a way that felt different from the gentle, steady currents in the streams where she usually bathed. The fish they caught were plump, salty. But then the lake had become a place for villagers to look for food when the farmers' crops struggled and the economy turned, and Jerusza had never brought her back.

"We have another forty-five minutes before the light is gone," Yona replied.

Aleksander beckoned to the group, and in silence, they filled their canteens and flasks with water—they each seemed to have one—and followed, wading across the stream and walking in a line as they pressed deeper into the woods.

"You asked about the gun," Aleksander said after a while. The sky above was turning inky, and Yona knew they'd have to stop soon. There was a clearing up ahead that she hoped would work. "We needed one. And there was a farmer near Mir who I knew kept a rifle in his salt cellar. I left the group one day and waited outside his barn until I saw him leave for the fields. I was in the cellar with the rifle in my hands when he appeared at the top of the ladder, pointing a pistol at me. 'Who is there?' he demanded, trying to see my face. I lifted my cap, and he stared at me for a whole minute before he said my name. He recognized me; I could hardly believe it. I had worked on his farm for a summer when I was a teenager. It's how I knew the gun would be there.

"I asked him not to shoot me, and though he didn't lower his gun, I somehow knew he was not going to. I held up his rifle and said, 'I'm sorry, but I need this.' He looked from me to it and then back at me. 'Where are your parents?' he asked. I told him they were dead. 'Your brothers?' Dead, too, I told him. He asked where I was living. The forest, I told him. Finally, he nodded, lowered his weapon, and stepped aside to let me up the ladder. I climbed up until I stood beside him. 'You must make me a promise,' he said. I will never forget the way he looked at me. 'If I let you take the gun,' he said, 'you must promise me that you will survive and tell stories of the things you have seen. That you won't let your family's deaths go unavenged.' I promised, and as I started to walk away, I turned and asked a question I needed to know the answer to. I asked him why—why he was letting me take a gun he must have needed himself. Why he was helping me at all when most of the farmers in their villages nearby would cheerfully turn me in for a bounty."

Aleksander paused as they reached the clearing, and he and Yona looked up at the sky together. It had almost reached full dark, and this place was as good as any; there was enough space for their group, and it was hidden by broad swaths of oaks, far enough from the stream that it wouldn't be an obvious place to look. Yona nodded at Aleksander, and he turned to the group and told them to start making camp.

"What did the farmer say?" Yona asked as she and Aleksander began stripping wide swatches of bark from trees. Behind them, in the clearing, she could hear Leib retching, his stomach upset from the rapid intake of water, but she didn't turn.

"He said that when he and my father were boys, my father had saved his life. He didn't explain, but he said that his parents wouldn't let him thank my father, because he was a Jew. They wouldn't even let him tell people that his life had been saved by Andrzej Gorodinsky. But he never forgot it and had always hoped to one day repay him." Aleksander paused and sniffed, turning away, and Yona's heart ached. "It was too late to repay my father, of course. But the farmer said he hoped that by helping me, he was giving my family a chance to go on."

Yona reached out and touched his arm. "I'm sorry about your parents, Aleksander. And your brothers. There aren't words enough to express that."

He turned to her, holding her gaze for a long time. "Thank you. But the farmer was right. I have to keep living. I have to go on. Or every trace of us, of the Gorodinsky family, of what we were, of what we could have been, will be gone. The Germans, they don't just wipe out our people. They wipe out our future. And I can't bear that."

Yona nodded. If there were words to say after that, she did not know them. It was the most she had ever spoken with another person, the most she had learned about the personal toll of what the Germans were doing, and her throat felt thick with grief. So she touched his arm again, so that he could hear the things she wasn't saying and understand that she was with him.

By the time they had constructed three makeshift shelters of bark and leaves, and Leon and Moshe had gathered kindling to make a fire, half of the group was already asleep, including all three children and their mother. Aleksander offered to take a turn keeping watch, and Yona sat beside the fire in the deep darkness of the wood, watching as Sulia and Miriam boiled water and pulled potatoes from one of the rucksacks. She'd never felt so hollowed out, nor so full of emotion, and she wondered how it was possible to feel both at the same time.

CHAPTER TEN

The night was clear and balmy, so the group didn't bother to build more than basic shelters before filling their bellies with watery soup and crawling off to bed. Leib took the first watch, followed by Aleksander, and when Yona rose in the morning, the sky just beginning to glisten at the edges, she lay still for a moment, watching him move in slow, steady loops around the perimeter of the camp.

He walked quietly—not as quietly as she did after spending a lifetime in the trees, but softly enough that she understood he was a fast study. By his own admission, the forest had never been his home, but he was quickly learning its mysterious ways. The thought filled Yona with a strange blend of relief and sadness—relief because it meant she could teach him enough to help his group survive the winter, sadness because it meant they wouldn't always need her. She had been with them for less than a day, and already she felt an unexpected attachment to all of them.

She had been right to insist they move—the longer they stayed in place during the summer, the more dangerous their situation became—but Yona also had to admit to herself that the group had fared well on their own. They had figured out a way to gather food, to tell basic poisons from basic sustenance, to build rudimentary shelter, even to arm themselves. It spoke volumes about Aleksander, Rosalia, Leib, and the others that they'd had a sense of what they needed to take from the villages and what they had to do to stay alive. Yona would help to make the upcoming winter easier, but even without her, it was possible they could all survive if they were fortunate enough to stay out of the path of those hunting them.

As Yona stood, she shivered, though the summer day was already warm. *Hunting.* The word lodged in her chest and throbbed there dangerously. She had hunted animals. She had *been* hunted by animals. But the thought of humans hunting humans—it was difficult for her to understand, and it made her feel ill.

She headed toward Aleksander, who turned and spotted her as she approached. "You should go back to sleep," he said. "Get some rest."

"I don't sleep much." It was true. Jerusza had taught her long ago that sleep, though necessary, was equivalent to weakness. Slumber left one vulnerable, useless. With the exception of her final few months, as she slowly passed from this world to the next, Jerusza had never slept more than four hours at a time, and she had often pursed her lips and chided Yona for sleeping for any period longer than that. Last night, though exhausted from the unfamiliar strain of human contact, Yona's brain had raced with thoughts about all the things she wanted to do in the coming days. She would need to teach the group to preserve fish, to dry bilberries and cawberries for winter, to gather and store mountain ash berries and tree cranberries. She had to teach them how to hunt without weapons, which wild animals would provide the most nutrition, which frogs and snakes could be eaten, which herbs could be picked to help make food more palatable, which could be gathered to help treat ailments. She would need to show them how to build winter shelters and to catch fish when ice had crusted the ponds. They were the secrets of the forest that villagers couldn't know, secrets that would mean the difference between life and death.

"You look troubled," Aleksander said after a moment.

She was, of course. She felt responsible for everyone here. But then she looked back at the camp—where Ruth lay clutching all three of her sleeping children, where Oscher and Bina held each other, where Miriam slept with one arm slung protectively over a snoring Leib—and a great peace settled over her, all the questions and worries fading to a whisper. "It will be all right," she said, as much to herself as to Aleksander.

"I'm very glad you are here, Yona. That we found each other."

She turned to him. The way he was watching her made her breath catch. "You were already doing a good job, long before I arrived. Everyone is alive and well-fed."

He smiled slightly. "I wasn't talking about survival, Yona. I'm grateful for *you*." His eyes held hers for a second more before he dropped his gaze. "For your company, I mean."

Her cheeks warmed, and as she looked back toward the group, she had the feeling that there was deeper meaning in his words. "And I am glad for yours, Aleksander."

The sky was light a half hour later, and the camp began to stir, the baby crying first. As Ruth pulled him to her breast, she jostled the girls, who both awoke muttering remnants of their dreams. Rosalia was awake next, then Oscher and Bina. Yona watched in silence as they all yawned and stretched, standing and wandering to the edge of the clearing, some of them taking swigs from the canteens they had filled last night, others taking turns relieving themselves in the privacy of the shadows beyond the perimeter.

By the time the sun had crested the trees, Rosalia was on guard, Aleksander had taken Moshe and Leon with him to show them how to use the gill net in the stream they'd passed the night before, the girls were cheerfully gathering berries with their mother, and Yona was teaching Sulia, Miriam, and Luba how to gather the pink Saponaria flowers that bloomed in the summer on hillsides, and how to crush the roots with small stones and mix in a bit of water to make a basic soap.

"Shouldn't we be doing something more useful?" Sulia asked, loudly enough for her voice to carry to the others, as she bent beside Yona to yank a handful of blooms from the earth. "This feels unnecessary."

Miriam and Luba glanced at her, but they didn't say anything. Yona could feel her chest constricting the way it sometimes did when she knew a predator had picked up her scent. "Without soap, you will have disease and lice," Yona replied. "We're fortunate that it is summer now, but by autumn, these plants will wilt. Before then, I'll teach you to make soap from hardwood ash and animal fat."

Sulia made a small noise in the back of her throat, but she didn't say anything else.

"Leib said you are very good at catching fish, Yona," Miriam said after a while. She had moved beside Yona, her skirt lifted in the front to create a basket for the hundreds of flowers she had gathered. She was quiet, and a hard worker, which Yona respected. Sulia and Luba had moved farther down the hillside and were chatting with each other.

"I have been fishing all my life," Yona replied. "Your son, he has good instincts. He will be a fine fisherman once he learns, and a good hunter, too."

"This wasn't the life I wanted for him," Miriam said after a long silence. "When children are small, mothers envision all the things they will do one day, the people they will become. Never did I think, when Leib was a boy, that he would be all I had left. Never did I think that my dreams for him would narrow so. Now I dream only of seeing him survive. To imagine more feels decadent." She paused and added, "It feels impossible."

Yona blinked a few times so Miriam could not see the tears in her eyes. She didn't know what to say, so she murmured, "I'm very sorry. For everything that has happened to you."

"It must be God's plan, though, yes? It is just that I cannot understand it."

"I don't understand it, either," Yona said, and she felt a stab of guilt. *One must never question God,* Jerusza had always told her. *It is our job on earth only to seek to understand him, never to doubt his will.* But this was madness, and Yona felt like the truth of it all was just beyond her grasp.

Miriam didn't reply, and after a moment, she returned to gathering flowers.

"How did you and Leib escape from the ghetto?" Yona asked a few minutes later.

Miriam sighed again and straightened, her eyes damp. "Leib is young, strong. That meant the Germans used him for work, for building things. One day they marched many of the other men from the ghetto out into a clearing. They made them dig a trench. And then they shot them all." She trembled as she drew a breath. "My husband was among those murdered. But Leib, he survived—Aleksander, too—because he was part of the work detail, and the Germans needed them. But we were no longer blind after that. We knew that it would be only a matter of time until they murdered us, too. And so Leib and Aleksander—whom we knew from our village—began to talk about escape.

"One day there was a rumor that they would be moving us all to the abandoned castle on the edge of town, a place that was fortified and would be impossible to escape from. Once we were there, they could kill us anytime; there would be no way out. Word spread around the camp that there were Jews meeting in the woods. 'Get yourself out of the ghetto, and we will find you,' they said. And so Leib and I made a plan. He would run from his work detail. We knew that it was a risk. When I kissed him goodbye that morning, I thought it was likely I would never see him again. But the Germans were busy that day preparing to shoot another group of Jews in the clearing, and Leib managed to escape. I hid in the ghetto—beneath an outhouse—until they already believed me gone. And then I fled, twelve days later, after they had stopped looking. If Leib had given up on me, I don't think I would have survived. But he was there in the woods, waiting, a small miracle in the face of so much loss."

"I'm very sorry about your husband and your other children, Miriam," Yona said after a while.

Miriam shook her head. "They are free now. And I still have Leib." But her voice snagged on the last word and became a sob. The silence that followed was an empty space that would never be filled.

For two more days, the group stayed in the clearing. Both days, Yona took Leib to the stream with the gill net, and together they gathered hundreds of fish. As night fell on the second day, Aleksander started a fire, and Yona showed the group how to smoke-dry fish to preserve them for winter, constructing a tripodlike tented structure from three tall, sturdy branches, lashing them with vines at the top, and using twine woven from grass to hang the fish. She covered the tented branches with bark to keep the smoke in, leaving a small opening at the top, and then she showed Leon and Oscher how to build a fire fueled by broken green alder branches. Once the fire was going, they had to transfer the coals to a hollowed-out spot in the center of the tent, where they would need to tend them until at least the next day to make sure both that they continued to smoke and that they didn't flame up. It was risky to let smoke rise in daylight, but they were deep enough in the forest that it was unlikely they'd be seen, and the thin plume that rose from a smoking tent was much less obvious than the clouds that billowed from the campfires they lit in the darkness to cook their food. Those could be seen for miles on a clear day, but not in the dark, for the night absorbed the clouds.

At night, Yona slept by herself under a canopy of leaves on the edge of the clearing, far enough from the others so she could watch them. After spending almost her whole life in the forest, her instincts were sharp enough that the slightest foreign noise would awaken her, and though Leib, Aleksander, and Rosalia maintained an armed perimeter patrol, she felt better knowing that she, too, provided a small layer of protection.

By the fourth day, though, Yona was growing uneasy. "We need to move again," she said to Aleksander, approaching him as he made his early-morning loops around the outskirts of the camp just before sunrise, the rifle propped against his shoulder, his eyes scanning the darkness beyond. She had awoken that morning in a panic she couldn't name, and she had barely stopped to pull her boots on before rushing outside to find him.

He stopped walking and looked down at her. "Move?"

"I can't explain it. We've been here too long."

"But it's only been four days. We have just gotten comfortable. And there's food here . . ."

"I know."

"Why, then?"

"I can feel things sometimes, bad things that are coming." She glanced up at him and then looked down. "I feel it now. There's darkness moving in."

She finally looked up again, and Aleksander studied her face in silence. His jaw, firm and square beneath his beard, flexed a few times, and she could see the cartilage in his neck bobbing as he swallowed. She had the strangest urge to reach out and place her fingers there, to feel his pulse and the rhythm of his breath, so she looked away again before he could read her eyes. "Yona?" he said softly.

She looked back at him. Her heart was still thudding with a drumbeat of danger the way it sometimes did before a raging storm. But there was something else there, too, a heat, an unsettling warmth. "Yes?"

He took a step closer. She felt the frisson between them again, the change in the air, and this time, she didn't stop her eyes from wandering where they wanted to go. His arms. The taut muscles

that ran the length of his neck. The way his broad chest strained
against his threadbare shirt. When she looked back at his face, he
was watching her closely, and there was something in his gaze that
hadn't been there before. She couldn't put a name to it, but it stirred
something in her belly, something she didn't know was there.

"Yona, I . . ." he began.

But then the low, plaintive call of a wolf nearby pierced the
quiet, and it was enough to shake her heart out of wherever it
had been, to remind her of the danger, to squeeze everything
else aside. Aleksander seemed to feel the shift, too, for he took a
step back and cleared his throat. "I'll—I'll go tell the others that
it's time to move," he said.

She made herself smile at him, but now that her belly was no
longer on fire, the tension that had knotted her insides was back.
Something was coming; she could feel it. "Thank you."

But after Aleksander had awoken the others and handed the
rifle to Rosalia, sending her out on patrol with a warning to
be on alert, they realized at the same time that Leib was gone.
"Where is he?" Aleksander asked Miriam, whose eyes were
wide and frightened.

"I have no idea," Miriam said. "He was beside me when we
went to sleep."

Yona quickly scanned the clearing. She had left the gill net
beside the smoker the night before, but it wasn't there anymore.
Smoke trailed lazily from the opening at the top of the tent, and
the hairs on her arms stood on end once more. "He's gone to the
river to fish, I think," she said to Aleksander. "I'll go."

"I'll come with you."

"No. Stay here with the others. Break up the camp and prepare to move."

She was gone, into the forest as quickly as her legs could take her, before he had a chance to protest.

She'd had this feeling before, this tightening of her abdomen, this tingling of her skin. Once, when she was just a girl, she had managed to scramble up a tree just before a trio of wolves emerged from the forest, running straight for her. When she was twelve, she had seen in her mind's eye a massive oak toppling on them during a storm the moment before it happened, giving her just enough time to awaken Jerusza and pull her away. The last time had been four years ago, when she'd found Jerusza, her ankle badly twisted from a fall, cornered by a snarling brown bear. Yona had shot the creature with an arrow in the back and carried Jerusza away while it lay dying.

You have a sixth sense, Jerusza had told her then. *There is a piece of me in you after all.* Yona had protested, insisting that she had simply been in the right place at the right time. But it had been more than that, and she'd known it then, just as she knew it now.

As she drew closer to the stream, she slowed her pace and slipped silently toward the water. Her body thrummed with something foreign, something dangerous. She spotted Leib first, on her side of the stream, his back to her. He was bent over the gill net in a splash of morning sunshine, quickly plucking fish. For a second, she let herself breathe more easily. He was fine. She was imagining the danger.

And then she saw the movement in the bushes several yards away, to her right. She flattened herself against a tree and held her breath, watching.

Time seemed to stand still as two men emerged from the woods, one skinny as a twig, the other one thick as an old oak trunk, both wearing the same tattered uniforms Yona had seen on the men she'd spotted last year with Jerusza before they'd fled to the swamp, the ones Jerusza had said were Russian partisans. Both had rifles drawn, both were moving with the quiet ease of practiced hunters toward Leib.

"*Ey, ty!*" the larger man barked suddenly, startling Leib so severely that he lost his balance and tumbled into the stream. He straightened immediately, whirling around, his eyes widening as they locked on the two men.

The slender one was leering at him. "*Ey, mne kazhetsya, on yevrey,*" he snarled. "*Eto tak? Ty yevrey?*"

Leib stared at them blankly, fear in his eyes. He was right to be frightened; they were pointing the rifles at him now, asking if he was a Jew. Slowly, her heart hammering, Yona tracked backward so she could approach the men from behind. She had to move slowly to stay silent, but she needed to get to them as quickly as possible before one of them pulled the trigger. "*Ja ciabie nie razumieju,*" Leib stammered—Belorussian for "I don't understand"—as he stood in waist-high water, dripping wet. There were many overlaps between the Russian and Belorussian languages, but in Leib's terror, he was having trouble interpreting words that weren't immediately familiar. He was in the worst possible situation; the water prevented his escape. He couldn't simply turn and run and hope that the men missed if they fired at him. He was a cornered target. Yona crept silently closer.

"*Ty yevrey?*" the smaller man repeated more loudly, his eyes narrowing, and Leib shook his head, clearly frightened.

"Of course he's a Jew, Vadim," the large man said in Russian as Leib began to back away. "Look at that nose. Look how dirty he is. He's probably one of the bastards who's been stealing from us."

"Dirty Jew." The smaller man spat on the ground.

"I think we make him pay. Make an example of him."

"String him up like a warning, yes, after we put a bullet in his head?"

The men both cackled, and Leib's eyes darted desperately back and forth from one to the other. It was clear he had little idea what they were saying but realized it was bad. Yona crept closer, close enough that she could smell them. They were both unwashed, stinking of sweat and saline, mud and adrenaline. They were so focused on the boy they were hunting that they didn't realize they, too, were being hunted.

Slowly, carefully, she reached for the knife that she kept strapped to her ankle, but to her horror, it wasn't there. She realized in a flash that she had left it beside her reed mat when she had gotten up that morning with panic knotting her insides. She had never done that before, not even when she was a child; she slept with the knife within arm's reach and then slipped it into its sheath the moment she awoke. Her blood ran cold, but there was no time to curse her terrible timing.

"All right, then. You want to do the honors, Tikhomirov?" the skinny one asked as he continued to leer at Leib.

The big one raised his rifle, pointing it at Leib, who was shaking now. Instantly, Leib raised his hands over his head. Yona had to do something. Her mind spun back to Jerusza's lessons.

"*Shis mikh nisht. Ikh bet aykh!*" Leib said in Yiddish, reverting in his panic to the language he'd been speaking in the woods. *Don't shoot me, please.*

"He talking that Jew language now?" the big one asked.

The other one laughed. "Think so."

"Last time he's ever gonna—"

But the larger man didn't finish, because Yona had leapt forward, silently, deftly, landing on his upper back, her legs instantly wrapped around his ribs to brace herself.

"What the—?" he began, his voice strangled, but that was all he had the chance to say, because Yona, stabilizing her body with her inner thigh muscles, hoisted herself higher until her head was above his, reached her left arm with lightning speed under his chin, wrapped her left hand around the back of his neck, and jerked up and back as hard as she could. She heard the snap and slid from his back as his body collapsed. She fell instantly behind him, using his body as a shield from the other man, whose face was white with fear as he swung his rifle wildly in her direction.

"Run, Leib!" she called, and as she had predicted, it was enough of a distraction for the confused man, who whirled in the direction of the stream. In the instant before he had turned fully back to her, she struck, first springing forward to gouge his eyes with the sharp index and middle nails of her left hand, and then, the second he tilted his head upward to scream in pain, slicing forward at his unprotected neck with the outer edge of her flattened right hand and thrusting sharply up into the hollow of his throat, crushing his windpipe. He slumped to the ground beside the other man.

Instantly, Yona put her aching right hand to her mouth. What had she done? She had acted on instinct, doing the things Jerusza had made her practice a thousand times, beginning when she was just a little girl. *There will come a day when you'll be glad I have taught you what I know,* Jerusza had said. Yona hadn't believed her then, hadn't really believed that taking another man's life could ever be necessary. But now, now she understood. There had been no other way; if she hadn't acted, they would have killed Leib for no reason at all. Still, that didn't negate the guilt that surged through her, hot and buzzing. She dropped to her knees beside the two bodies, her hand still over her mouth, tears stinging her eyes. She could hear Leib calling her name, but he sounded very far away.

"I killed them," she whispered, staring at the bodies. She felt as if she were in a trance, floating above the stream, looking down at the horrific scene. "I took two lives." She could feel eyes watching her, eyes she knew weren't really there. "Jerusza," she murmured. "I killed them."

"Yona!" Leib's voice was louder now, and then his hand was on her back, and he was pulling her up. "Yona, we have to go. What if there are others?"

She turned to him, dazed. His face, just inches from hers, looked blurry.

"Yona!" he said again, panic lacing his voice. "Yona!"

She could feel herself coming back to reality, but she still felt as if she were underwater, in the deepest part of Kroman Lake. "I think they were alone. But you're right. We can't be sure," she said dully. She had listened hard to the forest before she struck, and had heard no other human movement. They weren't with a Soviet unit; they were wandering the forest on their own. Were they trying to make their way home? Did they have wives, children they had hoped to return to? They shouldn't have been here at all, and now they were dead. "I killed them," she said more loudly now as Leib's face finally swam into focus.

"You did it to save me," Leib said. His eyes were bloodshot, damp, and Yona could see that he was trying hard not to cry.

"I . . ." Yona looked once more at the bodies of the two men. She shook herself out of it and reached for the rifle lying beside the smaller one. She stood and handed it to Leib. "Go back to the camp. Tell Aleksander what happened. Make sure they're ready to move."

He took the weapon uncertainly, his eyes never leaving her face. "What about you?"

"I'll be along soon. Go, Leib. Run."

He hesitated only a second more before nodding and dashing into the forest, the gun in his right hand.

The forest had grown quiet; even the birds had stopped singing. After the sound of Leib's footfalls had faded, Yona knelt once more beside the men. They both had eyes the color of marsh grass, eyes that would never see anything again. She gently closed their eyelids with the palms of her hands, the same hands that had taken their lives, and then, in the silence that surrounded her, she wept. She wept for their families; for the small, frightened group of refugees she had committed herself to helping; for Jerusza; for her own birth parents, whose hearts must have been broken years before when their daughter was stolen.

Finally, she straightened and, grimacing, methodically undressed both men, taking their clothing and boots but leaving their underclothes, for she couldn't stand to do them the final injustice of baring their bodies to the forest. She bundled their belongings into a pile to take back to the camp. The boots, especially, would come in handy as they moved deeper into the woods, as the cold of the autumn and winter moved in.

And then she rolled both bodies into the shallow stream, the only burial she could give them. The forest would silently absorb them, and by the time anyone found their bones, all traces of her would be long gone. As she watched them sink into the blue, she wiped her eyes. And then, grabbing the clothing and boots, the larger Russian's gun, and the gill net Leib had left behind, she ran, her feet carrying her into the dark of the forest.

CHAPTER ELEVEN

For the next two months, the group moved every week or so, deeper and deeper into the woods, always changing their location and leaving no trace. Yona taught them how to locate water sources below the earth and how to build simple wells. She showed them how to kill, skin, gut, and cook an adder, how to make a meal of May beetle larvae, how to find hedgehogs, frogs, and duck eggs, which were relatively easy picking when the weather was warm. She demonstrated how to trap and bleed small animals, how to field-dress a red deer, how to construct their own beds from reeds, how to lash together branches to make the frame for a temporary shelter, how to pitch their makeshift oak and pine bark roofs at a fifty-degree angle to keep the wind and rain out when the weather threatened. And slowly, they all began to prepare for the coming cold.

She had intended to stay for only a few weeks, until she was sure they'd survive without her. But somehow, the weeks had turned to months, and as the leaves began to change and autumn began to bare her teeth, she was still there.

"You need to find a place to shelter," she said to Aleksander one day in late September. The sun hung low in the sky, and a cold wind had swept in from the west. The whole group was hiking through a marshy area deep in the woods, hiding their tracks through sometimes ankle-deep water as they looked for a place to sleep for the night.

They were accustomed to moving by now, accustomed to subsisting on meager provisions, accustomed to burning nearly all the calories they took in. They had all grown leaner, stronger, even the children. Daniel had lost his chubby cheeks far too soon and was just as narrow-faced as his older sisters, who often trooped through the forest whispering and holding hands. They were all much too slim, but at least they were healthy, alive. Yona was thankful for that.

"Yes," Aleksander said, glancing down at Yona with a smile. "It is nearly dark. Let's look for a clearing on drier land."

"Yes. But I meant, too, that you need to find a home for the winter, a place that will keep you hidden, safe, and warm until the spring."

This time, his expression was confused. "But we must keep moving. You said it yourself. It is how we've stayed safe." The week before, on a quick mission into a village on the edge of the forest to get a new pair of spectacles for Moshe, and for Oscher this time, too, Aleksander and Yona had overheard a conversation between two local women who were talking about a small Jewish encampment a kilometer into the forest that the Germans had discovered the week before. Each of the sixteen refugees had been shot on sight, even two little girls. Yona had felt bile rise in her throat, and she'd had to cover her mouth as the women laughed. The chill in her bones hadn't gone away.

"But there is more to staying alive in the winter than staying hidden," she said now. They were quiet for a moment as they approached a flat patch of ground hidden in the heart of a cluster of spruce trees. By silent agreement, they stopped and gestured to the group that this would be their spot for the night. Without being asked, Rosalia and Leib, both carrying guns, disappeared to scour the area for signs of human activity.

"But if we stop somewhere for too long, we become easy quarry, don't we?" Aleksander asked as they set their packs down on the ground and began to collect logs and large sticks for make-shift shelters for the next few days.

"It is more dangerous to face the cold." Quickly, she pulled her axe from her pack and began to chop down some of the narrow, dead trees nearby. Silently, Aleksander removed his axe, too, and set to work splitting the long, dried logs into poles. They had established a routine since Yona had joined the group and had begun to teach them. Now, together, they could build a hut large enough for six or seven in under three hours, adding a roof of dead oak or live spruce bark when the cold or rain threatened, and Rosalia could do the same. The others had learned to build shelters, too, though they were slower. Yona liked that they had all developed a rhythm, a set of intrinsic responsibilities. It had never been like that with Jerusza; the two of them shared everything that needed to be done, except in the very end. But Yona had learned that a group this large worked best when there was a delineation of duties.

"Besides," she added after a few minutes as she and Aleksander set up their own small, individual lean-tos, just beside each other, as had become their custom. He was almost always the first person she saw when she woke in the morning, and she realized she liked that very much. "We are deep enough in the forest now that no one will find you once the snow begins to fall." On the other side of the clearing, Sulia—who usually shared a shelter with Luba and Rosalia—watched them as she lashed together her own gathered branches.

"But won't we leave traces in the snow?" Aleksander asked. "We'll be more obvious if they come looking."

"You will build shelters into the earth, both for warmth and to hide. And you will move about only when the snow is falling and will cover your tracks. The nights are long and the days are gray. It's easier to disappear in the cold."

Aleksander didn't say anything as he finished lashing his shelter and covering the roof with bark.

"When you speak of the winter, Yona, you never use the word *we*," Aleksander said finally, turning his gaze back to her. "Are you leaving?"

She was silent for a long time, for she didn't know the right answer. "That was always the plan, wasn't it? That I would stay only until you didn't need me anymore?"

Aleksander waited until she looked him in the eye. "We still need you, Yona," he said, his voice low.

"Aleksander—"

"Please. Don't leave."

"You'll survive without me."

"But I think I would miss you far too much." He cleared his throat. "We all would, I mean. You are one of us now. Stay— unless you don't want to."

She held his gaze for a long time, and in it, she saw a future she had never imagined for herself, a future filled with laughter and friendship instead of silence and loneliness. Maybe even a future filled with love. "I do," she said softly. "I do want to." But even as she said it, the wind whipped up, and she could hear it whispering to her, hissing a warning.

Two days later, they'd found a spot deep in the woods, a two-hour hike from the closest stream. Yona spent an additional day searching for an underground water source before digging a shallow well and returning to tell the group that they'd found their spot for the winter. No one argued.

They started with bark-covered huts for shelter, but by the second day, they were all burrowing into the earth with make-shift shovels, everyone but the children. The girls were running around the outskirts of the clearing, pretending to be wood fairies, while Daniel giggled at them from his bed of reeds. Their laughter made Yona smile, even as her muscles burned. This was what they were saving—a future of smiles for these three innocent children, maybe even for the children Pessia, Leah, and Daniel would have themselves someday. For the millionth time, Yona wondered at a world that would allow lives like theirs to be violently snuffed out.

By the end of the next week, following Yona's instructions, the group had finished two large *zemliankas* and a much smaller one. Unlike the temporary huts they had been constructing over the last few months, designed to be assembled and disassembled quickly, these were solid, permanent, protected. They were dug deep into the ground, with walls made of five-inch logs, wooden floors, and underground ceilings covered in earth and supported by log beams, each with a narrow stairway to the entrance aboveground. Now, before the first snowfall, the doors to the shelters were visible, but once the forest was under a blanket of snow, they would disappear. It would take the group a few more weeks to build mud-brick stoves and chimneys for warmth, and Yona would show them how; she had done it each year of her life with Jerusza as they prepared for the winter freeze.

The group also built a smaller, separate underground bunker for food storage, which Yona was eager to start filling before the cold made gathering harder, and a small latrine. In the end, in the space of two weeks, they all had real, semipermanent homes for the first time in years.

While Leib, Aleksander, and Moshe hunted and fished, the women gathered plants and berries, and Leon and Oscher tended a large smoker, Yona ventured out each day into the forest, gathering herbs to dry. Soon the ground would be frozen solid, and nature's medicines would be underground until the spring.

When she'd lived with Jerusza, they had done this each year, drying the plants they gathered, pulverizing some for teas and poultices and keeping others whole. But for a group of fifteen people—of all different ages—the need was greater. So Yona gathered yarrow, wormwood, chicory, and chamomile. She pulled leaves of *dziurawiec* for wound care, black lilac and yarrow for fevers, coltsfoot for coughs, nettle leaves for muscle weakness, rosemary for heart ailments, horsetail tips for swelling, and comfrey to treat broken bones and arthritis. By the time the air tasted like snow, she had assembled a whole arsenal of dried or mashed herbs that would take them through the winter.

On a morning early in December, Yona awoke before dawn, and, even from her nest beneath the earth, she could feel the change in the air. She pulled on her wool coat and made her way aboveground, where snowflakes were falling, clinging to the dirt for only a second or two before disappearing forever into the earth. Soon the snow would begin to stick, but for the first few minutes, it was as if the sky and the ground met, becoming one.

She tilted her head up and felt the flakes kiss her cheeks. The season's first snowfall in the depths of the forest was always magical, and though Yona had lived through nearly two dozen winters, the thrill of it never faded. Though she knew the sugar-delicate flakes were the harbinger of coming danger, of a winter that would test the resilience of all of them, there was no denying their beauty as they drifted down gently from a silent sky.

"Yona." She heard Aleksander's voice behind her, and she turned, startled out of her reverie. He was standing in front of the entrance to the larger zemlianka, watching her.

"Aleksander." She put a hand over her racing heart. "I didn't hear you. What are you doing up?"

"I couldn't sleep." He hesitated and crossed to stand beside her. Like her, he was in a wool coat, but she could still somehow feel the heat of his nearness as his arm brushed against hers. "It's beautiful, isn't it?"

They both gazed skyward, and for a moment, it felt as if they were alone in the forest. The others in their group slept, and the animals had all sought refuge from the cold. The only movement was from the snow itself. When Yona turned to look at Aleksander again, his eyes were already on her. "Is it wrong that I love the first snowfall so much?" she asked.

"Wrong?"

"The snow brings with it great peril. To welcome it feels strange in a way. It only means that life will become more complicated."

She wasn't sure he understood what she was saying until he reached for her hand. Neither of them had gloves, and so their fingers were freezing, but there was an instant warmth as they intertwined. "Perhaps the most complicated things are also the most beautiful," Aleksander said softly, and when she turned to look at him again, she found that she couldn't look away for a long time. When they finally turned their eyes to the magic of the sky again, it felt as if, for a moment, the world was at peace.

Later, when the others awoke and emerged into a world painted white, Yona felt an unexpected wave of warmth wash over her. To see the surprise, the joy, on the faces of the others was enchanting all on its own. The girls ran around in the clearing, laughing and trying to catch snow on their tongues, while Daniel simply stared at the heavens with his eyes wide and unblinking. Oscher and Bina held each other and swayed, and even Rosalia looked skyward with tears in her eyes.

But the snow would eventually force the group inside their bunkers for long periods of time, and so, as they all said good night that night and walked back to their zemliankas, the silence that descended felt heavy and dark, even if the world around them was turning the color of hope and peace.

Aleksander, Leib, Miriam, Bina, Oscher, Luba, and Sulia were sharing one of the larger shelters, while Moshe, Leon, Rosalia, Ruth, and the children shared the other. Yona had her own, the smallest and most basic of all, which she had built entirely by herself while the others had rested. It had worked out that way without discussion—a division similar to how they had sheltered each night when they had only temporary huts—and Yona had been glad that no one had tried to bunk with her. Being with a group after a lifetime of being alone was still unsettling and strange, and she needed those dark nights of solitude in order to breathe.

She had just drifted off on the night of the first snowfall when she heard a *tap-tap-tap* on her small zemlianka's door. She sat straight up, her eyes wide as she searched the darkness. Then, just as she was reaching for the knife she always kept beside her as she slept, she heard a soft voice from outside. "Yona? Yona, are you awake?"

In an instant, she went from frightened to confused. "Aleksander?" she asked.

"May I come in?"

Without answering, she rose from her reed bed and crawled across the tiny room to move the wooden beam securing the door. The other zemliankas had been designed with taller ceilings to make them feel more like aboveground homes, but Yona liked the feeling of being burrowed into the earth, safe from the world above. She needed only enough room for her bed, her small collection of belongings, and her stove for warmth.

As soon as she pulled the door open, the wind whipped through her small room, a burst of snowflakes entering in a gust. The fire in the corner stove flickered, sending shadows dancing across Aleksander's face. He was squatting by her door, his face red with cold. Instinctively, Yona searched the darkness behind him, but he was alone. "Quickly, come in," she said, and she moved aside so he could slide past her, then she pulled the door closed behind him, shutting the winter out.

This was the first time Aleksander had been here, had shared her space. He looked around for a few seconds, and she had to resist the urge to smile; the ceiling was only a meter and a half from the wooden floor, and his body was curved like a question mark to fit inside. "Would you like to sit?" she asked, and he nodded gratefully, settling in the only available place, on the edge of her reed bed. She hesitated before sitting beside him. "Is everything all right, Aleksander? Is anyone hurt?"

"No, no, everything's fine," he said hastily. He removed his cap and kneaded it between his hands. She realized suddenly that he looked nervous. "Your zemlianka. It's nice, Yona."

She laughed, but worry fluttered in her chest like an uncertain butterfly. "You came in the middle of the night to tell me that?"

When he turned to her, the firelight illuminating his features, his expression was serious, his face just inches from hers. "No. I—I came to thank you."

"To thank me?"

"For all of this. For everything you've done for us. For staying. I know you mentioned leaving once we were all right on our own. But now, I hope—I hope you won't go."

His words were punctuated by an eerie howl from outside, the wind rushing through a hollow of trees. The storm was picking up. She tried a smile. "I'm certainly not going anywhere in this weather, Aleksander."

He squeezed the cap in his hands a few more times and then looked at her again. He seemed to be searching her face, his gaze falling first on her eyes and then traveling to her mouth. "I didn't mean tonight. I meant . . . ever. I hope you will stay with us, Yona. What I mean to say is, I hope you will stay with *me*."

She didn't expect him to move forward then, to touch his lips to hers, but when he did, it felt just as she knew it was supposed to, though she had never been kissed before. She tensed for a second, surprised, and then she exhaled, her breath meeting his as she leaned in and closed her eyes.

His mouth was tentative at first, but when he felt her respond, Aleksander put a hand on the back of her head, pulling her gently to him, and as his tongue parted her lips, she could feel the vibration of the low groan that came from the center of his chest. She could feel him everywhere in her body, though it was only his lips and his hand touching her. Her skin tingled and warmth flooded through her. When he pulled away, instinctively she reached for him, already wanting him back.

She opened her eyes, breathless, and found him staring at her, searching her face. "Is this all right, Yona? I didn't know—"

She couldn't find words, so she pressed her lips to his, frantically, desperately, cutting him off. He hesitated only a second before drawing her to him, onto his lap, her legs spread over him. He groaned again, and she could feel it in her own chest as he put his hands under her hips and pulled her more firmly against him, kissing her more hungrily now. With his left hand still cradling her, he reached under her shirt with his right hand, and they both gasped as his cold fingers skimmed against one of her nipples, sending a shiver through her body.

"Still all right?" he murmured into her mouth.

"Mm-hmm." It was all she could manage, but instead of kissing her again, he paused and looked at her.

"Have you ever done this before?"

She was breathing hard, and she wondered if her pupils were as dilated as his were. She stared at him for a few seconds before whispering, "Aleksander, I never knew a man before you."

"We don't have to—"

"I know," she murmured, again cutting him off. "Don't stop."

He hesitated for only a second more before bringing his mouth to hers, moving both hands back to her hips. And then his hands were under her shirt, and he was pulling it off, then removing his own, so that in the cold chill of her tiny zemlianka, they both burned hot against each other, skin to skin.

There were no words left to say as he moved on top of her, slowly touching her everywhere, making her feel things she had never known before, guiding her hands across his body, so unfamiliar, and finally, pushing himself inside her. When she cried out, he paused, suspended above her, and whispered, "Should I stop?"

"No," she replied immediately, pulling him back and closing her eyes as she let the sensations wash over her.

When it was over, they lay on their backs in the cold, her head on his chest, his arm cradling her. She listened to his heartbeat and felt her own pulse race in the same rhythm. She closed her eyes and breathed him in, wondering what this all meant. She had read enough in the science texts Jerusza had given her to understand the biology of what had happened between them, but no one had warned her about the way her heart would feel like it could burst, how her body would feel both full and empty at the same time, how as soon as the silence set in, her mind would race to fill it with questions and fears.

But then Aleksander kissed the top of her head and murmured, "Yona, I think I love you," and the voices of doubt in her head finally went silent.

She buried her face in his chest. There would be time for wondering later. For now, all that mattered was this. "I think I love you, too, Aleksander." Did she? Was that what this feeling was? She smiled into his skin, astonished that the words were hers to say. "I love you, too."

CHAPTER TWELVE

No one in the camp seemed surprised to see Aleksander emerging from Yona's shelter the next morning, and Rosalia even put a hand on Yona's arm as they headed out to lay traps for animals. "I'm glad for you," the fiery-haired woman said, smiling slightly. "You deserve to find happiness. Both of you do."

"Is that what this is? Happiness?" In the light of day, Yona felt a strange blend of elation and fear. There was much to be lost by opening one's heart, and she had never understood that until last night, when the doors to hers had been flung wide. Now she felt naked, exposed, like she'd awoken in a den of sleeping bears without a weapon, without a plan. Yona felt foolish as she glanced at Rosalia. "Perhaps it meant nothing to him."

"Only a fool would break a heart in such close quarters. If Aleksander came to you, it is because he wants to be with you and hopes you feel the same."

Yona absorbed this in silence. "I think I do," she said at last.

"We've all lost so much. When we find happiness, especially where we didn't expect to, we must hold it close with all our might, don't you think?" There was a sadness to Rosalia's voice as she squeezed Yona's hands and added, "Please, don't worry."

But Yona *was* worried, and she couldn't stop herself. She was glad she had collected Queen Anne's lace and smartweed along with her other medicinal supplies, but she hadn't imagined she'd be the one needing them. She knew the herbs weren't foolproof, and that concerned her. A pregnancy in the midst of the dark wood could be deadly to both the mother and child, and with people hunting them, the innocent cry of a newborn could betray the whole group. Quite simply, Yona could not become pregnant, and she vowed that she would be more careful in the future—if there was a future for her and Aleksander.

After that first night, without a word of conversation about it, Aleksander moved into Yona's shelter, and every night, he slept with his arms wrapped tightly around her, as if even in sleep, he was terrified of letting her go. He continued to take a turn patrolling the grounds every third night, trading off with Leib and Rosalia, and when his side of the reed bed was empty, Yona felt a strange blend of freedom and loneliness. She still wasn't accustomed to sharing her life, even after a few months with the group, so having room to breathe was restorative. But she missed him when he was gone and often had trouble falling asleep, because when she closed her eyes, she imagined all the terrible fates that could befall him in the dark. It was the first time in her life she had cared for someone enough to worry about such a loss; she had always known that Jerusza would take care of herself. But now she understood that love left one vulnerable. It was a feeling she didn't like.

At the start of a frigid December, their bellies empty after a frustrating day of hunting, Aleksander whispered a reminder that

Hanukkah would begin the next evening. They were lying beside each other in the dark, and she was grateful that he couldn't see the unexpected tears that had sprung to her eyes. She knew well the story of the miracle of the ritual oil that the Maccabees had burned for eight days, but she had never known much of a celebration. Jerusza had always carved a menorah, and they'd dutifully lit candles, but they had done it quickly and quietly, and Jerusza had skipped the nights when she had other things to do. She thought for a moment of the longing she'd felt on a cold Friday night in 1931, watching from outside a window as a family celebrated the first night of the Festival of Lights. *The practice of dullards*, Jerusza had called it, but Yona had longed for the magic she saw reflected in the candlelit faces through the windowpane. Was it possible that she would finally learn one of the traditions she'd yearned for?

"My mother used to make latkes and *sufganiyot*. You know what those are? Doughnuts stuffed with jelly," Aleksander whispered in the darkness, oblivious to her tears. Yona could hear the smile in his voice, but also the sadness, the mourning for things lost. "We would light the menorah each night, and we'd sing 'Ma'oz Tzur.'"

Yona knew the song from the books she'd read, and from Jerusza reciting it aloud in an emotionless monotone. It had been the closest the old woman had ever come to acknowledging a celebration. "*Ma'oz Tzur Yeshu'ati, lekha na'eh leshabe'akh*," Yona murmured now.

Aleksander smiled and finished the verse for her in Hebrew, his deep voice coating the words in a haunting melody she'd never heard. "*My refuge, my rock of salvation! 'Tis pleasant to sing your praises*," he sang. "*Let our house of prayer be restored. And there we will offer you our thanks. When you will have slaughtered the barking foe. Then we will celebrate with song and psalm the altar's dedication.*"

Yona closed her eyes and rested her head against his chest. "That was beautiful." She could hear his heart thudding more quickly than usual. "You must miss your family very much."

He was silent for a moment, his breath heavy and warm, and Yona felt a tear slide from her right eye, onto the rough fabric of his shirt. If he noticed, he gave no indication. "They stole everything, Yona. Everything. How can that ever be forgiven? How can I carry anything but hate in my heart for the people who hate me, who hate my people enough to murder us all?"

The coldness in his voice made her shiver. "Maybe you can't," she said after a while. "Maybe you shouldn't. Maybe we can't rid ourselves of the things that torture us. Perhaps all we can do is move through them the best we can."

"I don't know how to stop it," he murmured. "This anger." He paused. "Sometimes I hate myself for surviving. And what do I do with that hate?"

The pain in his voice made her heart ache. There was nothing she could say to change the way he felt. Sometimes words could move mountains, and sometimes they could mean nothing at all. "There's a reason you're still here, I think, Aleksander," she said much later when she had finally found the words that felt right. "You have survived because God is using you to help save others."

But Aleksander was already asleep, his breath hitching as the shadows continued to eat away at his soul.

The next day, while snow drifted down and Aleksander went with Leib to check on some of the snare traps they'd set a half day's walk from the encampment, Yona came aboveground with her axe, chopped a large chunk of frozen deadwood, and brought it back into her small zemlianka. She hadn't whittled since she was a girl, desperate for company even if it came from imaginary creatures, but it came back to her in a flood. She could almost feel Jerusza's hands wrapped around hers as she pulled out her knife and began to slowly, expertly shave away strips of wood, slicing with the grain. Next she made smaller cuts, slicing the knife gently toward her own heart until the basic shape was hewn, and then she smoothed the wood and refined it for the next few hours until she was satisfied with the result. While she waited for Aleksander to return, she went to the group's larder, which was inside the largest zemlianka, and pulled out nine candles she had made that fall from nettle rope and gathered beeswax. Typically, the group saved the candles to usher in the Sabbath each Friday night, but there were enough to spare.

Back in her own zemlianka, Yona waited until Aleksander stepped through the door in a flurry of afternoon snow. She held up the object that had been a hunk of wood just hours before, and he stared at it, and then her, in disbelief. "You made a menorah?" he asked.

"I know it's not the most important of the Jewish holidays," she said. "But it means light in the darkness. The hope of a miracle. Deliverance from death. I thought that might mean something to everyone tonight."

Aleksander nodded slowly, and without removing his coat, he crossed to her, examining the fluid wooden lines, the spaces for eight candles all in a row, the elevated holder in the center for the *shamash*, the helper candle.

He looked up, his eyes round with awe. "Yona, it's perfect. I—I don't know how to thank you."

Fifteen minutes later, as the sun crept toward the horizon, the whole group gathered in the largest zemlianka, the one Moshe, Leon, Rosalia, Ruth, and the children shared. Yona was glad that they'd made the shelters larger than they needed, large enough to move around in; it made it possible to gather as a group, though there was little room to spare.

"Look what Yona has made," Aleksander said, holding up the menorah for all of them to see. There were a few gasps among the group, and nervously, Yona pulled the candles from her pocket and placed them into the holders. "Light in the darkness," Aleksander said, locking eyes with Yona. "The hope of a miracle."

Several among the group murmured words of astonished gratitude, and then the sounds faded to a hush as Leon, the oldest among them, stepped forward to light the shamash in the stove, then used the shamash to light the first candle. Moshe recited the menorah blessing, honoring God for his commandments and for the miracles for their forefathers, for granting them life and sustaining them. But somehow, even as Yona gazed around at the bowed heads, the somber expressions of the other adults, her loneliness lingered, and so, too, did the sadness. It was hard to imagine a miracle here, when they'd all lost so much, when their very survival seemed more like a fluke than a part of God's plan.

Two weeks into a frigid new year, the temperature rose by a few degrees, and what had been a blizzard of driving winds faded to a soft snowfall, the perfect weather to venture out in after nearly a month underground. Though the group still had a comfortable supply of dried chanterelles, smoked meats and fish, and berries, Yona was eager to check some of their animal snares and to show a few of the others how she fished in the winter, when the surfaces of the ponds were frozen solid. The snow was still falling enough to erase their tracks, but the day was temperate, which meant they'd be able to spend a few hours outside without freezing.

Rosalia agreed to patrol the camp's perimeter while Aleksander offered to take Leib with him to visit the traps spread around the forest. Luba and Sulia volunteered to melt some snow and use tallow soap to wash some of the group's clothing, while Moshe, Leon, and Oscher asked if they could come on Yona's ice-fishing expedition.

The going was slow as they set out from the camp, trudging carefully toward a frozen marsh nearby. Oscher's limp held them back, but Moshe lingered with him, offering his shoulder for support, while Leon walked a few paces ahead with Yona.

"We're fortunate to know you, Yona," Leon said after they had walked for a while in comfortable silence. He was a quiet man, a former teacher who spoke only when he had something important to say, who played his cards close to his chest. Yona respected that, respected the quiet, respected that he only used his voice when it mattered.

"I feel the same," Yona replied. "About all of you."

He tilted his head to study her. "This must be difficult for you. You are accustomed to being alone."

Yona nodded, and there was more quiet between them as the snow crunched beneath the soles of their boots. She was carrying a large willow basket on her back, one that she would use to catch the fish and transport them home, and it made her feel a bit as if she had wings. She looked back and slowed her pace slightly to allow Oscher, who looked like he was struggling, to keep up. She felt a surge of concern for him. Had it been a mistake to allow him to come? Had she put him in danger? Then again, surely it would have been worse to leave him behind feeling useless.

"It is the opposite for me," Leon said after a while, resuming their conversation. Around them, the snow continued to drift down gently through skeletal trees that had stood guard over the forest for hundreds of years. The world was silent, still, peaceful. "I am accustomed to being with people—with family, with friends, with shopkeepers, with the rabbi, with my neighbors. Here, I feel very isolated."

Yona tried to understand this. "Does it not help to share a shelter with Moshe, Rosalia, Ruth, and the children?"

Leon sighed. "It has been nice to have the children around. They don't know enough of the world to truly understand what is happening, which lets us pretend for a moment that we aren't running for our lives, living underground like rabbits. But Pessia often wakes up with nightmares, and I wonder at the demons that lurk in the dreams of someone so young. The others have been a comfort, certainly, but in a way, being together just amplifies our loneliness. They have become like my family, but they aren't really my family, are they? My real family is dead, all of them, and to feel others breathing around me at night is to be reminded of the breath that is no longer there, that will never be there." He sighed again and looked away. "I'm afraid that the longer we spend beneath ground together, the further away my old life feels. And I'm not ready yet to let that life go."

It was the most Yona had ever heard Leon say, and the stark words made her heart ache. "I don't think you have to let go of your old life to have a new one," she said after a while.

His smile was sad. "But of course we do. Are you the same person you were before you decided to join us? I don't think you are. We have to evolve, all of us, or we wither, but it also means that we spin further away from the past each day. And, Yona, I liked my past. I miss it terribly, the life I'd built, the people I loved."

"I'm sorry, Leon." The words were woefully inadequate.

"It isn't your fault, of course," Leon said, but what if he was wrong? What if her German blood made her culpable? It was something she had been thinking a lot about lately. If Jewish blood made one Jewish, what did her German blood make her? If the legacy of miracles was part of one's birthright, was the legacy of sins, too? "As I said," he added, unaware of the storm sweeping through her, "we are grateful for you."

They reached the marshy streambed in an hour, and it was, as Yona had said, frozen solid across the surface, tufts of dried grass punctuating the ice. She beckoned the others closer, and Oscher, breathing hard, gathered a pile of leaves and sat on them, wincing as he reached for his leg, rubbing it and muttering to himself.

"Are you all right?" Yona asked gently.

"Oh yes, fine, fine," Oscher said hastily, but his face was flushed, and his breathing still hadn't returned to normal. As Leon bent to put a hand on his shoulder, Moshe and Yona exchanged concerned looks. "Go on, Yona," Oscher added after a few seconds. "I'm all right, really I am."

Yona hesitated before nodding, pulling the willow baskets from her back, and bending to the ice. Soon Oscher would catch his breath, and then he'd be embarrassed by her concern. Better to focus on the fish. "The secret to catching mud loaches in the winter is simple," she began. "You see, there's little oxygen under the surface when it's frozen solid, and the fish are desperate for more. When we cut a hole in the ice, even a small one, they'll come right to us."

As the men watched, she used her axe to chisel out a hole in the slick surface five inches in diameter. They all bent to look, and Oscher, whose breathing was finally growing steadier, frowned. "But nothing is happening," he said.

"Wait," she said. She set one of the baskets upright and opened a small latch in the bottom, fitting it perfectly over the hole. Then she stood and beckoned to the men. "Now look."

The three men peered in, and she smiled as Moshe gasped. She knew exactly what they were seeing, even without looking herself, for she and Jerusza had fished countless times in the winter just like this. One by one, beckoned by the thrill of oxygen, the fat, snakelike fish were slithering from the hole, hoping for a taste of the air. But once they had left the water, the opening in the basket kept them from plunging back in, and so they flopped around the dried willow until they went still.

For the next hour, Yona collected the loaches as they stopped moving and shifted them to the larger basket as the smaller one continued to fill. When it was nearly overflowing, Yona finally moved the first basket away from the hole in the ice and watched as a final fish made a grab for the fresh air, landing on the ice and skidding away, flapping madly. She pushed the broken ice chunks back over the hole, once again enclosing the surface so no additional fish would lose their lives unnecessarily, and then she straightened to find the men staring at her. "What is it?" she asked, suddenly self-conscious.

"We will eat well for days, all of us," Moshe said quietly. "Yona, you're a miracle."

Yona averted her eyes, embarrassed. "It's not so difficult when you know the land. But we can't fish like this when it's colder; the fish won't come up. And we can't hike without a snowfall, because our tracks would be too obvious. Today was a lucky day."

The men murmured among themselves, and then Moshe offered to carry one of the baskets, and Leon the other. Yona nodded and handed the baskets over; then, as they began traipsing back toward the camp, tracing their own nearly vanished footprints, she fell back with Oscher and offered a shoulder to lean on. Though he refused at first, he was breathing hard after a few minutes, and when he stumbled and nearly fell, Yona placed a firm hand on his left forearm and didn't let go, bracing him as they moved through the snowy forest. "You two go ahead," she said to Moshe and Leon as they drew closer to the camp. Their earlier footprints were still barely visible, and she knew they could follow them home. "Oscher and I will be right behind you."

Leon and Moshe looked uncertain, but they hurried away, the baskets heavy on their backs.

"I'm sorry," Oscher said a few minutes after the other men had vanished into the forest ahead. "I'm holding you back, Yona. I shouldn't have come."

"No, I'm glad you did. And don't worry. There's no rush."

But the snow was falling harder now, the afternoon turning darker, the clouds gathering overhead, stealing the sun. Great gusts swept through the forest, and she could feel Oscher trembling beside her. Without the two men ahead of them to keep up with, his pace had slowed even further, and for the first time, Yona began to wonder what she would do if he couldn't go on. She was fairly certain she was strong enough to hoist him on her back, but would he let her? Certainly it would wound his pride. Jerusza hadn't wanted to be treated like an invalid, even at the end, and she suspected Oscher wouldn't want that, either. But she couldn't just leave him out in the cold, for in saving face, he would lose his life.

As he continued to slow, panting harder, Yona was still mentally running through her options—which must have been why it took so long to register the unfamiliar voice up ahead. Usually she was attuned to the forest, but in paying attention to Oscher, she had let her guard slip. Instantly she stopped, and with a hand across Oscher's chest, she halted him, too. She held a finger to her mouth, and then, in the stillness, she listened.

The voice was distant, too far away for Yona to discern the words, but it was male, and it was aggressive. Perhaps it was someone out hunting. Perhaps she and Oscher could just take a roundabout route back and avoid the stranger altogether.

But then her heart sank as she heard another voice: Moshe's, loud and worried. The stranger in the woods was barking at Moshe now, and every cell in Yona's body was suddenly on high alert.

"Wait here," Yona said. "Behind this tree." After a second, she pulled her knife from her ankle holster and handed it to Oscher.

"But you'll need this to protect yourself," he said, his face white with fear.

"I'll be fine." Of course giving her weapon away made her stomach roll, but Oscher was much more defenseless than she, and if someone came for him in her absence, the knife would give him a fighting chance. "I'll be back as soon as I can." Without another word, she raced toward the sound of Moshe's voice, her feet carrying her over the snow, her lungs bursting with panic.

She slowed her pace as the voices grew closer; if she could maintain the element of surprise, she had an advantage, even if the stranger up ahead was armed. She was close enough now to make out words, and she hesitated as the stranger's voice came again, speaking in Belorussian.

". . . no good reason to be out in the woods," the man was saying, his tone firm, his voice deep. "I will ask one more time what you are doing here. You are not hunting Jews, are you?"

Yona crept slowly forward until she could see Moshe and Leon, standing close together, cornered by a man with a square, stubble-covered jaw, broad shoulders, and a rifle. He had the gun pointed directly at the two men, but there was something about his expression, and in the careful way he said his words, that took Yona's panic down a notch. He had spoken his Belorussian slowly, as if it was not the language he was most comfortable with, and now she could see Moshe trying to do the same, trying to force out words in Belorussian when he'd spoken nothing but Yiddish for months now.

"No, we do not hunt Jews," he managed to say. "We are only fishing. See here? Here we have our fish." He gestured to the basket on his back, and the man stepped forward to look, lowering the gun slightly.

"Where did you get those?" The man was in what appeared to be a threadbare Russian military uniform, with military boots and a frayed overcoat, but the shirt and trousers looked too tight on him. Certainly his accent wasn't Russian.

"A stream about a kilometer from here." Moshe pointed away from the camp and away from the way he'd just come, obviously hoping to send the man in a direction that wouldn't result in him discovering Yona and Oscher or their hidden settlement in the woods.

The man's eyes narrowed. "There is no stream that way. Why do you lie to me?"

Something moved in the shadows behind the man, then, and in an instant, Yona's blood ran cold. It wasn't an animal; it was another person in the trees, another man. Why was he hiding? Who were these men? For a second she flashed back to the two Russian soldiers who'd been about to kill Leib for sport. But as she stared hard at the dark thatch of branches, her eyes adjusted, and she could just make out the form of a young woman with long, dark hair tied in a braid, crouching down and breathing hard.

Yona put her hand over her mouth as she understood what was happening. This wasn't a man who was there to hurt them. This was a man leading a group just like hers; she was almost certain. He didn't seem to understand that Moshe and Leon were in the same situation as he, and as he leveled his gun at them once more, Yona knew she couldn't wait a second longer.

"Wait!" she said in Yiddish as she stepped from the bushes. The man spun toward her, fear, then anger, then confusion flickering over his face in quick succession. "Please," she said in Yiddish. "We are like you."

She glanced at Moshe and Leon, who were staring at her in horror, and then back at the man, who hadn't said a word yet. As she walked close to the barrel of his gun, which was now trained directly at her, she wondered if she had made an enormous mistake. "You *are* Jewish, aren't you?"

The man looked uncertain, but she was close enough now that she could read his eyes. She could see that he understood her, which made her more certain that she was correct. A Belorussian villager wouldn't know much Yiddish, nor would a Russian partisan.

"Who are you?" the man asked, still speaking Belorussian, but his accent had slipped a bit more.

"Amkha." It was the first word Aleksander had said to her in the forest, the Hebrew word that meant she was part of the nation of people.

The man finally lowered his weapon and stared at her. "What are you doing out here? All of you?" He gestured to Moshe and Leon, but his eyes were still on Yona. He was speaking Yiddish now, which meant he believed her—and that she'd been right. She could feel the tension draining from her body like water through her fingers. "You are from one of the ghettos?"

It was too much to explain her own background, so she merely nodded. "Our group is. You are, too?"

"Yes." He hesitated and glanced behind him. From the shadows emerged the other man Yona had seen in the darkness, along with the woman with the long braid, who was younger than Yona had thought, perhaps only fifteen or sixteen. Behind them, Yona could see more movement, others hidden in the trees. "We have been walking for many days. We are hungry. Could you—would you share some of your fish with us? We won't be a burden after that."

"Of course." Yona's reply was instant. "How many of you are there?"

He took another step closer and studied her face. He was around thirty, with kind, gentle eyes, though his expression was still guarded. She could see him trying to decide whether he could trust her. He glanced once more at Moshe and Leon, and his face finally softened. "Eleven. Two are children. You?"

"Fifteen," Yona said. She had chosen to trust him, too. There was something about his eyes that was gentle but resolute. She could see it now, that he hadn't wanted to hurt Leon and Moshe, but that they had represented a threat to his people, and he would have done what he had to in order to protect them.

"How long have you been out here? Your group," the man asked.

"Months now." Again it was too difficult to explain to the man that her story was different, that she had always belonged to the woods.

The man blinked a few times. "You have survived all that time? Through the winter? But how? We left the Lida ghetto only two weeks ago. I thought I knew the forest well, but we—we are starving. I've never been out here in the winter, and I thought . . ." His voice cracked into helpless defeat.

Yona glanced at Moshe and Leon, and slowly, solemnly, Leon nodded. "Come," Yona said. "We will show you." Leon nodded at her once more, and she looked back at the man with the eyes that were kind, but frightened, too. She could see that now; she had mistaken fear for aggression.

He held her gaze for a moment longer before beckoning to the forest behind him. She watched as five more men, and one woman holding the hand of two little boys, emerged to join the man and young woman already standing there. Their expressions were exhausted, haunted, and their cheeks were hollow with hunger. Yona's heart ached, especially for the two children, who were only a little older than Ruth's girls. They looked frightened and weak, and Yona knew she had to help. She let her eyes move back to the first man, who was still staring at her, and then she turned to Moshe and Leon.

"Lead them back to our camp," she said. "I will go get Oscher." She looked back at the stranger and nodded. "There are enough fish for all of you to share. Leon and Moshe will show you the way. I'll be along soon."

And then she dashed back into the forest, her heart pounding as she wondered what she had just set in motion.

CHAPTER THIRTEEN

By the time Yona reached the camp with Oscher nearly an hour later, introductions had already been made, and it turned out that, by coincidence, the leader of the new arrivals had known Ruth and her parents a decade earlier, when Ruth's father had hired him to build a new roof on the family's house.

His name was Zusia Krakinovski, and he went by Zus, like the god of Greek legend. Most of the ten he'd brought with him were members of his family: his brother, Chaim; Chaim's wife, Sara; and three cousins, Israel, George, and Wenzel. The two boys, ages six and seven, belonged to Chaim and Sara, and there were also two men who were not related—Lazare and Bernard—and an orphaned fifteen-year-old girl named Ester who had begged to come along when she'd heard of their plan to escape.

They'd all come from villages near Lida, on the western edge of the forest. Unlike Aleksander and the group he'd arrived with in the spring, Zus and his companions knew the land, knew the woods. They'd all been farmers or laborers before the war, hunting and fishing in the forests for sustenance in the summer, growing their own crops of potatoes and beets for the winter.

"It is why I thought I could take care of them," Zus, his voice thick with worry, explained to Aleksander, gesturing to his group, who were all shoveling pieces of steaming fish into their mouths, sucking the bones dry. They'd been starving in the woods, something Yona understood more clearly now as the light from the fire in the stove illuminated gaunt faces, bloodied hands, collarbones so prominent they looked as if they belonged on birds rather than humans. They were all crammed into the largest zemlianka, the one where Moshe, Leon, Rosalia, Ruth, and the children slept, where the original group had spent the eight nights of Hanukkah not so long ago, and though there wasn't much room for anyone to move about, the collective body heat and the warmth of the fire seemed to be succeeding in thawing the newcomers. Ester, the girl with the long braid, had edged up next to Rosalia and was murmuring something with wide, sad eyes, and Chaim's two little boys, Jakub and Adam, were taking turns playing with Pessia's and Leah's reed dolls while Pessia and Leah watched with timid smiles.

"You did the right thing," Aleksander affirmed, reaching for another fish from the bowl Sulia had just set before them. He slid it into his mouth and sucked the flesh off the bones, tossing the slippery skeleton on the floor, where Sulia picked it up without a word.

"I'm not so certain." Zus sighed. "In the ghetto, at least, we had food."

"Not much, though, brother," Chaim said. He was slimmer and a few centimeters shorter than the broad-shouldered Zus. He was sitting with his back to his brother, rubbing Sara's shoulders with one hand as he grabbed a fish with the other, tossing it straight into his mouth. He paused to chew and pull the bones out. "And in the ghetto, they also had bullets for us."

"I don't forget that." Zus scratched his jaw and glanced at Yona for a few seconds before abruptly looking down. "But if I can't keep us alive in the forest, maybe we would have been better off."

"Penned like someone's livestock?" Chaim asked. "I would rather die out here, on our own terms."

"You will not die." Yona spoke before she could stop herself, and she was unsettled to feel Aleksander's eyes on her, as well as Chaim's and Zus's. She glanced at Aleksander, but his expression was unreadable. "You will not die," she repeated, looking back at Chaim and then at Zus, who was staring at her again in a way that made her stomach flutter. "We will not let you."

"Yona," Aleksander murmured, his tone a warning.

She glanced at him again, and she could see what he wanted to say, that they couldn't support eleven new, hungry mouths. But she couldn't send these people back out into the wild to perish during a harsh winter, either. Nature had given her a gift, and she couldn't turn her back on people who wanted only to live. "You will stay until the spring," she said, looking directly at Zus. "All of you."

Beside her, Aleksander murmured her name again, his tone sharper this time, but she didn't look at him. She had a say, too.

Zus looked from Yona to Aleksander and then back to Yona. "Thank you," he said, his voice deep and warm, but also uncertain. His eyes returned to Aleksander. "Thank you," he repeated, but this time, some of the warmth was gone.

Aleksander nodded at Zus, accepting the gratitude, but then he stood abruptly and left without a word, disappearing out the door of the zemlianka into the wind-whipped night. Yona watched him go, wondering if perhaps she could have handled things differently. He would understand later; he had to. She believed in speaking what was in her heart, but in a group, there were clearly roles they were all meant to be playing, roles that had been determined long before she got here, and she didn't entirely understand them yet. She had the sense she'd made a serious misstep.

"I'm sorry," Zus said a moment later, and by the time Yona turned back to him, Chaim had slipped into conversation with Sara and one of the cousins, and Yona felt suddenly as if she were alone with Zus, though they were elbow to elbow with two dozen other people.

"You don't need to apologize for anything," Yona said, looking away.

"I didn't mean to create a problem."

She turned back to him. His eyes were as green as oak leaves at the peak of the summer, and they were so full of sadness that looking into them for more than a few seconds made her own soul heavy with grief. Still, she held his gaze in silence. "Aleksander is just worried about everyone surviving, but we will. All of us will. I promise you that."

He studied her. He seemed to be trying to read her eyes, her thoughts, and she wondered what he was seeing. "Thank you, Yona."

She nodded, and as the light from the fire flickered across his face, sending shadows dancing across his eyes, she found she couldn't look away.

Aleksander wasn't in Yona's shelter when she returned an hour later after helping to sort the sleeping arrangements for the rest of the camp. There would be more time to talk about how to spread out tomorrow, but for now, the newcomers would take the second-largest zemlianka and the original group would take the largest. There was barely enough room in Yona's small shelter for Aleksander to share her space, so there was no mention of new occupants there.

It took Yona more than an hour to fall asleep, and before she did, she went out for a walk around the camp in the cold just to see if she could find Aleksander. He had not returned to the shelter, and she was worried. "He's in our group's zemlianka," said Leib, pausing in his patrol around the perimeter to press his gloved hands to his red, cold face. He blew steam into the air and looked at the sky, which was clouded and starless. There was a snowfall coming; Yona could taste it in the air. "Some were upset with the new arrangements."

Yona nodded and returned to her shelter, her stomach twisting. Why did it feel as if she had something to apologize for? The existing group was no more entitled to survival than the newcomers. Weren't they all obligated to help each other?

Once, Jerusza had told Yona of her travels south, down through Austria-Hungary, through Bosnia and Herzegovina, edging into Serbia, and finally the Ottoman Empire. She'd been a young woman then, and Yona had listened with fascination to this rare glimpse into Jerusza's life long before Yona had existed. Jerusza had been in the forests near Prizren, in the Šar Mountains, when the Albanians there had sworn a *besa* to preserve the integrity of their land, and that besa had come to mean, over the years, a word of honor, an obligation to help their fellow man in moments of need.

Yona had liked that, the idea that there was a term for that sense of integrity, of responsibility to all those who shared the earth. Over the last few months, she had found herself rolling the word around in her mouth, tasting it, reminding herself that though it was a concept that belonged to the Albanians, it was also a belief that should apply to all humankind. People should always help others in need; there was no other way for the human race to survive. And now, there was no choice but to extend that besa, that protection, to Zus and his group. Aleksander would have to understand.

In the morning, his side of the reed bed was still cold and empty, and as Yona emerged into a dim, foggy dawn, their footprints from the night before erased by a fresh blanket of pristine snow, she took a deep breath of damp, cold air and looked skyward for a second, wondering if it would snow again, whether they'd be able to return to the stream to fish some more. They needed the food. When she looked back down again, across the clearing, she locked eyes with Aleksander, who was standing in the woods, one of the rifles slung across his chest, watching her. She felt her heart skip, but she took another bracing breath and trudged across the snow toward him.

He leaned down to kiss her, but his lips landed on her cheek rather than her lips, and they felt cold against her skin.

"I thought Leib was on patrol," she said.

"I wasn't tired. I offered to take over."

"You could have come to bed."

He didn't say anything for a moment. His breaths were clouds, hanging between them before vanishing. "I needed time to think."

There was something about the way he said it, something about the way he averted his eyes, that made her uneasy. "Think about what?"

"Think about what? About our survival, Yona! About all the people I'm trying to protect. About the way you've put them all in danger!" His words burst from him, a series of tiny explosions.

She took a step back, snow crunching beneath her feet. "We can't let anything happen to any of them. You know that, Aleksander."

He made a noise in his throat, half grunt, half laugh. "You say it like you have control over it, Yona. Like you have some sort of deal with God. But you don't have that kind of power, and I'm not even sure God is listening. We're out here all alone in the middle of the woods, and it will be weeks, maybe months, before the snow thaws. We don't have enough food."

"We will gather more," she said softly.

"We don't have enough shelter!"

"Everyone fit last night. It might not be comfortable, but there *is* enough."

"And what about when the Germans come?" he shot back. "What then? With fifteen, we could hide, we could move. But with twenty-six? It will be twice as hard. You've exposed us to danger, Yona."

She watched her breath in the air for a moment, an unfamiliar ball of anger rolling slowly in her stomach. She had never felt that way toward Aleksander before, but now she wanted to grab him by the collar and shake him. "What would you have done without me?" she asked softly.

"What?"

"What would you have done without me? You are an intellectual, Aleksander. A bookkeeper. You said it yourself; you don't know these woods. Would you have known what foods could be stored for winter? How to hunt or fish when the animals became scarcer? How to hide? How to stay warm in the winter? How to build safe homes in the earth?" She hated to bring it up, but the fact was, he'd only survived because she had offered help, besa. Now it was his turn to do the same.

His eyes were hot coals as he stared at her. "Well, Yona, I suppose you've put me in my place, haven't you? I'm useless, yes? That's what you're saying? Good, I'm glad you've finally spoken the words aloud."

She took a step back. "Of course that's not what I meant. Not at all."

When he laughed, the sound was cruel. "No, Yona, your words were very clear. You're our savior, and I should just close my mouth and be grateful."

"That isn't what I—"

"Well, I suppose you should go back to your shelter." He'd said *your shelter*, not *our shelter*, and somehow this, more than everything else he'd said, felt like a blow. "It's cold out, and since we apparently can't survive without you, you should probably go rest up for all your future heroics."

"Aleksander—"

But he was already moving away, trudging back into the black expanse of the forest, defending the group from dangers that might be lurking in the darkness.

But what about the danger they couldn't see, the treacherous, icy water of their own decisions? Perhaps there was no protection against that.

"I'm sorry, Yona." Aleksander's words were soft, full of remorse, as he entered their shared zemlianka two hours later, his face red from the cold, snowflakes still clinging, frozen and resilient, to his lashes. Yona had already been to visit the other shelters, checking first on the newcomers, who were all grateful to have made it through another night, and then the original members of the camp, who were cramped but in decent spirits. Luba had a low fever and a cough, and Yona had returned to her own zemlianka, after a quick visit to the larder, with a handful of dried herbs to brew into a tea for her.

Yona didn't reply now, because what was there to say? When a person apologized, you were supposed to pardon them, she knew. But she couldn't do that here, because what Aleksander had wanted wasn't right. There was nothing acceptable about allowing innocent people to go to their deaths because their presence didn't suit your needs. That was what the people of Poland were helping the Nazis do to the Jews, wasn't it?

"I'm sorry," he said again. "I was only thinking of the people I brought out of the ghetto myself, because I feel responsible for them."

"I understand." She looked down. "But now the others need you, too."

"I know." He was breathing hard as he took a step closer. "You have a big heart, Yona."

But as he covered her mouth with his, as he pulled her to him, as he tugged off his overcoat and ran his frigid hands roughly up the front of her sweater, cupping her breasts with a low moan, she knew the words hadn't been a compliment, and the knot in her stomach twisted tighter, even as she closed her eyes and kissed him back.

It was barely noon when Yona emerged from the shelter, followed by Aleksander. The sun was filtering through the heavy clouds, and Sulia was across the clearing, staring at Yona, her jaw tight, as she sorted berries. Before Yona could stop herself, she trudged across the snow. Despite the months Yona had spent with the group, Sulia still hadn't warmed up to her. Perhaps it was time to try to change things.

"Can I help?" Yona asked, reaching for a handful of berries.

Sulia gave her a sideways look. "What, and dirty your hands with women's work?"

Yona blinked a few times as she picked out a couple of berries that had withered and begun to grow mold. It was important to periodically remove the bad ones before they destroyed the rest. "You don't like me," she observed, keeping her voice low and even. She had never known this kind of venom before, and she didn't understand it, though it reminded her a bit of the strange way Chana's mother had reacted to her after Yona had helped heal her husband.

Sulia's face turned pink as she ducked into her overcoat and busied herself with the berries, avoiding Yona's eyes. "I like you just fine."

"I—I don't think you do."

Sulia's jaw flexed and relaxed a few times, and then, as suddenly as a shot, her head snapped up. "It's just that you have no place here!" she exclaimed. "Who are you, anyhow? What kind of a person is raised in the woods with no human contact? It's unnatural."

Yona sat back on her heels. "I'm not—"

"I watch you sometimes with Aleksander, you know. The way you know how to talk to him, how to get him to do the things you want him to . . . I'm sorry, but you're not normal, Yona. You're up to something, and I won't let it happen. Someone has to protect him, protect the group, even if you have everyone else fooled."

Yona felt an unfamiliar tightness in her chest, a confusion. Her whole life had been straightforward, even her interactions with the perplexing Jerusza. Though the old woman had often gone about things in an infuriatingly roundabout way, she had never been anything but honest. Yona had always known where she stood, and why, even if she didn't always like or agree with it. But this feeling was alien to her, this sense that she had to defend herself against wild, unfounded accusations. "I don't—I don't know what you mean, Sulia."

"You're not one of us, Yona, and sooner or later, Aleksander will notice it, too. You act like a man, like you think you're better than me, than the other women. But you're not. And there's something else. I don't care who raised you. You're not like us. You call yourself a Jew, but ours is a religion that passes by blood or tradition—and you have no claim to either."

"Sulia, I—"

But Sulia was already standing, brushing the snow off her hands. She turned her back and trudged toward her zemlianka without another word.

Yona stood, her fingertips blooming red with berry stain as she closed her hands into fists. Did everyone in the camp feel the same way? She'd done nothing but try to offer her knowledge, her skills for survival.

She was still standing there, staring after Sulia, when Zus approached, trudging in from the woods to the east. "There you are," he said, his voice deep, warm. His stride was confident and long, and the way he carried himself reminded her of a mountain lion, proud and strong and sure. "I've been looking for you."

She turned, still a bit dazed, and tried to smile. "Zus."

He searched her eyes as he came up beside her. "Are you all right?"

She nodded, already feeling foolish. She had nothing to regret, nothing to be ashamed of. "Yes, yes, of course." She coughed and bent to grab the basket of berries Sulia had huffed off without. They'd need to be returned to the larder. She began walking in that direction, and Zus fell into step beside her.

"What is it?" Zus asked after a minute had passed. "You're not yourself."

Yona might have smiled if she hadn't been so upset. How did he already see her so clearly? "It's nothing." But when she glanced at him, she could see that he didn't believe her. "It's Sulia," she amended after a pause. "She said something about me not belonging. I—I don't understand why she seems to dislike me so much."

"She's jealous of you." Zus's reply was so immediate and matter-of-fact that it made her stumble. He caught her elbow with a smile, righting her.

"Jealous? What could she possibly be jealous of?"

He looked down at her, amused, and they both seemed to notice at the same time that his fingertips were still on her arm.

He hastily pulled away. "Well, your relationship with Aleksander, if I had to guess."

Now Yona stopped in her tracks. "What?"

Zus looked as confused as she felt. "Do you honestly not see it? The way she acts around him?"

Yona blinked a few times. "She *is* friendly, I suppose."

Zus laughed. "Well, that's one word for it." He glanced at her and sobered as she continued to look at him blankly.

As they walked in silence for a moment, Yona's mind spun. Falling together with Aleksander had simply happened. How could anyone begrudge her something that felt so natural? After all, if Sulia and Aleksander had had similar feelings for each other, wouldn't they have been drawn together in the same way before they met Yona? None of it made any sense, and Yona's frustration mounted; how was it that she was so easily able to survive but so confused when it came to what should have felt like a basic social interaction? She shook her head and sighed. "You said you were looking for me?"

"Oh, yes." He hesitated. "It's actually about Aleksander. He's the one in charge of the group, yes?"

Yona nodded. He was certainly the de facto leader, the one who made the decisions, though Sulia's accusations about Yona controlling him still rang in her ears. "He is. He led them out of the ghetto. They trust him."

"Good. That's good. I was thinking that perhaps I should meet with him, man to man, to discuss what we shall do for the remainder of the winter. I know we're a burden on all of you."

"You're not a burden."

His smile was weary. "Of course we are." He hesitated. "Can I ask you something?"

Yona nodded.

"You didn't come out of the ghetto with them, did you?"

She shook her head, but suddenly she felt exhausted. Was Zus, too, here to point out that she didn't belong? "Is it that obvious? I—I thought that they had become like my family. But now I think perhaps I was only seeing what I wanted to see."

He reached for the basket of berries, wordlessly offering to carry it for her as they trudged through the snow toward the larder. "All of us are family," he said after a few minutes. "I don't think the details matter."

She hesitated. "I was raised by a Jewish woman, but I wasn't born to Jewish parents," she blurted out. "So maybe you're wrong about me being family. Maybe I don't belong after all. Maybe I'm just fooling myself."

He accepted this in silence for a moment. When they reached the larder, she pulled the door open, and he held it for her as she ducked inside. He followed, and when her eyes adjusted to the darkness, she realized he was staring at her. "You *are* our family," he said when he caught her eye. "What matters is what's in your heart, I think, and that's so much more complex and personal than simply how you worship God. There's a farmer I know, Christian as they come, wears a big cross around his neck, has a brother who's a priest. And when the Germans came, he sheltered twenty Jews in his barn, and another five in his basement, without thinking twice. He helped because help was needed, and he couldn't turn his back on his fellow man. *He* was family."

"Besa," Yona murmured. "What a good man."

"And a dead man, I'm afraid. The Germans found the Jews. Killed them all, and then murdered him without a thought."

Yona could see his eyes shining in the darkness now. "That's terrible, Zus. I'm so sorry."

"I am, too." He hesitated. "Every time a good soul dies, I think the world gets a little darker."

Yona thought of Chana, of her innocent eyes, of the bullet hole in her head, of the rough laughter she'd heard through the trees. "Then it is very dark now indeed."

Zus nodded. "Yes. But there is light, too. In the times of greatest darkness, the light always shines through, because there are people who stand up to do brave, decent things. What I am trying to say, Yona, is that in moments like this, it doesn't matter what you were born to be. It matters what you choose to become."

Yona held his gaze for a long time. She didn't know what to say. Had she chosen anything at all, in fact, or had her life been dictated by the choices of other people? Was everything she was a product of Jerusza's decision to steal her on a warm Berlin night more than two decades earlier?

Still, though, Zus's steady gaze, his confident assurance, brought her unexpected comfort, and she nodded, the lump in her throat suddenly making it too difficult to talk.

CHAPTER FOURTEEN

As the winter wore on, the new group fell slowly into the old group's rhythm, and by the time the first buds of spring had begun to appear, they were an inseparable family. The time spent in close quarters had been undeniably difficult—the two large zemliankas were crowded, airless, packed too tightly with people. But the additional mouths to feed were outweighed by the hunting instincts of the new group— Zus and Chaim, in particular, had a sixth sense about finding and trapping animals that even Yona hadn't been able to procure, and in the dead of winter, thrice the group had feasts of stringy, hearty red deer meat, followed by two days of watery venison stew. It was enough to see them all through the winter alive.

The arrival of the newcomers had changed the spirit of Pessia and Leah, too, and seeing the little girls merrier, giggling at the things said by Chaim's boys, was like a tonic for the others. When the children's hearts were lighter, the nights were lit by laughter and contented sighs rather than quiet sobs and muted nightmares.

Even Sulia seemed to thaw with the changing weather, and though she never apologized to Yona for the things she'd said in the clearing, she glared at her less, though it was clear she went out of her way to avoid her. Sometimes, if Aleksander stopped to help Sulia with something, or if he led her into the woods to show her some rudimentary hunting skills, Yona noticed the other woman smiling triumphantly at her. But she always seemed to catch herself, pasting on a syrupy smile instead. It would never be a friendship, but the tension felt as if it had abated. Yona still didn't understand any of it, but she was glad.

The whole group was happier as they began to reemerge from underground, and though Yona knew the arrival of spring also meant that the danger of discovery increased, as there would be more enemy patrols in the forest, she was glad to be swept up in the joy of having survived to see yet another year. Nineteen forty-three was like a gift, and it wasn't until the trees had begun to sprout leaves once again that everyone seemed to believe that they had done the impossible: they had survived the winter without losing a single soul.

But at night, while the group sat around a campfire surrounded by the last icy patches of clinging snow, quietly singing Yiddish folk songs and passing around cigarettes rolled from dried sunflower roots, Yona, who often sat alone while Aleksander patrolled the forest, felt a sense of foreboding nibbling at the sweet edges of joy. Something was coming, something dark, and she couldn't put her finger on it. At night, while Aleksander snored beside her, his arm heavy across her, his head turned away, she closed her eyes and saw demons in the blackness.

A week after the last of the snow had melted, Yona woke up from a nightmare just before dawn and shook Aleksander awake, her heart still thudding with fear and certainty. "We must move," she said when he opened his eyes and slowly focused on her, coming back from whatever dream world he'd inhabited without her.

He blinked a few times. "We move in a week. You know this. We are still gathering supplies."

"No, we must go sooner." She couldn't explain it, couldn't describe the sixth sense that sometimes told her things. Even after all this time, she could still hear Jerusza's voice whispering to her, sometimes laughing at her, in the wind.

"How will I explain it to the others?" Aleksander asked, and Yona could see in his eyes that he didn't believe her.

"Tell them you're worried. That the Germans could be on their way now that the terrain allows it again."

"But is that true? It's still quite cold."

"You think that will stop them?" She closed her eyes for a minute, and all she could see were uniformed men spilling from the trees, gunfire exploding like tiny bursts of flame from machine guns designed to erase them all from the earth in the space of a few heartbeats. "It won't, Aleksander."

"But there are only twenty-six of us. Not worth the time it would take for them to come this deep into the forest."

"It doesn't matter. You know that. And now that the snow has melted, their dogs will be able to track us again. We're in danger and we must go. Please, you must believe me."

He stared at her for a long time, his mouth a thin line. "Not today, Yona. Tomorrow. We need time to get ready, and time to mentally prepare. We've been here all winter. Do you have any idea what it feels like to have a sense of home again? No, you wouldn't, because you've never really had one, have you?"

The words stung. "This feels like my home, too, Aleksander. That means something to me."

"Well then, you can understand why I can't just ask the group to abandon this place."

"You aren't asking that," she said quietly, so quietly that he didn't seem to hear her as he sat up and pulled a sweater on over his head. "You are asking them to trust you. To trust me. To *survive*."

His only response was to get out of bed, pull his coat on, and disappear without a word through the small door of their zem-lianka. As she sat in silence after he was gone, she looked around for a moment, taking in the gently sloping floors, the wooden walls, the shelter that had helped keep them safe and alive, living on borrowed time. She would miss it. But she could deal with an aching heart.

She spent a half hour packing her belongings; then, emerging from the shelter, she scanned the clearing. Several people were already up, enjoying the first temperate morning they'd had in months. The four older children were chasing each other around, laughing, while Daniel watched from Ruth's lap, clapping merrily. Yona was surprised to feel tears in her eyes as she paused for a few seconds to watch them.

Zus approached from across the clearing, where he'd been working with Chaim to clean the group's small collection of guns.

"Aleksander says we must leave sooner than planned?" he said, his arm brushing against hers as he turned to stand beside her, watching the children play.

"Yes." She could feel the tension in her neck, still there from the words she'd exchanged an hour earlier with Aleksander. "I know it's not convenient. But it's to keep the group safe. I'm sorry."

"You're sorry?" Zus waited until she looked up at him. His eyes were full of astonishment. "Yona, don't be sorry. You're doing what you can to keep us safe. We should all be kissing the ground you walk on."

She bit her lip and looked away. "You believe me?"

"Of course I do. It's clear by now that your instincts have helped save us. Why on earth would we ignore them now?"

She shook her head. "I don't know." Aleksander's words about her never knowing a real home still burned a hole in her chest. "Aleksander said that I can't understand how the rest of you feel because my past is so different. I think perhaps he's right."

"Yona." Zus's voice was deep, and she was surprised when he touched her arm, his fingertips lingering. She could feel goose bumps prickle where his skin met hers. "He's not. He's not right."

When she looked up at him, she was startled anew by the green of his eyes, which seemed to change with the weather, with his mood. Today, his eyes were bright, alive. "Perhaps you don't really know."

"Or perhaps you're listening to the wrong person," he said softly. "Don't forget to listen to yourself, Yona. No one knows what's in your heart but you." He walked away before she could say anything else.

Yona barely slept that night, worried about the day ahead and bothered by both Aleksander's and Zus's words. The group was on the move just after dawn the next morning. The traces of them in the forest—their zemliankas and the ground they had lived on, and under, for months—were too significant to erase, so Yona could only pray that the group was long gone by the time a German search dog found their camp.

She led them in a circuitous route, around thick underbrush, over patches of ice, even through a half-frozen swamp, which soaked their boots and made their teeth chatter. They would need to warm their feet and dry their clothing by the fire wherever they settled that night, but it was worth the risk, for neither man nor beast could follow their trail through this. She took them in directions that made no sense, trying to think of the choices trackers would make and leading them the opposite way. Finally, just before the light slipped from the early spring sky, she led the group into a small clearing surrounded by soaring pines, which would make a good camp for the night.

They were all exhausted; they'd been lulled into a false sense of security by their long winter slumber, and none were accustomed to moving the way they had that day. Their pace had been slow, largely because of Oscher and the children, but Yona knew that they had to keep moving, that they couldn't afford to do any less. The nightmares were always there now when she closed her eyes, shadowy soldiers lurking at the edges of her conscious thought. Danger was still too near.

They moved every two days, hunting and gathering on the days they remained in place, mending clothes, treating harsh blisters earned from all the walking, warming their frozen feet and hands by the fire at night, when it was too dark for the smoke to give them away. They were tired in a way they hadn't been during the long winter, but they were much more well nourished, now that the earth had returned to giving up her gifts. Day by day, the forest floor grew more abundant with bulbous porcini mushrooms, the bushes with bilberries, the streams with spawning fish. Animals emerged, shaking off the winter, and walked into the rudimentary neck snares that Zus's three cousins—Israel, George, and Wenzel—had learned to set, and most nights, the whole group had plenty to eat.

In April, they celebrated Passover with matzoh made from flour taken from a village, and though Ruth and Luba burned the unleavened bread in the makeshift mud-brick oven Yona had helped them make, it was a comfort to all of them to return to a familiar tradition. Leah, Pessia, and Chaim's two sons asked the "Mah Nishtanah," the four questions about the Passover celebration, and Leon and Oscher took turns telling the story of the Jews' exodus from Egypt. It was a night of peace that made Yona feel like a part of a family, and that made them all feel like survival might just be possible after all.

But late May brought a lice infestation in their camp, which made Yona's blood run cold. The tiny bugs were a nuisance—they made everyone's skin itchy and dry—but much more important, they were a danger. They often carried typhus, and if one among the group contracted the disease, they would all be exposed. Some would die. Yona knew they had to do something—and quickly.

"We need mercury," she said softly one morning, pulling Aleksander and Zus aside as the rest of the group gathered around a small fire. It was dangerous to create smoke in daylight, but they needed to burn the lice, so they had no choice. They picked the tiny bugs from each other's bodies, each other's hair, even their eyebrows and lashes, and flicked them into the flames. Yona could see Ruth crying as she picked at Daniel's curls.

"Mercury?" Zus asked, holding her gaze.

"You mean from a pharmacy?" Aleksander asked. "But that will be dangerous, Yona."

Yona took a deep breath. "I know. But I think it's the only way."

The three of them looked at each other for a moment. One of them would need to venture into civilization, to steal something in a dangerous mission, and disappear back into the woods without a trace. But they had tried all the other things Yona knew how to do: holding their belongings over the flames, washing their clothes in boiling water, even wiping their bodies with their own urine in hopes that the acid would kill the lice. But the lice were stubborn, cheerfully embedding themselves in pores to wait out the various assaults, jumping from host to host and multiplying.

"What will mercury do?" Aleksander asked.

"The woman who raised me taught me a trick long ago that she'd learned from some Russian soldiers she helped feed for a month during the Great War," Yona replied. Jerusza had, in fact, made Yona repeat the information back several times, warning her that she would need it someday, because lice were ruthless, dangerous invaders. "Mercury mixed with an egg, soaked in fabric and worn across the body. It's the only thing that drives them away for good."

Aleksander scratched his head. "That just sounds like the babbling of an old woman."

Zus shot him a look. "It sounds more promising than anything we're doing now. I'll go. I know a town with a pharmacy."

Yona gave him a grateful smile. "Then I will go with you." Her reply was immediate, and Zus looked startled, but he didn't refuse.

"No, you should stay here, Yona," Aleksander said. "I'll go with Zus."

She turned to him. "Zus knows the villages, Aleksander, and I know the forest. It makes the most sense. You can stay and protect the others."

Aleksander searched her eyes for a moment. "No, Yona. It's too dangerous. If something happens to you . . ." He hesitated and shook his head. "No. I can't let you do that."

She wasn't sure whether he was objecting because he loved her or because he was acknowledging her importance to the group. Maybe he was only trying to establish that he was the one who wrote the rules. Regardless, he was wrong. Getting swiftly to and from a village under cover of darkness and disappearing into the forest in daylight would be dangerous and would require someone who knew intimately how to vanish in the trees. She opened her mouth to explain, but Zus spoke first.

"Yona, I think Aleksander is right," he said, turning his warm gaze on her. "You *would* be the best person to go, but that's why you must stay, in case something happens. The group needs you. I will take Chaim. We both know the land. I even know the pharmacy we'll visit, unless it is no longer there. There's a chemist in Lubcha who hired my father to repair his windows many years ago after a break-in. My father did good work, like he always did, and afterward, the man refused to pay. Called him a dirty Jew, accused him of shoddy work, then said he hadn't actually done the work at all." Zus smiled slightly, but there was sadness at the edges of his mouth, anger in his eyes. "It will be nice to pay him a visit for old times' sake. I think Chaim will feel the same."

He looked at Aleksander, and Aleksander nodded. "It's decided, then. How soon can you go?"

"We can leave within the hour. We should be at the forest's edge by midnight. Can you make camp here for a couple of days so we can find our way back to you?" Zus looked at Yona.

She thought about it for a few seconds, her mind still spinning uneasily through all the fates that could befall Zus and Chaim in the forest, especially if they were discovered. But they had managed to lead nine others, including children, out of the ghetto and into the woods undetected. They would survive, as long as nothing went wrong. "Yes," she said. "We will stay here unless something forces us to move. I think we are safe for a few days."

Zus nodded. "I'll go tell Chaim."

She watched him go and then turned to Aleksander. "I really should go with them. It will increase their chances of getting back alive."

"You are better off here." There was something cold in his tone, something that caught her off guard and made her look up sharply to meet his gaze. He looked away. "It's decided. They know the forest. They will be fine."

As he, too, strode away, she rubbed the back of her neck, trying to untie the tension knotting her muscles, the lingering feeling that something terrible was coming. As Zus emerged from one of the shelters across the clearing, Chaim following close behind him, his eyes found Yona's, and for a few seconds, she sensed he shared her foreboding.

Zus and Chaim left within an hour, both armed with the rifles Yona had taken from the dead Russians the summer before. Before they went, Zus paused in front of Yona and murmured,

"We'll return with the mercury. I promise." His words were soft, and she could feel them against her cheek.

"Just be safe. Please."

He nodded, and then the brothers were gone, the forest swallowing them whole.

The next night, Aleksander was out on patrol, and Yona went to sleep alone in the hut they'd built the day before. As they had the previous summer and fall, the group slept in smaller clusters again, now that they had emerged from hibernation, two or three to a hut, some of them—such as Rosalia and Zus—choosing to build their own one-person lean-tos and sleep alone.

Yona still couldn't shake the feeling that something bad was coming, but she was good at sleeping for a few hours at a time even when her mind raced, for sleep protected against illness and was essential to survival. Though she was worried about Zus and Chaim, she drifted off just as the moon reached its zenith in the sky; there was no rain in the air, so she and Aleksander had opened their makeshift roof to watch the stars, which brought her peace.

She awoke with a start a few hours later. She had dreamed of a great cloud of ravens, so numerous that the moon and stars disappeared under a canopy of black. As they all croaked at once, their voices reverberating, she sat bolt upright, her heart thudding. Dreaming of ravens meant imminent death. She was out of bed and running into the clearing before she could stop herself.

"Aleksander!" she hissed into the darkness. It took a few seconds for her eyes to adjust, and when they did, she could see the outlines of the group's huts, lit by a nearly full moon. She heard people sighing in their sleep, someone shifting on a reed bed. Otherwise, the night was silent, ominous. She could still hear the echoing call of the ravens in her head.

She stood motionless and listened until she could hear footsteps, just a single pair around the perimeter, moving in a steady circle. It was Aleksander on patrol; she needed to find him quickly and tell him that something was wrong. Her heart continued to hammer in her chest as she set out in the direction of his footfall. "Aleksander!" she whispered again.

But when she reached the perimeter and saw a man's shadow coming toward her, she stopped, startled. It wasn't Aleksander.

"Leib?" she asked in confusion as he quickened his pace to approach.

"Yona? What is it?" His voice was laced with fear. "Has something happened?"

She shook her head as he stopped beside her. "Where is Aleksander, Leib?"

When Leib's eyes settled on her, they were dark, shuttered. "He's not here."

"But he was on patrol tonight. If he's not here, where is he?" She blinked and saw the ravens again, calling out their warning in her mind's eye. She scanned the forest, but nothing moved in the darkness. "Leib?"

"He's . . ." But he didn't finish his sentence. Instead, he shifted uncomfortably and stared down at her. When she looked up and met his eyes, the depth of the pity there knocked the breath out of her, and all at once she knew. He wasn't in danger. That wasn't what her dream had been foretelling at all.

"He wouldn't," she whispered.

"Yona—" he began.

But she was already moving back toward the camp, and she knew exactly what she would find even before she reached the shelter that Sulia and Luba shared, the one with the web of woven marsh grass draped across the front for privacy. Slowly, her heart slamming against her rib cage, she pulled back the curtain of green and peered in.

On one side of the sloping lean-to, Luba lay on her side, snoring softly. On the other side lay Sulia. And on top of her, his back bare, moving in a rhythm that Yona recognized with a sick, immediate certainty, was Aleksander.

"Oh!" Despite herself, Yona let out an audible gasp, which was enough to make Aleksander turn awkwardly, rolling away from Sulia.

"Yona!" he choked as he scrambled upright and hastily tugged his trousers back over his hips.

It all seemed to be happening in slow motion. Sulia was protesting, reaching for Aleksander, even as he distanced himself from her, his face white in the shadows. Sulia grabbed for her dress, her face a mask of fury as she tugged it over her head and said Aleksander's name. But he was already moving away from her, moving toward Yona, as he stammered an explanation. In the corner, Luba continued to snore heavily, oblivious.

Yona didn't wait to hear what Aleksander had to say. Instead, she took a few steps backward, into the clearing, and then she turned and ran, stumbling into her hut, the one she had shared just the night before with a man she had believed loved her.

But it had all meant nothing, and now, as she lit a piece of pine bark with shaking hands and hastily gathered her things, tears coursed down her face like rivers. She ignored Aleksander as he entered behind her.

"Let me explain, Yona!" he said, reaching for her, but she twisted away.

"What could you possibly say?" She didn't look at him. She was shaking, and she didn't trust herself not to fall apart. She had never felt this way before, and she had no idea what to do.

"You don't know, because you don't come from society like we do," he began.

"Enough of that! Enough of trying to make me feel like an outsider! I *know* I'm an outsider, Aleksander! I just didn't think it mattered to you!"

"That's not what I meant, Yona!" He touched her arm again, and again she pulled away. "Just that you're different than we are."

She snorted. "I'm different, so I couldn't possibly understand what it feels like to be betrayed?"

"That's not what I'm saying! What I mean is that it's not like what you've probably read in your books, Yona. It's a whole different world out here. I was just trying to find some happiness for a little while, to forget the misery . . ."

"And you couldn't do that with me?"

He opened and closed his mouth a few times before looking away. "You don't look at me anymore the way Sulia does. She needs me to save her."

"So you don't want me because I'm not helpless?"

He looked back at her, his jaw set. "It's just . . ." He raked his hands through his hair. "It's more difficult with you. And with Sulia, it is easy. Isn't life hard enough?"

Her heart suddenly felt hollow. "I make your life more difficult?"

"That's not what I mean, Yona. Please, just stop packing your things and listen to me for a moment. You don't understand."

Indeed, Yona had little experience with the way people were supposed to interact with each other. But she knew enough to know that when a man loved a woman, he didn't do this. Not a good man, anyhow. And she knew, just as surely as she knew her own soul, that she couldn't stay here for another second. She may have helped the group to find their way, to survive the winter, but they knew the things she knew now. And they were Aleksander's group, not hers, as he and Sulia had just made abundantly clear. Yona had ignored Jerusza's warnings, had opened her heart incautiously, had made an enormous, unthinkable mistake by believing she was actually a member of this family. Even now, she could hear Jerusza's laughter, soft and cruel in her memory.

It was time to go.

It took her only five minutes more to put everything she owned into her knapsack. She turned to Aleksander, who was still behind her, still talking, saying things that didn't matter. She put a finger to her lips, and finally, he stopped, his eyes shining with desperation in the darkness. "Yona?" he asked, his voice high, pleading. "It is the woods. The rules are not the same. We are all just trying to survive."

"I shouldn't have stayed so long," she said softly, and when his eyes widened and he began to protest, she held up her hand and waited until he went silent again. "It was my mistake. When Zus and Chaim return with the mercury, gather several eggs from nests nearby. Use just the whites. Mix them with the mercury, and dip strips of fabric into the solution for everyone to wear across their chests for a day, then across their backs for a day. It should rid you of the lice. You know how to hunt now, how to trap, how to fish, how to stay on the move. Zus and Chaim are with you now, and they know the woods better than you do, so don't let your pride get in the way, or you'll die out here. Listen to them. And never let your guard down, for the Germans will find you. May God watch over you all."

She turned to go, and when he grabbed her wrist to stop her, her pain bubbled to the surface as a white-hot streak of anger. Twisting away, she dug her nails into his forearm, squeezing until he yelped in pain and let go. "You will *never* touch me again," she said.

"But the woods—"

"Are where we learn who we really are." And then, extinguishing her pine light in a puff of breath, she hoisted her pack onto her back and slipped into the dark night.

Across the clearing, Sulia stood outside her shelter, her dress askew, a small smile on her face, as if she believed she'd finally triumphed by driving Yona out. But it hadn't been Sulia to make her go. Yona should have been gone months ago, but she had foolishly opened her heart to the wrong person, which made her ignore all the things she knew to be true. Now she was wiser. Now she would return to the world she knew, the world in which she flew alone, a dove in the wilderness, untethered. Her wrist throbbed with purpose as she turned and strode toward the trees.

Later, when her anger had faded and the heartbreak crept in, the thing that would hurt most was the fact that when she left, Aleksander didn't follow, nor did he try to stop her. She didn't turn to look back, but she imagined him standing beside Sulia as they watched her go, the woman who had helped them to survive already no more than a footnote in their story.

CHAPTER FIFTEEN

Yona had walked for only thirty minutes—tears streaming down her face, no sense of direction in the thick forest, where the moonlight was nearly lost—when she heard footsteps approaching. Her grief was pushed immediately aside by fear, and she slid quickly behind a tree, holding her breath. She could tell by the footfalls that there were only two people trudging through the darkness, both men, judging from the sound, and her mind spun. If they were Germans, there might well be others not far behind. She had a chance to stop these two, for she had the element of surprise, but what about a whole German unit? Would it be too late to protect the group?

But as the men drew closer, she heard their voices, and she recognized them immediately with a great swell of relief. It was Chaim and Zus, returning from their mission. She closed her eyes and put her hand on the tree to brace herself, weak with gratitude that they were safe. For a few seconds, she considered letting them pass. After all, she was embarrassed by the pain she knew was written across her face. But she needed to know whether they'd been successful, because if they had the mercury, she would sleep better knowing that the group would be able to eliminate the imminent threat of typhus. If not, she would have to go back, wouldn't she?

Taking a deep breath, she stepped from behind the tree when they were just a few feet away, and she was encouraged to see that their reaction was instant; their guns were on her immediately, even though their guard had been down just seconds before. With instincts like that, they'd have a fighting chance.

"It's only me," she said softly, and they both blinked at her, alarm still firing in their eyes as they lowered their guns.

"Yona?" Zus asked, stepping forward. He reached out as if to touch her face and then seemed to think better of it, pulling his hand quickly back. "What is it? What's wrong? Has something happened?"

She shook her head. "The group is fine. I just— I couldn't stay any longer."

In the silence between them, the words seemed to unfold without a sound, and after a pause, Zus blinked in understanding. "Aleksander. What did he do?" When she didn't answer, his jaw clenched. "He was with Sulia?"

"You *knew*?" Another wave of despair threatened to wash over her.

"No, Yona, I didn't. It was just—it was a guess. I'm sorry."

Yona was embarrassed to feel tears in her eyes again. "Yes, well, he said I didn't understand because I am not like him. That things were easy with her." She delivered the words in a monotone, embarrassed by how deeply they had wounded her.

"Those are not the words of a man with a backbone," Zus said instantly, and Yona could hear the fury in his voice. "And they speak entirely of his character, not yours."

She looked at the ground. "Is it supposed to hurt this much?"

"Yes, I'm afraid it is." Zus frowned and then turned to Chaim and nodded. An understanding passed between the brothers and Chaim stepped several meters away, out of earshot. Zus turned back to Yona. "I didn't know, Yona. I wouldn't have kept a secret like that. I don't believe in betraying the people who care for us."

"I know." And she did. She understood, even with her limited exposure to people, that Zus was a different kind of man than Aleksander was, with a different kind of heart. She had felt it from the moment she first met him, and it had confused her then the way it confused her now. Aleksander had seemed like everything she needed: safety, security, a place to belong. In the end, he had been none of those things, and she wondered just how blind she had been. Certainly, she had been a terrible judge of character—and terrible at discerning what lay in her own heart. She wiped her tears away. Inside her chest, sadness was fighting a prolonged battle with fury. "Did you get the mercury?" she asked.

He nodded, opening his coat to show her a large knapsack of vials. Relief flooded through her, making her knees weak. Zus reached out to brace her, and their eyes met.

"Thank God," she murmured without looking away. "Thank you, Zus, for doing this. I know it was dangerous."

He seemed to hardly hear her. "Where are you going, Yona?"

"Away."

They held each other's gaze, and for the first time, Yona had the sense that he could read her like a diary, that perhaps he'd always been able to. The thought should have unsettled her, but instead, it filled her with a strange peace, an unfamiliar sense of being entirely understood. "Don't go. Please," he said.

"I have to. I should have gone long ago. It was a mistake to get comfortable, a mistake to stay. I never belonged. I see that now."

"You're wrong. You can't let Aleksander force you out, Yona." Zus took a step closer, and this time, when he reached out to touch her face, she didn't resist, and he didn't stop himself. His touch on her cheek was rough and gentle at the same time. "You didn't see it, but he was never worthy of you."

"Or maybe there is something broken in me." Somehow, speaking the words aloud felt like releasing a flock of birds to the sky. "Perhaps I just don't know how to love."

"You will know, Yona. When it is the right person, you will know." Zus took a deep breath. "And you're not broken, Yona. It's the cracks in us that make us who we are, and you . . . you are stronger than anyone I have ever met, I think. Stay, Yona. Please. We need you."

"I'm sorry, Zus," she said softly, stepping away. His hand fell from her face, and the sadness in his eyes was as deep as a well in the earth.

"Yona—"

She smiled sadly. "I am a dove, Zus." She held up her wrist, which was throbbing with purpose now, warning her. "And doves are meant to fly." She took another step away from him. "Protect them, Zus. I know you will. They listen to you now, all of them. They respect you. I do, too."

"But—"

"Be well, Zus." She turned, because if she let him hold her gaze for a second longer, she might stay forever. Then she ran, stumbling through the undergrowth, knowing that he wouldn't follow—not because he didn't want to, but because he knew the choice was hers.

Jerusza had always taught Yona to move east when there was trouble, always flying toward the sunrise, never the sunset. *Always move toward the beginning of the day, not the end.* The old woman's words rang now in Yona's ears as she fled in the wrong direction, wanting only to be free of Aleksander. She needed to clear her head, to run from the guilt of abandoning the group, even if some no longer wanted her there.

She had done what she could for them, and she'd left them with the tools they'd need to survive. They might well have made it through the winter without her anyhow; they didn't know the forest as well as she, but they were all smart, resourceful. It was likely they could have figured out on their own how to eat, how to shelter, how to hide themselves from the Germans. Maybe she had meant nothing to them at all.

Besides, though she understood now that Aleksander was not to be trusted, he had led the group well, had made good decisions about their survival. Zus had become a leader, too, and together, they understood the things the forest would require of them.

She wasn't a savior. How had she let herself believe that she held their fate in her hands? That had been foolish, selfish. They didn't need her, no matter what Zus had said. So why did his voice echo in her ear now? *Stay, Yona. Please.*

For three weeks, Yona meandered through the forest, venturing out now and again on the southwestern edge of the trees, hoping to catch a glimpse of other people just to assuage her loneliness. She could hardly believe that after a lifetime with only Jerusza's company, she no longer knew how to be by herself. She missed the feeling of thinking she mattered, even a small bit, to others. She missed seeing others' smiles, hearing laughter, sharing meals. She even missed the comforting heat of Aleksander beside her at night. She hadn't realized that once one opened the door to one's heart, it was impossible to fully close it again. At night, in those hazy moments before she fell asleep in the hollows of lonesome old trees, she often heard the voices of the children—Pessia, Leah, Daniel, Jakub, and Adam. She missed them most, for they were the most in need of her protection. They were the ones who haunted her when she tried to rest.

Twice she considered turning back, but she forced herself to keep moving, though her pace was slow. Alone, she was usually swift as an eagle, but she found herself lingering, staying within a few days' walk of the group, just in case. But she couldn't live in this limbo forever. She had to put some distance between herself and the group so she didn't turn around, didn't follow the heartbeats that drew her back to the east.

Jerusza's words were haunting her now, too, as she continued west, the direction from which she'd originally come, so long ago. *Behaimstrasse 72 in Berlin. Siegfried and Alwine Jüttner.* Her parents. Jerusza had said she mustn't return to them, but what if the old woman had been wrong all along, terribly wrong, and had taken Yona from the life she was meant to have? What if finding her parents now could banish the crushing sense of loneliness that threatened to overtake her?

But the thought was foolish, and Yona knew it. Europe was at war. She couldn't simply cross through Poland and waltz over the German border, could she? And who knew if twenty-one years after their child had been taken from them, the Jüttners were still there. What if they had moved, or worse, died? But when Yona had asked Jerusza on her deathbed whether she would see them again, Jerusza hadn't denied it; she had merely delivered another confusing proclamation. *The universe delivers opportunities for life and death all the time.* But what did that mean? Was finding her parents an opportunity for life? Was that why her feet continued to carry her west? She felt as if she were being swept across the continent by forces greater than herself, and for once, still swimming in grief, she let the current take her.

She was moving toward the Białowieża Forest, the Forest of the White Tower, where she had lived for a time with Jerusza, the forest where she'd met a young man named Marcin almost a decade ago, startling her out of her isolation. It was a place that felt like home to her, and now she longed for its embrace—but that meant she had to cross a land that was far more populated with both villagers and soldiers than it had been when she and Jerusza last traversed it years before. She knew how to disappear in public, though, not by looking down but by walking with her head held high, meeting people's eyes for fleeting instants instead of shying away from their gaze. It made her look as though she had nothing to fear, nothing to hide, but she also knew to avoid the kind of extended eye contact that made bears, wolves, and men feel as if she was an aggressor.

She washed herself in a brook, scrubbing her face pink, scraping the dirt from her knuckles and nails, lathering her hair with Saponaria flowers and rinsing it until it gleamed. She changed from her familiar shirt and trousers into the dress that lived at the bottom of her pack, the one she used only as an extra layer in the depths of winter. Jerusza had stolen it for her years before, telling her she must always keep it with her, for if she needed to venture into a village, her rugged shirt and torn trousers would immediately mark her as suspicious. Since Yona would have to slip through a few dots of civilization before reaching the safety of the woods to the west, she would need to look as if she belonged.

She was just passing the outskirts of a large village she didn't know, grateful that she'd almost reached another cluster of trees, when she heard a burst of machine-gun fire, a scream, and then—after a congress of startled crows had lifted off, darting away from the danger overheard—only cold, eerie silence. Yona froze.

Suddenly, there was movement up ahead, near an old church on the edge of the town. It was enough to snap Yona out of it, and at last she scrambled into a thatch of trees up a hill, hiding behind a large oak as a woman hurried into view. It was a nun, wearing a black habit, but the distinctive white yoke and hood were stained with blood. She was carrying a small child, a little girl with long blond ringlets whose bare feet dangled lifelessly from the nun's arms.

The nun was crying as she approached a small house behind the church. "Father Tomasz! Father Tomasz!" she called. "Please, are you there?" The woman couldn't knock on the door, for the child hung heavy in her arms, but surely if there had been someone inside, he would have heard her. No one came, and the nun's moan of despair a moment later shook Yona to her core. She dug her fingernails into the tree, waiting. If the little girl was dead, there was nothing she could do. But if she was still alive . . .

And then, suddenly the girl stirred, and Yona was halfway down the small hill before she could reconsider. The nun turned at the sound of footsteps and looked startled, but she must have seen something in Yona's eyes that spoke silent volumes, because she held Yona's gaze and said simply, in Belorussian, "She has been shot. You are someone who can help? I don't know how to save her, but if we don't do something, she will die."

"I will do what I can," Yona said, and the nun nodded once, then handed the limp child to Yona and gestured for her to follow her to the church several meters from the house. Together they swept through the back door into a darkened vestibule. The nun lit a candle, and then another as Yona laid the girl gently on the floor and put a hand to her neck. She still had a pulse, a strong one, and Yona exhaled in relief. "Water," she said, turning to the nun. "I need water, and alcohol for the wound, if you have it. And yarrow to help clot her blood. Does yarrow grow near here?"

"One of the sisters keeps a small basket of medicinal herbs. I will see what she has." The nun stood, wiping the blood from her hands onto the cloth of her habit, where it seemed to disappear, taken by God. "Please. Do not let her die."

"I will not." Yona didn't know what made her issue a promise she might not be able to keep, but it seemed to reassure the nun, who nodded and hurried away.

Yona turned her attention back to the girl, whose lips were moving, as if she was trying to say something, though she was still unconscious. Her face was white, and when Yona put a hand to her forehead, it was clammy and cool, covered in a sheen of perspiration. Yona unbuttoned the child's dress and saw the wound where the bullet had entered her tiny body, tearing through her just below the collarbone and under her left shoulder. Another two or three centimeters to the right and it would have shredded her heart.

As gently as possible, Yona lifted the girl slightly, bending her own head to see the child's back. There was an exit wound, too, which was a blessing, but she was bleeding heavily. Yona laid her back down and the girl groaned, her face constricting.

The nun was back within a few minutes with everything Yona had asked for, and without a word, Yona quickly set to work, first disinfecting the wound with the vodka the nun handed her—encouraged when the child flinched—and then spreading a paste from hastily ground yarrow on both the little girl's chest and back. Gradually, the bleeding slowed, and when Yona put her cheek on the child's chest, she could hear a strong heartbeat and steady breath. Sighing, she straightened up and met the gaze of the worried nun.

"She is still alive," the nun said, and Yona could see that the woman was crying.

Yona nodded. "Someone should get her parents."

"Her parents are dead." She wiped her eyes, but new tears sprang up in place of the vanished ones. "The Germans shot them. They thought they'd killed her, too."

Yona could feel her heart constrict in her chest. "They are Jewish?"

The nun shook her head. "They thought her parents were communists." Her tears were falling more quickly now. "The Jews of our town have been mostly taken away—taken away or murdered." She put both palms to her cheeks and drew a deep breath. Her eyes—a watery, crystal blue, framed by laugh lines that hadn't been used in a while—locked on Yona's. "Some of those soldiers probably believe themselves to be good Christians. But shooting an innocent family . . . How could anyone believe that God approves of that? I've been searching my soul about it, and I'm no closer to an answer than I was the day they arrived."

"I'm—I'm not Christian," Yona blurted out, and then immediately felt foolish, exposed. Why say such a thing? It was just that she couldn't bear the way the woman was looking at her, her eyes begging for an explanation.

The nun nodded slowly. "Jewish, then?" Her tone was even, and Yona couldn't tell what she was thinking.

Over a long few seconds of weighted silence, Yona considered the question. In the woods, though she had felt as if she didn't belong, she had also felt a deep kinship with the people who believed the same things she did, even if she wasn't always familiar with their customs. "Yes, I think I am," she whispered, though it was surely foolish to admit such a thing, even to a nun who seemed kind. It was impossible to know whom to trust anymore, but she had to trust God, didn't she? And she couldn't betray him with a lie, not in a church where people came to worship him.

Yona waited for the nun's expression to change in judgment, but instead, she looked relieved. "Good. So you believe in God, then."

Yona blinked a few times. "Of course I do."

"Well, that's what matters, don't you think?" The nun sighed and looked down at the girl. "I believe the things I believe, but we all come to God in different ways, don't we? This, though, this is not the way."

Just then, the girl stirred. Her eyelids fluttered, and then she blinked several times, looking back and forth between Yona and the nun, the fear in her expression deepening each time her eyes opened again. "Who are you?" she asked in Belorussian, her voice barely a whisper as her gaze settled on Yona.

"My name is Yona. And this is Sister—"

"Sister Maria Andrzeja," the nun filled in softly.

"We are here to help you," Yona said. "What is your name?"

The child looked from Yona to the nun and back again, and some of the terror left her expression. "Anka," she whispered.

"Anka," Yona said, hearing the tremor in her own voice. "It's important that you stay very still for now. You are hurt, and we are helping you."

The girl looked down at her chest, and her eyes widened when she saw all the blood. She raised her gaze back to Yona. "My mother and father?"

Yona couldn't speak over the sudden lump in her throat, and so, with her eyes never leaving the girl's, she shook her head.

Anka blinked a few times, absorbing the news, and then her face crumpled and she began to cry. "I saw them, you know, when my eyes were closed. My mother, she was saying goodbye to me."

Yona choked on her own stifled sob and had to turn away for a second to gather herself. Sister Maria Andrzeja moved in beside her to hold the child's hand. "You are here with us now, and we will protect you."

"But where is here?"

"The Church of Saint Helena," the nun replied. "Here we help people in need."

"But I am not Catholic," Anka whispered. "My father, he did not believe in God."

"But God believes in you, my dear," Sister Maria Andrzeja

replied immediately. She looked up and held Yona's gaze. "And that makes us all the same, all over the world."

Later, with the girl hidden in a small room beneath the church, finally asleep though she whimpered while she dreamed, Yona sat on a pew in the church's main room, staring up at the gold crucifix above the altar. She had never been inside a church before, never seen such a detailed depiction of the Jew who was said to have sacrificed his life on the cross for the world's salvation. As she studied him now, in candlelit darkness, she felt a great sweep of sadness. Was faith futile in times like these? Where was God in all of this, in this world where people starved to death or perished at the hands of cruel and heartless men? Where was God when neighbors turned against each other?

"It is easy to question our faith," Sister Maria Andrzeja said, coming to sit beside Yona. She had changed her clothing, and now the collar that framed her face was a stark white, all traces of the little girl's blood erased. "And much more difficult to maintain it."

"I don't understand how God can let these things happen," Yona whispered, looking at the nun and then back at the altar, where the gilded Jesus watched in silence. "All of this. This heartache. This death. This suffering. The woman who raised me taught me never to question God, but sometimes lately, I can't help myself."

Sister Maria Andrzeja was quiet for a while. "Throughout all of mankind's history, God has tested us, has tested our faith. Do you know the story of Job?"

Yona nodded.

"Then you know that God protected Job, and Job prospered. Job was a good man; the Old Testament describes him as blameless and upright, a man who feared God and shunned evil. Satan came to God, and God gave Satan permission to test Job, to test his faith, by taking everything from him but his own life. And so Satan did, taking all Job held dear. Job cursed the day of his own birth, but he never cursed God. He did not understand why God was testing him, but he still believed in the Almighty."

Yona shook her head in frustration. "But at the end of Job's life, God restored everything. That is not happening here. God is letting innocent people die, so many of them, at the hands of evil. The little girl in the basement, what did she do to anyone? Why would God let so many people like her be tested?"

"Do not abandon faith, my child." The nun's eyes were a deep well of sorrow. "We can only pray to be his servants, to do what we can to ease the suffering and to save the innocent."

Yona looked down. "What if I am failing in that?" She thought of the way fate had put her in the path of the refugees in the forest. God had given her a chance to help them, and at first, she had answered the call. Had she failed God by turning her back now?

"You can only do your part. You can do your best to strike a match in the darkness, to light the way. God is with you, always, and he sees what's in your heart." The nun folded her hands over Yona's. "Today you saved that child's life. That was God working through you. Tomorrow you might help someone else. As long as you are doing good, you are doing God's work. You are making a difference."

"Whoever saves a life, it is considered as if he saved an entire world," Yona murmured to herself.

"The Talmud."

Yona looked up in surprise. "*You* know the Talmud?"

Sister Maria Andrzeja smiled slightly. "Those of us who seek spend a lifetime trying to find God, to know him, to understand him. Perhaps we can hear him where we least expect. But we must always listen. We must never turn our backs."

Yona felt tears in her eyes as she nodded. The nun, solid in her Catholic faith, was as spiritually far from Jerusza as one could get. And yet they'd both been on the same journey to understanding.

"I don't know where you're coming from, or where you're going," the nun continued after a moment. "But there is a room in the attic. Won't you stay for the night, at least?"

Yona's heart skipped. "Oh, I couldn't possibly—"

"It is probably dangerous to ask you to remain here. But it is not for my benefit. Or for yours. It is for the child. I may need your help."

Yona bowed her head. The nun was right. She couldn't leave without making sure the girl had a chance to live. "Yes, of course."

"Good." The nun stood and patted Yona's hand. "Do not be afraid to ask your questions. But you must always be sure your heart is open to hear the answers."

CHAPTER SIXTEEN

Yona slept fitfully on the wooden floor of the church's small attic, somewhere beneath the steeple and the cross that stood above it. It was the first time in more than two decades that she'd spent the night anywhere but the woods, and the stillness of the air and the quiet of the old building made her uneasy. Twice she stood up to leave, but each time, she could smell Anka's blood on her own clothes, and she reluctantly lay back down.

She found herself thinking of the last time she'd slept under a real roof. She had been just two years old when Jerusza took her, and perhaps it was the sudden, drastic change that had ensured some of her memories of her life before the woods were frozen in her mind forever. She could see moments like distant photographs, always just beyond her reach. Her mother's dark curls. The sharp angles of her bedroom walls. The smooth lines of her father's face. She traced those lines now, a familiar rhythm, and she fell asleep still thinking of the parents she had once known, a world and a lifetime away.

Long before dawn, she rose and made her way in silence down the ladder to the church's vestibule, then down to the basement, where the girl was hidden. Sister Maria Andrzeja was there with her, fast asleep in a chair beside the child's small cot. The little girl was asleep, too, her chest rising and falling steadily, and Yona could see that some of the color had returned to her cheeks. If they could stave off infection, she might well pull through. But then what? Where would the poor child go?

Yona laid a hand on Anka's forehead and was heartened to find it warm but not hot. She was a fighter, even if she didn't know it yet. But she would need more to survive, the kind of care that Jerusza had taught Yona, and the nun had mentioned that the sisterhood's supplies of medicinal herbs were running low.

Yona slipped out before Sister Maria Andrzeja awoke, making her way out of the church and into the still, predawn morning. The nun would likely have told her it wasn't safe to venture into the forest, but she didn't know that Yona could move with the wind and disappear into the trees. She didn't know that without the forest, Yona couldn't breathe.

The setting moon was still bright and full, lighting her way, though the horizon hadn't yet begun to pale. Not a single light burned in the village; not a candle flickered. In the stillness, it felt deserted, otherworldly. In the forest, even if you couldn't see them, you could always hear the animals moving, burrowing, settling, awakening. Here, though, it was as if the whole town were holding its breath, waiting.

As she made her way toward the town's edge, which blurred with the forest, she saw two German soldiers at a distance, smoking on a street corner, the tips of their cigarettes tiny sparks in the darkness. She hugged the shadows, moving in silence, and just before she reached the comfort of the trees, she spotted a dozen more young soldiers in a cluster, all of them wearing swastikas on red bands around their arms. She drew closer, but they didn't notice her. She, however, could hear them talking in low, somber tones. She strained to hear what they were saying, but they were moving away, and she dared not follow. A chill ran through her as she finally moved into the trees and saw hundreds of bullet casings on the ground, and a huge swath of freshly turned dirt several yards away. It took her a few seconds to realize it could only be a mass grave, and she choked on the bile that rose suddenly in her throat. She could almost hear the spirits reaching out to her, begging her for help. Her heart thudding, she turned, her eyes blurred with tears, and ran for the woods.

In the next hour, as dawn arrived reluctantly, she gathered yarrow, linden flowers, burdock, and Saint-John's-wort, greeted the awakening birds like old friends, picked ripe berries and fat porcinis to eat, and, with her knife and a bit of quiet stillness, killed a fat hare to make a rich soup for the nun and the child. She had seen it in their faces; both were starving. The little girl, in particular, would not survive without sustenance. She tucked the supplies into the deep pockets of her dress.

By the time she slipped back into town, the streets were beginning to awaken, but she was accustomed to being invisible. She hugged the shadows, keeping her head down. She was nobody, nothing, a nondescript woman from the village out on her morning errands.

"*Sie!*" A harsh German bark cut through the quiet morning, and she was careful not to react too quickly. Perhaps he wasn't addressing her. "*Halt!*" he added.

Slowly, she raised her gaze, keeping her expression neutral, her eyes level and calm. "*Dobraj ranicy*," she said calmly. The German staring at her from a few feet away was older, at least in his forties or early fifties, and his uniform was different from the ones she had seen on the younger men—an officer, she guessed. Carefully, she added with deference, "*Guten morgen*." She spoke the German words slowly, uncertainly, as if she had just learned them.

"What are you doing?" he asked in uncertain Belorussian, his emphasis landing on incorrect syllables, his pronunciation all wrong. She guessed, from the way he retrieved the phrase so handily, that he'd been here for a while, but that he didn't have the intelligence or depth to have truly grasped the new language.

"Coming from my mother's house." She was glad she had hidden the things she'd brought from the forest in the folds of her dress, for how would she explain them?

"So early?"

"I sleep there sometimes when she is afraid. And lately, you see, she is afraid all the time."

The German studied her. She stared back, refusing to blink. Finally, he lowered his gaze, and when he looked at her again, his eyes were cold, steely. "And your mother? Where exactly does she live?"

"Gesia Street," she answered calmly. She had taken note of a street name just on the edge of town in case she needed it. "In the small house with the blue shutters. She painted them herself when I was small, after my father died. She tends the roses in the garden each day, but they haven't bloomed yet this year. Every night, she falls to her knees and asks God when he will send the flowers."

She continued to stare at him as he attempted to translate her long string of Belorussian words. Jerusza had taught her that she should never deceive people if she could help it, but that if ever she was cornered, staying calm and spinning a story with useless details was the best way to sell a tale. Someone trying to avoid the truth would naturally speak less, not more. Season the story with meaningless facts and it immediately became more palatable. The fact that the officer was struggling with the language simply made the trick that much more effective.

"Well. You should not be out so early," he said, taking a step back, effectively releasing her. And then, as he studied her, something in his face changed. He took a step closer again, and her pulse began to race. Had she slipped up somehow? Still, she stared him down silently, refusing to drop her gaze, for to look away would be to signal fear. She had the feeling that this would be the kind of man who would only be encouraged by a whiff of it.

"Your eyes," he murmured at last. "One blue, and one green . . ."

She blinked. It wasn't what she had expected him to say, and the observation threw her for a few seconds. Her eyes were her greatest weakness, the one thing that kept her from blending in if someone got too close. She'd nearly forgotten; it had been a long time since anyone had made a point of mentioning them. "Yes, that's correct," she said after a moment.

When he still didn't say anything, she finally looked reluctantly back up. He searched her eyes again. "It's just that . . ." He stopped and shook his head. "Nothing. I'm being foolish. You are Polish, of course, yes? Or Belorussian or whatever you people are right now? Your borders change so often, I can't keep track."

Yona nodded.

"Of course you are," he murmured, more to himself than to her. "Of course. Well, be on your way." And then, abruptly, he turned and walked away from her. She didn't linger, for she didn't want him to change his mind. As she hurried away, his strange reaction spun in her mind.

She walked briskly to the church, head down, and let herself in through the same door in the back she'd slipped out of a few hours before. She went straight to the basement, where she found Sister Maria Andrzeja tending to Anka, whose eyes were still closed.

She turned as Yona entered, but her expression was guarded. "I thought you'd left us."

"No." Yona withdrew the hare, the mushrooms, and the fruit, along with the yarrow and herbs. "The girl needed medicine to fight her fever. And I thought you might be hungry."

The nun stared at the hare for a long time before looking back up at Yona, her eyes wide. "You went to the forest?"

Yona nodded.

"That was foolish. They execute people who look as though they are sneaking around, you know. You might well have been caught."

Yona didn't mention that she almost had been. "You need food. I can see it on your face. You and the girl."

The nun took a deep breath. "It is not just me. There are others, too. We are eight nuns altogether, and there's a priest on the grounds as well."

"Then I will return to the forest tonight and bring back more."

"No. Absolutely not. It's far too dangerous." The nun hesitated, eyeing the hare again. "But tonight, we will eat together. Thank you, Yona. But please, do not risk this again."

Yona bowed her head. How could she tell the nun that running to the forest hadn't felt like a risk at all? It was the return to the church that had felt like a danger.

That evening, one of the nuns, a woman named Sister Maria Imelda, stayed with a sleeping Anka, while the others gathered around a narrow, splintered table in the small wooden house behind the church. A slender woman with sloping shoulders and graying hair who went by Sister Maria Teresa had prepared a rich hare and potato soup, and another nun, the youngest among them, a blond woman with big blue eyes and a tiny, delicate nose, had baked bread that, though it smelled like wood shavings, made Yona's mouth water.

"A feast," murmured Mother Bernardyna, the gray-haired, plump nun with the kind eyes who seemed to be in charge. "We are grateful, Yona. You have come from the Nalibocka Forest?"

Yona nodded, and the nuns around the table—six of them, including Sister Maria Andrzeja, who sat just beside her—all regarded her curiously. But there was no judgment in any of their gazes, and for the first time, Yona felt as if she was surrounded by people who saw her for what she was and accepted it. She had not expected that on the grounds of a Catholic church.

"And Sister Maria Andrzeja says that you are Jewish?" the older nun continued, her expression not changing.

Yona gave Sister Maria Andrzeja a look. "I am," Yona said

cautiously, and around the table, there were only nods of understanding, and a few smiles. "I'm sorry. I don't mean to bring danger to your doorstep by being here. I understand how things are. If you would prefer I leave . . ."

Sister Maria Teresa began to bring bowls of steaming soup to the table, setting one down in front of Yona first before serving the other nuns. "Dear, the danger is already at our door. And you are always welcome here."

"We have helped many like you," said the blond nun, though one of the older women hushed her.

"And yet the lives the Germans have taken far outweigh those we've saved," Mother Bernardyna said softly, and the other nuns sobered. "We pray each day for an end to the terror, but the murders continue." She looked around at each of the nuns, her gaze finally settling again on Yona as Sister Maria Teresa delivered the final bowls of soup and sat down herself.

Together, the nuns said grace in Latin, while Yona bowed her head and wondered if God could hear them. "*Benedíc nos Dómine et haec Túa dóna quae de Túa largitáte súmus sumptúri. Per Chrístum Dóminum nóstrum. Ámen.*"

When the prayer had ended, Yona looked up to see tears in Mother Bernardyna's eyes. "I'm afraid I have news," the older nun said.

"Yes?" Sister Maria Andrzeja's voice was hollow, and it seemed to echo in the sudden quiet.

"The Germans have arrested a hundred villagers," Mother Bernardyna said, her voice calm, even. "They are to be executed."

Yona's gasp seemed to pierce the room, and suddenly, all

of the nuns' eyes were on her. When no one said anything, she finally whispered, "But why?"

Mother Bernardyna glanced at Sister Maria Andrzeja before looking back at Yona. "There was a German soldier ambushed on the outskirts of town last week and beaten senseless. The Germans have made it very clear in the past that there will be consequences for such things."

The words settled over Yona, and she swallowed hard, her throat dry. "So they plan to kill a hundred people?"

"As a warning." Sister Maria Andrzeja's voice was flat. "Men and women, old and young. Chosen at random."

"But . . . we can't let that happen."

The older nun smiled gently at her. "Dear girl, your heart is in the right place, but it is not your battle to fight."

"But we can't just let them murder innocent people," Yona protested. "There must be something we can do." She watched as Mother Bernardyna and Sister Maria Andrzeja exchanged looks again, speaking volumes in the silence. "What is it?" she asked when no one said anything.

"In the morning, I will go speak with the German commander," Mother Bernardyna said after a long, heavy silence.

"But if he doesn't listen . . ." Yona's voice trailed off in desperation. She couldn't imagine that the kind of man who would order the execution of a hundred innocent people would be swayed by the pleas of a nun.

"That is why we must pray that he will." The older nun's tone was firm. She held Yona's gaze for a long time and then smiled sadly. "I hope you will pray for us, too, Yona. Now eat, everyone, before the soup grows cold."

But no one moved to touch the food, and on the table before

them, the steam stopped rising, the soup cooled, and an uneasy silence descended once again.

In the church basement early the next morning, Anka awoke, and Yona gave her some linden tea to reduce pain and inflammation. Then, as Sister Maria Andrzeja tended to the child's wounds, humming a haunting tune to herself, Yona ground the rest of the herbs and tied them up in cloth bags to give to the farmer's wife on the edge of town who had agreed to take the girl in. "She is a good woman," Sister Maria Andrzeja said to Yona after Anka had fallen back asleep. "She knows people who can move the child. She will keep her safe." But Yona knew as well as the nun did that there was no guarantee of safety anywhere in Poland, perhaps in all of Europe.

"And what about you?" Yona asked softly. "Who will keep you safe? What if Mother Bernardyna's plan to talk with the German officer today puts all of you in danger?"

Sister Maria Andrzeja didn't say anything.

"Who will protect you?" Yona asked into the silence.

"We believe in God's plan," the nun said after a long time. "And if that plan eventually means the end of our time on earth, we believe in heaven. And we believe that by his death and resurrection, Jesus has opened that heaven to us. We believe that in heaven, we will find paradise beyond what we can imagine. In heaven, we will all meet again."

Yona felt a surge of despair. "But you don't believe Jews get to go there, too, do you?" She was thinking of little Chana, of the murdered families of the group in the woods, and even of

Jerusza. What was on the other side for them if heaven was re-served only for those who worshipped Jesus?

"Of course I do." Sister Maria Andrzeja's answer was firm, unequivocal, and Yona was surprised to feel tears in her own eyes as the nun went on. "I believe that Jews who live good and holy lives will achieve salvation, because they, too, are following the light of God."

"I thought Catholics believed that people must accept Jesus to find salvation."

The nun smiled slightly. "I can see you are well-read in your theology, Yona. And I wish I had a better answer for you about how exactly God works. But deep within us lies the reality of God. Find that reality, hold fast to it, and I believe that those of us who live good lives in his image will be reunited in the afterlife." She paused and put her hands over Yona's. Her palms were warm, reassuring. "Now go, my child. Go before it's too late. The woman who will protect her is Maja Yarashuk, one of our parishioners. You will know her by the scar on her cheek, in the shape of a cross. Her husband was killed by the Germans, and she fiercely opposes them. She lives on the eastern edge of the town, not far from here, in a farmhouse painted white, with the window frames painted red, the colors of the Polish flag. There is a weather vane with an eagle, and the eagle is missing a portion of its left wing. That is how you will know you are in the right place. When she asks who sent you, tell her 'the Siberian iris,' and she will know it was me."

"The Siberian iris?"

Sister Maria Andrzeja smiled. "My very favorite flower, in the most glorious shade of blue." For a second, her gaze was far off, but then she seemed to snap back to the present. "Wait!" she exclaimed before hurrying away, returning a moment later with a handful of documents. "My identity papers," she said, thrusting them at Yona. "They might be of use to you."

Yona took a step back. "I can't take them from you. What if you need them?"

"I will not," the nun said firmly, reaching for Yona's hands and placing the papers there before Yona could pull away again. "I won't be going anywhere but this church, and the others will vouch for me. But they might help you if you're stopped on the way to deliver the child." Yona glanced down and saw on top an identity card with the nun's picture. In it, she was younger, and without her nun's habit she looked like a different person altogether. Her hair was as dark as Yona's, and though their faces were contoured differently, they were papers that might work on first pass.

Yona hesitated only a second more before nodding, taking the papers, and slipping them into her pocket with a murmur of gratitude. "I'll bring them back," she promised.

"Don't." The nun smiled. "After you've dropped Anka off, you must go, Yona. Things are happening here, bad things."

"But—" Yona began to protest, but she was interrupted by Anka, who moaned in her sleep.

"It's time," Sister Maria Andrzeja said.

She didn't wait for Yona's reply; instead, she shook the child gently out of her slumber. As Anka blinked up at them, Sister Maria Andrzeja explained, her tone impossibly light, that Yona would take her to a place where she would heal and be safe until the end of the war. Anka looked uncertain, but when Sister Maria Andrzeja bent to kiss her forehead, she lifted her head and kissed the nun on both cheeks. "Thank you," she murmured. "Thank you for saving me."

The nun turned before Anka could see her tears, and then she pulled Yona into a brief, tight hug. "God be with you, child," she whispered in Yona's ear, and then she turned and hurried out of the church basement without looking back.

CHAPTER SEVENTEEN

Anka was light as a bird in Yona's arms—too light. Holding her precious cargo, she hurried past a cluster of German soldiers who paid her no mind, past a queue of empty-eyed townspeople outside a butcher shop with cobwebs on the windows, past a deserted school. Across the town, curtains were drawn tight, most shop fronts were closed, and the few people who walked around did so with eyes downcast, their clothing as gray as the buildings surrounding them, as if they were trying to disappear.

By some miracle, she and Anka reached the edge of town without anyone stopping them. Then again, the town was quiet, waiting. Heart pounding and arms aching with the weight of the child, Yona quickened her pace and headed east on a dirt road toward the safety of the forest until she spotted the farmhouse Sister Maria Andrzeja had described, the white one with red window frames and a broken eagle's wing on the weather vane.

"Is this it?" Anka asked weakly. She had been drifting in and out of sleep, and now she opened her eyes and peered around as Yona walked up the dirt drive to the farmhouse. Out back, a weathered gray barn stood stubborn against the bleak morning sky, its back to the trees beyond. Looking past it, to the edge of the forest, made Yona's heart lurch unexpectedly. She belonged out there, in the wood, not here in this village. But Jerusza had always told her never to question God's plan, that even when things felt like they were falling apart, there was always a reason, always a purpose.

The door to the farmhouse opened, and a tall, slender woman in her fifties stood there staring for only a second or two before rushing toward them. She looked once into Yona's eyes, nodded, and put a hand on Anka's forehead. She pulled quickly away as if she'd been burned. "Who sent you?"

"Er . . . the Siberian iris. You are Maja?"

The woman pursed her lips and nodded. "Into the house, before anyone sees you," she said, and though there didn't appear to be another soul around, Yona followed, realizing that in this world, as in hers, invisible eyes could watch from the darkness.

Inside, the farmhouse was dimly lit and smelled of yeast and straw. Dust coated the chairs and table. Without a word, the woman led Yona, still carrying Anka, into a room in the back and closed the door. "There is a trapdoor in the floor, beneath the rug," she said, finally turning to them. Her words were clipped, tense. "Not a good solution for the long term, but good for you to know if you were followed today."

"We were not."

The woman's eyes flicked to Anka and back. "You should put the child down," she said without waiting for an answer. She gestured to the small, threadbare sofa to the side of the room, and Yona gently lowered the girl, who groaned softly. "She is wounded, I see." Maja's forehead creased in concern. "Badly."

"Yes. She was shot. We have cleaned the wound, and the bullet is gone, but she needs to heal."

The woman muttered something under her breath, an indiscernible expletive, and then she studied the girl for a long, silent moment before turning back to Yona. "I will help. I give you my word. But who are you? How have you come to bring her to me? You are not her mother."

Yona wondered how Maja could see that so clearly. "I—" She began to speak, but then she stopped. How could she explain who she was, what she was doing here? She could hardly understand it herself. "Her parents are dead," she said at last.

Something shifted and then softened in Maja's expression. "They all are these days. So many children without parents." She shook her head. "What is her name, then?"

"Anka. She will live if you keep the wound clean and her fever down. I have brought you some yarrow, which—"

"I know," Maja interrupted. She smiled slightly. "I know the forest's secrets, too. Before I married my husband, before I came here to live, I was a nurse. It is why the sisters send people to me from time to time, people who need healing." She bent beside Anka, who was watching them with wide, confused eyes, and said slowly, "Hello, Anka. I am Maja Yarashuk. I will keep you safe."

Anka blinked at her but didn't say a word.

"What will you do with her?" Yona asked.

"I have friends. They help people disappear. But I will wait until she is stable and well." She stood abruptly.

"Here in this house?" Yona looked uncertainly toward the front windows. If anyone had an inkling that there was something suspicious going on here, there would be nowhere to hide.

Maja stared at her for a long time, evaluating her. "There is another trapdoor in one of the stalls in the barn. That is all you need to know. Now go. The sooner you are gone, the safer she will be."

Yona knew the words weren't intended to wound her, but they did. Was she only meant to preserve life for a moment before being driven away? It was a strange role to play, and it stirred in her a great feeling of loneliness, a sense of belonging nowhere. But Maja was right: better for the girl to be absorbed into this house, hidden and healed, and then sent on to start a new life somewhere else, God willing.

Yona knelt beside Anka and placed a hand on the little girl's forehead. It was still cool, a good sign. "You will be safe here," she murmured, touching the girl's hollow cheek.

"How do you know?" Anka asked in a whisper.

Yona looked up at Maja, who was watching them. "I know," she said, looking back at Anka. "We must trust Sister Maria Andrzeja. She risked her life to save you, and she trusts Maja. We must believe in her, too."

Anka searched Yona's eyes, and then she nodded. "All right." She glanced up at Maja and then back at Yona. "All right."

Yona stood and nodded at Maja. "Shall I bring you some more herbs? Some food?"

Maja glanced at Anka and then led Yona out of the room. Over her shoulder, as she went, Yona raised her hand, a silent goodbye to Anka. The little girl raised hers in return, touching the air where Yona had just been.

"I'll say it again: you must not return," Maja said firmly once they were out of the girl's earshot. "It is for the girl's own good. And for yours."

"But I—"

"Thank you for bringing her here. But you cannot save everyone all by yourself. Trust me to do my part." Maja's voice was firm, and had there not been kindness in her eyes, Yona might have gone back for the girl immediately, taken her with her. But she could read the honesty in Maja's face, the grit, the weariness, and she knew Anka would be as safe here as anyone could be in the midst of a war. "Now, go."

Yona drew a deep breath and then, without allowing herself to look back, she slipped out the front door and scanned the quiet morning. She would need to cross through the heart of the village to make it to the woods on the other side. Anka would be safe. Maja was right: she couldn't save everyone all by herself. And now, as the nun had said, it was time for her to go.

Yona had been gone for only an hour and a half when she reentered from the dirt road leading into town. A young German soldier, who hadn't been there before, was blocking the road as she approached.

"Halt," he said in Belorussian. "Who are you and where are you coming from?"

For an instant, instead of fear, Yona felt instead a great sweep of sadness. The man's accent was foreign, but his words were perfect; unlike the officer she had met earlier, he was obviously bright. But instead of spreading his wings in a university somewhere, using his intelligence to make the world a better place, he was here, an anonymous soldier on a dirt road to nowhere, doing the devil's work in a foreign land.

"Do you not speak Belorussian?" he asked after Yona's silence had gone on too long, and now she felt less pity for him, because there was a curtness to his tone. "Damn it, I can't make heads or tails out of these towns. Are you Polish? Do any of you peasants even know what you are? No matter, soon you'll all be speaking German."

She looked up and met his gaze. His eyes were icy blue, his narrow nose sharp as a bird's beak. "I am on the way to pray in the church," she replied in perfect Belorussian.

He arched an eyebrow. "And you are coming from where?"

"Milk. I went to see if any of the farmers on the edge of town had milk they could spare." It was the first thing she could think of.

"Milk? For whom?"

She thought instantly of Anka. "My daughter."

His eyes moved to her belly, flat as a board, and then back to her face. "Your daughter?"

She refused to look away. "She is four years old and starving."

The soldier continued to study her. "But you have no milk."

"None of the farmers had any to give. I—I could not pay."

The soldier snorted. "And you hoped that someone would give you some out of goodness? Madam, there is no goodness left here. Don't you know?"

"That is why I am going to church. I will ask God to help provide."

He shook his head, his gaze sliding away. "God is not there this morning, madam, I assure you. Go home if you know what's good for you."

Her heart skipped in her chest. "Has something happened?" She thought of the nuns' conversation the night before, the hundred innocent townspeople, Mother Bernardyna's intention to argue their case with the Germans.

Anguish flashed across his face, replaced quickly by anger. "Please, just take my advice and go home to your child, all right?"

She forced herself to relax. "Yes, sir," she said, and he nodded, apparently satisfied that he had properly put her in her place. "Thank you." She hurried past him, relieved that he'd let her go without asking for her papers. She had the ones Sister Maria Andrzeja had hastily insisted she take, but she suspected they would fool only someone less intelligent.

"Wait!" he bellowed behind her, and she froze. Had he realized, after all, that she'd been lying?

She turned slowly, forcing innocence across her face.

He strode toward her, and she stood stock-still, holding her breath. He studied her face once more, as if trying to decide something. Then, hastily, he withdrew a small object from his pocket and handed it to her. "Here. For your daughter."

She took it, and he was already walking away, back to his post, before she realized what it was. It was a small bar of chocolate, German lettering on the wrapper. For him, it must have been a piece of home, and yet he'd given it to her, concerned for a starving four-year-old. Her heart squeezed. It was a shred of decency in a world gone mad. "Thank you!" she called out, but he didn't turn. He merely raised his right hand in acknowledgment, and after a second's pause, she, too, went on her way.

The road to the church was silent, unnaturally so. This time of morning, people should have been bustling about. As she drew closer, she could hear raised voices and the murmurs of a crowd, could feel a ripple of terror in the air the way one might feel a coming storm. She wanted to break into a run, but it would look suspicious, and so instead she walked as quickly as her legs would take her until she rounded the corner, bringing the square in front of the church into view. Immediately, she had to clap her hand over her mouth to stop from screaming.

The square teemed with townspeople, at least two hundred of them, jammed elbow to elbow, some of them whispering, some crying. On either side of the crowd, Germans with rifles kept watch. Ahead of them, on the steps of the church, stood the nuns, all eight of them, with Sister Maria Andrzeja on one end and Mother Bernardyna on the other. They were standing in a row, all of them watching in silence as the body of a young priest swung lifeless from a lopsided, rudimentary gallows that had evidently been constructed from several broken church pews. Yona felt her stomach lurch, tasted bile in her throat. What had happened in the short time she'd been gone?

"This," a stout German officer was bellowing to the crowd in heavily accented Belorussian, "is what happens when you choose to fight us! You brought this on yourselves! Do you understand? The blood of this priest is on your hands!"

Yona stood frozen, staring at Sister Maria Andrzeja's face. The nun's eyes looked straight ahead, and her jaw was set, her chin thrust upward, defiant, angry. How had the sisters wound up in this position? Yona had to do something, but what?

She took a steadying breath and began to move quietly forward through the throng, which parted easily, for no one wanted to be visible today; they were all jostling to hide behind one another. In a minute, she found herself at the front of the crowd, which was filled almost entirely with young women, small children hidden behind them. Their courage made Yona draw a deep breath; they had all placed their bodies here deliberately to protect the youngsters behind them. They didn't understand that their flesh and bones would offer no shield against a volley of bullets.

"This priest!" the German officer was saying as he paced, his face flushed with anger. "He is dead because of all of you. A week ago, there was an attack on a German soldier, and the assailant got away. Yesterday, we arrested a hundred citizens of this village, with the intention of making them pay for the crime, as an example to all of you. But this priest stepped forward this morning and offered his life for theirs. So, too, did these eight nuns."

Yona gasped aloud, the sound absorbed by the anguished murmur of the crowd. Suddenly, she understood. The nuns had been planning this all along; when Mother Bernardyna had mentioned last night the bargain she'd hoped to strike, this had been it. This morning, Sister Maria Andrzeja had given Yona her papers because she knew she wouldn't need them any longer. "No," she murmured.

"We accepted their bargain," the German continued, shouting at the crowd. "All of you must be punished today, so that the lesson sticks, which is why you're gathered here to watch. You're like children, all of you, and this is the only way children can learn. Maybe today, you will understand."

Yona tried to catch Sister Maria Andrzeja's eye, but the nun continued to stare resolutely ahead. Yona was so focused on staring at the nun that it took her a few seconds to realize that there were eyes on her, too. She turned to see the German officer she'd encountered yesterday, the one who had seemed so perplexed by her eyes, standing off to the side in a cluster of other officers. He was watching her, a strange look on his face, and as their gazes locked, he murmured something to the officer next to him, a tall man with graying dark hair, whose back was turned to the crowd.

The taller officer turned slowly, and as he did, time seemed to stop for Yona. In the background, she could still hear the German on the steps, and the rumble of the frightened crowd, but it was as if her field of vision had suddenly narrowed as the man's face came into view and his eyes met hers.

His face was creased like worn fabric, and though his mouth pulled down at the corners, though his eyes had sunken farther into his face with age, she recognized him in an instant, the sight of him triggering long-latent, milk-scented fragments of memory. A face above her long-ago infant bed. A smile at her first step. A hand slipping into hers, huge and warm, to steady her.

And here he was, impossibly, more than two decades later, more than nine hundred kilometers from the apartment on Behaimstrasse in Berlin where she'd seen him last.

It was Siegfried Jüttner, the man who'd once been her father.

CHAPTER EIGHTEEN

His eyes never leaving hers, Jüttner started down the steps toward her, trailed by the officer who'd spoken with her yesterday, and as she stood there, paralyzed, she registered dully that he was a high-ranking officer, his uniform decorated with elaborate, silver-braided shoulder straps and collar patches. He had almost reached her before she snapped out of her shock and began sliding backward away from him, away from this man whose blood she shared. Her whole body was shaking, and her legs trembled as she melted into the crowd, never taking her eyes off him.

Lives are circles spinning across the world, and when they're meant to intersect again, they do, Jerusza had said on her deathbed. Now, suddenly, Yona understood. The old woman had foreseen a moment like this, a terrible reunion. Perhaps the current had been pulling Yona west after all, to this. But why? *We believe in God's plan,* Sister Maria Andrzeja had said just that morning, but how could any of this be it?

Up on the church steps, the angry officer was still bellowing. "So you see? Now you will witness the deaths of these eight nuns!" he barked, and the ensuing panic of the crowd was enough to let Yona slip deeper into the mass of people, hidden from her father, who was now scanning faces wildly as he moved closer. Heart thudding, tears prickling her eyes, Yona made herself smaller and smaller, letting the frantic crowd swallow her. "And maybe you will remember this the next time you consider crossing us!"

The crowd stirred, mothers bending to their young children, old men falling to their knees to pray, teenagers mumbling about rebellion and powerlessness. On the church steps, the officer was beckoning to eight soldiers, one for each of the nuns, to step forward with handguns. Suddenly, Yona stopped in her tracks. She could still see her father, but he couldn't see her, though he was scanning the crowd desperately. She felt suddenly ill, and though she didn't have the right vantage point to see the nuns anymore, she could feel their pain radiating out over the assembled group.

And at that instant, before the German soldiers raised their guns, before the order was given, Yona knew that everything in her life up to this moment had been designed to lead her here, to this place, where she might be the one person with the power to halt what was about to happen. She didn't know why, but she knew what she had to do. As others crossed themselves and cowered, as the nuns raised their eyes to God, she took a deep breath, stood, and turned in the direction of the man who'd given her life. "Stop!" she cried in German. "Siegfried Jüttner! Please, stop this!"

At the superior officer's name, the stout man on the steps turned, sneering at the crowd as he searched for the source of the voice. But Yona wasn't looking at him. She was looking at her father, who had finally found her in the throng. He was staring at her, slack-jawed. "Stop this, please," she said, and now, as he drew closer, she was speaking only to him. "You can do that, can't you? Please. I am begging you to spare the lives of the nuns."

"Inge?" When Jüttner spoke, even his voice was familiar to her, so familiar that it tugged at a corner of her heart she thought had been closed long ago. Without looking behind him, he gestured to the officer on the church steps, telling him with a single wave of his hand to pause. Yona had been right: he was the senior officer here. Shaking his head in disgusted disbelief, the officer on the steps signaled to the eight soldiers as Jüttner began to walk again toward Yona, who had to force herself to stand still, though it went against her every instinct. But if she ran, the nuns would die.

The silent crowd parted like the Red Sea as the tall Nazi officer moved through them, stopping just inches from Yona. The other officer, the one who'd seen her yesterday, was scrambling behind him. "You see? It's just like I told you! Her eyes! Just like—"

"Enough." The world around them fell silent as Jüttner stepped so close to her that she could feel his breath on her cheek. His uniform was creaseless, his gaze appraising and guarded. He stared directly into her eyes, as if trying to see into her soul, and then, without a word, he picked up her left wrist and gently turned it over. As he stared down at it, she watched him. The dark dove throbbed as he brushed it with his thumb, as if making certain it was real. Something changed in his eyes, a vanishing of doubt. When he looked up at her, his eyes were filled with tears. "Inge?" he whispered. "Is it really you?"

It had been her name once upon a time, before Jerusza crept from the shadows and spirited her away. Slowly, she nodded. "*Papa*," she murmured, her first word so long ago, a word she hadn't uttered in more than two decades. She struggled with how to think of this man before her; he was the father of her hazy memory, but now he was a stranger in a Nazi uniform, a stranger who had allowed the murder of a priest, who had been about to oversee the execution of eight innocent nuns.

"How are you here?" he asked, and when she looked back at the church steps, his eyes followed hers, to where the red-faced officer was staring at them with confused disgust, and to where Sister Maria Andrzeja was watching, her mouth agape. "You have been alive all these years?"

She took a deep breath. "I will tell you everything. But first you must stop this. Please. The nuns have done nothing. You've already made your point with the priest."

He nodded slowly, as if in a daze, and turned to the officer standing inches behind him, who'd been watching their exchange with wide eyes. Jüttner murmured something, and though the man looked perplexed, he nodded and hurried up the church steps, where he repeated the command to the red-faced officer who'd been about to order the execution. The officer looked furious, but he nodded curtly and ordered the soldiers to stand down. Then he barked an order at one of them to lead the nuns into the church and to guard them until the situation was resolved.

Yona watched until Sister Maria Andrzeja vanished inside, shooting Yona one last look of confusion and terror. And then, as the officer on the steps disappeared inside the church, too, and the crowd continued to shrink away from her, she turned back to Jüttner. "*Danke*," she said, thanking him in German.

"It is only temporary, until I understand what you are doing here." He stared for a moment longer. "My daughter," he murmured to himself. As he took her hand in his, his long fingers crushing hers as he began to lead her away, her stomach churned. The nuns had been granted a reprieve, but for how long? And what would be the price for their salvation? This time, when Jerusza's words spoke to her on the wind, they were unmistakable. *You fool. What have you done?*

Jüttner's hand was coarse and cold, but when he glanced back at her, he must have seen the fear on her face, for he loosened his grip slightly. "All will be well," he said as he led her past the line of soldiers who had been set to execute the nuns just a moment earlier. Now they all stared at her in confusion.

"Wait," she said, stopping abruptly, which forced him to stop with her.

When he turned around, his expression was a strange blend of tenderness and impatience. "Yes? What is it?"

"The nuns. How do I know they will be safe if I come with you?"

He glanced at the soldiers, all of whom were watching, and she could see a shadow cross his face. "Because I am in charge here. My men do what I say."

"The nuns haven't done anything wrong. They don't deserve to die."

He looked as if he was about to protest, but instead, he frowned and tightened his grip on hers. "You don't understand yet." He turned sharply, leading her up the steps of the church. He shoved the wooden doors open, sending a burst of light into a sanctuary that had been destroyed.

Pews were tipped and splintered, and the scent of ash lingered in the air. In the corner, the eight nuns stood holding hands and praying while the officer who'd been about to order their murder watched from several feet away, his face still the color of a summer beet. A soldier stood guard nearby, his gaze flicking uneasily between the nuns and the gold crucifix that hung over the altar.

Yona could feel Sister Maria Andrzeja's eyes on her as Jüttner pulled her past the destroyed rows of pews, to the other officer.

"What is this, then?" the man asked, staring hard at Yona.

"This is my daughter," Jüttner said, his voice catching on the last syllable. Sister Maria Andrzeja's eyes widened, and a few of the nuns exchanged glances.

The officer's upper lip curled. "Your daughter is a Pole? What, you screwed a Polack whore twenty-odd years ago, Jüttner?"

"My *daughter* is a *German*," Jüttner said sharply, and the other man took a step back and looked at the floor for a second. "You will not disrespect either of us."

When he looked back up, the doubt in his expression was obvious. "Yes, well, what does she have to do with this?"

"Until I return, you will keep these nuns safe." It wasn't an answer. "You will not proceed with the execution." He said it as casually as if he was telling the other man not to order dinner without him.

"But—"

"Do you under*stand*?" Jüttner's voice rose to a bellow, and the other man looked away. "I have given you an order."

"Yes, sir."

Satisfied, Jüttner nodded and looked down at Yona, whose hand he still grasped. "Come."

Yona looked once more at Sister Maria Andrzeja, whose

eyes were narrowed now. Yona could imagine what the nun was thinking—that Yona had deceived her, about her name, about everything. Perhaps she would have the chance to explain it all to the nun one day, to make her understand that none of it had been a lie, that it was possible to be two people at once, and that what mattered was what lay in one's heart. But there was no time for that now, and so Yona turned away as Jüttner led her out of the church and back into the sunshine, where the square now stood empty, the crowd having dissipated quickly after a reprieve they didn't understand.

Wordless, Yona followed Jüttner, whose hand was still wrapped around hers like a vise.

Jüttner led her on a brisk, winding walk to a grand stone house in the center of town that had obviously been commandeered from a once-wealthy villager. "My home," he said brusquely, without looking at her. He nodded to two soldiers stationed outside, then he released his grip, unlocked the front door, and led her inside. The windows were swathed in heavy crimson curtains, the walls painted a delicate eggshell white, the white furniture well-made and immaculate. Rugs that looked as if they had come from another land covered the polished wooden floor, and on the walls along the staircase there were faded rectangles where Yona imagined family pictures must have hung. What had happened to the people who once called this place home?

Jüttner hesitated after closing the heavy door behind them, enclosing them in the dim light of the foyer. "You will be needing a bath," he said, and for the first time, Yona was conscious of the thin layer of grime coating her skin, which usually didn't bother her. She looked at the floor as he added, "You'll find a tub in the back room, just there, already prepared by my maid for the bath I had intended to take. The water will be cold, but a cold bath braces one's constitution. I will get you some clothing from the closet. There was a girl who lived here once, about your size."

"I'm fine. I don't need—"

"You will be dining with me. You must be presentable." He softened his tone a bit. "It is better for you. You will feel better."

"All right," Yona said, but she didn't move, and neither did Jüttner.

"Is it really you, Inge?" he whispered after a moment.

She looked up at him and met his gaze. She could see him searching her unusual eyes, confirming what he already knew. "It is," she said, and his gaze traveled once more to the dove on her wrist. "My name is Yona now." He stared at her wrist but didn't acknowledge her words.

"Go. Clean yourself up." It was an order, and Yona found herself walking away, down the hall.

Twenty minutes later, she emerged from the washroom, where she'd bathed in a deep, white clawfoot tub, leaving a ring of dirt behind, even though she tried to wipe it away. Wrapped in a white towel, she opened the door to find a chair sitting just outside, a cream day dress draped over it. She lifted it carefully, examining it with wonder, for she'd never worn anything like it. The fabric swirled like a waterfall and was impractical in every way, but as she retreated back into the bathroom and slipped it over her head, she found that it fit almost perfectly and fell to the floor, covering her knife and her ankle sheath neatly. Still, in something so feminine and foolish, she felt naked, exposed.

Her hair was still wet when she walked into the sitting room a few minutes later. Jüttner, still in his full uniform, was pacing with a frown, and he jumped when she entered. "I've brewed us some coffee. Do you drink coffee? And I've fetched us some biscuits made by my housekeeper, Marya. She comes each day. She will launder your things for you tomorrow. You will sleep in the bedroom at the top of the stairs." He seemed to realize he was babbling, for he quickly clamped his mouth closed and gestured to one of the sofas, which was so stiff it looked as if it had never been sat upon. "Inge, join me. Do you take cream?"

Yona shook her head as she crossed the room and carefully sat down, the many layers of her dress swishing as she did. As he poured her a cup of steaming black coffee and then fixed one for himself, with generous splashes of cream and sugar, she marveled at the casual decadence of it. Most of the people in this town likely hadn't seen cream or sugar since the start of the war.

His hands shook as he raised his cup to his lips. "I don't know where to begin."

Neither did Yona, and so she bought time by taking a sip of her own coffee. It was like nothing she'd ever tasted before—smooth and black and fragrant—and she coughed, choking it down. She'd only ever had pale acorn coffee in the woods.

"How did you know who I was?" he finally asked. "After all these years?"

She searched his face. She wanted to hate him for what he was now, but she couldn't stop her mind from spinning back, back to a different time, a different place. Even his scent, cedarwood with a touch of lavender, triggered latent memories. She tried to push the familiarity away, but it was impossible. "I have never forgotten."

He looked away, and when he turned back a few seconds later, his eyes were wet. "One of the other officers told me he'd seen someone with eyes like yours, the right age . . ." He paused and shook his head. "I never imagined it could really be you. I thought he was crazy. So many times in that first year, after you disappeared, your mother swore she saw you. But she was always wrong."

The words sent a stab of pain through her heart. In her foggy recollections, her father had been distant and removed, but her mother's face had shone with warmth. Once upon a time, Yona had been loved. "My mother." She said the words carefully, tasting the strangeness of them on her tongue. "Is she still in Berlin?"

Jüttner's expression turned hard. "She died two years after you were taken. The doctor said it was grief, a broken heart."

Tears stabbed at Yona's eyes. "I'm very sorry," she said, and though none of it had been her fault, she felt the heavy burden of responsibility.

"But where *were* you, Inge?" Jüttner asked after a minute, his voice cracking. "Where have you been all these years?"

His voice had fallen to a desperate whisper. "My name is Yona now," she told him again, and again, he seemed not to hear her. "I was taken by a woman named Jerusza."

He studied her, digesting this, his features twisting in confusion. "And she took you here? To Poland?"

"Eventually."

"But where did you live? Where have you been?"

"Nowhere. Everywhere. The forest."

"A village near the forest, you mean?" Perspiration gleamed on his brow.

"No. Never a village. She—she didn't trust people. We lived off the earth, built shelters to sleep in at night, foraged for our food."

"But how do you speak such perfect German if you were raised by a savage in the wilderness?"

"Jerusza wasn't a savage. She was . . ." Yona trailed off, for how could she explain the old woman? Words could never be enough. "She believed that the more knowledge we possess, the better prepared we are to face the world. She taught me things. How to survive. Many languages."

"And this—this woman? She harmed you, Inge?" The anger in his voice was barely controlled. "Where is she now?"

"She died. And no, she never harmed me." But wasn't that a lie? She had stolen a well-cared-for child from her home and made a desperate, hungry warrior out of her.

"But what, then, was her motive?" His face had reddened, and a thick vein bulged in his neck now. "Why us? Why you?" Yona didn't say anything for a moment, and at her silence, her father sat heavily on one of the sofas and put his head in his hands. "*Why?*" he whispered. "Tell me why."

"I don't know." Yona hesitated before adding, "She always said she was saving me."

He looked up in astonishment. "*Saving* you? From what? A warm, safe home with parents who loved you?"

The words sliced into her deeply. "Did you?" she asked in a small voice. "Love me?"

"Of course I did. I'm your father." His voice broke, and he stood abruptly. He began to pace. "She destroyed us, Inge. She made a fool of me."

"Jerusza said . . ." Yona paused and swallowed. "She said you were bad people."

"*We* were bad people?" He choked out a strained laugh. "She kidnapped our child! That's a bit like throwing stones in a glass house, no?"

"But here you are now, overseeing the murder of many innocents. So perhaps she wasn't so wrong."

Anguish washed over his features. "The orders are never mine, Inge. You must understand that."

"But you carry them out."

"What choice do I have?"

She held his gaze. "You always have a choice."

He stood quickly and began to pace. "No. It is easy for you to say that. You do not know what it's like. To go against commands I'm given would be to lose my life."

"And instead, thousands of people should lose theirs?"

"You don't know!" His eyes were alight, almost feverish, as he whirled on her. "You don't understand! There will be peace here the moment they all stop fighting back!"

"And the Jews?" Yona asked softly. "There will be peace for the Jews, too, in this world you imagine?"

"The Jews?" He seemed to choke on the word, as if the taste of it was vile. He began to pace again. "The Jews worked against Germany in the Great War, Inge. Do you understand that? The German army was winning, and it was the Jews who destroyed it all at home. It was the Jews who brought war upon us in the first place, too, you realize. They control everything, the banks, in and out of Europe. You understand? If we allow them to gain the upper hand again, they will destroy Germany. The Jews are a poisonous race who live off German wealth and weaken us. We must destroy them before they destroy us."

Yona stared at him. "That's nonsense, all of it. You think that thousands, maybe millions, of people deserve to die so that Germany can rise? You believe that there's any God who would condone that?"

"You were raised in the wild by a madwoman. You know nothing of God."

"Yes, I do." She waited until he looked at her. "You do, too. You know in your heart that what you're doing is an affront to him. I can see it in your eyes." She knew she had gone too far, but still, she pressed on. "Won't you do the right thing and release the nuns?"

He stared at her in disbelief. "Again with the nuns? You ask as if any of us has a choice. You ask as if fate is in your hands or mine."

"But it is. Isn't it?"

He opened his mouth as if to respond, but then he shut it again and stormed abruptly out of the room, heading for the stairs. A moment later, she heard the slam of a bedroom door.

Yona looked to the door of the house. If she left now, if she could somehow slip past the soldiers out front, she could run for the woods and be gone before Jüttner knew she was missing. But in doing so, she would seal the nuns' fate. Jüttner had said that if she came home with him, the nuns would be safe. She needed to stay, at least until she could figure out a way to persuade him to order their release. But then what?

Eventually she walked upstairs and entered the room he'd said was hers, a small bedroom with a squat bed covered in a lacy cream quilt. Atop it, neatly laid out, was a nightgown that appeared as if it would fit her. She closed the door behind her and picked the gown up, feeling the diaphanous fabric slip between her fingers, and then she set it back down again. She couldn't imagine a world in which she'd wear something so impractical, even to sleep. On the nightstand was a small, clear globe with several trees inside, a dusting of snow on the ground. When Yona picked it up to look more closely, the snow shifted. Entranced, she turned it over and then flipped it back, watching the snow drift slowly, silently down under the glass dome. It made her long suddenly, powerfully, for the safety of her beloved forest.

Finally, she set the globe down and sat on the bed, testing the weight of it. She had not slept in a bed since the night before her second birthday, and it felt strange, unfamiliar. The ground beneath a person should feel solid and reassuring, not spongy and soft, for that was false comfort. Then again, all of this was false. After a few minutes had ticked loudly by on the grandfather clock near the window, she lay on top of the covers, placing her head on one of the pillows, which was filled with feathers. After a second, she climbed out of bed and lay on her back on the floor.

She was staring at the ceiling sometime later when there was a soft tap on the door.

"Come in," she said, sitting up as the door handle turned and Jüttner entered.

"I apologize," he said gruffly, and for a split second, she thought perhaps she'd gotten through to him, but he added, "I must remember that you were raised by a lunatic in the wilderness. It will take you some time to understand things. But you are my daughter, and I will teach you."

Yona didn't reply, and after a pause, he cleared his throat.

"What are you doing on the floor?"

"The bed is too soft."

He looked at her like she was crazy. Maybe she was.

"What will become of the nuns?" she asked.

"I don't know yet. But there will be no decision tonight. I give you my word."

She searched his eyes for signs he was lying, but she found only deep sadness and fear there. "All right."

"Get some sleep. We can talk more when you awaken."

Yona nodded, and he gave her a strange half smile before closing the door behind him. A second later, she heard a bolt click, and she knew, even before rising to twist the knob herself, that he had locked her in. She crossed the room and tried the window, which slid open readily. She shut it again, relieved that she had an easy way out if she needed it. Still, she was unsettled by the fact that he'd thought not only that he could trap her, but that he had the right to do so.

She lay back down on the floor and closed her eyes, for she would need all the energy she could get for whatever might come next. She knew she wouldn't sleep well, though, for she was under the roof of an enemy, even if he was her own flesh and blood.

CHAPTER NINETEEN

I t took Yona an hour to relax, but eventually she slipped into a strange half sleep and dreamed of Jerusza. In the dream, Jerusza was walking toward her through the woods, her eyes burning with anger, but when she spoke, the whipping wind whisked her words away. Each time Yona took a step closer, desperate to hear what Jerusza was saying, the old woman became more and more translucent, until she disappeared altogether into a spill of sunshine. She was gone, and her words—surely a warning—had vanished, too. Yona awoke with a start, her heart hammering, her forehead damp with perspiration, and for a few blurry seconds, she couldn't remember where she was. She looked wildly around, taking in the genteel furnishings, the embroidered curtains, the plush bed she was lying beside. Her pulse slowed as it all came rushing back to her.

Then again, this is what her life might have looked like if Jerusza hadn't come for her all those years before. Would her mother have been alive? What kind of a person would Yona have become?

But when life opens a door, the others behind it slam closed. It was impossible to know what would have been, what could have been, because the choices Jerusza made forever altered the future. There was no sense in looking over her shoulder. And the ghost of Jerusza could shout all she wanted into the wind, but the old woman didn't belong here, not in this moment. She couldn't save Yona from the past.

Sometime later, Yona drifted once again to sleep, but this time, her slumber was dreamless, and when she awoke to light streaming through the windows, she felt well rested for the first time in weeks. She sat up, startled that she had slept so soundly. How could she have let down her guard? Quickly, she got to her feet, smoothed her dress and her hair, and headed for the door, which opened easily; Jüttner must have unlocked it when he'd risen that morning.

"The nuns?" she asked without greeting as she entered the kitchen. "They are all right?"

Jüttner was in full uniform, sipping a cup of coffee at the small table. He looked up and smiled indulgently, almost as if she were a child asking for an extra serving of cake. Yesterday he'd looked as if he was unraveling. Today he looked polished and unflappable. The swift transition chilled her. "Good morning, Inge. And how did you sleep?"

"The nuns?" she repeated.

"They're fine, Inge."

But his eyes were cold and hard, and she didn't believe him. "Show me. Please. I must see them."

He gestured to the seat across from him, and as she sat, slowly and reluctantly, he rose to get the silver coffeepot. He poured her a steaming cup and then sat back down. "I was just about to go myself."

"Take me with you." Yona held his gaze.

He hesitated. "That would make you happy? Very well. But first, you will have some coffee and some food. You are my guest." Jüttner didn't wait for an answer before pushing a hunk of bread with a fat pat of butter toward her. Yona stared at it in disbelief; she couldn't imagine any Polish citizen had tasted butter since the start of the war. There was cheese, too, and a small platter of cold sausages. Yona hadn't eaten since the day before, but the food, the utter bounty of it, made her stomach turn. She began to push the bread away, but then she saw Jüttner's expression, and instead she picked it up and took a small bite, which earned her a nod of approval.

"Thank you," she said once she'd swallowed, though the words tasted as bitter as the bread.

"You're welcome." Jüttner's eyes slid away. "I thought you might try to leave during the night."

Yona bit her lip before she could ask if that was why he'd locked her in her room like a prisoner.

"You see, Inge," he said, his eyes returning to her. There was something softer there now, something more familiar. "It would have broken me."

She felt a surge of pity for him, but she wouldn't forget who he was, what he had become. "I am still here."

He bowed his head. "You cannot go. I haven't been whole since . . ." He paused and then stood abruptly, busying himself with carrying his plate and cup over to the kitchen counter. "It would be a humiliation." He cleared his throat a few times, his back to her, and then he was silent.

"The nuns," she said after a few minutes had passed. "Please. Will you take me to them?"

He wiped at his eyes before turning around. "We'll leave in

five minutes. Finish your bread, Inge." He brushed crumbs from the corner of his mouth and smiled. "There are people starving out there."

In the bright light of morning, the quarter where Jüttner lived was both beautiful and eerily deserted. As they walked in silence toward the church square on the north side of town, their footsteps were a conspicuous *tap-tap* on the stone, and Yona imagined people peering through slits in the curtains of the windows above, wondering who she was, what she was doing with a Nazi commander. They would assume she was like him. They wouldn't know she was only here to save the women in the church.

But it was more than that, wasn't it? She was also rooted in place by the familiarity of Jüttner's face. He was a part of her, even if she abhorred the role he was playing in this war. Yona had never known what it felt like to be part of a family, and here was a man who, despite all his enormous flaws, had once loved her. Perhaps he still did. But was craving that love, even in part, a silent acquiescence to the choices he had made? Or was it simply human nature? And if that was it, how would she ever turn those feelings off? She couldn't stay forever, but once she departed, she'd be alone again, and in the process, she might be breaking her father's heart anew. Did she bear responsibility for the pain that would inevitably come?

"Be careful there," Jüttner murmured, touching her arm to help steer her around a puddle in the street. It was only as she passed that she realized the water was pink with stale blood and that there were bloodstains on the sidewalk and against the base of the storefront to her right, a butcher's shop that had been boarded up and abandoned. Her stomach turned, and she pulled away from Jüttner, hating herself for being warmed, even in part, by his concern for her. People had been murdered here, and recently—she could still smell the metallic scent of death.

"No need to run, Inge," Jüttner said, a smile in his voice as he quickened his pace to keep up with her. But she couldn't even look at him, couldn't acknowledge the lighthearted admonition, for there was, in fact, every reason to run, to fly into the woods as quickly as her feet would take her, without looking back.

The church was guarded by two soldiers, who straightened to attention and gave Jüttner the flat-palmed salute of the Germans, their hands tilted downward as if shielding their faces from God. He saluted back and led Yona past them and into the church. She could feel their eyes burning a hole in her back until the church door swung slowly, heavily, closed behind her, shutting out the sunshine.

It took a split second for Yona's eyes to adjust to the church's dim light, and another split second to register that all eight of the nuns were lined up on the altar, all of them still alive, all of them seated with their hands bound behind them. She exhaled audibly, and the Nazi officer from yesterday, who was standing beside them, glared at her before saluting Jüttner, who saluted back.

"See?" Jüttner said proudly, nudging Yona as they strode down the aisle toward the prisoners. She recoiled from his touch, but he didn't seem to notice. "What did I tell you? They're perfectly fine."

Yona nodded, but she couldn't bring herself to speak. In any case, Jüttner was wrong. Though the nuns were still alive, which was a great relief, they looked terrified, all except for Sister Maria Andrzeja, who was sporting a black eye and a gash on her cheek, and who looked angry and resolute. As Yona moved toward her, the Nazi officer made a move to stop her, but Jüttner held up his hand.

"No, let her approach, Schneider," he said. "She feels a fondness for them."

The other man's eyes narrowed and then flicked from Jüttner to Yona and back. "I don't understand."

"You don't need to," Jüttner said. "She will speak with the nuns now. It is my order."

The man glowered at her but stepped aside and began to speak in low tones with Jüttner as Yona reached Sister Maria Andrzeja's side. The other nuns scooted aside a bit to allow Yona room to squat there.

Neither Yona nor Sister Maria Andrzeja said anything for the first few seconds. The nun searched Yona's eyes, as if trying to answer a question, before finally saying in a hoarse whisper, "You are the daughter of a German commander?"

Yona bowed her head. "By blood only."

Again there was silence between them. Behind her, Yona could hear the low, angry murmurs of Jüttner and the other Nazi officer.

"You should have told me," Sister Maria Andrzeja said at last, and Yona looked up, relieved to find that some of the nun's anger and suspicion had faded, though the confusion remained. "Why didn't you?"

"I didn't know it myself."

The bafflement in the nun's expression deepened. "What do you mean?"

"I was stolen from my parents when I was just a baby."

After a few seconds, she nodded, accepting this. "But then why are you here now? In this church?"

"I needed to know that all of you were safe. I needed to know what happened. I—I want to help you."

The other nuns were watching her, some with suspicion, some with pity and sadness. Sister Maria Andrzeja didn't say anything.

"Is it true?" Yona asked after a moment. "The German officer said on the steps that you offered your lives in exchange for the hundred townspeople they planned to execute."

Sister Maria Andrzeja didn't say anything for a long time. When she finally looked back up at Yona, her eyes were so full of despair that Yona felt the air knocked out of her own lungs. "We've been praying about this, all eight of us, for a long while now," the nun said softly. "Praying for the safety of the town. Praying that the Germans would let us live in peace. First, they came for the Jews, and we did little to stop them. And then, last year, they executed sixty townspeople for no reason at all, among them the two pastors of the church on the other side of town, which is now closed. Since then, the town has been holding its breath, waiting. But in the silence, God spoke to us."

"But to sacrifice yourselves . . ."

"This is the only answer. We will save innocent lives. And the Germans will feel that they've gotten a prize, because surely it will frighten the town to see eight nuns in their habits murdered right in front of them." When the nun looked up and met Yona's gaze, her eyes were gleaming with purpose. She lowered her voice to a fierce whisper. "But we also believe this might light a fire of resistance. The Germans don't believe that Poles and Belorussians have it within them to fight back. But we do, you see. All of us do. Perhaps our deaths will inspire a change, will force people to ask God themselves what their role is."

"But then won't more people die?"

The nun's eyes filled with tears. "People will die either way. I am hopeful, though, that fewer of those deaths will be in vain."

Yona touched Sister Maria Andrzeja's arm. "There must be another way."

"There is not. We came here to help the people in this town, to help save as many as we could, to remind them that God always loves them. God has finally given us an answer about the role we are meant to play in all of this. The Nazis need someone to make an example of. Who better than us, if our eight lives can spare a hundred? It is the path God has given us."

"But . . ."

"Remember, Yona? Whoever saves a life, it is considered as if he saved an entire world."

Yona sat back on her heels and stared, first at Sister Maria Andrzeja, then at the others. She could see the determination in their eyes, but there was fear there, too. "I won't let it happen," Yona said. "What if God sent me here to save you?"

Sister Maria Andrzeja waited until Yona looked back and met her gaze. "Or perhaps *we* are meant to save *you* by reminding you of your goodness, of your responsibility to your fellow man."

"But—"

"We accept our fate. All of us. You must do the same." A single tear rolled down the nun's cheek, disappearing into the wound that stretched from her nose to her ear. "Never forget, Yona, God is your father, and he is always with you."

Yona's own eyes filled, too. She didn't say anything. Jerusza had always taught her that the forest was her parent, both mother and father, and what was the forest but God's creation, anyhow? Perhaps even when Yona had felt most alone, she'd always been surrounded by a father who loved her just as she was.

"And the little girl?" Sister Maria Andrzeja asked after a moment, lowering her voice to a whisper. "She is safe?"

"She is."

Sister Maria Andrzeja closed her eyes briefly. "Praise God." She turned her gaze back to Yona. "Thank you, Yona. You have been brave and kind, but it's time now for you to go. Leave us to our fate. We all accept it."

Yona glanced at the other nuns. Some were watching her, some had their eyes closed and appeared to be praying. "But you mustn't give up. I will do all I can to help. I will talk to Jüttner. My . . . my father."

The nun's smile was sad, and she didn't meet Yona's gaze. "False hope is dangerous, Yona. They cannot release us now. Remember, a trade was made. Our lives for a hundred. If the Germans allow us to live, someone will have to pay."

"There must be a—"

"Inge!" Jüttner's impatient voice boomed from behind her, and she turned to find Jüttner watching her. The other officer had stepped away and was halfway down the aisle, his stiff back turned to them, his hands balled into fists.

"Shall we go now?" he asked Yona, his tone almost jaunty, as if he'd entirely forgotten that there were eight hostages nearby.

Yona glanced back once more at Sister Maria Andrzeja, but the nun's eyes were closed, her lips moving, and somehow, Yona

knew the nun was praying for her, which was wrong, unde-
served.

"Come on, then," Jüttner said with a sharp edge of impatience, and before Yona could reply, his hand was on her arm
and he was leading her away.

"Yes, good day, *German daughter*," the other officer said as
they passed, and Yona could hear the sarcasm lacing his words,
the annoyance. Jüttner nodded at the other officer, who nodded
back, and then pulled Yona with him out into the sunshine outside the church.

"Can't you order their release?" Yona asked as she and Jüttner
walked home from the church.

"It isn't that simple." He didn't look at her.

She thought of what Sister Maria Andrzeja had said. "Because you would have to execute a hundred townspeople if you
released them," she said flatly.

He nodded slowly. "It was the nuns themselves who came to
us with this bargain. You are trying to save people who do not
want to be saved."

"We all want to be saved."

He glanced at her. "Some must sacrifice for the greater
good."

Yona swallowed the lump in her throat. "So you intend to
kill them after all?"

"I know this matters to you. But I don't know what to do."
He looked down at her as they turned a corner. The circles be-

neath his eyes were pronounced, his forehead creased with fatigue. "You must understand that I am merely a cog in a wheel, Inge."

"But you're in charge here. Surely you can do something. Surely you can—"

"Enough!" His voice was low, but she could hear the fury in his tone, the frustration. "You know nothing about it. You think I want to be living in a godforsaken Polish town on the edge of nowhere? You think I wouldn't prefer to be in Berlin? No, Inge, I am here for a reason, and I can't let myself become distracted. If I let myself forget, I will fail. And that is not an option. We have work that needs to be done, and soon, but first the villages must be controlled. And that means people must know the consequences of undermining us."

"Why *are* you here?" Yona asked as they turned another corner. They were near Jüttner's home now, but at the end of the long avenue, the forest loomed in the distance. As Jüttner looked directly at it now, and then quickly away, as if he hadn't meant to let his eyes travel there, Yona understood in a sharp instant of clarity. They were here for the Russian partisans—and the Jews—hidden in the trees. Suddenly, she couldn't breathe. "The woods," she managed to say.

His expression hardened. "There are people out there making trouble for us, blowing up our railway lines, killing our men. And what are they? Russian deserters and Jews who ran like cowards from their fate. They don't deserve to live."

Yona felt her blood run cold as ice, and she shivered. "Who are you to decide that?"

He stopped walking and whirled to face her. His eyes traveled over her, peeling back layers like those of an onion. "That's where you were before you came here, isn't it? With one of those groups?"

Yona didn't say anything, and after a moment, he grabbed her arm and squeezed so tightly that she yelped in pain and surprise.

"Jews or Russians?" he hissed. When she still didn't answer, he shook her, hard, and she could feel his eyes burning into her. "*Jews or Russians?*"

Still she stayed silent, and after a few more seconds, he dropped her arm with a sneer of disgust. "Jews, I'm guessing. The Russians use their whores up and discard them."

She bit her lip so hard she could taste blood.

"Well, you're here now." He was trying to console himself. "Perhaps you had no choice when you were all alone, but now you are with me. And certainly you know that the Jews are lazy and conniving. They're a drain on all of us. If you feel sympathy for them, you have been conned."

"No, *you* have." She finally found her voice. "You've been brainwashed, and you're too foolish to see it."

His face turned red, and his whole body seemed to stiffen. "How dare you." His voice was flat, emotionless, but she could feel the anger rolling from him in waves as he grabbed her arm and began walking again, pulling her with him. She stumbled a bit, but he didn't slow his pace; he merely tightened his grip. They were silent as they turned onto his street and as he nodded at the soldier outside his house. Neither of them spoke again until they were both inside, the door closed behind them.

"You will never speak to me that way again," he said, his tone lower now, deadly.

"When?" she asked softly, ignoring his words, though they made her feel as if she'd been plunged into the Neman River in the dead of winter. "When are you coming for them?" In her mind's eye, she could see Ruth and her three small children, Oscher with his limp, Chaim's young sons. She could see all of them, one by one. But the face that lingered was that of Zus. *Stay, Yona*, he had said, his eyes boring into hers as he touched her face. *Please. We need you.*

"You aren't thinking of going back?" Jüttner's eyebrows were raised so high that they nearly disappeared into his hairline. He sputtered a laugh of mocking disbelief. "No, no one would be that foolish."

She refused to react. "*When?*" she repeated.

He flexed his jaw, and then, he smiled slightly. "Two weeks from today."

"Please, don't." She hated that her voice shook, that it sounded so desperate. "Please stop it." He didn't say anything, and after a few seconds, she added, "Please, Father. *Papa*."

It hurt her to call him that, but she could see the reaction it elicited. He flinched as if she'd hit him, and she knew the word had made a difference. He sighed, and at last he met her gaze. "It has nothing to do with me, Inge. The woods are full of Russian partisans who wish to destroy us. They are our first target. There is also a man named Bielski in the woods. A Jew, a swine from Stankiewicze. He has taken hundreds of Jews into the Nalibocka, and they work to damage the German train lines, the German transports. You see why we have no choice? Why we must strike back? There's another group of Jews, too, under a man named Zorin, and they do the same. These are not innocents, Yona. They are fighting against us. This is war."

"They are only trying to survive," she protested, ashamed of the flicker of selfish hope that went through her when she realized he was targeting the larger groups, groups whose location she didn't know.

"But they have no right to survival, Inge," he said after a long pause.

"Who are you to decide such a thing?" she demanded.

Before he could say another word, she was running for the stairs, desperate to put distance between them. Her mind was spinning. She had to warn Zus, Aleksander, and the others that the Germans were coming. She had to find a way to get to the Zorin and Bielski groups, too, to tell them to be ready. But how could she leave the nuns? They would be executed the moment she left. How could she put one life above another? Who was *she* to choose?

She refused to join Jüttner for dinner that night, and she cried herself to sleep, safe in a warm room granted by the enemy, as an inevitable darkness moved in across the night sky, inching closer and closer to everyone she cared about, blotting out the stars.

CHAPTER TWENTY

Jüttner refused to take Yona to the church the next morning, but when he returned that evening, just as twilight was settling over the town, his first words to her were a promise that the nuns were still safe.

"I spoke with your Sister Maria Andrzeja myself today," he said stiffly. "She asked me to tell you she's praying for you."

Yona couldn't imagine the two of them having a conversation, and she wondered what had prompted Jüttner to speak to the nun himself. "Thank you." It was hard to force the words out, to express gratitude for anything at all.

He sat down in the parlor and gestured for her to do the same. She settled across from him, her stomach swimming. He sounded lighter today, more cheerful. It made her uneasy. "I've come up with a solution, I think." He was beaming at her proudly when she finally dared look at him.

"A solution?"

"The nuns will be taken to the woods. There will be guns fired, eight shots. And then they will be taken in a truck to another part of Poland, far from here. They will be ordered not to return, or they'll be shot on sight. No one in town would need to know that a punishment has not been handed down."

Yona stared at him. "You would spare them?"

"On two conditions. When I leave for the forest the week after next, you will return to my home in Berlin, where you belong. I have already arranged transport for you." He waited for her to reply, but when she didn't, he went on. "The second condition is that you will tell me where the Jews are hiding. You will direct me to the Bielski camp."

"I have never seen that group," she answered honestly.

"Don't lie to me, Inge. I am trying to help you."

"It's not a lie."

"Then who were you with? The Zorin group?" His voice was rising.

"No. I was alone." Was it really a lie? After all, even when she'd been with the group, she'd been on the outside looking in, no matter what she told herself. "But there's a group in the western part of the Nalibocka, just south of the big road that crosses the river. I saw them."

It was a part of the forest where she was almost certain no one was hiding, for she had traversed it just the week before, and there had been no signs of human life. It wouldn't have been a logical spot to hide, either; the trees were younger, thinner there; there were fewer animals to snare, fewer streams to fish, fewer places to hide. But certainly Jüttner knew none of that.

Still, he narrowed his eyes at her after a moment. "You're lying."

"I'm trying to save the nuns," she hissed. "We are making a deal, right?" She took a deep breath and channeled Jerusza, inventing details to sell her story. "You think I feel good about betraying people who haven't done anything wrong? But there are at least thirty people hiding there, in tents made of marsh grass. At least some of them are armed; I could hear them hunting deer when I passed by."

After a few long seconds, his expression cleared. "Good. I'm glad you're seeing things my way. You've done the right thing."

"Have I?"

He frowned. "I understand that this, what lies between you and me, is very fragile right now. I am trying, Inge. I will keep your nuns safe."

The words sat between them, and Yona's throat felt dry. Emotion rolled over her in waves: relief for the nuns, guilt for the fact that she'd leave as soon as the nuns were safe, for she needed to warn the group in the forest. She was taking something of value from Jüttner under false pretenses, and she knew it. "Schneider agreed to this?"

"I have organized this without his knowledge. As far as he is concerned, they will be dead in two days' time."

"He won't insist on carrying out the executions himself?"

"As you pointed out, he takes orders from me." Jüttner was silent for a moment before clearing his throat. "I hope you realize I am making an attempt to give you what you want."

She swallowed the lump in her throat. "I know you are."

"I realize you think I'm cruel. But I hope that once you get to know me again, you will realize that I am only doing what I need to."

To Yona's surprise, the words brought some comfort, for she, too, had things she needed to do, things that would hurt him. "I know you believe that."

Later, over a dinner of hearty veal-head soup, prepared by Jüttner's silent Belorussian housekeeper, Yona blurted out the question that had been gnawing at her for days. "How do you live with it all?"

Jüttner paused, his spoon halfway to his mouth. His hand shook as he lowered it back down to the bowl. He took his time wiping his mouth on his cloth napkin before asking, "Live with what?"

"The things you've done. The deaths you've been responsible for?"

His eyes narrowed, and color rose in his cheeks. For a moment, she feared that she'd gone too far. But his shoulders slumped, and he shook his head. "Frankly, I have not yet figured out how to do that, Inge."

"So why do you continue?" she pressed after a few seconds. The clock in the foyer ticked loudly in the silence, reminding her that time was running out: for her, for the groups in the forest, for the nuns. She would have to leave as soon as the sisters were safe. "Why don't you abandon your post and try to redeem yourself?"

His laugh was sad and empty. "It isn't that simple. Don't you see? If I abandon my post, as you suggest, I'll be arrested and executed as a traitor. Is that what you want for me?"

"Of course not." She stared at him, surprised by how emphatic her answer felt. He might have been a terrible man, but she didn't want to see him dead.

"Then you see that I have no choice."

They ate in silence, Yona taking only small tastes of the soup to be polite, for once again, she'd lost her appetite. "Is it my fault that this is who you've become? Did the theft of your child, and the death of your wife, turn you into this?"

He blinked at her a few times. "I don't understand what you're asking."

But Yona could see in his eyes that he did. Might he have turned the other way, to goodness, if he'd known the unconditional love of a child? If he and his wife had grown old together? Had Jerusza herself shaped his fate, and that of everyone who died at his hand, with her decision to steal Yona long ago? Or if Jüttner had become someone different, would it merely have been another man in his jackboots doling out death? The answers were terrible and unknowable. "I'm very sorry," she said softly.

He cleared his throat. "You have nothing to apologize for. You were a victim, as was I." He paused to take another bite, and for a moment, though the space between them was filled with sadness and regret, there was a sliver of understanding there, too, a bridge connecting them at long last.

That night, Yona dreamed of the forest, but instead of clear, burbling water, the familiar streams ran red with blood. In the middle of the night, she awoke in a sweat, certain she'd heard gunshots, a sharp series of *crack-crack*s in the distance, but when she sat up in bed, she realized it had been merely a dream. She went to the window and opened it to let the cool night air in, peering out at the alley below. Overhead, the sky was dusted with stars, and a full moon bathed the rooftops. She listened, the silence convincing her once and for all that the sounds hadn't been real. Still, when she lay back down again, sleep eluded her for hours.

She awoke late, still groggy from her restless night, and when she descended to the kitchen, she found Jüttner already gone, the maid, Marya, scrubbing the dishes.

"Good morning." Yona greeted the maid in Belorussian. She guessed it was the language the woman spoke, though she'd never heard her say a word. "Is Jüttner here?"

Marya turned, her eyebrows raised. "Your *father*?" she asked in Belorussian, her voice dripping with barely concealed hatred. "Yes, he's gone. You had a leisurely sleep, I see. How nice for you."

Yona wanted to protest that Jüttner wasn't her father, not really. That she wasn't accountable for his sins. But she was sleeping under the roof of a Nazi commander and eating the food his position provided. "I'm not him," she murmured.

Marya regarded her suspiciously. "And why do you speak our language, then? You are German, no?"

"I was not raised there."

"Yes, I've heard. Your father's vanished girl. And how have you come to be here now?" Suspicion glinted in her eyes. "At this moment? In this town? It is all very suspicious."

Yona thought of Sister Maria Andrzeja's words. "Perhaps it was God's plan."

The maid snorted, but she didn't say anything more.

"Was this your home?" Yona asked after a moment. "Before the Germans came?"

"No." Marya paused, as if considering how much to tell Yona. "But I worked for the people who lived here."

"What happened to them?"

Now there was something else in her eyes: rage. "The father, shot in the street. The mother and children, shot in their beds.

The youngest was just four. Russian sympathizers, the Germans said. You tell me how a four-year-old can be a Russian sympathizer, hmm?"

Yona put a hand over her mouth. "The room I've been sleeping in . . ."

"The teenage daughter. Czesława. She died right where you've slept." Marya crossed her arms over her chest, looking both smug and devastated. "The snow globe on your nightstand? The beautiful one with the forest and the snow? She used to look at it every night and dream of a future far away. And now, because of people like your father, she is dead, buried in the dirt here. She never even left the town where she was born."

Yona quickly crossed the kitchen and retched into the sink. When she straightened, the maid was still staring at her. "I'm sorry," Yona said.

The maid just grunted. "That does not bring them back, *Fräulein* Inge."

Her given name coming from Marya's mouth sounded strange and wrong, even worse than when it was uttered by Jüttner, who had at least known her as something else a lifetime ago. "It's Yona," she said softly. "My name is Yona now."

Marya scowled. "You think you can escape who you were born to be? None of us can. Can't you see that?" She turned away without another word and swept out of the room, leaving Yona alone, the taste of bile and regret in her mouth.

She dressed quickly, once again donning the dead girl's clothes. Her own things were neatly folded in the corner; Marya had laundered her dress, her shirt, her trousers, her underthings, even mended the holes in her socks. They seemed to taunt her now, reminding her that this was no time to play dress-up, but it had to be. If she could just keep the ruse of being a dutiful daughter going a little longer, she could save everyone. Wasn't it foolish not to try?

She was relieved not to see Marya as she slipped downstairs again, but the relief faded when she peered out the front door and saw two soldiers outside, both of whom turned to stare with curiosity until she'd closed the door once more.

It took her a full minute to realize that if there were two soldiers out front, one of them might be the one who was supposed to be guarding the alley. Quickly, she flew across the house and flung open the back door. She looked left and right and saw not another soul. Without hesitation, she slipped into the alley, closing the door softly behind her, and then, hugging the shadows, she walked quickly to the end of the block, where a glance told her that the street was deserted. She didn't wait another second before breaking into a run, putting as much distance between herself and Jüttner's stolen home as she could.

She slowed to a brisk walk on the main street, so as not to arouse suspicion. What was her plan here? She slowed slightly as she neared the church. She would go to one of the stained glass windows near the altar and peer in; there was a side door to the church with a particularly translucent pane, the flesh tones of Jesus's mother. If she pressed her face against the glass, she should be able to see inside, though the view would be hazy. It would be enough, though, to count eight nuns, seated and alive. She would then rush back to Jüttner's home before he discovered her missing, and there she would agonize about her next move. She would need to be ready to flee to the forest the moment the nuns were safe.

Just before she rounded the corner into the small square out-side the church, she heard raised voices and froze. It took her a few beats to recognize one of them as Jüttner's, his words a sharp, threatening hammer of anger. She was too far away to make out what he was saying, but as she crept forward for a glimpse of the argument, hugging the shadows as she went, she could see him standing just outside the church door with a cow-ering Schneider, poking a finger at the other man's meaty nose as he yelled about something. Schneider's face was red, and he was attempting to get a word in, but Jüttner kept going, rolling furiously over him.

Yona bit her lip and slipped backward, letting the shadows swallow her. Something was wrong. Her heart pounding rap-idly, Yona hurried up the narrow street, doubled back down an alley, and crept toward the door of the church near the altar. She would just glance in, reassure herself about the nuns' safety, and then depart as quickly as she'd come.

There was no guard at the side door, which didn't surprise Yona; there hadn't been a guard posted here the last few times, either, and Yona had assumed that the door had been locked. What she didn't expect to see was an unguarded door that had been left slightly ajar. The tempo of her heartbeat quickened.

She hesitated before slipping inside, as quiet as a breeze. The church was silent and dark, and in the stillness, Yona smelled the blood and the spent bullets before she saw the bodies. She clapped a hand over her mouth as her eyes adjusted to the dim lighting. There on the altar, lined up in a neat row, lying on their backs, were seven of the eight nuns, bullet holes in their heads, their open eyes looking sightlessly up toward God. The eighth nun was just a few feet away, on her knees and slumped to her right, facing the crucifix above the altar, a bullet hole in her back. She had died in prayer, staring up at Jesus. Yona knew before she approached and gently turned the body over that it was Sister Maria Andrzeja.

The kind nun's eyes were open and empty, her lips just slightly parted. Yona could imagine her whispering to God, quickly saying her final words, even as the other gunshots rang out. Or had Sister Maria Andrzeja been the first to die?

"I'm so sorry," Yona whispered, but there was no forgiveness in the nun's lined face, no absolution in her eyes. She wasn't here anymore; her soul had already flown. The dove on Yona's wrist throbbed as Yona bent quickly to kiss the nun's cold forehead. With the palm of her hand, she gently closed Sister Maria Andrzeja's eyes and stood frozen for a few seconds. Then she straightened and put her hand over her mouth again as she looked at the seven other nuns, forever silent now. She backed away and said a quiet prayer in the darkness, then she slipped out the way she'd come and gulped the fresh air outside. She could still hear Jüttner's raised, angry voice coming from the church's front steps, and she knew this hadn't been what he'd wanted.

He had tried to stop the execution, but perhaps the end had always been inevitable. Yona had been fooling herself in believing she could make any difference.

But she could still help the group in the woods.

Jüttner had said that the plans to enter the forest were already well underway, but what if it wasn't too late to do something? *Whoever saves a life, it is considered as if he saved an entire world.* She could still hear the quote from the Talmud in Sister Maria Andrzeja's soft, gentle voice. As she turned and walked quickly away, trying her hardest to look casual and nonchalant instead of like a sobbing mess, Jüttner's voice faded behind her, and she moved away from the past forever.

She knew she would never see him again.

Twenty minutes later, Yona reentered Jüttner's house through the back door, changed into her own dress and sturdy boots, and grabbed what she could from the dead girl's closet: two pairs of shoes, a dozen socks, two sweaters, and a beautiful red wool coat that was impractically bright for the forest but would provide much-needed protection against the freezing winter. She went back out the way she came, and, wiping away tears that wouldn't stop, she strode quickly along the road leading to the farmhouse near the forest's edge, the one with the red window frames and the eagle with the clipped wing. She had to make sure Anka was safe before she left the town forever. It would bring her peace to know that amid the madness at least one life had been saved, that one of Sister Maria Andrzeja's last acts could be her legacy.

"Halt!" A voice rang out from the side of the road, and a German soldier stepped into her path, a few crumbs hanging from the corners of his narrow lips. He'd been eating as she approached, a clear dereliction of his duty, and his startlement upon seeing her was obvious. It took her only a second to register that it was the same German she'd encountered on her way back into town three days earlier, and he seemed to realize the same thing a few beats later. "Ah, it's you," he said in his smooth Belorussian. "You're after more milk for your daughter?"

She mustered an embarrassed smile, which served to hide her relief. He hadn't been there in the square that day when she announced herself to Jüttner; he didn't know that she was anything but a simple villager. "She is very hungry, sir." She bowed her head and added, "Thank you for the chocolate."

When she looked back up at him, his pale blue eyes were deep wells of despair. "It is not something to be mentioned. I wish I had more to give you."

She glanced at the remnant of his hunk of bread, lying by the side of the road, half eaten. He followed her eyes and then met her gaze, guilt with an edge of annoyance etched in the creases of his face. "I'm hungry, too, you see."

He looked perfectly well-fed, and though she appreciated his kindness with the chocolate, she saw it now for what it was: a way for him to sleep at night, to pretend to himself he'd made a difference. "I'm sorry to ask again, sir," she said, coating her words with honey so he wouldn't hear the venom or the sadness. "But might I pass? I just need to feed my child."

He frowned down at her. "You have money this time? For the milk?"

She hesitated. "A bit."

He licked his lips, catching the crumbs. For a moment, she thought he was going to demand that she produce the cash, which of course she couldn't do, because there was none. Instead, he merely nodded and stepped aside. "I'll see you when you come back this way."

She nodded. "I might be a while. You see, I don't have much, and I will need to bargain with the farmers."

He nodded and raised his eyebrows, his mouth twisting into a knowing smirk. He looked her up and down, appraising her, no doubt wondering what else she might have to trade. She hated him for the implication.

"I see," he said, now openly leering at her.

She forced a blank smile. "I'll see you in a few hours."

"I'll be waiting." His step was jauntier now as he turned his back on her and returned to his bread.

She walked for a half hour, just to make sure she wasn't being followed, before finally approaching the white farmhouse with the red shutters, silent on the far edge of town. There was a dog in the yard, skin and bones, which was probably the only reason he hadn't yet been killed for meat. He lifted his head as Yona approached, his eyes watery and baleful. She pulled her gaze away and knocked lightly on the front door.

There was no answer, so she knocked again, more loudly this time. Perhaps Maja was merely being cautious, but when Yona peered in the window, the room inside looked still, untouched, particles of dust dancing in the stale air. She swallowed the fear rising in her throat and backed away, heading for the barn and the trapdoor in its floor.

Yona was running by the time she reached the rambling structure on the edge of the property, and as she slipped in, she was terrified that she'd see Maja and Anka splayed out on the hay, a mirror of the scene at the church. But as her eyes adjusted to the darkness, she breathed a sigh of relief. There were no bodies, no blood, no tinny smell in the air. There was only silence.

Quickly, she went from stall to stall, pushing aside hay in the deserted spaces until she found a small square in the barn floor. It was the trapdoor. She used the edge of a shovel to pry it open before sweeping over her tracks in the sawdust so if anyone else came looking, they wouldn't be able to follow her footprints. She lowered herself into the hole and pulled the door closed above her, plunging the space into blackness.

She felt her way along the wall in silence, walking in the pitch dark. She had assumed that the trapdoor led to a hidden room, but instead, it seemed to be a narrow tunnel that went on and on. Her tension rose as she walked farther along without the benefit of sight. Where was this invisible path taking her?

She was just about to turn back when she stumbled against something heavy and warm.

"Oof," said a high voice in the silence, and Yona began to back away.

"Who's there?" came a more confident voice, and in the blackness, a match flared, illuminating the shining, defiant face of Maja Yarashuk, who was standing protectively over a crouching Anka. The child was who Yona must have run into. She seemed to recognize Yona at the same moment Yona recognized her, and they both sighed in relief. "What are you doing here?" Maja asked. She reached into her pocket and pulled out a piece of pine bark, which she lit. In a few seconds, it was bright enough to see down the length of the tunnel, which seemed to dead-end several hundred yards away. "You should not have come."

She glanced down at Anka, who was watching her with bright, frightened eyes. There was no need for the girl to know what had befallen the nuns, so Yona stepped closer to Maja and quickly whispered their fate. "I needed to warn you," she concluded, and Maja nodded once, then looked down at Anka with concern.

"Thank you. But I think we are safe here for now. I moved her into the tunnel last night; my contact should be coming this evening to take her to another village."

"And you?" Yona asked.

"I will stay here. There is more work to be done."

"But if the Germans find out about you . . ."

"Then I will see my husband again sooner than I'd planned. I accept my fate. But you must go now. Surely you are no longer safe in the village if you were seen with the nuns."

Yona looked away. Maja didn't know the half of it. "I must go back to the Nalibocka Forest. There is a retaliation planned against some of the groups there. I need to warn them." She looked back to see Maja and Anka staring at her with wide eyes.

"It will be dangerous," Maja said. "I could send you along with Anka instead, help you to disappear."

Yona shook her head. "This is something I need to do."

"I understand." Maja nodded toward the far end of the tunnel. "Walk that way until the tunnel ends. There is a door above that opens into the woods."

Yona stared at her. "A door that opens into the woods?"

"It is how we move the children in and out without being seen. My husband, he built it during the last war. One day the Germans will find it, and I will be done for. But I don't think it will be today. Now go, carefully. Once you emerge into the woods, head north for an hour, and then to the east. You will eventually find yourself back in the Nalibocka."

"And Anka?"

"She will be taken the other way. She will be safe."

Yona bent to the little girl, who had been watching the exchange with wide eyes. "How are you feeling, Anka?" she asked.

"Better." Indeed, her cheeks were brighter, her voice stronger. "Where is Sister Maria Andrzeja?"

"She is not here," Yona said gently. "But she is here." She tapped the little girl's chest on the left side, just over her heart.

Anka accepted this in silence. "Like my mother and father," she said after a moment.

Yona could only nod.

"Then I will be safe." Still, the little girl looked uncertain.

Yona took Anka's hands and held them tight. "With so many people watching over you, how could you not be?"

The girl smiled a small smile, and then Maja tapped Yona on the shoulder and nodded toward the end of the tunnel. "Go," she said. "Godspeed."

"And to you," Yona said. She didn't look back as she hurried down the length of the tunnel, climbed up the ladder that hung there, and emerged into a dense cluster of trees. Then she ran for the Nalibocka, her feet already carrying her toward the only home she'd ever truly known.

CHAPTER TWENTY-ONE

The forest absorbed Yona quickly, ingesting her into its darkness. But as she moved deeper into the trees, moving east as quickly as her legs could take her, she didn't feel comforted by the familiarity. She felt sick. The nuns were dead. She hadn't been able to stop it. And she hadn't done a thing to avenge their deaths. But vengeance would only taste sweet for a second, and then it would be a permanent stain on her soul. No, she was doing the most important thing she could: fleeing to warn Aleksander, Zus, and the others. But could she find them in time? It felt already as if precious minutes were slipping away like sand in an hourglass.

Yona stopped often, breathing into the stillness, waiting for approaching footsteps that never came. She had to be certain she wasn't being tracked, that she wasn't leading the Germans straight to their quarry. She walked on leaves and grass and strode through streams so her footsteps would vanish. And though grief weighed her down—she couldn't take a step without seeing Sister Maria Andrzeja's empty eyes—she also felt lighter, untethered at last from a past that had always been an invisible weight. She was not Jerusza's—she never had been, and she knew that now. But neither was she her German father's. She belonged only to herself, a dove of the dark forest, the forest that called to her now.

She walked for three days, pausing for only a few hours here and there to sleep in the hollows of fallen trees when the sun crested the sky. She ate berries and leaves, caught fish in the streams, picked green-capped russula mushrooms, and slowly felt like herself again as she put distance between herself and the carnage. By the second day, she found herself talking to Sister Maria Andrzeja, apologizing at first and then pleading for guidance, for some sign of a way forward. But the nun never replied. Jerusza had remained after she died, whispering from time to time in the wind, but the nun's soul was already far away. By the third day, Yona began to talk directly to God, asking why he would let such terrible things happen to his earth. Couldn't he hear them?

But it was Jerusza's voice in the breeze answering the question. *The universe is always in balance*, she said. *Summer and winter. Day and night. Sustenance and poison. Good and evil. To know the light, you must also know the darkness.*

"I've seen too much darkness!" Yona answered in an angry whisper, the wind carrying her words skyward. "We all have! When will it end, Jerusza?"

There was no reply.

She knew she was getting close to a group on the move when she found several bushes picked entirely clean of their bilberries, and three spruce trees stripped of their bark. There were burned logs and dace bones in a clearing, and as she bent to inspect them, she knew they'd been discarded no more than a day before. Judging from the number of fish bones, it was a group the size of the one she'd left behind, and this was in the same part of the forest she'd left them in a month earlier. She felt a surge of hope. Had she found them so easily? But there was fear there, too, for in discarding the bones instead of burying them, in leaving the traces of a fire and a meal behind, they had drawn a map for their hunters. Yona's pulse pounded; she needed to make them disappear.

It wasn't until she had walked another half day that it hit her; when she found the group, she would have to face Aleksander for the first time since she'd fled. It was enough to make her stumble, nearly fall, though the ground beneath her was flat and even. She caught her balance on a sapling, her lungs constricting. She hadn't thought of him much at all in the last few weeks, but distraction wasn't an impenetrable dam.

She forced herself to begin moving again. It didn't matter, did it? There was nothing he could do to wound her more than she'd already been wounded. *It's the cracks in us that make us who we are*, Zus had said, and perhaps he'd been right. When a linden tree broke, it often grew back, stronger and more beautiful in its damaged places. What if the same was true for man?

And so it was Zus's deep voice in her ear, not Aleksander's, when she finally found footprints that had been made within the last hour—a man's footprints, alone, the path curving into a wide arc. It was almost certainly one of the group's patrols, and if Yona had found them simply by walking east, they would be far too easy to find when the Germans came. She closed her eyes briefly and then snapped them open again, because the image she saw in her mind's eye was one of carnage.

Just then, she heard footsteps, and hastily she slipped behind a tree. Within a minute, she could make out a man's broad-shouldered form approaching from the darkness. A few seconds later, her heart lurched. It was Zus, his brow furrowed, muttering something to himself as he walked his patrol, a rifle slung over his shoulder. She stood frozen for a few seconds, simply watching him, taking in the growth of his thick stubble, the few white hairs that had found their way into the darkness of his hair. How had she never noticed them before? And then summoning her courage, she stepped out from behind the tree, her hands up in surrender.

Zus spun on her immediately, his gun raised and aimed as easily as if it were an extension of his own body. But in a split second, suspicion changed to relief, fear turned to surprise, anger turned to something tender and sad that she couldn't quite name. When he lowered his weapon and said, "Yona," she was sure it was the most beautiful sound she'd ever heard: her own name—not the name that had been given to her years ago by strangers—spoken in a deep voice that cracked with emotion.

"Zus," she said as he strode quickly to her.

"It's really you," he said, stopping abruptly just inches away, as if he'd thought to embrace her but had changed his mind. "Yona, I was afraid you were . . ." He trailed off, his voice thick. "Thank God," he said, his voice so deep and low, it almost vanished into the breeze.

She wanted to stay in this moment forever, pinned by the familiar weight of Zus's gaze, but she couldn't. "We have to move, Zus," she said, and he blinked a few times, as if pulling himself back from somewhere far away. "The Germans," she added. "They're coming."

On the way to the group, Yona repeated what she knew about the planned infiltration of the forest, though she couldn't bring herself to explain how she was privy to such a secret. Zus accepted it without question, though, going silent for a while as he absorbed the news and what it meant for them. As they drew closer to the group's camp, he filled her in on the events of the past month, and Yona was surprised to learn that the settlement had grown by seven in the short time she'd been gone. Two complete families had arrived from a village where they'd hidden for months together in the storage area beneath a farmer's barn until the farmer was killed in a raid by the local police, who suspected him of harboring fugitives. The families had been looking for a group led by a man named Tuvia Bielski, which was rumored to be large enough to function like a small society. It was the group Jüttner had mentioned, too, the one that was hiding hundreds of Jews. Instead, the newcomers had happened upon this group, and they'd been welcomed immediately.

Zus, it seemed, had stepped into more of a leadership role in the weeks since Yona had been away. "We all feel that we owe our survival to you," Zus said, his voice deep with warmth and something stronger. "And to see Aleksander and Sulia act as they did felt like a betrayal of all of us."

The words made Yona's heart thrum with confused gratitude. "No one needed to fight my battle with Aleksander."

"There is no battle," Zus said simply. "Just a clarity about the type of man Aleksander is."

They said no more about it, and ten minutes later, as they walked into a bustling camp, her eyes filled with tears when she saw the children chasing each other around, and Zus's cousins, Israel, George, and Wenzel, their heads bent together as they knelt beside a log, grinding acorns into powder. Oscher was mending a boot, and fifteen-year-old Ester was methodically picking through a basket of berries. Little Pessia was the first to spot Yona, her face breaking into a grin.

"Yona!" she called, jumping up and racing toward her, and Yona forgot for a few seconds about the danger that had brought her here so quickly. She had thought that this was Aleksander's family, that she was the interloper, but as Pessia threw herself into Yona's arms, followed quickly by Leah, she knew that she'd been wrong to run. She belonged here, in the heart of the forest, at the heart of this family, which was hers after all.

"I'm so glad to see you," she whispered into Pessia's ear, and then she kissed Leah before straightening up to face the others. They had all emerged from huts or walked in from the forest to see what the commotion was about, and as she looked out at the small sea of smiling, familiar faces, dotted with a handful of strangers, her eyes prickled with tears of gratitude. "I'm sorry," she said, raising her voice so it carried across the clearing. "I'm so sorry I left."

"You have nothing to apologize for." Zus's deep voice came from behind her, and as she wiped away a tear, she could see a few of the women nodding. Aleksander still hadn't emerged, and Sulia hadn't, either, but Yona saw plenty of glances toward a small lean-to, just big enough for two.

"We're just glad you're home, Yona," Ruth said. She was holding Daniel, who had grown even in the month that Yona had been gone. Life had unfolded without her, and the thought of that made her heart throb with regret over what she had missed.

"I'm glad, too," Yona said, and just then, Aleksander emerged from the small structure, followed closely by Sulia, who appeared to be reaching for Aleksander's hand, though Aleksander ignored her.

"Yona?" he asked, and in his expression, she saw both relief and trepidation. "I didn't expect you to return."

Yona was surprised when the words didn't wound her. Aleksander was no one to her now, nothing more than any of the others. He was someone whose life she needed to save, just like everyone else. "Yes, well, life is full of things we don't expect, isn't it?" she said evenly, glancing at Sulia, who at least had the decency to look away. Zus cleared his throat, and Yona was certain that the sound covered a laugh.

"Yona has come with news," Zus said, and as all eyes turned to him, expectant and waiting, Yona was struck by how much attention he effortlessly commanded. Before she'd left, he'd seemed content with a secondary role, but in her absence, he had filled a void. It was more than she'd hoped for; he was a good man with solid instincts for the forest. He had kept the group safe. "Yona, you can meet the Sokolowskis in a moment, and the Gulniks, too," he continued. "They are the new families who have joined us." In the small crowd, the newcomers nodded at her. "But for now, we must listen to you."

Yona gave Zus a nod of gratitude before turning back to the group. "The Germans are moving into the forest very soon," she said without preamble, and a few of the people gasped. She saw both of Chaim's little boys look up instantly at their father, and he put his hands on their heads, as if he could protect them with his touch. "We must move. Now."

"Move where?" Sulia asked, her voice high and harsh. "We live here." Aleksander took a step away from her.

Yona took a deep breath. She had been thinking about this during her whole journey here. Where could they go that the Germans couldn't track them, wouldn't find them? "Into the vast swamp just to the west of the forest's heart." *Safe*, whispered the voice in her head, an echo from the past.

"A *swamp*?" Sulia spoke again, disgust in her tone, and this time Aleksander turned and shushed her loudly.

Yona turned to Zus, who was nodding thoughtfully. He looked up and met her gaze; she could see the agreement in his eyes. "The Germans will not think we might hide there, for it's an inhospitable environment. And they won't risk coming in after us."

"And that's where you want us to go? We'll be standing shoulder-deep in water, won't we?" Zus's cousin Israel said. "God knows what creatures will get us there."

"The leeches will not kill you," Yona said.

"I can't swim," Miriam murmured, and several others nodded.

"We will help each other," Yona said. "There are a few places in the swamp that are too deep to walk, and we will avoid them. The adults will carry the children. The strongest among us will help those who are struggling. There is an island I know of in the middle, small, but dense with trees." She thought of the time Jerusza had taken her there, the water hissing its comfort. "It is large enough for all of us to stay for a time. We can shelter there until the Germans pass."

"Who's to say they will pass us by?" one of the men asked.

"We are small," Yona said. "We are not the group they are looking for. They are searching for Russian partisans, and big groups led by men called Zorin and Bielski."

"Tuvia Bielski," one of the men from the new families said. "He owned a store in Subotniki. His is the camp we were looking for when we came into the woods."

Yona nodded, though her only knowledge of the Bielskis was what Jüttner had told her. "Do you know roughly where the Bielski camp is?"

"Yes. We stumbled upon you first, but I believe it should be a few days' walk to the south."

"But in this swamp, as you say, how will we eat?" asked one of the women from the new families.

It was Zus who stepped up beside Yona to answer. "We will bring the food we've preserved already. It's enough to get us through a few weeks, at least."

"That food is for the winter." Aleksander's voice was stiff. "That was the plan."

Zus didn't even look at him. "Now the plan has changed. We will begin again for the winter when we are safe. But first, we must survive this."

"There will likely be some food on the islands in the swamp, too, though not enough. Zus is right; we must bring what we have. But we must go now," Yona said. "The Germans have the advantage. I believe they are still a week away, but they'll cover thrice the ground we can in the same time. There's no time to waste."

Most of the group nodded their understanding as Zus spoke. "We will gather our things now and move within the hour." He leaned in, put a hand on Yona's shoulder, and added in a low voice, "May I speak with you for a moment?"

"Of course." As she followed him to the other side of the clearing, she could feel Aleksander watching her, but she didn't care as much as she thought she would. "What is it, Zus?"

His eyes were sad as he looked down at her. "I think we must try to find the Bielski group, to warn them. The Zorin group, too, if we can. Otherwise, we are as guilty as the collaborators at the forest's edge."

Yona sighed. "I was thinking the same. But it will be dangerous."

"I know. And this is the last thing I want to be saying right now, Yona, but I think we should separate. You know the forest better than any of us, so I think you should take most of the group to the swamp. And I know the area near the edges of the forest where the Bielski and Zorin groups are likely to be hiding, so I'll take a few of our people with me to warn them. It makes the most sense."

Yona nodded, her heart heavy. "We are stronger when we are together, but right now we don't need strength. We need speed, and we need to be able to disappear. And we need to make sure the other groups in the forest have time to do the same."

"Yes," Zus said. "Let's go tell everyone." But neither of them moved. After a few seconds, Zus cleared his throat. "I—I wish things were different, Yona."

"So do I." She looked up and met his gaze. "But we will both be safe. God will watch over us. He has to, doesn't he?"

Zus didn't say anything, but she could read in his eyes that he didn't entirely believe her words. She wasn't sure she believed them herself. Side by side, they walked back to the others, who murmured to each other as they approached. Zus glanced once more at Yona. "Everyone, Yona and I have spoken. The best thing to do will be to divide."

"Divide? That makes no sense," Aleksander blurted out, and several people in the group shot him looks of ice.

"Let him speak, Aleksander," said Moshe, the tailor, before turning back to Zus and nodding. "Go ahead. I know you do not suggest this lightly."

Yona glanced up at Zus, whose eyes were sad. "It's too dangerous to have the children and some of the older members of this group trying to find the Bielskis before they find safety—but we cannot ignore our responsibility to our brothers and sisters hiding out there in the forest. And one or two of us should not go alone; that would be too dangerous, too easy to be outnumbered. Yona will lead one group into the swamp; I will lead the other to find the Bielski and Zorin camps." He turned to Yona. "I will send Chaim with you." It wasn't a question. She nodded, and Zus turned and addressed his brother, who stood in the middle of the clearing. "You, Sara, and the boys will go with Yona."

Chaim nodded, and Yona smiled at Jakub and Adam, who looked uncertain, and at Sara, who met Yona's gaze with a single nod.

Yona looked around and quickly evaluated the rest of the group. "I will also take Oscher and Bina, Leon, Moshe, Ruth and the children, as well as the Sokolowskis and the Gulniks, since they both have children with them."

"Take Rosalia, too," he said. "She will help you. I'll take Aleksander and Leib, Leib's mother, my cousins, and Bernard and Lazare. Sulia should come with me, too; she's fast."

"I'll go, too," Luba said. "I'm in no rush to have leeches sucking me dry."

Yona and Zus exchanged looks. Luba was older, but she was healthy and could cover ground quickly. And an extra pair of capable hands could help the smaller group. Zus nodded.

"All right, it's decided, then," Yona said. "Now, we must move swiftly. Pack up your things, and fill your packs and your pockets with all the food you can."

"Go, everyone," Zus said, and then, putting his hand gently on Yona's arm, he steered her toward the newcomers, the Sokolowski and Gulnik families, who were still standing in place, staring at her as if she were a visitor from another planet. In fact, she must have seemed like one—a woman they'd never seen, arriving from nowhere, and ordering the camp to disband.

"Yona," Zus said as they stopped in front of the seven strangers: two men, two women, and three children. It was only then that Yona realized that one of the women was heavily pregnant. She sucked in a sharp gasp without meaning to at the sight of the woman's swollen belly and felt terrible when the woman's eyes filled with tears. Yona would protect her; she had to. But there was much danger in escorting a pregnant woman through the forest with the Germans on their tails. "This is Shimon Sokolowski and his wife, Elizaveta," Zus said, nodding to the pregnant woman. "And their son, Nachum." A wide-eyed boy of about six looked up at Yona and nodded. "And these are the Gulniks, Leonid and Masha, and their children, Sergei and Maia." Sergei was a boy of about fifteen, and Maia a dark-haired girl of four or five, her cheeks hollow with hunger but her eyes alight with what looked like determination. Yona liked her immediately and smiled at the girl first before greeting the rest of the family. "I trust Yona with my life," Zus added, "and you should, too."

Leonid looked skeptical as he studied Yona. "But she's only a girl."

"She knows the forest better than all of us combined," Zus said instantly. "I believe in her more than I believe in anyone else I know."

Yona looked up at Zus and saw tears in his eyes. He looked quickly away. "Thank you, Zus," she said softly. "I believe in you, too."

He nodded and then strode away before she could say more. She turned back to the newcomers, all of whom were studying her curiously.

"How far along are you?" Yona asked Elizaveta, who was protectively cradling her pregnant belly.

The woman's eyes were full of worry as she blinked at Yona. "I should deliver in about two months. I'm—I'm sorry. We did not mean for this to happen."

Yona reached for the other woman's hands, though her own throat was thick with concern. "Never apologize for bringing life into the world. We will make do." She smiled once more at Maia, the little girl, and then she nodded at Leonid, Shimon, and their wives. "There is work to be done. I will see you soon."

Two hours later, the camp had been packed up, and all the adults were loaded down with as many supplies as they could carry on their backs. They were leaving many things behind—fabric, extra clothing, pots, pans, cups—but the hope was that when the Germans left the forest, the group would be able to return for their things. They would leave everything in holes dug into the earth, making it harder to plunder if the Germans came upon this spot.

Shimon Sokolowski had drawn a detailed map to the location where he'd been told the Bielski group had made camp, but he had declined to join the group on the southern route; he wanted to stay with his son and his pregnant wife.

Zus approached from across the clearing and put a hand on Yona's shoulder. "Would you take a walk with me?" he asked in her ear, and she nodded. She glanced once more around the camp, where everyone was milling around, anxious, in motion. There was a frisson of excitement, of anxiety, in the air. As she turned and walked toward the woods with Zus, she could feel eyes on them, and when she turned, she saw Aleksander standing still, watching. She looked away.

"Yona," Zus began once they were alone, deep enough into the trees that no one could see them. "There is something I must say to you."

His voice caught, and when she looked up at him, she was surprised to see that he looked uneasy. Did he have doubts about the plan? "What is it, Zus?"

"I—I regretted not saying something to you before you left last month."

"Zus . . ." She opened her mouth to tell him that whatever it was could wait, that she knew she would see him again in a few days' time, once they'd reunited on the island deep in the swamp, but there was something in his gaze that stopped her.

"Yona, you see yourself through a different looking glass than we see you, perhaps because you've been alone for so long." His words fell quickly, as if he was trying to force them out before he could change his mind. "I just want you to know, in case we are separated, that I think you are extraordinary."

"Zus—"

He held up a hand to stop her, his voice deepening. "Perhaps you still love Aleksander. But I—I wish my own heart was not so broken, Yona, because if it was whole, I think I would fight for you. I would tell you that I refuse to let you go, that I will not let you disappear into that forest without me ever again. But I don't think I am capable of that, of all that comes with those kinds of feelings. And perhaps you don't want to hear these things anyhow, so I will simply tell you good luck. And I wanted you to know, in case we do not see each other again, that I think you are far more special than you seem to see."

His eyes didn't leave hers as he waited for a reply, and in the quiet between them, she could hear them both breathing heavily. "We *will* see each other again," she said at last. "We will reunite in the swamp in a few days, and then the Germans will retreat, and we will find our way back here together."

He held her gaze. "I pray to God you're right."

"May I say something, too?" She hesitated, fighting the urge to look away from him. "I don't know much about these things. But I think that broken hearts heal. I think that perhaps the only way through that kind of pain is to move forward. I think that losing people you love changes you forever, but I think that God finds a way to let the light in."

He blinked a few times and nodded. "Perhaps," he said. He hesitated for only a second more before stepping closer and kissing her once, gently, on her right cheek, his warm lips lingering there for a long time. By the time she opened her eyes, he was already walking away, back to the camp, back to the forest that lay before them.

CHAPTER TWENTY-TWO

Yona had been to the swamp only once—with Jerusza, in that strange summer of 1941—and as she walked through the forest now, deeper and deeper into the darkness, she wondered if Jerusza had taken her there because she saw this moment coming. But if she had seen the world descending into madness, why hadn't she warned Yona? Why hadn't she told her that in two years' time, she would need to help lead a group of innocent people into the forest's invisible heart to save their lives?

Yona walked ahead while the rest of her small group followed slowly behind her, Oscher doing the best he could with his limp to keep up, Bina beside him for support, Rosalia bringing up the rear several paces back, a gun over her shoulder as she silently scanned the forest. Yona was glad that Zus had suggested that Rosalia accompany Yona's group; Yona trusted her more than anyone else in the camp except for Zus himself, and she felt safer knowing that she was there. Chaim, Leonid Gulnik, and Shimon Sokolowski each carried a gun, too; the two new families had each arrived with one.

As she led the group deeper into the dark woods, Yona found herself thinking about Zus and the things she should have said before they parted ways. He had told her that she was more special than she could see, but why had she missed the opportunity to tell him the same? After all, it was Zus she had thought of during her long walk back from the village, and it was his voice, his words, that had led her home. The way he commanded the respect of the others, through his gentle compassion, was something that moved her, but she didn't know how to put it into words. Now, though, the things she'd left unsaid tugged at her heart.

After an hour or so of walking, Chaim fell into step beside Yona, his wife and boys several paces behind. They were all moving slowly northeast, deeper into the heart of the forest, navigating by the setting sun. At nightfall, Yona planned to stop and let them rest for three hours before moving again. To avoid the Germans, they would need to shelter during the day and walk at night from now on.

"My brother is a good man, you know," Chaim said gruffly after they'd walked side by side in silence for almost thirty minutes.

His words, out of the depths of his silence, startled her. "How did you know I was thinking of him?"

"I didn't." He smiled. "But I hoped you were. I believe he is thinking of you."

Yona shook her head. "He sees me as more than I am, I think."

"No. He sees you for exactly who you are. And that is very difficult for him."

"Difficult?"

Chaim scratched his jaw and paused before speaking again. "It nearly destroyed him when Shifra and Helena, his wife and daughter, died. It's not my place to tell you, Yona, but he is not able to talk about it himself yet. And I think . . . I think he would want you to know."

"What happened to them, Chaim?"

Chaim was silent for a long time, and it wasn't until Yona turned her head that she realized he was trying not to cry. "Shifra had been married to Zus since they were teenagers, for more than ten years. She was a very good woman, and Helena, their daughter, she was only four. She was intelligent. Funny. Kind. She would have grown to be a good person, like her father. He loved them both with his whole heart, and I loved them, too."

"I'm so sorry." It was all Yona could think to say, though it would never be enough. Chaim didn't seem to hear her.

"The Germans came. Zus, he had made a name for himself as someone people respected. We think that's why they targeted him, to eliminate anyone who might speak up against them, who might encourage people to resist." Chaim took a deep breath and went silent again. Their footsteps crunched over the fallen leaves, and the birdsong had gone silent, as if the forest were waiting for the remainder of the story, too.

Chaim's voice was hollow as he began to speak again. "The day they came to move us all to the ghetto, they bound Zus's hands and feet tightly, tied him to his stove so he couldn't move. They beat Shifra unconscious, right in front of him, and then shot her and little Helena while he begged for their lives. They left, laughing, saying that by the time anyone found him, he'd be dead, too, but in the meantime, he could think about how it was his fault that his family was dead. They must have thought that no one would come to save him, since the Jews had all been moved. But five days later, I was able to sneak out with a work detachment, and I made my way back to our village. I found Zus, delirious, still tied to the stove. He had stopped trying to escape; he had given up. I brought him back to the ghetto, because I couldn't abandon my own family, and I knew nowhere else to take him to nurse him back to health. His body eventually healed, but the rest of him . . ."

Yona choked on a sob as Chaim paused.

"He was whole once, Yona," Chaim said after a moment. "He laughed all the time. He loved life, but they broke him. He's broken."

"We all are," Yona murmured, but she knew now that Zus had been shattered in a different way than she had. You can't heal a heart that has been smashed to pieces; you can only move forward, doing your best to hold the shards together until they eventually form into something new.

"He cares for you, Yona," Chaim added after a few minutes. "I didn't realize it at first, maybe because he was so careful to respect the fact that you were already with Aleksander. But when you left last month, I saw some of the light go out of him. If we're fortunate enough to make it through this alive, you must promise to never leave again, not without warning. Please. We are your family now. All of us. But Zus . . . No matter what you feel for him, you must know that in a corner of his heart, something blooms for you."

Yona bowed her head. She wanted to give Chaim her word that she wouldn't leave, but she didn't know what the future would bring. All she could say was, "I care for him, too, Chaim."

He must have heard the truth of it in her voice, for he nodded, and after a while, he fell back and rejoined his family, leaving Yona to walk alone once again.

Yona's group had just begun their second evening of walking, after a long afternoon break to eat and rest, when they heard the first signs of the German incursion. She had been wondering how Zus's group was doing as she led them past an overgrown, abandoned dirt road that didn't look like it had been used in months, but now, as twilight fell, the warm evening stillness was broken by the rumble of approaching trucks. Instantly, Yona hushed her group and pulled them back behind the trees. Less than two minutes later, two large vehicles passed, each loaded with several German soldiers, each bearing a swastika flag that whipped in the wind.

"They're really here," Rosalia whispered once the trucks had disappeared into the distance. The vehicles were heading southeast, and Yona had to swallow a lump of fear in her throat before she replied. What if Zus's group was in the convoy's path? What if she had let him go straight into harm's way? She would never forgive herself.

"We're only a day or so from the swamp now," Yona said, trying to hide her fear. She looked back at Rosalia and forced a resolute smile. "We must keep moving."

Rosalia nodded, but from the way she avoided looking Yona in the eye, Yona knew the other woman doubted the plan, perhaps even doubted that there was, indeed, a swamp where Yona had said it would be.

The following evening, the group paused by a stream to drink and gather some berries. They were all exhausted and hungry; they'd been eating little so their supplies might last, for they didn't know how long they'd have to wait out the Germans, or what food might be available to them in the swamp. They were almost there; Yona felt certain of it. The ground beneath them was losing its firmness, the moss and ferns growing lusher.

Yona had just bent for a drink beside Maia, the little daughter of the Gulniks, when the first gunshots rang out, a staccato hail of them, one flying close enough to Yona that she could feel it as it passed above her head. Immediately, she flattened herself on her belly, pulling the girl down with her. Rosalia hit the ground, too, but some of the others merely looked confused; Oscher actually took a step out into the open, craning his neck as he scanned the forest curiously.

"Get down!" Yona hissed, crawling forward and tugging at his pants leg, and then at Bina's leg, too. They both looked down at her, blinking, bewildered, but after a moment, they crouched beside her, then flattened themselves on the earth, too. "Is everyone all right?"

There was a mumbled chorus of assents, a panicked glancing around to ensure that everyone was accounted for. They were, thank God, and now Yona gestured silently for the others to follow her, keeping low. There were more bullets overhead, and then a German shouting in the distance, *"Juden, Juden, kommt raus, wo immer ihr seid!"* followed by a chorus of laughter. "Jews, Jews, come out wherever you are," the German voice repeated in a singsong, and then there were more bullets whizzing around them. In that instant, Yona understood that they weren't actually being fired upon; the Germans didn't know they were there. This was merely posturing between the soldiers, an amusement. They were playacting at the sport of hunting men.

Within a minute, Yona and Rosalia had led their small group to a thatch of bushes a hundred meters from the stream. It wasn't perfect cover, but it would have to do; as they neared the swamp, the area around them was devoid of many of the trees Yona had come to rely on for concealment, giving way to saplings struggling for purchase in the soft earth.

"Where did the shots come from?" Rosalia whispered, moving beside Yona, little Maia wedged between them. Maia's eyes were squeezed shut, and she was whimpering.

"A few hundred meters away," Yona said. "We must wait and see if they move closer."

"They are going to kill us, aren't they?" Maia cried, and Yona pulled her close.

"No, they are just playing a game," she said, keeping her tone as light as possible. Rosalia met her gaze over the child's head, her eyes dark with worry and foreboding. "It is quite a stupid game, yes?" Yona added with more forced levity.

Maia took several seconds to digest this. "Mami says not to say 'stupid,'" she said at last, her voice tiny and unsure. "It's not nice."

"And your mama is right," Yona whispered. "But I think she might make an exception for these silly German boys."

Maia nodded solemnly and then buried her face in Yona's arm. Her parents, several meters away, crouched behind another bush, watching in silence. Masha, the mother, was clinging to her son Sergei's arm and crying silently.

There were more shots, but they were farther in the distance, moving away. The voices were fading, too, but there was no sense of relief. The Germans could turn back toward their hidden group at any moment. They had to stay quiet, still, hidden. Maia continued to sob softly; everyone else was silent, waiting.

"The Lord is my shepherd," Rosalia said softly after a few seconds. Maia looked up at her, and Rosalia smiled reassuringly down at the girl. "I shall lack nothing."

Yona stared at Rosalia as the other woman continued to effortlessly recite the Twenty-third Psalm. "He lays me down in green pastures; he leads me beside still waters."

Chaim was listening, too, and he chimed in, keeping his voice low, saying in unison with Rosalia, "He revives my soul. He directs me in the paths of righteousness for the sake of his name."

By the next verse, there were more people whispering, Shimon and Elizaveta Sokolowski now, too, Shimon holding their son, Nachum, and Elizaveta's hands cradling her own pregnant belly. The bullets had stopped flying; the German voices had faded away. "Though I walk in the valley of the shadow of death, I will fear no evil, for you are with me; your rod and your staff, they will comfort me." Chaim's wife and two boys were speaking the words aloud, too, and so were Oscher and Bina, Leon and Moshe. Yona joined in, as did Maia's parents and brother, as they all said, "You will prepare a table for me before my enemies; you have anointed my head with oil; my cup is full."

Ruth pulled her children close, all three of them safe and breathing, and whispered with the rest of them, "Only goodness and kindness shall follow me all the days of my life, and I shall dwell in the house of the Lord for many long years."

"Amen," whispered little Pessia, and as silence fell around them again, wrapping them in safety, the word was repeated

by each of them in turn as they all realized that they'd survived against the odds yet again. Still, they stayed just where
they were, motionless and frightened, for another hour, until the
Germans were long gone.

Late the next evening, just as the sun was sinking toward the
horizon, the group finally arrived at the edge of the swamp,
which flowed seamlessly from the more solid forest floor, the
distinction invisible to the naked eye. But as they walked, the
mud was suddenly at their ankles, sucking them down, pulling
at them, and Yona smiled in relief, even as the wet cold seeped
into her shoes. "We're here," she said, hardly believing it herself.

There was a small whoop of collective glee from the group,
and a few of them surged forward despite the muck. Yona held
her hand up to stop them. "The terrain gets deeper from here,
and soon we'll be wading through water up to our waists. We
must move with caution and stay together."

"It's a damned lake," Leonid said twenty minutes later as
they emerged from a cluster of trees, their feet already submerged. There were a few gasps as others arrived at the edge
of the swamp and saw muddy water stretching out before them,
dotted with drooping trees, tiny islands, and fallen trunks, as far
as the eye could see.

"Don't worry," Yona said, though her own heart was thudding with uncertainty. The swamp had risen since she'd last
been here, and she was no longer certain how easy it would be
to make it across. "It is not deep, and you can see there are trees
to hold on to the whole way through." She paused, her mind

spinning. "Everyone, please pull out any extra clothing you have brought with you in your packs. We must work quickly, while there's still sunlight. We will use the clothing to tie ourselves together, two or three to a group. None of us will go down."

For the next half hour, the group worked on fashioning shirts and trousers into makeshift ropes, and then Yona and Rosalia divided them into pairs or trios, giving the children enough slack in their lines so they could be hoisted upon shoulders when necessary. The leftover clothes were shoved back into packs, and the group set off.

Full dark had fallen, but the sky was clear, and a half-moon lit their way, the stars tiny pinpricks of light in a blackening sky. The children all looked up in awe, and even Leon, who at seventy was the oldest among them, sighed in contentment. "It has been many months since we've fully seen the stars," he said, and the group murmured their assent. "You can hardly make them out above the trees. They disappear deep in the forest, don't they?"

"So do we, if we're lucky," Moshe said, and a few of the others laughed.

"Yes," Leon said, tapping his chest, where once upon a time, the star of David had marked him as a lesser citizen, as a target for elimination. But the forest knew no difference when it came to race, religion, or gender; it smiled and frowned upon all of them in equal measure, sometimes providing protection, sometimes peril. "By the grace of God, may we all be vanishing stars."

Despite the chill of the mud, and the fact that there was water now, too, dragging at their calves, and then at their knees, the group made good progress for the first hour. "Do you think we'll see the others soon?" asked Bina after a while. They were all trying to be quiet, but it was hard not to talk now and then, just to remind themselves that even in the darkness, they still existed. "Perhaps they're already at the island."

"They might be," Oscher said. "If they found the Bielskis quickly, they could have made it here before we did."

"We will see." Yona hoped that the knots in her stomach were simply a fear of the unknown rather than a harbinger of approaching trouble. Jerusza had always taught her to be attuned to her own body, to the messages it gave her even before events unfolded, and now, though she was trying to explain away her rising sense of discomfort, she couldn't ignore it.

"Are we almost there?" Maia asked an hour later, her voice small and weak.

"I'm afraid not," Yona said. This wasn't the time to remind them that they would have to wade through water of varying depth for another day more before reaching the island. "But look up ahead. I think we've found some solid ground. Let's take a rest."

The group quickened their pace and found that though the ground Yona had seen was thick with mud, it appeared to be stable. It was barely large enough for all of them, and Yona cautioned them to leave their ties in place and to use the extra clothing from their packs to fasten themselves to trees and bushes, whatever they could find, so they could sleep in peace without worrying about drowning. Still, though her head throbbed and her eyes were heavy with exhaustion, Yona refused to sleep. She kept watch while the others slumbered, their clothes and hair caked with mud, their lips cracked with thirst, their bodies twitching in the throes of deep dreams.

It was dawn when she stirred them awake, urging them to

move again. Now that they were in the swamp, they no longer had to be as wary about moving in daylight; the Germans would have to wade in after them even to catch a glimpse, and Yona felt sure that wouldn't happen unless the soldiers had some indication they were here.

"Are you all right?" Rosalia murmured, coming up beside Yona as the group untied themselves from the trees and made sure the knots connecting them to each other remained secure for the trudge ahead. "You didn't sleep."

"I'm fine," Yona reassured her, but as they waded once again into the mud, Yona could feel the exhaustion in her bones, and she worried that it would blunt her instincts, make her less capable of spotting trouble ahead. She started off leading the group, but after a few hours, Chaim, who'd been walking behind her, offered to switch off for a while, and Yona gratefully accepted the reprieve.

By noon, the water was up to the middle of their chests, and all the children had been hoisted onto the shoulders of adults so they wouldn't slip beneath the muck. Yona untied herself and moved toward the back of the line, where Rosalia was supporting almost the full weight of Oscher, who was having trouble moving forward.

"We'll never make it," he moaned as the sun beat down, turning them all redder by the hour, blistering their skin. In the depths of the forest, they were shaded enough not to burn, but out here, the light ate at them, and though Yona paused the group so they could all tie clothes around their heads for protection from the sun's rays, it wasn't much relief.

"Are we almost there?" Leon whispered in the early afternoon, and Yona was startled that she hadn't realized how much he had slipped behind, how he was faltering, gasping for breath.

"Can we take another break?"

They were nearly up to their necks now, so deep that it was impossible to have any perspective on the distance to land. All they could see ahead of them were endless fallen trees, tangled vines, and marsh grass. But something was tingling in the pit of Yona's belly now, a feeling that they were close. She could hear Jerusza whispering in the breeze, *Keep going*, and she almost wanted to tell the old woman to be quiet, because they had no choice.

Instead, she moved back to walk beside Leon, and then she snaked her arm around his back and held tight, forcing him to lean into her for support, even if he was too proud to do so.

They were approaching another twilight, a few of the brightest stars already appearing overhead as the sun crept toward the horizon, when Chaim, who was still leading the group, let out a muted whoop.

Yona's head snapped up. Was it possible that they had found the island at last? She hardly believed it, but ahead of her, the single-file line of haggard refugees began to rise from the mud, footstep by footstep, until they were standing on a wide swath of solid land.

"My God, it's real?" Leon asked aloud before shooting Yona a guilty look. "It's not that I didn't believe in you."

"I hardly believed in myself," Yona admitted as the two of them took their first steps onto firm ground. Soon, all the group was on the shore of the island, which was larger than Yona remembered, and for the first time in days, she felt safe again. The Germans would not find them here. They had reached the shelter in the midst of the swamp that would give them refuge until the storm passed. "Quickly," Yona said, "let's move into the trees so we're less visible, just in case."

But as they did, her heart sank, for though their group was safe for now, the island wasn't large enough to hide a second contingent. Zus and the others hadn't made it yet.

As night fell over the island and the exhausted travelers quickly ate some of their stored provisions, settled down, and fell into a deep sleep where they lay, Yona looked up to see Chaim and Rosalia just as alert as she was, despite their exhaustion. In the moonlight, she met their worried gazes, and she knew that they were wondering, as she was, if the others were all right.

It was midnight before Yona finally drifted off, and she slept soundly until she was awoken, just before dawn, by the piercing sound of a woman's screams.

CHAPTER TWENTY-THREE

Yona sprang awake, already on her feet and clutching her knife before her eyes adjusted to the darkness. But Rosalia, who had been sleeping beside her, put a hand on her arm to still her.

"It's Elizaveta Sokolowski," she said. "Her baby is coming."

And though this should have consoled Yona—the screams hadn't been about the Germans approaching or a wild animal attacking in the night—it instead filled her with fear. "It's too early," she whispered to Rosalia, lowering her weapon. "She said her baby would not arrive for another two months."

"Yes, well, the baby seems to have its own plans," said Rosalia, her face white in the moonlight.

Together, they moved to Elizaveta's side. Her husband, Shimon, knelt beside her, weeping, and Masha had taken their son to a spot several meters away, behind a bush, so he could not see or hear his mother's distress.

"She must keep quiet," Chaim hissed in the darkness. "It is so still out here."

"I know," Yona murmured. She put her hand on Shimon's arm. "Shimon, you must help me now. You must help calm

Elizaveta," she said, and his eyes flashed with a dangerous blend of anger and fear.

"She will die out here!" There was panic in his voice. "Have I saved her only to let her perish in the wilderness?"

"No." Yona was firm. "We will keep her safe. But you must help her stay quiet or we will all die. Think of her, and think of your baby. Think of your son, Nachum."

He seemed to search Yona's eyes, and then quickly he nodded and moved to murmur in his wife's ear. She was writhing, her face red, her forehead beaded with sweat, her lips contorted in a pain Yona couldn't imagine, but she seemed to understand what her husband was telling her.

"I didn't intend for this to happen," she said to Yona, the sentence beginning as a whisper and ending in a gasp of anguish as a contraction racked her body and she fought not to cry out. "I'm sorry."

"You have nothing to apologize for," Yona said when the woman was still again. "What can I do to help you?"

Elizaveta was in no shape to be dispensing medical advice, but still, she whimpered, "Sterilize what you can, I think. That's what the midwife did when I had Nachum."

The words snapped Yona into action. She had read about childbirth, for Jerusza had insisted that her base of knowledge be broad and deep. She understood infection and the risks it would pose for both mother and child. But she couldn't let Elizaveta or her child perish simply because they were stuck in the midst of a filthy swamp. There had to be something she could do.

"Who has alcohol?" Yona called out to the camp, which had now come awake with people watching, their eyes wide with fear. No one replied, and Yona tried again. Rudimentary distilled spirits, bimber, often wound up in the camp after food missions to nearby villages—most farmers kept many bottles—and though she had always discouraged drinking in the camp because it made the senses less sharp, she knew it was still wide-spread, a way both to cope and to ensure that liquid was pu-rified. "I know you were not meant to bring it with you. But please tell me one of you disregarded my words. Please."

It was Bina who finally spoke up. "In my pack," she mur-mured. "I'm sorry. I—I have it for Oscher's pain. This trek has been difficult."

"Bina," Oscher murmured, but there was no time to discern whether he meant to offer explanation or apology, for time was of the essence.

"I need it now," Yona said, and in a few seconds, Bina had placed a bottle, half-full, in her hand. It was some sort of miracle that, after the trek through the forest and the swamp, the bottle was still intact, but Yona didn't have time to thank God for that now. She poured some of the moonshine over her own hands to sterilize them as much as possible, and soaked a portion of the rope Moshe handed her with more. She edged between Elizave-ta's open legs and saw to her horror that the baby's head was already there. Elizaveta would need to push or the baby might not be able to breathe.

"Someone give us some clean cloth!" Rosalia called, and rags and a scarf appeared from nowhere, thrust forward into the darkness. The scarf Yona gently laid beneath Elizaveta's hips the next time they rose and bucked, and the scraps of fabric she handed back to Rosalia for when the baby emerged.

Elizaveta cried out again, her voice strangled, and then, in a rush of liquid, the baby—a girl—slipped from her body and into

Yona's waiting arms, tiny and still and blue, membranes covering her silent face like a burial shroud.

"No," Yona whispered, frozen in place, unable to accept that
Elizaveta's child could be stillborn. It was Ruth who came from
behind her, her voice solid and commanding in a way none of
them had heard before from the shy mother of three.

"It's the cord," she said. "It's wrapped around the baby's
neck."

Yona saw it then, too, but Ruth was already in motion,
unwrapping the umbilical cord. Yona stared at the baby, paralyzed, before remembering that the cord was supposed to be cut.
Wasn't it? Was that why the baby wasn't moving yet? Taking a
deep breath, she reached for her knife.

"No!" Ruth cried, flinging her hand out to stop Yona. "No!
Don't cut the cord yet. It is the baby's only source of oxygen
until we can get her breathing."

Horrified, Yona dropped the knife, and for a long second,
she and Ruth just stared at the motionless baby. Then she shook
herself out of her horrified trance and reached for the tiny infant, hardly bigger than a sparrow. "Make sure Elizaveta is all
right," she said to Rosalia, and Rosalia nodded, moving away
from her and back to Elizaveta, who was whimpering, a sound
that filled Yona with relief, for it meant she was alive and alert
enough to be scared.

Yona prayed now as she tore her own shirt off and laid the
baby down on the fabric, faceup. She rubbed the baby's stomach
and chest, and then tapped on the bottom of her feet. Still nothing. Yona stopped her conversation with God as she took a deep
breath and bent to the tiny child. She would need to breathe for
her, the way Jerusza had taught her so many years before, one

in a countless number of scenarios the old woman had prepared her for, just in case. Would she remember how? Jerusza's voice whispered to her from somewhere far away as she placed her lips over the baby's mouth and nose and pushed a small burst of air into her lungs.

All around them, their small island, and the swamp in which they floated, seemed to have gone silent. The stars held their breath, the moon hid behind a cluster of clouds, and even Elizaveta had stopped sobbing. It was into this silence that the most beautiful sound Yona had ever heard emerged: a tiny sputter, then a cough, then a mewling that sounded like a kitten's, coming from the lungs of the tiny baby before her.

And just like that, in the midst of an inhospitable wilderness, another life came into the world, a tiny, impossible miracle that reminded them all that even when there were those trying to wipe them from the earth, they could survive by the grace of God, and by the sheer force of will. Before Yona passed the crying baby to her mother, she looked into the child's eyes and saw a future there, long and beautiful and bright, a future that would go on after Yona herself had passed from the world, a future still unwritten. Whatever else she would do, Yona vowed she would make sure this baby survived, and she would fight to the death for all those who had gathered here, under the stars, on this night.

Elizaveta and Shimon named the baby Abra, which meant mother of nations, and she carried the hope of all of them. Though she was tiny and struggled for life in her first few weeks, the other adults in the group gave up a portion of their meager supplies without being asked so Elizaveta could eat enough to make milk to nurse the infant to health. At night the baby cried, and Elizaveta muffled the noise so that it sounded like little more than the grunts of a bear cub finding her voice.

Against the odds, Abra began to thrive, but the rest of the group was withering; the island had almost no food available beyond the edible flowers and mushrooms they had already picked clean, and though the water around them was plentiful, it seemed to be making some of them sick. They couldn't stay here forever, and they were all worried about Zus and the others, and so after a month had passed in the swamp, Rosalia and Chaim set out to venture to the nearest town to see if the Germans had gone.

It was five days before they returned with eight loaves of dried, brittle bread, a bottle of vodka, and good news. The Germans had departed a week earlier, and though they'd caught a few dozen fleeing Jews and a handful of Russian partisans on the outskirts of the woods, they'd been mostly unsuccessful, missing both the Bielski and Zorin groups, and had abandoned the forest after torching many of the villages in retaliation for their failure.

"We will return to our camp," Yona said an hour after everyone had finished eating the bread and swigging from the bottle. "Let us pray that the others are waiting there."

She was greeted with silence, and she realized that the others feared, as she did, that the other half of their group was dead, that they were among those the Germans had swept from the safety of the forest before retreating. But she wouldn't speak the words aloud, nor would she allow anyone else to, for perhaps if they believed strongly enough in a God who would spare them, he would listen. That was foolish, fruitless thinking, Yona knew, but it was all she had, and as she came up beside Chaim and put her hand on his, she reinforced the folly by speaking it aloud.

"They will be there, waiting," she said firmly.

Chaim hesitated. "But they were meant to meet us here."

"And there must be a reason they chose not to," Yona replied. "I believe that. Don't you?"

Chaim looked away. "I don't know what I believe anymore."

But as they began their long walk back through the watery swamp to dry land, toward the camp they'd abandoned weeks before, she could overhear him more than once telling his sons the fun they would have with their uncle Zus, once they were all reunited. And she knew he wouldn't dangle hope that he believed to be entirely false; there was a sliver of possibility that the others were still alive.

Yona found herself thinking of Zus in the long moments of silence as they moved slowly, quietly, through the muck. Since the conversation she'd had with Chaim on the way to the swamp the previous month, she'd been thinking a lot of him, in fact. Aleksander's betrayal had made her feel as if she wasn't worthy of love, that she was as disposable as the shelters they used for a few days at a time. But in Zus's eyes before they parted ways, she had seen herself as something more. There was so little she understood about dealing with others, and she had blamed herself for how complicated things had gotten with Aleksander. But perhaps things didn't have to be difficult at all.

"We are lucky to have found you, Yona," Chaim said as they walked side by side on the fourth night of their trek back, their first out of the swamp, after they'd paused for a few hours to rest, drink, and eat all the berries they could pick on dry land.

Tomorrow they would pause to fish, and in two days' time, they would know whether the others had returned. She could barely stop herself from running ahead to find out, but this group needed her.

"I am lucky to have found you, too." Yona hesitated. "I have never known what it felt like to have a home. And though we move often—"

"Home is not a place, but the people you choose to love," he said, finishing the thought she hadn't quite known how to put into words. And she *did* love these people, from tough Rosalia, to quiet and honest Chaim, to hardworking Moshe, to the children whose survival every day was a triumph against the odds.

"I'm frightened by it, though," she said after a while. "For when you love, you stand to lose so much." She thought of the nun whose empty eyes she had pushed closed. She thought of little Chana, a bullet through her head, and of Anka, whose parents had been stolen from her so violently. And she thought of Zus and how he had been forever transformed by the terrible things that had happened to his family.

"But I think you stand to lose far more when your heart is closed," Chaim said. "That is no life."

Yona thought of Jüttner, the father who had been made cold and hard by the loss of his child and then his wife, and she felt a surge of guilt for the pain she had surely inflicted by leaving. "You're right," she murmured.

Two days later, after sleeping mostly during the days and walking by the light of the moon, the group was finally approaching the camp they'd left behind six weeks earlier. Yona could feel it, taste it, and she and Chaim, who were walking ahead, both quickened their pace. It was nearly dawn, and if the others were there waiting, they'd just be waking up to start their day. If the camp was occupied, there would be some sign of a guard any moment now.

But the forest was quiet, the only sounds the stirring of animals emerging to greet the day and the rustling of leaves and grass in the breeze. Chaim gave Yona a look of despair, and she swallowed hard. He was thinking the same thing she was, that it was too still, too deserted. The missing group couldn't be up ahead.

But then the new baby broke the silence among them by letting out a long, plaintive wail, and all at once, there was movement in the trees ahead. In that moment, Yona knew that God had been with them all along, for Zus emerged from the forest, his gun leveled at them. He stopped abruptly, blinking in confused recognition, and as Yona ran forward without pausing to think, he lowered his weapon and stumbled forward into her arms, clinging to her like he never intended to let go again.

"You're alive," he murmured into her hair, his voice husky with emotion, and then they were forced apart by the tidal wave of others rushing forward to greet Zus with hugs and handshakes and tears of gratitude. "What's this?" Zus asked with a smile, eyeing the new baby, and as Chaim's sons began to regale their uncle with a rapid, scattered story about their adventures, Zus looked up, his gaze meeting Yona's again and lingering there. When the boys were done talking and Zus had greeted the new baby with gentle kisses on her tiny cheeks, and on Elizaveta's cheeks, too, he gestured for Yona, Chaim, and Rosalia to step aside with him.

"We lost four," he said, his voice gruff, his eyes downcast as Rosalia gasped and Chaim grunted as if he'd been punched in the gut. "I'm very sorry. I tried my best to keep everyone safe . . ."

"Whatever happened, it couldn't have been your fault,"

Yona said. "I am to blame for being so willing to let you go without a fight." The weight of that realization had sat heavy on her for weeks.

He looked up at her. "Yona, you are blameless. It was the only choice. We couldn't just protect ourselves if there was a chance to save other lives. All of you survived?"

Yona nodded.

"Praise God." He sighed and looked down for a long time before raising his head again. "Lazare and Leib were killed by Germans when they ventured out on a food mission," he said, his voice flat. Yona put her hand over her mouth and blinked back tears. Poor, sweet Leib, only eighteen, a man before his time, who never had the chance to reach true adulthood. Miriam must be beside herself. "I'm sorry. We were starving. I offered to go, but instead I stayed to help protect the group . . ." He cleared his throat. "We lost Luba, too. An illness. It's what slowed us down, prevented us from reaching the Bielski group in good time. She became sick only a day after we left camp, and we had to move more slowly. She did not wake up on the third day." His eyes went to Yona again, and he held her gaze as he added softly, "We also lost Aleksander. I'm sorry, Yona. He died bravely; two Belorussian policemen came upon us in the woods, and he moved to protect my cousins, who were fishing and did not hear them approaching. He saved their lives, but in the gunfight, he was shot, and he perished a day later. He was a hero in the end."

Tears flowed down Yona's cheeks, and the depth of her grief confused her; Aleksander had hurt her, discarded her, but she had still shared a season of her life with him. She had loved him, even if that love had been misguided. She wiped her face, drew herself up to her full height, and looked Zus in the eye. "I think he would be proud to know you feel that way." She took a deep breath. "How is Sulia? She is grieving?"

Zus hesitated. "She seems to be."

"I'm sorry for her." Yona meant it. No one should know the pain of such a loss. "You reached the Bielski group?"

Zus shook his head. "We found their settlement, exactly where Shimon said it would be. But it was deserted; it appeared that they had fled a day or two before. It was a whole society in the woods, Yona; there must be a thousand of them there. It was incredible. We've been praying since then for their survival; it would be difficult to hide a group that large."

Yona nodded; it was just as Jüttner had said. "When Rosalia and Chaim ventured into some villages, they learned that the Germans' mission had not been successful. They did not find the Bielski group."

"We heard the same. It gives us hope that they are still alive."

"And the Zorin group? Did you reach them?"

Again Zus shook his head. "We tried. It is what kept us moving for so long in the wrong direction. But we never found them, and then we heard that the Germans had retreated. After we lost Aleksander, we began to move back here in hopes of finding you." Zus glanced at Chaim and Rosalia before looking back at Yona. "There's more. We have added to our group. Eight newcomers, six men and two women. They are all heavily armed, and they were wandering the forest alone, looking for a way to fight the Germans."

"They are Jews?" Chaim asked.

"Yes." There was awe in Zus's voice as he added, "They came from the Nowogródek ghetto. Like the Sokolowskis and the Gulniks, they were looking for the Bielskis and did not find them. But they came upon us, and when we told them about our settlement here, they asked if they could stay. They want to help us. They came with machine guns and ammunition, taken from Germans they ambushed in the forest."

"If they bring their own guns, they are very welcome to stay," Chaim said, and he and his brother shared a weary smile.

"Come," Zus said, raising his voice to address the whole group. "There is much to tell all of you, and I want to hear everything about what happened to you, too. Shall we go have a meal?"

Laughing and chattering, with the clouds overhead temporarily parting to let in the light, the group that had followed Yona into the swamps began to walk back toward the place they had come to know as home.

That night, after meeting the eight newcomers—all between the ages of eighteen and twenty-four, and all bright-eyed with anger and grief for loved ones slain by the Germans—Yona walked a hundred meters away from their camp and found herself alone in the woods for the first time in weeks. It was safe here in the camp, as safe as it could be, and even Chaim and Rosalia had let down their guard and crawled off to sleep. Israel and Wenzel, who had come back with Zus's group a week before and were well rested, were on patrol tonight, and Yona could hear their distant footsteps moving through the trees. But still she was able to close her eyes and block out the sound as she sat by the edge of a burbling stream.

The soft rushing of the water comforted her, gave her leave to let go, and before she knew it, tears were running down her face, and then she was sobbing, her body heaving with the sudden effort of drawing a breath. The moon shone down, peaceful and quiet, the stars twinkled overhead, and Yona wept at last for all the things that had been lost: for the people who should still be here, for the father she'd never see again, for the death of Aleksander, for the senseless loss of young Leib's life, even for Jerusza, who seemed farther away than ever. *The Germans, they don't just wipe out our people*, Aleksander had said to her long ago. *They wipe out our future.* Aleksander's family line, and Leib's, were forever erased now. How many futures had the Germans snuffed out the same way?

She was crying so hard that she didn't hear anyone approaching until warm, callous fingers touched her arm. She jumped up, whirling around, and found herself face-to-face with Zus. The scream in her throat melted into a whimper, and without a word, he folded her into his arms and simply held her as her shoulders shook. When she finally pulled away, she knew that her face was streaked with salt and dirt, and her eyes were bloodshot, but when Zus reached out and gently tucked an errant fall of hair behind her ear, she saw herself reflected in his eyes, and she saw none of those flaws.

"I'm sorry about Aleksander," Zus said, his voice rough as he broke the silence between them. "I know what it is to lose someone."

"I'm not crying only for him," Yona said, and there was something about the way that his shoulders sagged slightly in relief that made her heart beat a bit faster. "My tears are for everyone we've lost. All the lives that should not have been extinguished."

Zus nodded, and they looked skyward at the same time.

Yona watched as a splash of stars, an infinite galaxy far away, disappeared behind a dark cloud, and then she looked back at Zus.

"They took my wife and daughter," he said, his voice flat. He was still looking at the space where the stars should have been. "Right in front of me. I—I could not stop it. Did Chaim tell you?"

Yona nodded. "I'm so sorry, Zus."

She reached for his hand, and he laced his fingers through hers. After a moment of silence, she followed his gaze back to the sky.

"I'm broken, Yona," he said, still not looking at her. "I always will be, no matter what I do, no matter how many lives I help save."

She hesitated before moving closer and resting her head on his shoulder. "I'm broken, too. But sometimes it's the jagged edges that allow us to fit together. Sometimes it's the breaks that make us strong."

Zus didn't reply, and for a moment she was certain she'd said the wrong thing, that in trying to make him feel less alone, she had instead made him feel as if she were comparing her losses to his. But then he placed his index finger under her chin and gently tilted her face up. He studied her eyes for a few seconds, his gaze stormy, and then, wordlessly, he leaned in and kissed her, so softly that at first his lips barely touched hers. When she leaned in and kissed him back, he turned slightly, angling his body toward hers and pressing her against him.

When he finally pulled away, the light had returned to his eyes. He looked as if he wanted to say something, but there was no need for words. After a few seconds, she placed her head on his shoulder again, and he rested his head against hers, and she wondered if maybe their broken edges had been a perfect fit all along.

CHAPTER TWENTY-FOUR

For the next month, it was as if the night had never happened, as if they hadn't held each other in the starlight until dawn and opened their hearts for a moment to let a bit of light in. A thousand times she had replayed it in her mind and wondered if she should have pulled away in those few seconds before he kissed her. He had mentioned his wife and child, and perhaps his grief for them had clouded his judgment for a few minutes. Perhaps it had been up to her to stop him from making a mistake, up to her to stop her heart from suddenly wanting something she shouldn't.

But she often caught him looking at her, his gaze tender and penetrating, and sometimes, when she looked up and met his eyes, it felt as if they were the only ones in the world. The feeling confused her, as did the way her skin tingled whenever he brushed against her, which had never happened with Aleksander. But she pretended nothing was wrong, for what could be gained from harping on feelings she didn't understand, when their survival was at stake?

She focused instead on checking on little Abra, who was, blessedly, a quiet baby, and on the eight newcomers: the Ro-

zenberg brothers, Benjamin, Maks, Michal, and Joel; Regina
and Paula, who were the wives of Benjamin and Michal; and
the two men who had come with them, Rubin Sobil and Harry
Feinschreiber. All were young, angry, and ready to fight back,
and already, their arrival had changed the mood in the camp.
Now there was a restlessness to everything, a feeling of waiting.

The Germans had fallen back for now, leaving in their
wake an eerie silence, a feeling that the worst was still to come.
The more immediate problem, though, was that winter was
fast approaching and the group's food supply had dwindled to
nearly nothing, since they'd taken so much of the preserved
food with them when they fled into the swamps. There were
more mouths to feed now, and much less food. They would
not survive the winter with what little they had left, and when
Benjamin and Maks Rozenberg brought up the idea of am-
bushing a German supply convoy to steal food and weapons,
Yona couldn't dismiss it, though she hated the idea of putting
any of them in harm's way.

"There is no choice," Zus murmured one day as he sat down
in the clearing with Yona, Chaim, and Rosalia. "We must eat."

"And the villages have been bled dry," Chaim said. In the
time since they'd been back at their camp, several of them had
taken turns venturing out to the towns on the edges of the forest
to see what had been left behind. They were desperate to find
stores of food, but instead they found bodies and burned buildings everywhere they went. The Germans had torched farms
and slaughtered livestock to prevent refugees from finding any
nourishment. Still, there had been some beets remaining in the
ground, and Chaim and Zus had found a small underground
bunker filled with potatoes, which they'd transported back to

camp in big sacks. It was a start, but the food wouldn't last the winter; they needed more.

It was Rosalia who replied. "Something must be done. They have forced us into the woods, murdered our people, taken all that we hold dear. It is time they pay."

Yona didn't know Rosalia's history, what had brought her into the forest, but for the first time, she understood that something terrible had happened to her. There was a crack in Rosalia's cool exterior now, and it made Yona shiver.

"Why now?" Yona asked.

When Rosalia turned to her, her eyes were on fire. "Because it is no longer enough to simply survive. How long are we supposed to go on like this? Our bodies may be enduring, but what about our souls? What about our pride? What about the things that make us who we are beyond our flesh and bone?"

The others nodded, all except Yona. When she looked at Zus, he was watching her. "What do you say, Yona?"

"I thought we were talking about taking food from the Germans, which is dangerous enough," she said slowly. "But revenge? I think, at best, revenge would be a short-term salve, and at worst, it could be dangerous." There was no right answer here on earth, so she looked for reason elsewhere. "'You shall neither take revenge from, nor bear a grudge against, the members of your people,'" she said at last. "'You shall love your neighbor as yourself.'"

Zus looked stricken. "Leviticus 19." He took a deep breath. "'You shall not hate your brother in your heart,'" he said, quoting the same chapter, his eyes not leaving hers.

"But they are not our brothers." Rosalia's voice had grown colder, and Chaim was nodding slowly along with her now, something dark flickering in his eyes. "The German soldiers are not our neighbors. They have invaded our home. They have turned our countrymen against us. Moses himself commanded revenge against those who murdered the children of Israel. 'Go to war against the Midianites so that they may carry out the Lord's vengeance on them,' he said."

"But God spoke to Moses and commanded it," Yona said. "He has not spoken to us. All we have is conscience to be our guide."

"I would not lose a moment of sleep over harming those who seek to erase us from the face of the earth." Rosalia's eyes were as steely as her tone as she turned to Yona. "You don't know what it is like to watch your loved ones murdered before your eyes, Yona. You don't know what it is to carry that anger inside of you for months that become years," Rosalia said, her voice softening. "You are kind and good, but I think maybe you can never understand if you are not one of us, if you haven't suffered the things we have."

"Rosalia, how can you say that?" Zus said at once. "Has she not risked her life for yours a hundred times? For all of us?" But in the silence that followed, Yona's heart ached. She understood what Rosalia meant, and she wasn't wrong.

"I'm sorry, Yona," Rosalia said, bowing her head and then looking up with eyes full of remorse. "I should not have said that."

"But you were right." Yona had no place in this choice, for she hadn't lost the same things they had, and so she looked to Zus, whose expression was troubled. "I will trust your decision." They held each other's gaze for a long time, and she could see the anguish in his eyes, the conflict.

"We go after the Germans," he said at last. "Far from here, so they can't trace us. Not for the purpose of taking lives, but for the purpose of obtaining the food and supplies we need. It's not revenge. It is seizing what we need from the people who have stolen it from us, and perhaps letting them know in the process that we have it in us to fight back, that we are proud and free. Are we in agreement?"

Chaim nodded first, stepping forward to shake Zus's hand. Then Rosalia murmured her assent, and all of them looked to Yona. She knew the forest better than anyone, and if there was to be an ambush, she would need to decide where it would take place.

"The road into the forest from Nowogródek," she said at last. "It is two days' walk from here, so they won't know where we came from. It is one of the transport roads the Germans use." She had seen their trucks herself when she fled Jüttner's home and made her way back into the forest. "If we can stop a transport truck, we can take their weapons and ammunition, as well as provisions for our people."

"Right out of the Germans' mouths," Chaim said, nodding in agreement. "Won't it anger them, though?"

"That's what the raids this summer were about," Yona said. "The Bielski group and the Russian partisans have been launching attacks like this one. The Germans tried to strike back, and they failed. I think it is very likely they are still licking their wounds. If we stop only one truck, and if we manage to get away, the impact of it will be so small that they won't come after us." She knew she sounded more confident than she felt, but she was counting on the fact that the Germans would want most of all to save face.

Zus was studying Yona with a frown. "But it would still be dangerous. We could be killed."

She looked first at Rosalia, then at Chaim, and then finally back at Zus, who had lost so much. "Rosalia is right, though. We would be fighting back at last. Maybe it *is* time."

Zus finally nodded, and turned to his brother, quickly running down a list of who they could take with them and how quickly they could move. As they talked, Rosalia edged up next to Yona and put a hand on her shoulder.

"I'm sorry," she said. "I should not have said you are not like us."

"You were right." Yona blinked and could see Jüttner's face in her mind, not his cold, lined face now, but the face of a younger man leaning over her cradle all those years before, looking down at her with tenderness. She blinked again, and the image disappeared. "Who did you lose, Rosalia? I'm sorry I've never asked you before."

Rosalia looked away, and when she looked back, there were tears in her eyes. Yona had never seen the other woman cry. "Everyone. Including my husband and our two sons."

"I'm so sorry," Yona said, reaching for Rosalia's hands, but Rosalia pulled away. "I—I never knew you were a mother."

"It is in the past." Her voice was clipped, but Yona could hear it trembling, and she understood in an instant that there had always been far more to Rosalia than she knew.

"How old were they? Your boys?"

Rosalia took a deep breath. "Two and four. Their whole lives were in front of them. And now I am the only one still here. It is no longer enough to merely get by, Yona. This has to end, all of it. I'm tired of running. I'm tired of hiding. I want to salvage a life from the ruins. I want to honor my children."

"You will honor them by surviving," Yona said.

"Perhaps," Rosalia said. "But I must also make them proud."
And then, before Yona could say another word, Rosalia turned
and walked away, deeper into the forest.

Two days later, Zus and Chaim had assembled a team; Leonid
Gulnik would come along, as would Bernard, Rosalia, six of
the newcomers, and Yona. Israel and Wenzel would be in charge
of guarding the camp while they were gone. Sulia had begged
to join them, but Zus and Chaim had decided against it; they
needed to be able to trust everyone on their mission, and none
of them believed she would put the group's safety ahead of her
own. She had huffed off angrily after her request was denied, but
now, though she was still shooting Zus and Yona dirty looks,
she seemed to have accepted the decision and was flirting with
Harry Feinschreiber, who looked bewildered to be on the re-
ceiving end of her attention.

They would leave the next morning before dawn, bringing
with them all but one of the machine guns and all but two of the
rifles; they would need as many weapons as possible to take on
the fully armed Germans, but of course they couldn't leave the
camp undefended. They had carefully laid out their plan—shoot
out the tires of an approaching German transport; then, in the
melee, rush forward from all directions and shoot as many of the
soldiers as possible before the Germans returned fire. It would
be dangerous, and they'd likely be outnumbered, so the element
of surprise would be everything. And then, most important,
they would have to disappear as quickly as they'd come, melting

into the forest without a trace, for certainly the Germans would come looking for them.

Yona had just laid her head down in her small hut, in hopes of quieting her mind and getting at least a few hours of sleep, when there was a rustling just outside, then the sound of someone clearing his throat. "Yona?" It was Zus, and Yona immediately went to greet him.

The rest of the group was all tucked away, the fire from dinner extinguished, the night quiet. The moon was a mere sliver, and the sky was dark, so he was barely more than a shadow in the blackness. "Is everything all right, Zus?" she asked.

"May I come in?"

She nodded and moved aside. When she lit a candle in the darkness, light flooded the small space, and she had to stop herself from reaching out and touching his face. She waited in silence for him to speak.

"Yona, I'm frightened," he said at last, his low, deep voice reminding her of a distant rumble of thunder, soothing and dangerous at the same time. He took a step closer. They were inches apart, as close as they'd been the night he'd kissed her. "What if we are making a mistake? I couldn't live with myself if I let something happen to Chaim." He hesitated and then looked into her eyes. "Or to you."

She blinked a few times, trying to escape the power of his gaze. "Chaim makes his own decision, as do I. You are not responsible for either of us, Zus."

"But he is my brother. I love him, and I don't want to lose him. And you are . . ." He trailed off. "You are *you*. You are . . ." He didn't seem to know how to finish the sentence, but she could hear it in the tremble of his voice now, see it in the pain reflected in his eyes. "What you said about broken pieces, Yona, I—I know you're right. I am trying to find my way back to life, you see. It's just taking me longer than I expected."

She wanted to lean forward and kiss him. But she held herself back, because she had never explained the fact that perhaps she was irredeemable from the start by the very act of her birth. So she took a deep breath and gestured for him to sit down beside her. They settled on her reed bed, and he searched her face.

"What is it?" he asked.

"I've been thinking about what Rosalia said," she began softly. "There's something I should tell you."

He touched her cheek. "There's no need."

"But there is." She took a deep breath. "When I was gone this summer, I met my father."

He blinked a few times. "Your father? I thought you were raised by an old woman. That you didn't know your parents."

"I was with them until my second birthday. Sometimes at night I could see their faces in my mind, frozen there, like a piece of my past I couldn't touch but would always remember."

He looked puzzled, but he nodded, encouraging her to go on.

"That's why I recognized my father, I think, though I never expected it. He was always there, just beyond my reach." She dared a glance at Zus and then hung her head in shame. "He's a German officer, Zus. He's the one who told me the Germans were coming to the woods."

He hadn't moved away, but he looked as if he'd been slapped. "Yona . . ."

"You see, I'm not like you after all. Your family is dead. Mine is perhaps responsible for that. Maybe . . . maybe I was born to be something terrible," she concluded in a whisper.

He didn't say anything, and as she looked down, she feared that he agreed, that he was appalled. But then he reached out and wrapped his hands around hers. He waited until she looked up before speaking. "We all come into this world with our fate unwritten, Yona. Your identity isn't determined by your birth. All that matters is what we make ourselves into, what we choose to do with our lives. You are no more a Nazi than I am a creature from outer space who flies among the stars."

Despite the tears in her eyes, despite the gravity of their discussion, she couldn't stop herself from choking out a laugh. He touched her face, tilting her chin up so she had to look him in the eye.

"You are you, Yona, and you are extraordinary. It doesn't matter who your parents are, or even who raised you. Who are you here?" He tapped her chest, just above her left breast, and then he lingered there, his palm against her skin. She could feel her heart beating against his hand.

"I don't know," she whispered.

"But I do. You are a warrior. You are a hero, and a fighter, and a savior. You are a caretaker and a life giver." He took a deep breath and waited until she looked up at him. "And you are the woman who has reawakened a heart I thought would sleep forever." He reached for her hand and placed her palm on the left side of his chest so that they sat in the quiet, their hands over each other's hearts, feeling the steady rhythm of life. "You are a woman I hope can forgive my shortcomings, and a woman I hope might one day find space in her heart for me."

At this, her eyes filled with tears. "You are already there, Zus. Can't you feel it?"

His palm pressed into her chest, absorbing the beats of her heart, which seemed to march in time with his. Slowly, he nodded.

"I'm just not certain that there will ever be space in *your* heart," she said softly. "And I understand if there's not."

He looked into her eyes. "You are already there, too, Yona."

And then his lips were on hers, and it felt different from the last time. There was no hesitation, no question hidden in the way they touched, nothing left unsaid. Zus knew now that Yona understood his past, and she knew that he understood hers. None of it mattered, not in this moment. As she blew out the candle and felt the weight of him on top of her, his body covering hers and his hands entangled in her hair, she closed her eyes and released her fear. The only thing that remained was the only thing that mattered: love—the kind that could be found in the darkness when all pretenses had disappeared, the kind born of pain and despair and hope, the kind that was a shelter in the storm.

CHAPTER TWENTY-FIVE

I n the morning, Zus was gone, but when she saw him in the
clearing an hour after daybreak, his eyes were warm, and when
he reached out to touch her hand, his fingers brushing gently
against hers, she could feel the current running between them, a
shared energy she'd never felt with Aleksander.

"Are we sure about this?" he asked, leaning in close, and
for a second, she thought he was asking if she was certain about
what they'd shared the night before. But when she looked into
his eyes, she understood instantly that he was asking instead
about the mission they were about to embark on. Already,
Chaim, Rosalia, Leonid, and Bernard Zuk were clustered
near the remnants of last night's fire, talking to the Rozenberg
brothers, and the two Rozenberg wives, Regina and Paula,
who were handing out guns. Shimon was on the other side of
the clearing with Rubin Sobil and Harry Feinschreiber.

"There is great risk." Yona's gaze settled on Rosalia. "But I
think it is something we must do."

Zus nodded slowly. "Then it is time."

He stepped away from her and called to the others. All

around them, the members of the camp emerged from their huts one by one to listen.

"If all goes well," Zus began, "we will be back here in four and a half days' time with enough food to last the winter. Our group is small, but we cannot survive on what we've gathered from the forest, and as you all know, the Germans have stolen from us the option of taking foods from the villages and farms. It is time we fight back."

A murmur of approval ran through the small crowd. Everyone was nodding in agreement, even those who looked frightened.

"It will be dangerous, though," Zus continued. "But all of us who are risking our lives to take on the Germans, to feed our camp, know the risks. We are all ready to fight for what is ours."

Rosalia stepped forward. "We stand up now. We stand up for those who are not here anymore to stand up for themselves."

Something shifted in Yona's belly, a swell of nerves. This wasn't what the mission was about, but the murmurs in the group rose to cheers, and a few people clapped and whistled.

"Stand up for my mother!" called out Elizaveta, who had sleeping baby Abra pressed against her chest. "She was on her knees begging for mercy when the Germans shot her."

"Stand for our son Natan and his wife and children!" Oscher called out. Bina was by his side, tears in her eyes, nodding.

"For my daughter, Ryka, and my wife, Sosia!" called Rubin Sobil.

"For my daughter, Dolca!" cried Moshe.

Ruth grasped Leah's hand and hoisted little Daniel higher on her shoulder. "For my children's father, Chiel."

"For Aleksander, and Leib, and Luba, and Lazare!" yelled Ester.

All around the camp, names rang out. Husbands, wives, mothers, fathers, children, friends, loved ones. They'd all lost more people than could be counted, and that's why it was time. Yona and Zus exchanged glances, the understanding of that truth passing silently between them.

"Take what is ours!" Chaim's wife, Sara, called out, her voice thick with tears. "But come back to us, all of you. The best revenge is your survival."

Chaim nodded solemnly, and so, too, did the others, all except for Rosalia, whose face was as still as carved stone. Once the grief for her lost family had finally come to the surface, it had settled there, heavy and immovable, making her almost unrecognizable.

Ten minutes later, after exchanging hugs and kisses and handshakes with those who would remain, the small group set out toward the west. All around them, the forest was shedding her green, preparing for the winter. The world drifted down around them in all the colors of fire and flame, and they could still smell the smoked ruins of some of the villages on the forest's edge. It smelled like autumn, too, of leaves crisp and spent, of grass turned to straw, of mushrooms taking their last gasp of air before the forest turned cold. Rabbits and chipmunks fled ahead of them as the group marched on, and ravens lifted off with great caws of warning.

They stopped at nightfall and ate a small meal from their knapsacks, each of which was stuffed with blankets taken from neighboring towns, which Moshe had hastily fashioned into giant sacks to transport whatever foodstuffs they managed to obtain. That night, they didn't bother with shelters; they built beds of sticks and reeds, covered them with fallen leaves and let exhaustion overtake them. Sometime during the night, Zus, who slept in a makeshift bed beside Yona's, reached for her hand, and they didn't let go until the first rays of dawn pierced the sky. It was time to move again.

The group walked until midafternoon on the second day, when Yona quickly jogged to the front of their exhausted line and held up a hand to stop them. "What is it?" asked Rosalia, who'd been leading the charge through the forest.

"We're getting close," Yona said. Within an hour, they'd reach the road. "Let's rest here until midnight." She gestured to a cluster of fallen oaks a hundred meters away. "We can find some shelter there. We'll move again in the darkness, and we'll find our places along the road so we're there to greet the Germans in the morning."

They all gathered, sharing potatoes and dried berries they'd brought from camp. They passed around a bottle of bimber that the brothers had brought along and talked in low voices about the plan for the morning. They would position themselves so they would immediately surround an approaching transport. They would be cautious not to fire on a truck that contained only soldiers, for it would yield no food and would be more dangerous. They would also avoid convoys of multiple vehicles and wait for a truck traveling on its own.

As the group settled in for a few hours of rest, softly singing folk songs everyone but Yona knew, Zus sat beside her, his arm around her, and though a few people looked at them with curiosity, no one said anything. After nightfall, instead of building beds, most of the group found refuge in the hollows of the fallen tree trunks, sleeping alone, except for Zus and Yona, who slept beside each other on a bed of leaves, her head on his chest.

Just past midnight, Chaim, who had taken the second shift guarding the group, shook Yona gently awake. "It's time."

Indeed, the nearly full moon shone down, bathing the forest in more light than Yona would have liked. They were close to civilization, so the trees here weren't as dense as they were in the deeper parts of the forest, nor were the canopies overhead as thick. The stars that were often hidden in the forest's depths looked here like spilled sugar across the blackness of the sky.

"Are you ready?" Yona whispered to Chaim before helping him to wake the others.

"To ambush a German convoy? No, I don't think I ever will be. But we are in desperate times, yes?" He sighed. "I just want to feed my family and make it back to them. I want to live to see Jakub and Adam grow into adults. Is that too much to ask?"

"No," Yona replied. Beside her Zus stirred and sat up. "It is the very least any of us deserves."

In fifteen minutes, the group was awake, their knapsacks packed, their guns loaded, adrenaline buoying them. "We'll be to the road in an hour," Yona said, looking at the assembled group one by one. Beside her, Zus was studying his brother with concern. Yona watched as Zus crossed to Chaim, put a hand on his shoulder, and said something into his ear. Chaim nodded and looked up, sharing a moment of silent understanding with Zus, and then Zus looked to Yona and nodded solemnly.

They moved through the woods in darkness, their path lit only by the moon and stars above, silent except for the crunch of leaves beneath their feet. The light disappeared behind clouds for a bit, plunging them into darkness just as they had to cross a small river, but it returned in time to illuminate the wide road ahead, which seemed to slice the forest in two.

"There it is," Rosalia whispered almost reverently.

"There it is," Chaim echoed, but his tone was different, filled with trepidation.

"All right," Zus said as the group began to whisper among themselves. "We must get in position. We don't know how early they come through. Rosalia, you go a hundred meters east with Leonid. Remember, we will only stop a cargo vehicle, and only one that is alone, or it will be too dangerous. You two will fire the first shots to disable the vehicle. Aim at their wheels; the best we can hope for is that they spin out of control, disorienting the soldiers for a few seconds. After that, we lose the element of surprise. Joel, you and Maks head down there, across from Rosalia. If another transport truck comes up behind it, you'll need to disable them quickly so the tables don't turn on us. The rest of us will split up, here, there, and there." He gestured to two spots on the other side of the road. "We will have to be ready the moment Rosalia and Leonid begin shooting, because it will be only seconds before they return fire. Anything else, Yona?"

She shook her head slowly. The assuredness of his plan reminded her how little she knew about his past; he spoke like someone who had led military missions before.

"Once upon a time, I trained to be in the army," he said softly, reading her mind as the group began to disperse to their assigned locations. "I'll tell you all about it one day." The words were an unspoken promise that they'd both survive.

Yona wound up beside Zus and Chaim, in the shadow of a giant oak that reached over the road. Across the way, Benjamin and Michal hid behind trees several meters apart, each accompanied by his wife. As clouds drifted across the moon, Yona could see only the white of their eyes in the darkness until the sun began to rise, pinking the sky to the east.

It could have been hours before the first transport came through, but instead, just as the sun crept above the horizon, they heard the low rumble of a vehicle in the distance. Up the road, Rosalia stood and waved everyone down. Yona's heart thudded against her rib cage; what had seemed like a good idea moments before now seemed like a recipe for disaster.

Time seemed to stand still as the noise got louder and louder. A shadow appeared from around the bend, and a few seconds later, a large truck rumbled into view. It was a German Opel Blitz, a cargo truck with a dozen soldiers seated in the open rear. With that many men back there, it couldn't be carrying many provisions, and Yona assumed Rosalia would notice the same thing and hold her fire. But then, in a flash, Rosalia rose from the bushes, her gun leveled, and fired once, calmly, accurately, into the Blitz's front left tire.

There was a giant bang as the truck swerved sideways, lurching into the bushes beside the road and slamming headlong into a tree. Zus cursed, and as some of the soldiers were thrown from the truck and others scrambled down, their guns drawn against an invisible enemy, there was no choice but to open fire, even though this was the wrong truck, a truck that couldn't possibly provide ample food for the winter, a truck whose only real bounty was men.

Yona ran forward with the others, all of them firing at the Germans. Some of the soldiers had reached for their weapons; others simply stood there, stunned. One soldier lay in the middle of the road, still and bloodied, apparently knocked unconscious after falling from the vehicle. The driver of the truck clambered down from the cab, his cap askew as he searched the forest wildly. A bullet sliced through his neck before his feet hit the ground, and he slumped face-first into the earth.

Most of the soldiers fell, one by one, dropping to the ground in clouds of their own blood, but impossibly, two remained standing long enough to fire back. Their bullets ricocheted off the trees, whizzing like crazed bumblebees as they shot haphazardly at a threat they couldn't see, panic rendering them careless. But it was too late for them; a bullet found the head of one of them, and a spray of machine-gun fire from one of the brothers shredded the chest of the other, and then, with all the Germans finally lying dead, the forest fell silent.

Yona slowly lowered her weapon, her legs quaking beneath her as the full reality of what they'd done began to sink in. They had murdered these soldiers for no good reason; there was no assurance they were carrying anything of value aside from their weapons and the clothes on their backs.

"That was for our parents," Maks Rozenberg said, kicking one of the Germans. His brother Joel spat in the dead man's face.

"Come, quickly," Zus said, shouldering his gun and grabbing Yona's hand. "Come, all of you. We must take what we can and disappear before another truck arrives."

It was too sloppy, all of it, and Yona felt sick. Rosalia had acted without considering the consequences, her hatred temporarily squeezing her common sense aside. Yona scanned the road, looking for her as the others gathered themselves. Her heart skipped as she realized the fiery-haired woman wasn't there. "Rosalia?" she called out.

The others stopped what they were doing and turned, looking for her, too. It was Yona who saw her first, facedown on the ground, her beautiful red hair splayed around her like a lion's mane. "Rosalia!" Yona cried, rushing to her side and dropping to her knees. She put a hand on Rosalia's back; the other woman was still breathing in shallow gasps. Yona knew even before she gently rolled her over that Rosalia was dying.

Her face no longer looked like stone; as she tried in vain to drink the air, there was a softness to her that Yona had never seen before. Zus came to kneel beside Yona, and then Chaim was there, too, all three of them looking down helplessly as Rosalia opened her eyes, struggling to focus on them. Yona could hear one of the Rozenberg brothers exclaiming over something he'd found in the truck, one of the wives urging them to hurry. But their voices sounded very far away. There was a gaping hole in Rosalia's chest, and Yona could see blood bubbling out each time she took a breath.

"I had to," she managed through gasps for air. "They took so much. My children would be proud that I stood up for us."

Yona could feel tears in her eyes as she reached for Rosalia's hand and held tight. Zus put his hand on Rosalia's chest to try to stop the blood, but Yona shook her head at him sadly. It was no use.

"Yes, they would be," Yona said, and Rosalia smiled a wobbly smile.

"I will tell them," she whispered, and then she took one last shuddering breath, and the light went out of her eyes.

Yona could feel herself choking on a sob, but before she could say anything, Chaim had grabbed her arm and Zus's and was pulling them away. "We have to go," he said, his voice thick with both grief and urgency. "*Now.* We've been here too long."

Yona looked up in a daze to see the others waiting by the edge of the road, the giant packs Moshe had made for them stuffed full. Yona blinked back tears; there had been more supplies in the truck than she had imagined. The Rozenbergs had worked quickly; the Germans lying on the road had been stripped of their guns, boots, and coats, too—an impressive stash with which to survive the winter.

"Come," Chaim urged again, his tone panicked now, and then Zus grabbed her hand and was pulling her along, toward the woods.

"What about Rosalia?" she asked, though she already knew the answer.

"We can't waste any more time," Zus said, squeezing her hand. Chaim nodded his agreement. "We must honor her by surviving. And when the Germans find her, perhaps they'll feel that they've gotten their pound of flesh. She may yet save our lives once more."

He was right, of course, but Yona couldn't resist one last look back at Rosalia, who lay silent forever among the dead Germans, her sightless eyes staring up at the sky. Yona whispered a prayer to God, and then she followed Zus and the others as they fled back into the woods, heading for the river to hide their footprints, making them impossible to follow.

They ran for an hour and then waded downriver for another mile before emerging into a part of the forest that was unfamiliar to everyone but Yona. They had gone far enough that the Germans wouldn't track them. The group finally stopped to rest in the shade of a thatch of oaks. Without a word, the Rozenbergs began to unwrap the bundles they'd been carrying, and Yona and Zus, who had been balancing a large bundle between them, did the same. Chaim and Leonid each had a small bundle, and in a moment, everything they'd taken lay on the ground before them.

Yona gaped at the treasure. She'd had no idea what they'd been carrying, but now, with all of it spread before her, she wondered if perhaps Rosalia's death hadn't been entirely in vain after all.

There were a dozen new machine guns, four pistols, and plenty of ammunition. In the bag she and Zus had been carrying, she was stunned to find two dozen loaves of hard bread, boxes of cigarettes, at least a hundred wrapped candy bars, and dozens of tins labeled *Rinderbraten*, *Truthahnbraten*, and *Hähnchenfleisch*. Chaim and Leonid had similar hauls, as did Regina and Paula, who were also carrying packages of pellets labeled *Erbswurst*, and bags of hard crackers. The bread and cigarettes had been soaked, but everything else looked mostly intact.

"What is all this stuff?" one of the Rozenberg brothers asked.

"The tins are beef, chicken, and turkey," Yona said slowly, reading the labels as she reeled from the unexpected bounty. "And the pellets are to make pea soup."

"Soldiers' rations," Zus murmured, and Yona nodded. It made her hate the Nazis a bit more for plundering villages and destroying crops when their own survival was already assured.

"With this, we'll have enough for the winter," Yona said. "This is what we were after."

They exchanged looks as the weight of what they'd taken settled over all of them. It was Chaim who broke the silence. "We should go," he said. "We have a lot of ground to cover."

Everyone mumbled agreement, and they hastily bundled the supplies into heavy packs once more. They would walk until they couldn't take another step, and then they would rest for a few hours, continuing their homeward trek before dawn.

"Are you all right?" Zus asked, his voice low, as he fell into step beside Yona, who was leading the march through the woods.

"No," she whispered after a moment.

He nodded, and she knew he wasn't, either. They had all known the risks today, but losing Rosalia felt senseless.

"*Yitgadal v'yitkadash sh'mei raba b'alma di-v'ra chirutei*," Zus began after a long silence, and Yona felt her heart flutter in recognition. "*V'yamlich malchutei b'chayeichon uvyomeichon uvchayei d'chol beit yisrael, ba'agala uvizman kariv, v'im'ru: amen.*"

It was the mourner's kaddish, spoken in Aramaic to honor the dead. She took a deep breath.

"*Y'hei sh'mei raba m'varach l'alam ul'almei almaya*," they said together, their voices joining as one. Yona whispered along as Zus continued with the rest of the prayer, and she knew, from the way his voice cracked, that he'd said it many times for many people he'd lost. To say it now, alone in the forest without a quorum of ten men, wasn't tradition, but it brought Yona comfort. They would say it properly later, just as they had for Aleksander and the others. But for now, this was enough to keep Yona moving forward, to keep all the survivors headed home.

CHAPTER TWENTY-SIX

The winter moved in swiftly that year, frosting the forest in ice before the group had the chance to finish building their zemliankas. Still, they had managed to hollow the ground out before it froze solid, so they were fortunate; all that remained was to build the roofs and stoves, and that they had accomplished by the first heavy snowfall.

There would be just enough food to see the group safely through the cold, thanks to the autumn attack on the German truck as well as a few supply missions to neighboring villages. With the Germans mostly dispersed from the area now, it was easier to venture in and forage for food left behind. Before the world was frozen, they had brought home half-rotten potatoes, a dozen hens that had somehow managed to escape the Nazi slaughter, and even some bags of grain from a hidden basement in a barn.

With the cold of the winter, too, came a warmth Yona had never known. Without saying a word about it, she and Zus had drifted together, spending more and more time with one another and eventually moving into the same zemlianka, where they huddled together at night under a shared blanket, absorbing the heat of each other's bodies. There hadn't been time to build smaller shelters this year, so they were living with eight others, packed in wall to wall. Modesty prevented them from doing more than holding each other at night, but the way he kissed her gently and cradled her like a treasure was enough. Yona knew how he felt, and her heart echoed his.

"You've found love in the madness," Ruth said to her one day with a small smile as they stood in the clearing watching Leah, Pessia, and Daniel play with the Gulniks' little girl, Maia. Daniel was toddling now, unsteady on his skinny legs, and the girls delighted in being teachers, showing him how to put one foot in front of the other and giggling with him when he tumbled into the snow. "What a blessing."

Yona hugged her arms around herself and gazed around the camp. It was relatively warm for a winter day in the forest, the biting wind absent for a change, though the snow was falling enough to erase the traces of them when they went back beneath the earth. Elizaveta was outside bouncing a giggling Abra on her knee, while Nachum tossed a ball made from Moshe's yarn back and forth with Chaim's boys. Four of the adults were playing cards with a tree stump for a table, and a few more were laughing at something while passing a bottle of bimber back and forth. It felt strangely normal. The threat wasn't gone, and there was still a smattering of Germans in the area, but on this day, no one was thinking about survival. They were simply enjoying the moment, a rare luxury in the woods, and it was beautiful. "I think we've all found love," Yona said at last, smiling as she watched the children. She hadn't realized it was happening, but somehow along the way, they had all become her family, each and every one of these refugees. She had thought she was teaching them how to live, but now she realized that in many ways, she had been the student all along.

Ruth nodded and put a hand on Yona's arm. "Thank you, Yona. I'm not sure if I have said this before, but I don't think we would have survived without you."

Yona looked away, embarrassed. "You would have. I only helped a bit."

"Yona, you saved us." Ruth cleared her throat. "You are a true gift from God, and I thank him for you every day."

Yona looked once more at the scene before her, normalcy in the midst of madness. "I thank God for all of it."

That night, the whole group crowded into the largest zemlianka, and in their hiding place beneath the earth, they sang the Hebrew songs Yona had come to know, and Ruth told the children fairy tales of elflike creatures called *shretelekh*, who brought goodness to those who were good to them. It was an evening that should have felt magical, but Yona found herself thinking instead of the winter before, and the first night the group had lit a menorah together. Hanukkah would begin again in a few days, but so many of the people from that celebration were no longer here. Her heart ached for all that was lost.

Sulia was with Harry Feinschreiber now, having moved on from Aleksander almost as if he'd never existed, but the past never really disappeared, did it? There were ghosts in the woods that night—Rosalia, Aleksander, Leib, Luba—but it wasn't just their ghosts. It was the sense of countless lives snuffed out, the hopeless cascade of future generations lost. She glanced at Zus, who sat in the shadows, and when he turned to look at her, she had the strange sense that he was thinking the same thing.

And though the night of celebration eventually ended and Zus came to bed with Yona as he always did, his body warm against hers in the stillness, he didn't say a word, and it felt as though a cloud had moved in front of the stars, obscuring all the light in the world.

Later, long after the sun had disappeared, the whole camp was asleep, tucked away in their winter homes beneath the ground. Yona awoke with a start in the pitch darkness and realized right away that she was alone in her reed bed. Zus was gone.

She sat up, blinking into the blackness. Her eyes adjusted slowly, but she could make out only the vaguest shapes in the zemlianka, and Zus was not among them. Wrapping her blanket around herself, she pulled her boots on, then made her way toward the door, opening it quietly and stepping into the cold world outside.

The snow was drifting down gently, silent in the soft moonlight, falling only from a few scattered clouds that trekked slowly across the sky, allowing glimpses of the stars. It was still a few hours before dawn. The sky stirred while nature slept, and for a few seconds, Yona simply stood still, taking in the silence and the peace, letting the snowflakes kiss her cheeks. Then she looked down and found Zus's footsteps just barely visible in the freshly fallen snow. Worried, she set off in the direction he'd gone, tracking his path deeper into the woods.

She walked for twenty minutes, and she was beginning to panic when she finally saw him, his back to her, his hands clenched in fists by his sides as he stared into the black depths of the forest. She exhaled in relief. As she walked toward him, he heard her and whirled around, his eyes wild and unfamiliar. He didn't have a gun with him, but he was crouched in a defensive posture, ready to fight. "Yona?" he asked after a few seconds, straightening back up, the shadow over his face clearing, but not all the way. "What are you doing here?"

"I was worried about you." As she walked closer, he took a step backward, away from her, and that's when she realized he'd been crying. There were tear tracks down his cheeks, and his eyes were bloodshot. "Zus?"

"I didn't want you to see me like this." He took another step backward, forcing distance between them, and though she wanted to pull him into her arms, to promise him that everything would be okay, she knew that might be a lie.

"What happened, Zus?" she asked, trying to keep the fear out of her voice. "Are you hurt?"

He shook his head, and another tear fell from his left eye. He swiped it away angrily. "It's Helena," he said, his voice strange and strangled, and it took Yona a few seconds to realize he was speaking of his daughter. He had never said her name aloud in Yona's presence before; even when she had gently asked about his past, he had shaken his head, pressed his lips together, and told her that he could not open that door without falling apart. It was only from Chaim that she knew the truth.

"Oh, Zus," she murmured.

He turned his back to her, staring out into the wilderness again. Overhead, the sky watched in silence. In a few hours, it would be dawn, and the forest would be alive again, the world would be alight. But for now, it felt like just the two of them in the moonlight.

It was a long time before Zus turned back around. "She would have been six today. It should have been her birthday. But I—I couldn't save her. How can it be that I am still alive and she has been gone from this earth for two years now?"

He began to cry again, heaving sobs this time, and Yona hesitated before stepping forward and putting a tentative hand on his shoulder. He flinched, but he didn't pull away, so she took another step, pulling him against her. He didn't resist, and after a moment, his arms were around her, and he was sobbing into her hair. She absorbed the tremors of his grief.

"There are no words that can tell you how sorry I am, Zus," she whispered when finally his tears had stopped falling. "I wish I had known her."

He took a deep breath and pushed away, creating a sudden gap between them. He looked disoriented, defensive. "But don't you see? If I had not lost her, if I had not lost Shifra, my wife, I never would have met you. This life that I have now with you, these feelings I have . . ." He shook his head. "It is only possible because they are dead. How can I embrace that? Am I not betraying them?"

She blinked as he took another step backward, away from her, widening the distance. It wasn't just sadness eating at him, it was guilt, and she was at the center of it. "Zus, I—"

"There's nothing you can say, Yona. There's nothing anyone can say."

It was the first time she'd heard him sound cold toward her, and it sent a chill down her spine. She knew it was his grief speaking, but it still felt like a blow. She knew that things with Zus were different than they had been with Aleksander, that what she had with him was real and true. But was love transitory? Could it run its course, disappear at a moment's notice? What if that was what was happening here? Could a person simply decide to turn his heart off? There was so little she understood; a lifetime of reading books deep within a lonely forest had not prepared her to open her own heart the way she had.

"I'm sorry," she whispered at last, and when he looked at her, his face softened a bit.

"Yona, I didn't mean—" His voice caught and he stopped abruptly. She could see the storm in his eyes, the confusion, and she hated that she was the cause of it. Still, when he reached for her hand, she squeezed back, and when he pulled her to him, so that her head rested against his heart, she held him tightly. "I wish you had known them, too, Yona. I wish that life was different. That it had taken a different path. None of us should be freezing to death in the damned woods. People shouldn't hate us in the name of God. But they do. And we are here. We are surviving. We are living to honor our dead." His voice broke again. "We have to. Don't we?"

She listened to his heartbeat before speaking. It was rapid and insistent, thudding against his rib cage like it was trying to break free. "I knew a nun once," she whispered. "She told me that those of us who live good lives will be reunited in the afterlife. Do you believe that? That you will see Helena and Shifra again someday?"

He didn't reply right away, and in the quiet, she could hear him sobbing again, could feel the tremors of grief that shook his body. "I do," he said at last.

"Then maybe they are closer than you think, Zus." She imagined the ghost of his wife watching them now in the forest, the way Jerusza sometimes watched her, and it was enough to make her pull away from him. Would the woman who'd loved him begrudge Yona for being here, in his arms? Would she hate Yona for taking a place she would never again be able to fill? "They are with you always," she added after a moment. "As they should be."

Zus sighed, but he didn't step closer, didn't take her back into his arms, and somehow, though she'd been the one to put distance between them, she was hurt by his inaction.

He looked away again, deep into the impenetrable dark of the forest. "I love you, Yona," he said at last, not looking at her. "I love you, but that love breaks my heart. The further I step into this life with you, the more I leave my life with them behind."

And then, without warning, he turned away and ran, his footfalls heavy on the dusting of snow, the woods closing around him before Yona could dislodge the lump in her throat. By the time she could speak past her shock and sadness, he had vanished, and with him, her newfound sense of belonging.

She wiped away tears she hadn't known she was crying and then wrapped her arms more tightly around herself. The snow continued to drift down, and as she looked skyward, a few flakes landed on her cheeks, washing away the salty rivers.

Behind her, the camp slept, and the night was still. She couldn't go back, not yet, and so she walked in the opposite direction from which Zus had fled.

Ahead of her lay a cluster of fallen trees, and she settled on one of the toppled trunks, studying the stump it had broken off from. It had been here for a while, from the looks of things, and over time, the sharp lines of the tree had softened. Now they were crusted in ice, hard and unforgiving, and Yona wondered if she'd been wrong when she told Zus that their broken edges were meant to fit together. Maybe the jagged pieces never fit anywhere again. Maybe they were destined to wear thin at the edges, and to freeze over, impenetrable and incompatible. Had she been fooling herself to think that she and Zus could fill each other's empty spaces?

She lost track of time as she sat on the stump, staring up at the soft snow and the dark, moonlit sky, and the gentle canopy of branches above. Finally, she closed her eyes and sighed. She had to keep moving forward, and so did Zus. Their pasts would always be with them, but that didn't mean there wasn't some sort of future ahead. Dawn was coming, the sky to the east just beginning to lighten as the stars continued to keep watch overhead in patient silence. She was just about to get up to return to camp—surely the group would be worried if they awoke and found both her and Zus gone—when she heard distinct footsteps to the west, crunching in the snow. She leapt to her feet, all her senses suddenly on alert as she stared into the dark, impenetrable depths of the forest, trying to see the source of the sound. It had been something large, as large as a man. Could it have been a bear? A large wolf? She hadn't brought a gun, but she reached for the knife in her boot, the one that was always strapped against her ankle. She had just closed her hand on its hilt when a voice came from behind her.

"Yona?"

She spun again and saw Zus standing there, his eyes wide with concern. She stared at him, confused. Grief had thrown her senses off; she had thought the footfalls were coming from the opposite direction, but the sound must have echoed across the cluster of trees, confusing her trained ear. She blinked a few times to right herself, and Zus's forehead creased.

"Yona, are you all right? What is it?"

"I—I thought I heard something." She shook her head and forced a laugh. "Perhaps I've been out in the cold too long."

He smiled and stepped into the small clearing of fallen trees. He was still several meters away, illuminated by the faint light of the coming dawn. "I'm sorry," he said, his voice gruff. "I'm sorry for the things I said. I didn't mean to hurt you."

"Of course you didn't, Zus. I know that."

All around them, the stars twinkled and the snow continued to drift quietly down. For a second Yona felt as if they were suspended in a world that wasn't theirs, like the tiny trees in the snow globe in the bedroom of the home Jüttner had commandeered.

"Zus—" she began.

He took another step closer, putting up a hand to stop her. His expression was tender, anguished. "Please. Yona, there's something I need to say. I shouldn't have—"

But his words were lost, for in the middle of his sentence, something crashed through the trees behind them, and they both whirled, alarmed, expecting to see a wild animal.

Instead, it was a man, crouched like a beast. His eyes were wild, his hair and beard bushy and unkempt. He was wearing a tattered wool coat with swastika-emblazoned epaulettes. "Hello, daughter," he said, his voice a growl, and in a terrified flash, she recognized him behind the beard, the fury, and the anguish.

"Jüttner," she murmured. And in the silence that followed, she could hear the cocking of his pistol, which was now aimed straight at Zus's heart.

CHAPTER TWENTY-SEVEN

Yona could hear the sharp intake of Zus's breath, could feel his shock and fear as he took a step closer to her, stopping abruptly when Jüttner waved his gun and growled in warning.

"So is this why you fled back to the forest? For this dirty Jew? I bet you didn't tell him about me," Jüttner said in German, jerking his head in Zus's direction. Spittle flew from the corners of his dried, cracked lips. How long had he been wandering the woods? His cheeks had hollowed, and the coat hung from his frame like a garment from a hanger. "I bet you didn't tell him that your father is a Nazi."

Zus inched a bit closer to Yona as if he could protect her, but he was still several meters away. "Yona is nothing like you," he said in careful German. Yona hadn't even known he spoke the language.

Jüttner's eyes darkened. "Her *name* is *Inge*," he spat.

"What are you doing here, Papa?" Yona asked quickly, trying to keep her tone even. She used the term of endearment in hopes of relaxing him, and it seemed to work a little.

"I came for you, Inge." His voice softened a bit, and some of the anger went out of his eyes. He lowered his gun, and she exhaled in relief. He was looking only at Yona, almost as if he had instantly forgotten that Zus was there. "You left because of the nuns, but that was not my fault. Surely you can see that. I was trying to save them for you."

Her heart ached; she could still see Sister Maria Andrzeja lying dead on the altar, before God. "I left," she said softly, "because I never belonged there with you. I could not stay."

"You only believe that because of the woman who took you. She made you forget who you are, Inge. But you are my *daughter*. You belong to *me*." His voice, a low whine, was rising again. "You humiliated me, Inge. What do you think it looked like to have my daughter run away so soon after she came back? They mocked me, Inge. I've been looking for you for months now. I've come to save you, to show everyone where you really belong. To bring you home."

"But *this* is my home."

Jüttner looked confused, as if it was not the answer he expected. His eyes flicked to Zus, back to Yona, and to Zus again. "And this Jew? He is forcing you to stay here, yes?" His gun went up again, pointed at Zus. Yona could feel her heart slamming against her rib cage.

"No." She took a deep breath. She could pretend he meant nothing to her, and then her father might let him go. But what if he killed Zus anyhow? She couldn't let his last memory be one of denial, erasure. And so she stood a little taller and looked right at Zus as she murmured, "His name is Zus. And I love him. I will never forgive you if you harm him."

"But he's a Jew!" The fury in Jüttner's voice was gathering like the clouds before a terrible storm. "He has tricked you! That's what the Jews do, Yona. He is only using you."

"He loves me, too," Yona said softly.

"Don't be a fool, Inge. Jews aren't capable of such a thing. They're animals! How could you let him influence you this way, take you away from the life you could have with your family?"

"He's my family now. He's my future." Yona knew she should stop. Jüttner had a gun, and he looked unhinged. But it was as if all the light and pain poured into her heart had finally burst the vessel, and she couldn't keep it in anymore. "How could you think I would come back with you? Do you see what you've become?"

"Enough!" her father roared, his anger suddenly exploding. He waved his gun wildly, and Yona felt a pang of fear. Jüttner was gaunt, exhausted. If she and Zus turned to run, there was a chance they could get away from him before he began firing, and in minutes, they could vanish into the forest. But if his instincts were still sharp, they'd both be dead before they took a few steps. It was too risky. "You are my daughter," her father said, his voice sinking to a low growl. "You will leave all of this foolishness behind and come with me now."

"She is not going anywhere with you." Zus's words were firm and calm.

"You think you can tell me what to do? She is my *blood*," Jüttner spat, spinning unsteadily toward him. "Don't you people care about that, too? That you're a *Jew* because of what's in *your* blood?"

Zus didn't say anything.

"What, you can't speak now, you filthy Jewish dog? Answer me! What makes a Jew? In your fancy religion, with all its rules and its plans for taking over humanity, *what is the one thing that makes a Jew?*"

Yona could feel the tension escalating.

"According to halakha, a child with a Jewish mother's blood is always Jewish," Zus said calmly. "Is that what you're referring to?"

"Stop, Zus," Yona murmured. He was making it worse. She could see Jüttner beginning to spin out of control, his eyes bulging, his movements growing more erratic. He looked crazed, and with a loaded gun and a simmering hatred of Jews, there was only one way this could go.

"And you think that by tricking my daughter into loving you, you can purify your own dirty soul? That if you have children, they won't be Jews like you? Is that it? That's your plan?"

"I—" Zus began, but Jüttner cut him off.

"Well then, joke's on you, Jew. You want to know *my* dirty little secret? *I married a Jew.*" He turned to Yona, his features twisted, his eyes wild. "She lied to me about it, but your mother was a half-Jewish whore, the daughter of a Jewish mother and a Christian father. She tried to hide who she was, but you can't hide a thing like that. Not in Germany. She didn't even tell me, the ungrateful bitch. She was long dead by the time the records surfaced. And it's a good thing, because I might have killed her myself. She could have ruined me, Inge. You understand that, right?"

She felt as if the breath had been knocked out of her. "My mother was Jewish?" she whispered.

Jüttner's laugh was cruel. "Oh, she fell to her knees in church every Sunday, just like everyone else did. You never would have known that her blood was tainted. She was hiding it, Inge. Hiding it from *me*."

Yona's head was spinning. Was *that* why Jerusza had chosen her? Not just a random desire to steal a baby from a blooming

Nazi, but a premonition about the day the truth might be revealed? Had Jerusza realized that if things had unfolded without her interruption, Yona and her mother might have one day been sent away to their own deaths by the man who was supposed to love them most?

"I've been Jewish all along," Yona murmured.

"No," Jüttner said firmly. "*No.* You are a *Mischling* of the second degree, not a Jew. My blood is strong, Inge. I have done enough for Germany to erase the stain of your mother's lies. It's why I had to bring you back. It's why I've been wandering the woods for months now, looking for you. I have to save you, Inge, before someone sees what you really are."

She finally found her voice. "I don't need saving. Not by you."

"But you do!" He waved his arms wildly. "It's obvious now! Don't you understand? The second you join your life to his, you become once again a full Jew by law."

Yona took another step backward. Why wasn't Zus moving away? "Papa." She tried the word again, to soften the tension, but it was too late. Jüttner seemed to hardly hear her.

"You were stolen from me once!" He was almost screaming now. "I won't let it happen again!"

Now he raised his gun with purpose, pointing it at Zus, his eyes suddenly focused, his gaze hard and steely. No longer was he an out-of-control madman; he was every inch a determined German officer prepared to carry out an execution he deemed necessary. "Look away, Inge," Jüttner said, his voice suddenly flat, emotionless. "It will be better that way."

"Don't do this."

"It is for the best. You will understand one day."

Zus was moving slowly backward, his hands raised defensively, but as time slowed to a crawl, Yona knew it wouldn't be enough. Jüttner would not miss.

It was her choices—and perhaps the war in her blood, too—that had led all of them here, to this moment, and she couldn't let this happen. She couldn't be responsible for the death of the only person on earth who loved her for who she was, not for who she might become. Her parents had barely known her, and if her mother was trying to hide her heritage from her father, perhaps a baby had only been a regret, a complication. Jerusza had always wanted more from her, too, an apprentice in her image rather than a child with her own hopes and fears and dreams. Her father wanted her to be a Nazi like him, and even Aleksander had wanted her to change, to become meeker, more servile. But she could only be herself, and Zus knew that and loved her not despite it, but because of it. She could see it in his eyes every time he looked at her, even through his grief, even now, through his fear.

The world was frozen in time, the seconds drifting down like the soft snowflakes all around them. As Jüttner leveled his gun and took one step, then two, toward Zus, who was still backing away, Yona found herself flying forward, stride after stride, her legs stretching with the strength of a lynx until finally, she leapt, her body arcing between the two men at the exact moment Jüttner fired.

And then, time moved again. The snowflakes fell, the crows overhead cawed in agony, the rabbits near the clearing fled in fear. And in the fading moonlight of early dawn, Yona tumbled to the ground, the driven snow around her suddenly crimson with her blood.

"What have you done, Inge?" Jüttner's voice was suddenly anguished, and he sounded very far away. "Oh God, what have you done?" Then suddenly he was beside her, kneeling at her left shoulder, his face appearing from the blurriness of the world, his eyes full of grief. He was still clutching his pistol, but he seemed unaware of anything but Yona's body in the snow, the blood pumping slowly, surely out of the hole in her torso.

"Yona!" It was Zus, and he was beside her, too, on her right side, separated only by Yona's body from the man who had tried to kill him only seconds before. She wanted to tell him to run, because the second Jüttner stopped to gather his thoughts, he would finish what he started. But she couldn't make her tongue work, couldn't get her mouth to say the words. All she could do was breathe in and out, in and out, as the snow around her melted and she drifted nearer to the frozen ground beneath.

"Yona, no, no, you can't leave me," Zus said, and he was crying now, his whole body heaving as he begged her to stay.

"Please," Yona managed to say, and then it was her father's face hovering above her, just as it had once hovered over her cradle, one of the few memories she had of life before Jerusza had taken her. She listened for Jerusza's voice now, but it wasn't there. Nothing was. The world was silent, though she could see the lips of both men moving as they hovered above her, pleading with her to stay alive. She could feel the light leaving her, seeping out with her blood, and already, she weighed less than the air. She was a dove, ready for flight.

But there was one last thing binding her to the earth, for the moment Yona died, Jüttner would kill Zus, and she could not let that happen, could not let her final legacy be the death of a good man, a man who deserved to live. And so she summoned the last of her strength and reached slowly, slowly for the knife at her ankle. As her father leaned over her, his tears falling, grieving the daughter he'd never known at all, she held his gaze, and before she could vanish into the deep well of grief and hatred and fear she saw in his eyes, she brought the weapon up to his left wrist and sliced, cleanly and perfectly, taking the blade swiftly up the length of the radial artery, and splaying it wide open, nearly to his elbow just as Jerusza had taught her long ago, the summer she was eight, the summer Yona said she could never imagine taking a man's life.

And then the world had sound again, and the man who had once been her father was falling back on the snow, his blood red and angry and mingling with hers. He gasped for breath, gasped for life, and Yona found her voice at last. "I'm sorry," she whispered, using the last of her strength to turn her head toward him. He was lying on the snow beside her, his head tilted toward her, and so their eyes met once more, and in them, she could see disbelief and a great, deep fear of what was to come. "I'm sorry," she murmured again, and then he gasped once more, and the light in his eyes went out forever, leaving behind an empty, ruined shell.

Yona closed her eyes, exhausted. Zus was safe now, though it was impossible to know whether her father had been alone. What if he'd been traveling with other deserters? What if another angry German had heard the gunshot and was already on his way here? "Run," she whispered, forcing her eyes open again. Zus hovered over her, his tears falling. "Danger . . . You must run," she managed to say.

"No." His voice was choked but firm. "No, Yona. I never had the chance to tell you what I came back to say. I came to tell you I was wrong. That I want to open my heart again. That I want to spend the rest of my life with you."

She could see a future stretching before him, beautiful and bright. Children. A solid home. Food on the table and flowers in the garden. But it wasn't her life, wasn't her future. It was his, and she wanted him to live it, to be happy. "Go, Zus," she whispered. "If you don't, you will die."

"Then so be it." He was firm through his tears. "But I will not lose you, Yona."

"Zus," she began, but she couldn't manage to say more, for she could no longer hold the air in her lungs, could no longer remember how to pump blood through her veins. So instead, she gazed up at his face, his beautiful face, as he picked her up in his arms. She was weightless, floating, suspended in air, and then, because it hurt too much to see the pain in his eyes, she looked past him, up at the vast sky visible above the skeletal trees. There, the night stretched on forever, a road to a heaven that had been there all along.

As the last of the light slipped away, he carried her out of the clearing, back toward the camp, his tears falling warm on her frozen face as the world faded around her and the stars vanished from the sky.

CHAPTER TWENTY-EIGHT

Seven months later, thousands of refugees once marked for death poured from the mouth of Poland's vast forests, alive and free, though the world they'd once known lay in ruins. The final weeks in hiding had been the deadliest; all through the woods, the Germans had struck back as they retreated from the advancing Red Army, felling scores of innocent Jews who had survived the war only to lose their lives in its waning days. Shimon and Leonid were among the final victims; they had been on patrol when a dozen fleeing Nazis had approached the camp, and the men had managed to open fire, killing four soldiers, before being shot themselves. The Rozenberg brothers, roused from their sleep by the noise, had run into the woods and doubled back, encircling the Germans from behind and finishing them off before they could reach the main camp.

In the months since Yona had been shot, the group had grown, eventually numbering fifty-three by the time the spring thaw came. When they reemerged into the world, with Chaim as their leader, his wife and boys beside him, there was joy at the war's end, but also great sadness at all that had been lost. In

Nowogródek, in Pinsk, in Lachowicze, in Lida, in Mir, in all the towns they'd come from, they found the homes they'd once lived in occupied by others. They found news of countless loved ones who hadn't returned and never would. They found synagogues burned to the ground and townspeople astonished to see Jews who had survived. They found a world that no longer felt as if it had a place for them in it.

Those who had survived the war, though, knew that they had to find a way to go on. And so they lived and thrived as best they could, some resettling in the towns they had once called home, most leaving tattered Slavic villages behind for a new life somewhere else. Chaim, Sara, and their boys went to Israel, as did Miriam, Oscher, and Bina, and the families of Shimon and Leonid, the wives vowing to start over to build a new life, a safe life, for their young children. Ruth, Pessia, Leah, and Daniel immigrated to Israel, too, hoping for a new start, and sixteen years later, when Daniel lost his life on a reprisal mission after an attack on his adopted country, Ruth and her daughters grieved deeply, but they were proud that Daniel had died fighting bravely for the rights of Jews to live in peace. It was a war that seemed to know no end.

Some who had survived the Second World War in the great woods would spend the rest of their lives trying to forget the things they had endured, the things they had lost. They started over, lost touch, tried to move on. Others stayed in place, forever conscious of the impossibility of ever righting the scales, of ever taking back the moments that had been stolen. All of them, though, were forever tied to the dark forests of eastern Europe—the forests that held their secrets, the forests that held their dead.

Many years later, well into the next millennium, children still told tales of the old woman who lived deep in the heart of the Nalibocka Forest, the one with one green eye and one blue. Some wondered if she was real at all, though others swore they had seen her singing to the stars, speaking to the squirrels, swaying with the trees. They believed she was a witch, and they whispered stories of terror and fright about her in the hallways of schoolhouses where children of all races and religions now learned side by side.

But they didn't know the old woman at all. They did not know she had been the wife of a man whose heart had opened once more, jagged edges and all, and who had stayed by her side until his own peaceful, quiet death at the age of eighty-nine. They did not know that she was the mother of two children, well into their sixties now, who—though they had moved out of the forest long ago, one to Israel, one to France—loved her with all their hearts and visited her whenever they could. They did not know that she was a proud Jewish hero who had discovered who she was in the darkness and who had helped give life to many who might not have otherwise lived.

And that was just fine with her. She belonged there, among the trees, in the night that always embraced her, under a ceiling of sky splashed with endless stars. And on the sixteenth of July, 2019, she died quietly in the little cabin she had built with her own hands, both of her children beside her, under the light of the first full moon of her hundredth year of life, just as an old woman had promised she would, so many years before.

AUTHOR'S NOTE

On December 5, 1941, the life of Aron Bielski changed forever.

The youngest of twelve, Aron, then fourteen, was out doing chores in his small Polish village of Stankiewicze, when he saw a police vehicle pulling down the lane. Dropping everything, he ran and hid in the barn.

He had good reason to be terrified. The Bielskis were the only Jews in town, and the Germans—who had occupied Poland months earlier—had been hunting his older brothers for months, in conjunction with local authorities who collaborated with them. In fact, Aron hadn't spoken a word since the day that summer when the police had tried to elicit his brother's whereabouts by forcing the frightened boy to dig his own grave—and then lie in it—at gunpoint.

As he watched from his hiding place, the men arrested his parents, Beila and David, and took them away. It was a Friday, and by Monday morning, they were dead—murdered along with more than four thousand other Jews and dumped into a mass grave just outside the nearby town of Nowogródek. Also killed that day were the wives of two of Aron's older brothers, as well as his baby niece.

"My husband cannot forgive himself," Aron's wife, Henryka, told me in July 2020, just days before Aron's ninety-third birthday. "All were killed, and he survived."

Aron fled into the woods, where he reunited with two of his older brothers. By March, there were seven others with the three Bielskis, and by the summer, their group had grown to thirty, including a fourth brother, Tuvia Bielski, the oldest among them.

For the next two years, as the Germans moved Jews first into ghettos and then to concentration camps, the group grew, moving deeper and deeper into the dense woods, until they numbered twelve hundred. Remarkably, almost all of them survived the war.

Their story unfolds in startling, breathtaking detail in the 2008 Edward Zwick film *Defiance* (starring Daniel Craig and Liev Schreiber), as well as in the 1993 nonfiction book of the same name by Nechama Tec, on which the film is based. Both were resources I used in writing *The Forest of Vanishing Stars*, which sets the main character, Yona, on a collision course with a group similar to the small Bielski group in the summer of 1942, before it grew in size. It's important to note that though the fictional group in this novel is similar in location to that early Bielski group, the fictional characters are not directly based on any real people; in fact, I wrote the rough draft of the first half of the book before I ever spoke with Aron and Henryka.

Still, it was enormously important to me to get the details right, and that's one reason why I did a huge amount of reading and research—and why I was so grateful to talk to Aron (who changed his surname to "Bell" after moving to the United States). The conversations I had with him—and with Henryka, also born in Poland—gave a beating heart to the vast collection of details I had accumulated. "Sorrow," he told me in our first conversation, "teaches a person how to live, how to survive, what to do next."

But life wasn't always sorrowful for Aron—or for the many Jews who lived in Poland before the German occupation. The Bielskis had a good life. They owned a mill, and Aron has happy childhood memories of riding horseback, playing in the nearby forest, and even walking six miles to school. "I was a king," he told me with a shrug. "I was beginning to be a king."

But then, of course, life changed. "The Germans came," said Henryka, "and everything turned upside down."

In the heart of the Nalibocka Forest—the same forest where Yona spends much of the novel—the Bielskis set up not just a camp but a society. "They had their own hospital, their own jail, they had a place that was a kitchen, a sewing place where they were fixing clothing, because there were twelve hundred people," Henryka explains. "They were self-sufficient. They had doctors, nurses, everything."

But most of all, they had each other. They found community, and they survived the war because they found trust, life, and hope in the darkness.

After speaking with Aron, I found myself thinking often of his parents, who were taken away to a horrible fate, just as six million Jews were across Europe. Henryka told me that to this day, when Aron first wakes up in the morning, he often sees his father before him. "He was so scared in the forest," she said. "But his father is always with him, always."

When I thought about the guilt Aron has lived with his whole life—the guilt of surviving while so many others died—I wondered what his parents would have thought to know their youngest son has lived into his nineties. His very survival is a triumph over evil, and his whole life—as well as the existence of his three children, fourteen grandchildren, and thirteen great-grandchildren—is a testament to that.

During our conversation, Aron paused at one point and said, his voice trembling, "You have to remember one thing for the rest of your life: hardship teaches a person life." I can't think of a more important message as we emerge from the shadow of 2020, the year in which I wrote this book. I think many World War II novels remind us that there is always a light at the end of the tunnel, and that as a human race, we can all triumph over the darkness. But this year I needed to hear that—and to internalize it, to make sure it found its way into both my life and my writing—more than ever. To hear it from a survivor was even more impactful.

On a personal note, I'd like to add that much of the Jewish side of my own family, on my father's side, actually hails from an area of eastern Europe not too far away from where *The Forest of Vanishing Stars* takes place—something I didn't realize until my brother sent me a link to a family tree he was putting together on Ancestry.com. (Thanks, Dave!) It was amazing to discover that my great-great-grandparents—Rudolph and Rose Harmel—had in fact emigrated from Poland to the United States in August 1888, fifty-one years before Hitler's army invaded their former homeland. Rudolph died in 1932, but Rose lived until 1941—long enough that she must have known of the horrors that were beginning to befall the people she'd left behind. I don't know if I had distant relatives—perhaps sisters, brothers, or cousins of my great-grandparents—who were caught up in the Nazi terror, but I would imagine I did. It's incredible to think about fate and how the decisions our ancestors made—mine's decision to leave Poland in 1888, for example—affect us so much to this day.

In *The Forest of Vanishing Stars*, as in real life, many Jews in Poland made decisions that impacted the future, too. They stood up. They fought back. They survived. And when you think of the odds they faced in Poland, that's truly incredible.

According to Yad Vashem, the world Holocaust remembrance center based in Israel, more than 3.3 million Jews lived in Poland on the eve of World War II—more than any other country in Europe. In fact, they made up 10 percent of Poland's population, the highest percentage of Jews anywhere in Europe. According to the United States Holocaust Memorial Museum, between 2.8 million and 3 million Polish Jews were murdered during the war. That's somewhere between 84 percent and 91 percent of the entire Jewish population of the country.

Think about that for a moment. *Approximately three million Jewish people were murdered in a single country.* Jewish casualties in Poland far outweighed those in any other country during the war—and yet people somehow found a way to survive against those staggering odds. It's incredible and inspiring, and as I spoke to Aron Bielski, I felt almost as if I were having a conversation with a real-life superhero. He was young during the war, and it was certainly his older brothers who did the most to build their society of salvation within the woods. But Aron played a role, too, and he's still here to talk about it. What a gift to us all.

I'd love to give you a few notes on the real historical basis of *The Forest of Vanishing Stars*. I played around slightly with a few dates and minor geographical details to make the story work, but everything was based on the real history of the area.

Chana's family, whom Yona meets toward the beginning of the novel, fled from the Volozhin ghetto, just north of the Nalibocka Forest. Just like the other ghettos mentioned in the book, the one in Volozhin was real. In August 1941, more than three thousand Jews from Volozhin and nearby villages were moved into a tiny ghetto. They were often shot at random, such as during an October 1941 *Aktion*, during which three hundred Jews were brought, ten at a time, to be killed in a field just outside the ghetto. In May 1942, the Germans oversaw a mass execution, carried out by local collaborators, in which more than fifteen hundred Jews were shot dead and then incinerated in a field. Another eight hundred were rounded up and machine-gunned down in a building. In August 1942, three hundred Jews were burned alive. The ghetto was finally "liquidated" in 1943.

Aleksander's group comes from the Mir ghetto, about fifty-five miles south of Minsk. There, the killings began early. On July 20, 1941, the Germans rounded up nineteen Jewish and three non-Jewish intellectuals and murdered them in the forest. In October and November of that year, another two thousand Jews were killed, and the remainder of the Jews in the area were moved into a ghetto. Jews there received a ration of just 4.4

ounces of bread each day. In May 1942, the surviving Jews were moved into the large, run-down Mir Castle, to which there was only one entrance, making it harder to escape. But a Polish Jew named Oswald Rufeisen managed to infiltrate the local police station as a German translator. He tipped off ghetto prisoners that a liquidation was coming—and he helped distract police while an escape took place. More than two hundred escaped into the forest, as did Rufeisen himself, who later converted to Catholicism, became a friar, and moved to Israel. The remaining 560 Jews in the ghetto were murdered in August 1942.

Zus's group comes from the Lida ghetto, which was established in September 1941. In May 1942, around a thousand workers and their families were pulled aside, and the remaining Jews—5,670 of them—were murdered. Soon, Jews from other settlements were moved into the Lida ghetto, and in March 1943, there was another round of killings; some two thousand Jews were shot just outside town. The ghetto refilled with Jews from elsewhere once again, eventually numbering four thousand, and the ghetto was liquidated in July 1943, with the remaining prisoners sent to the Majdanek death camp.

Escapes took place from all three ghettos—and from others nearby, too. Many of the Jews who found their way to the Bielski encampment had escaped from ghettos. In fact, members of the Bielski group—including Aron—ran rescue missions into the ghettos to persuade people to leave, and to show them how. "Aron was a tiny boy," Henryka recalled during our conversation. "He was going into a hole under the gate into the ghetto to get people out. One day, they made a huge mission. One hundred fifty people escaped through a tunnel they had dug by spoon. It led one hundred fifty meters, maybe two hundred, under the fence, until they finally escaped out of the ghetto."

Those escapes were miraculous, seemingly impossible. The vast majority of Jews did not make it out—and those who did faced nearly insurmountable odds on the outside, too. Finding their way to larger groups, where refugees could pool their knowledge and resources, was key.

I'd like to touch on a few other historical elements of *The Forest of Vanishing Stars.*

The nuns Yona encounters in the middle of the book were loosely inspired by a real-life group of eleven nuns known today as the Blessed Martyrs of Nowogródek. In the summer of 1943, life had become very difficult in the town of Nowogródek, near the Nalibocka Forest. The Jews of the town had been executed or deported, and sixty townspeople, including two priests, had recently been murdered. In the middle of July, 120 townspeople were arrested by the Germans and slated for execution, and the nuns, led by a woman named Sister Maria Stella, decided to offer themselves in exchange for those prisoners. The Germans accepted the nuns' offer, and on the morning of Sunday, August 1, the eleven sisters, ranging from age twenty-six to fifty-four, were driven into the woods, shot, and buried in a mass grave.

Fifty-six years later, the nuns were confirmed as martyrs by Pope John Paul II, and they were beatified on March 5, 2000, which means that they are recognized by the Catholic Church as "blessed" and thus have the ability to intercede on behalf of individuals who pray in their name. "Before the war and during the occupation, they zealously served the inhabitants of Nowogródek, participating actively in pastoral

care and education and engaging in various works of char-
ity," Pope John Paul said at the time of their beatification.
"Their love for those among whom they fulfilled their mission took on special significance during the horror of the
Nazi invasion. Together and unanimously, they offered their
lives to God, asking in exchange that the lives of the mothers
and fathers of families and that of the local pastor be spared.
The Lord graciously accepted their sacrifice and, we believe,
abundantly rewarded them in his glory." Their feast day in
the Catholic Church is celebrated each year on August 1—the
anniversary of their death.

The nuns in *The Forest of Vanishing Stars* are not meant to
represent the Martyrs of Nowogródek, whose story and deaths
unfolded differently, but I hope their story serves as a reminder
that even in moments of death and despair during the war, God
was there—and that there were people from all walks of life
standing up to injustice in the face of evil.

Another historical element I want to mention is the swamp
where half of Yona's group flees during Operation Hermann
(the German incursion into the forest in the summer of 1943).
In real life, the Bielski group escaped the German forces during
the summer of 1943 in a similar way. They abandoned their
camp and fled to a large swamp in the middle of the forest called
Krasnaya Gorka, where they knew the Germans were unlikely
to follow. As they trudged through the mud, they tied themselves together so they wouldn't sink, and at night, they tethered
themselves to trees so they wouldn't drown. They ate mushrooms and berries, and flour made from tree bark, and they
were near starvation when the Germans finally retreated, torching many villages behind them.

I tried to stay as accurate as possible in terms of the things the forest refugees would have eaten, the way they sheltered, the way they fought back. Any errors or omissions are my own.

I used what felt like a million nonfiction books in the research of this novel, including: *Defiance* (Nechama Tec), *Fugitives of the Forest* (Allan Levine), *Polish Customs, Traditions & Folklore* (Sophie Hodorowicz Knab), *How to Eat in the Woods* (Bradford Angier), *Masters of Death* (Richard Rhodes), *Fighting Back* (Harold Werner), *Kabbalah: The Mystic Quest in Judaism* (David Ariel), *Do Not Go Gentle* (Charles Gelman), *Jack & Rochelle* (Jack and Rochelle Sutin, with Lawrence Sutin), *When Bad Things Happen to Good People* (Harold Kushner), *They Fought Back* (Yuri Suhl), *The Cruel Hunters* (French L. MacLean), *Kill or Get Killed* (Col. Rex Applegate), *Slavic Witchcraft* (Natasha Helvin), *Fairy Tales of the Russians and Other Slavs* (Ace and Olga Pilkington), *Survival Wisdom & Know-How* (from the editors of Stackpole Books), *Smithsonian WWII Map by Map*, and *Historical Atlas of the Holocaust* (United States Holocaust Memorial Museum).

Perhaps one of the most helpful books I used was *Naliboki Forest: Land, Wildlife and Human* by Professor Vadim Sidorich, a zoologist and doctor of biology. But Vadim's assistance went far beyond the sweeping book he authored; he also works as a Naliboki Forest ecotourism guide, and I reached out to him for help. He gave me detailed notes on many of the scenes in this book, and he answered every question I asked, bringing to life the flora and fauna of the Naliboki Forest the same way Aron

Bielski brought to life for me the plight of Jewish refugees during the war. His help—and his willingness to answer even the most minutely detailed questions—was absolutely invaluable, and I could not have written this book without him, nor could I have written as accurately about the deep forest that held so many lives in its lush heart.

Vadim went so far as to trek into the depths of the forest to send me photos of abandoned World War I bunkers where my characters might have sheltered, hollowed-out oak trees large enough to hide multiple people, and molds my characters might have used to form mud bricks. Because of Vadim, I know things I would never have otherwise learned, such as the fact that during the war, the main varieties of mushrooms eaten by refugees included boletus, Russula, chanterelle, and honey fungus, and that half also ate sulphur shelf mushrooms. I know that if you're building a roof for your dugout, you should either use oak bark from a dead tree or spruce bark from an old live tree, and that hedgehogs—a great source of food—are easiest to catch at twilight in the warm season and under big spruce trunk bases in the cold season. I know that the larvae of the May beetle were easy to find during the war and could be used for making fatty breads, and that refugees often collected and fried their larvae, too. Vadim was incredibly generous with his vast knowledge, and I will be forever grateful. If you are ever in Belarus and would like to see the forest for yourself, look no further than the Naust Eco Station, run by Vadim and his wife, Irina. You can find them online at www.wolfing.info, a site that also contains many photographs and articles. It's a great resource if you're interested in learning more about the terrain after reading this book.

If you're wondering why the forest is referred to in the book as the Nalibocka, and in Vadim's book (and in some of my notes here) as the Naliboki, it's because the former is the Polish spelling, while the latter is the Belarusian (formerly "Belorussian") spelling. When the events of the book took place, the forest was within Polish borders, and the forest was known by the Polish name; now, it lies within Belarus because of the shifting of national borders that took place during the twentieth century. Similarly, the city called Nowogródek (the Polish name) in the book is now called Navahrudak or Novogrudok. There are many other such instances, but in the book, I've tried to retain the Polish spellings wherever possible, since those would have been accurate in the 1940s.

For translation help, I'd like to thank German translator Jens, Russian/Belarusian translator Anna, and Yiddish translator Arik. I struggled the most with the Yiddish translations, because they involve transliteration (in this case from Hebrew letters to Roman letters), which is never a perfect art, but which was further complicated by regional dialects and the fact that Yiddish is largely a slang language. To that end, I also consulted Rebbetzin Hindel Levitin of the Chabad House Palm Beach, and my friend (and foreign rights agent) Heather Baror-Shapiro, as well as Shiri Shapira, who works as a Yiddish translator for Armchair Publishing, my beloved Israeli publishing house, and Shiri's colleague Arun Schaechter Viswanath. In the end, the translations I used came mostly from Shiri and Arun, because they took into account the regional dialect and accent that best fit the story. All the aforementioned Yiddish speakers gave me invaluable input, and if I've slightly missed the mark, the error is mine—though I promise, it's not for lack of trying. I had several sleepless nights, and one nightmare, worrying about just the three short Yiddish sentences in chapter 1! Rebbetzin Levitin also went out of her way to help with the accuracy of a few other passages, for which I am deeply grateful.

I also need to thank Tamara Vershitskaya, the researcher and curator of the Museum of Jewish Resistance in Novogrudok, who answered several questions for me, as well as my friend Pam Kancher, the executive director of the Holocaust Memorial Resource & Education Center in Maitland, Florida, who is always willing to provide help and answers when I need them. It means so much when people are willing to spend their time, energy, and resources lending a hand, and I appreciate it deeply.

When I talked to Aron Bielski, I asked him what he thought made ordinary men like him and his brothers rise up and do something so extraordinary. He was silent for a long time and then said softly, simply, "God."

I was especially struck by that, because to hear Henryka and Aron tell it, there wasn't much time for religious observance during those years in the forest; their focus had to be on survival. "You cannot do it; you have to go fight, you have to go for a food mission," Henryka explained. "But there was a rabbi who taught religion, and they celebrated high holidays, too. They celebrated the best they could." Aron said he couldn't recall if they even lit candles for Shabbat. "I don't remember that," he said. "But if you didn't have a candle, you took a piece of wood."

Even in the darkness, that light burned. God was with them all along, in the big moments and the small. I think they felt it then, and Aron still feels it now.

Today, eight decades after the Germans swept through Poland and took so many lives, Aron and Henryka are concerned about the way the world sometimes seems to be splintering once again. "We worry because of what's going on in the world now with the hate between nations, between religions, between races," Henryka said. Added Aron, "It was, it is, and it always will be."

As for the message Aron would like to share with the world today? "Be nice if at all possible, and help always poorer and weaker individuals. Hopefully there will not be such a war again, although there is still too much hate, and you never know what the world will get. . . . We hope it will never happen again, but there is no guarantee."

Let's not forget the past. Let's not forget the heroes who fought so that others could survive. Let's not forget to be kind to our fellow man.

Be nice if at all possible. It's such simple advice, but if we can all do that, every day, maybe we can be the change. Maybe we can stand together. Maybe we can build the world a better future. Here's to lighting a candle, or a piece of wood, in the darkness—and to letting that light carry us through.

ACKNOWLEDGMENTS

I wrote *The Forest of Vanishing Stars* entirely in 2020, the strangest year any of us could have imagined.

This could have been a year of sadness, and in many ways, it was. But for me, it also became a year defined by community. And at the heart of that community was *Friends & Fiction*, the Facebook group, live weekly show, and podcast I cofounded with Mary Kay Andrews, Kristy Woodson Harvey, Patti Callahan Henry, and Mary Alice Monroe in the first few weeks of the pandemic shutdown.

Our community has grown to tens of thousands since then, and every day it has brought me solace and a sense of belonging. Mary Kay, Kristy, Patti, and Mary Alice have become very dear friends of mine (we probably exchange about a hundred texts a day), as have Meg Walker (our managing director) and Shaun Hettinger (our audio/video guru). Each week, we've interviewed other authors (including Kristin Hannah, Delia Owens, Brit Bennett, Lisa See, and William Kent Krueger), and day after day, I've felt a little less alone. I've realized we're all in the same boat. And I've found such comfort in being a part of a vibrant community of active, engaged, compassionate readers who are on our page all the time, giving each other advice, sharing their lives, and discussing the books they love.

I'd also like to thank our *Friends & Fiction* assistants, Rachel Jensen and Grace Walker; our book club leaders, Lisa Harrison and Brenda Gardner (and book club cofounder Michelle Marcus); our production company, Audivita Studios; and our many wonderful community members, including Annissa Joy Armstrong. (There are *so* many more of you to thank, too! Where would I even begin?) We appreciate *all* of you so very deeply. You changed the whole course of 2020 for all of the "Fab Five," and we hope that, in some small way, we've made a difference in your lives, too.

Of course, as always, I owe a huge debt of gratitude to Abby Zidle, who has been my trusted editor and cherished friend since 2011 (happy tenth, Abby!), and to Holly Root, the most wonderful and miraculous literary agent in the world. To Michelle Podberezniak (Gallery) and Kristin Dwyer (LEO PR): I could not ask for two better, kinder publicists or friends. And to Kathie Bennett (Magic Time Literary Publicity): I'm fairly certain you've cloned yourself, because I'm not sure how else you get so much done at once. You're amazing! To Danielle Noe: Thanks a million for your friendship and marketing expertise. To all of you, thank you so much for being the dreamiest of dream teams; it's an honor and privilege to work with you.

To my foreign rights agent, Heather Baror-Shapiro: You have changed my life in so many ways, and I'm endlessly grateful. To my film agent, Dana Spector: Thanks for all your guidance (and your over-the-weekend read of my script!) this year. I'm so lucky to work with both of you. This year also brought me two enormous, unexpected gifts in the form of Anna Gerb (one of the most generous, hardworking people I've ever met—you're a true joy to work with) and Jonathan Baruch (with whom I bonded instantly), both of whom I'm now so honored to call friends.

To Jen Bergstrom: Can you believe I've been a Gallery author for a decade now? I couldn't be prouder to work with you. One of the best things that 2020 showed me was that at Gallery, I'm part of a *family* in ways I couldn't have imagined before this year. Jen, you—as well as Abby, Michelle, Jen Long, and Eliza Hanson—had my back every step of the way when we hit a pandemic-related shipping issue, and I'll never forget the love and dedication I felt from all of you. Thanks also to Sara Quaranta, Molly Gregory, Sally Marvin, Anabel Jimenez, Lisa Litwack, Chelsea McGuckin, Nancy Tonik, proofreader Susan Bishansky, Wendy Sheanin and the rest of the incredible Simon & Schuster sales team, and, of course, Jonathan Karp. And thanks as well to my awesome team at S&S Canada, including Catherine Whiteside, Gregory Tilney, Adria Iwasutiak, Shara Alexa, and Felicia Quon. I smile every time I see one of your names in my in-box!

Last year, in *The Book of Lost Names*, I wrote a bit in my acknowledgments about the magic of books, and how booksellers and librarians can change lives. I had no idea when I penned those words—before the pandemic began—just how important that sentiment would become. When the world shut down in early 2020, so many bookstores and libraries were impacted, often devastatingly so; but still, countless bighearted booksellers and librarians stuck with it and found new and inventive ways to connect with readers. You were lifelines for all of us over the past year; we needed books more than ever to anchor us to the world outside our doors. You continued to get books into our hands, to send us on adventures in our own imaginations, and to give us a reason to connect with one another over stories we love.

A special thank-you to some of my other dearest writing friends: Linda Gerber, Alyson Noël, Allison van Diepen, Emily Wing Smith, Wendy Toliver, Kristina McMorris, Fiona Davis, Lauren Elkin, and Jay Asher. I was also so privileged to get to know so many other author friends better this year, including Susan Meissner, Kristin Hannah, Stephanie Dray, Melanie Benjamin, Nguyễn Phan Quế Mai, Heather Webb, Hazel Gaynor, Susan Elizabeth Phillips, Rachel McMillan, Julia Kelly, Alison Hammer, Christina Lauren, Kelly Rimmer, Lauren Willig, David James Poissant, Larry Loftis, Genevieve Graham, Caroline Leavitt, and more. I think it's extraordinary, in a business that could be so competitive, that so many authors are kind, generous, and eager to lift each other up. As Mary Kay Andrews so often says, "A rising tide lifts all boats." I'm so very honored to be sailing these waters with all of you.

A huge shout-out to all the bloggers, bookstagrammers, librarians, booksellers, reviewers, hosts, podcasters, and overall magic-makers who do such a wonderful job of celebrating the community of authors and booklovers—especially Ron Block, Laura Taylor, Lauren Zimmerman, Cathy Graham, Serena Wyckoff, Linda Kass, Melissa Amster, Kristy Barrett, Robin Kall, Susan McBeth, Robin Hoklotubbe, Andrea Peskind Katz, and more.

There's a question we ask each week on *Friends & Fiction*: "What were the values around reading and writing in your childhood home, and how did that shape you into the writer you became?" So, as always, Mom (Carol Harmel), thanks for opening my world to books from a very early age and for letting me surround myself with words. Thank you, too, for all the times you patiently read my childhood scribbles or attentively watched the "plays" I wrote for my siblings to star in. And speaking of siblings, thanks to Karen and Dave (stars of those early, ridiculous plays!) and your families, and to Dad (Rick Harmel) and Janine, who are always so encouraging and enthusiastic about my books. Thanks to Wanda (who stepped up in a big way to help me out this year during some of my craziest weeks!), Mark, and all the Troubas, Lietzes, and Riverses (the best in-laws anyone could possibly ask for) and to all the Sullivans (a special shout-out to Aunt Donna Foley, who made reading cool when I was a kid!) and Harmels (especially Courtney Harmel, who has given me a New York home-away-from-home for more than two decades). I truly hit the family jackpot with all of you.

The biggest thanks this year, though, goes to my husband, Jason, and my son, Noah. We kept Noah out of school because of the pandemic for most of 2020–21. I taught him at home, since there was no virtual pre-K option at his school, and that changed life enormously for all of us. Normally I work during Noah's school hours, but since there no longer were any, and I was now working with him on a pre-K curriculum for at least two hours a day, our whole schedule changed. Jason, you stepped up to give me early mornings and weekends to write, and Noah, you were such a trouper during all the times I had to miss bedtime for online events, or had to take calls or Zoom meetings during our days together. I couldn't have done any of this without the understanding and love of the two of you guys this year. Thanks for being the best husband and son I could possibly ask for. I love you both so deeply. And, Noah, I probably owe you lots of LEGOs.

Finally, to all the readers: Thank you so much for all your support. One of the great privileges of *Friends & Fiction* over the past year, as well as so many of the virtual events I did in 2020–21, was finally getting to meet and interact with so many of you. Please know how much you *all* mean to me. Writing is, by nature, rather solitary, but you remind me every single day of the potential power and reach of words. Thank you for picking up this book, sticking with me, and for being the kind of people who find worlds within the pages, and who open your minds and hearts to stories. I hope to meet more of you this year at virtual chats and maybe even at in-person events. And please do drop by *Friends & Fiction* (www.Facebook.com/groups/Friendsand Fiction), my website (www.KristinHarmel.com), or my Facebook page (www.Facebook.com/KristinHarmelAuthor) to say hi; it's always such a pleasure to connect. Thanks so much for reading *The Forest of Vanishing Stars*, and please stay safe and well.

WELBECK

PUBLISHING GROUP

Love books? Join the club.

Sign up and choose your preferred genres to receive tailored news, deals, extracts, author interviews and more about your next favourite read.

From heart-racing thrillers to award-winning historical fiction, through to must-read music tomes, beautiful picture books and delightful gift ideas, Welbeck is proud to publish titles that suit every taste.

bit.ly/welbeckpublishing

WELBECK

ANDRE DEUTSCH

MORTIMER

MORTIMER

WELBECK